W9-BIC-948

FROM BLOOD AND ASH

Also From Jennifer L. Armentrout

Fall With Me
Dream of You (a 1001 Dark Nights Novel)
Forever With You
Fire In You

By J. Lynn
Wait for You
Be With Me
Stay With Me

The Covenant Series
Half-Blood
Pure
Deity
Elixer
Apollyon
Sentinel

The Lux Series
Shadows
Obsidian
Onyx
Opal
Origin
Opposition
Oblivion

The Origin Series
The Darkest Star
The Burning Shadow

The Dark Elements
Bitter Sweet Love
White Hot Kiss
Stone Cold Touch
Every Last Breath

The Harbinger Series
Storm and Fury

FROM BLOOD AND ASH

AND
ASH

#1 *NEW YORK TIMES* BESTSELLING AUTHOR
JENNIFER L. ARMENTROUT

From Blood and Ash
A Blood and Ash Novel
By Jennifer L. Armentrout

Copyright 2020 Jennifer L. Armentrout
ISBN: 978-1-952457-12-8

Published by Blue Box Press, an imprint of Evil Eye Concepts, Incorporated

All rights reserved. No part of this book may be reproduced, scanned, or distributed in any printed or electronic form without permission. Please do not participate in or encourage piracy of copyrighted materials in violation of the author's rights.

This is a work of fiction. Names, places, characters and incidents are the product of the author's imagination and are fictitious. Any resemblance to actual persons, living or dead, events or establishments is solely coincidental.

Acknowledgments from the Author

Laura Kaye and I were standing in the Cincinnati airport in 2016 when I told her about From Blood and Ash. She was the first person who said, I need you to write this right now. I didn't. It was a high fantasy, something I'd never written before, and I kept telling myself that I needed time to see if I could take this crazy idea and pull it together into something that made sense. I didn't find that time, not in 2016, 2017, or 2018. It wasn't until I was talking with JR Ward about writing books of the heart—books that weren't exactly what was expected from us, but needed to be written nonetheless. It was that conversation in September of 2019 that gave me the courage to finally say now is the time to write this book. So Laura Kaye and JR Ward, I owe you two a world of thanks. Without both of you, From Blood and Ash would've never made it from an idea to a fully fleshed novel.

There were others involved in making sure I finished this book. It was Brigid Kemmerer, whose excitement when I told her about the book, gave me the courage to continue writing something that was unfamiliar to me. It was Hawke's Harem of Two—Wendy Higgins, who sent the most lovely and inspiring words to me after reading the book. It was Jen Fisher, who fell in love with Hawke by chapter three and provided unmeasurable feedback. It was Andrea Joan who sent me paragraph length texts about the book as she read. It was all the JLAnders who immediately hopped aboard the mystery teaser ship, willing to take this journey with me.

I'd originally planned on self-publishing this book. There were a lot of reasons, but there were two reasons that were most important to me. One was my goal to get this book out to you as soon as possible. The other was the need to write and publish this book without expectations and pressure, but then I heard about Blue Box Press, and knowing all the amazing work they do on their 1001 Dark Nights novellas, I reached out to Liz Berry. I had no idea what she would think when I told her what I was writing and how I wanted to publish it. I really thought she'd "nope" right out the discussion, but she didn't. In one phone call, she not only wanted the book but, I swear, had a marketing plan that lined up with what I wanted before even reading the book. I knew FB&A was in amazing hands. To MJ, Liz, and Jillian (and Steve, because STEVE BERRY STORY TIME), thank you for taking this unexpected leap with me. Your excitement, love, support and feedback has been invaluable in finishing this story and in getting it into the hands of readers. To the whole team behind this book: Chelle Olson, Jenn Watson, Kim Guidroz, thank you!

Thank you to Sarah J. Maas for your support. I'll try not to creepily pet your hair the next time I see you. Lexi Blake—without your advice I'm pretty sure we'd still be going back and forth on the back cover jacket. Thank you. And Hang Le, you are so incredibly talented. I can tell you three things: swords, arrows, and a bloody forest, and with that scarce description, you created the most amazing cover I've seen in a long time. You are the bomb diggity. Thank you to Stephanie Brown for taking care of all the things and Ernesto Floofington III for sounding like a little gremlin racing around above my head while I worked. To all the JLAnders Reviewers who knew this book was coming a lot sooner than anyone else, thank you for keeping it quiet and for always giving your honest reviews. Finally, thank you to YOU, the reader who will pick this book up and read it. Without you, none of this would be possible.

Sign up for the Blue Box Press/1001 Dark Nights Newsletter
and be entered to win a Tiffany Lock necklace.

There's a contest every quarter!

Go to www.1001DarkNights.com to subscribe.

As a bonus, all subscribers can download
FIVE FREE exclusive books!

Dedication

To You, the Reader.

Chapter 1

"They found Finley this eve, just outside the Blood Forest, dead."

I looked up from my cards and across the crimson-painted surface to the three men sitting at the table. I'd chosen this spot for a reason. I'd…felt nothing from them as I drifted between the crowded tables earlier.

No pain, physical or emotional.

Normally, I didn't prod to see if someone was in pain. Doing so without reason felt incredibly invasive, but in crowds, it was difficult to control just how much I allowed myself to feel. There was always someone whose pain cut so deeply, was so raw, that their anguish became a palpable entity I didn't even have to open my senses to feel—that I couldn't ignore and walk away from. They projected their agony onto the world around them.

I was forbidden to do anything but ignore. To never speak of the gift bestowed upon me by the gods and to never, ever go beyond sensing to actually doing something about it.

Not that I always did what I was supposed to do.

Obviously.

But these men were fine when I reached out with my senses to avoid those in great pain, which was surprising, given what they did for a living. They were guards from the Rise—the mountainous wall constructed from the limestone and iron mined from the Elysium Peaks. Ever since the War of Two Kings ended four centuries ago, the Rise had enclosed all of Masadonia, and every city in the Kingdom of Solis was protected by a Rise. Smaller versions surrounded villages and training posts, the farming communities, and other sparsely populated towns.

What the guards saw on a regular basis, what they had to do, often left them in anguish, rather it be from injuries or from what went deeper than torn skin and bruised bones.

Tonight, they weren't just absent of anguish, but also their armor and uniforms. Instead, they donned loose shirts and buckskin breeches. Still, I knew, even off duty, they were watchful for signs of the dreaded mist and the horror that came with it, and for those who worked against the future of the kingdom. They were still armed to the teeth.

As was I.

Hidden beneath the folds of the cloak and the thin gown I wore underneath, the cool hilt of a dagger that never quite warmed to my skin was sheathed against my thigh. Gifted to me on my sixteenth birthday, it wasn't the only weapon I'd acquired or the deadliest, but it was my favorite. The handle was fashioned from the bones of a long-extinct wolven—a creature that had been neither man nor beast but both—and the blade made of bloodstone honed to fatal sharpness.

I may yet again be in the process of doing something incredibly reckless, inappropriate, and wholly forbidden, but I wasn't foolish enough to enter a place like the Red Pearl without protection, the skill to employ it, and the wherewithal to take that weapon and skill and use them without hesitation.

"Dead?" the other guard said, a younger one with brown hair and a soft face. I thought his name might be Airrick, and he couldn't be much older than my eighteen years. "He wasn't just dead. Finley was drained of blood, his flesh chewed up like wild dogs had a go at him, and then torn to pieces."

My cards blurred as tiny balls of ice formed in the pit of my stomach. Wild dogs didn't do that. Not to mention, there weren't any wild dogs near the Blood Forest, the only place in the world where the trees bled, staining the bark and the leaves a deep crimson. There were rumors of other animals, overly large rodents and scavengers that preyed upon the corpses of those who lingered too long in the forest.

"And you know what that means," Airrick went on. "They must be near. An attack will—"

"Not sure this is the right conversation to be having," an older guard cut in. I knew of him. Phillips Rathi. He'd been on the Rise for years, which was nearly unheard of. Guards didn't have long lifespans. He nodded in my direction. "You're in the presence of a lady."

A lady?

Only the Ascended were called Ladies, but I also wasn't someone anyone, especially those in this building, would expect to be inside the Red Pearl. If I was discovered, I would be in...well, more trouble than I'd ever been in before and would face severe reprimand.

The kind of punishment that Dorian Teerman, the Duke of Masadonia, would just love to deliver. And which, of course, his close confidante, Lord Brandole Mazeen, would love to be in attendance for.

Anxiety surfaced as I looked at the dark-skinned guard. There was no way Phillips could know who I was. The top half of my face was covered by the white domino mask I'd found discarded in the Queen's Gardens ages ago, and I wore a plain robin's egg blue cloak I'd, uh, *borrowed* from Britta, one of the many castle servants who I'd overheard speaking about the Red Pearl. Hopefully, Britta wouldn't discover her missing overcoat before I returned it in the morn.

Even without the mask, though, I could count on one hand how many people in Masadonia had seen my face, and none of them would be here tonight.

As the Maiden, the Chosen, a veil usually covered my face and hair at all times, all except for my lips and jaw.

I doubted Phillips could recognize me solely on those features, and if he had, none of them would still be sitting here. I would be in the process of being dragged back, albeit gently, to my guardians, the Duke and Duchess of Masadonia.

There was no reason to panic.

Forcing the muscles along my shoulders and neck to ease, I smiled. "I'm no Lady. You're more than welcome to talk about whatever you wish."

"Be that as it may, a little less morbid topic would be welcomed," Phillips replied, sending a pointed look in the direction of the other two guards.

Airrick lifted his gaze to mine. "My apologies."

"Apologies not needed but accepted."

The third guard ducked his chin, studiously staring at his cards as he repeated the same. His cheeks had pinkened, something I found rather adorable. The guards who worked the Rise went through vicious training, becoming skilled in all manner of weaponry and hand-to-hand combat. None who survived their first venture outside the Rise came back without shedding blood and seeing death.

And yet, this man blushed.

I cleared my throat, wanting to ask more about who Finley was, whether he was a guard from the Rise or a Huntsman, a division of the army that ferried communication between the cities and escorted travelers and goods. They spent half the year outside the protection of the Rise. It was by far one of the most dangerous of all occupations, so they never traveled alone. Some never returned.

Unfortunately, a few who did, didn't come back the same. They returned with rampantly spreading death snapping at their heels.

Cursed.

Sensing that Phillips would silence any further conversation, I didn't voice any of the questions dancing on the tip of my tongue. If others had been with him and had been wounded by what most likely had killed Finley, I would find out one way or another.

I just hoped it wasn't through screams of terror.

The people of Masadonia had no real idea exactly how many returned from outside the Rise cursed. They only saw a handful here and there, and not the reality. If they did, panic and fear were sure to ignite a populace who truly had no concept of the horror outside the Rise.

Not like my brother Ian and I did.

Which was why when the topic at the table switched to more mundane things, I struggled to will the ice coating my insides to thaw. Countless lives were given and taken by the endeavor to keep those inside the Rise safe, but it was failing—had been failing—not just here, but throughout the Kingdom of Solis.

Death....

Death *always* found a way in.

Stop, I ordered myself as the general sense of unease threatened to swell. Tonight wasn't about all the things I was aware of that I probably shouldn't be. Tonight was about living, about...not being up all night, unable to sleep, alone and feeling like...like I had no control, no...no idea of who I was other than *what* I was.

Another poor hand was dealt, and I'd played enough cards with Ian to know there was no recovering from the ones I held. When I announced that I was out, the guards nodded as I rose, each bidding me a good evening.

Moving between the tables, I took the flute of champagne offered by a server with a gloved hand and tried to recapture the feelings of excitement that had buzzed through my veins as I'd hurried through the streets earlier that evening.

I minded my business as I scanned the room, keeping my senses to myself. Even outside of those who managed to project their anguish into the air around them, I didn't need to touch someone to know if they were hurting. I just needed to see someone and focus. What they looked like didn't change if they were experiencing some sort of pain, and their appearance didn't change when I concentrated on them. I simply *felt* their anguish.

Physical pain was almost always hot, but the kind that couldn't be seen?

It was almost always cold.

Bawdy shouts and whistles snapped me out of my own mind. A woman in red sat on the edge of the table next to the one I'd left. She wore a gown made of scraps of red satin and gauze that barely covered her thighs. One of the men grabbed a fistful of the diaphanous little skirt.

Smacking his hand away with a saucy grin, she lay back, her body forming a sensual curve. Her thick, blonde curls spilled across forgotten coins and chips. "Who wants to win me tonight?" Her voice was deep and smoky as she slid her hands along the waist of the frilly corset. "I can assure you boys, I will last longer than any pot of gold will."

"And what if it's a tie?" one of the men asked, the fine cut of his coat suggesting that he was a well-to-do merchant or businessman of some sort.

"Then it will be a far more entertaining night for me," she said, drawing one hand down her stomach, slipping even lower to between her—

Cheeks heating, I quickly looked away as I took a sip of the bubbly champagne. My gaze found its way to the dazzling glow of a rose-gold chandelier. The Red Pearl must be doing well, and the owners well connected. Electricity was expensive and heavily controlled by the Royal Court. It made me wonder who some of their clientele was for the luxury to be available.

Under the chandelier, another card game was in progress. There were women there too, their hair twisted in elaborate updos adorned with crystals, and their clothing far less daring than the women who worked here. Their gowns were vibrant shades of purple and yellow and pastel hues of blue and lilac.

I was only allowed to wear white, whether I was in my room or in public, which wasn't often. So, I was fascinated with how the different colors complemented the wearer's skin or hair. I imagined I looked like a ghost most days, roaming the halls of Castle Teerman in white.

These women also wore domino masks that covered half their faces, protecting their identities. I wondered who some of them were. Daring wives left alone one too many times? Young women who hadn't married or were perhaps widowed? Servants or women who worked in the city, out for the evening? Were Ladies and Lords in Wait among the masked females at the table and among the crowd? Did they come here for the same reasons I did?

Boredom? Curiosity?

Loneliness?

If so, then we were more alike than I realized, even though they were second daughters and sons, given to the Royal Court upon their thirteenth birthday during the annual Rite. And I...I was Penellaphe of Castle Teerman, Kin of the Balfours, and the Queen's favorite.

I was *the* Maiden.

Chosen.

And in a little under a year, upon my nineteenth birthday, I would Ascend, as would all Ladies and Lords in Wait. Our Ascensions would be different, but it would be the largest one since the first gods' Blessing that occurred after the end of the War of Two Kings.

Very little would happen to them if they were caught, but I...I would face the Duke's displeasure. My lips thinned as a kernel of anger took root, mingling with a sticky residue of disgust and shame.

The Duke was a pestilence of overly familiar hands and had an unnatural thirst for punishment.

But I wouldn't think about him either. Or worry about being disciplined. I might as well go back to my chambers if I was going to do that.

Dragging my gaze from the table, I noted that there were smiling and laughing women in the Pearl who wore no masks, hid no identities. They sat at tables with guards and businessmen, stood in shadowy alcoves and spoke with masked women, men, and also those who worked for the Red Pearl. They weren't ashamed or afraid to be seen.

Whoever they were, they had freedom I deeply coveted.

An independence I chased tonight, because masked and unknown, no one but the gods would know I was here. And as far as the gods were concerned, I had long ago decided that they had far better things to do than spend their time watching me. After all, if they had been paying attention, they would've already taken me to task over numerous things I'd already done that were forbidden to me.

So, I could be *anyone* tonight.

The freedom in that was a far headier sensation than I imagined. Even more so than the unripe poppy seeds provided by those who smoked them.

Tonight, I wasn't the Maiden. I wasn't Penellaphe. I was simply Poppy, a nickname I remembered my mother using, something only my brother Ian and very few others ever called me.

As Poppy, there were no strict rules to follow or expectations to fulfill, no future Ascension that was coming quicker than I was prepared for. There was no fear, no past or future. Tonight, I could live a little, even for a few hours, and rack up as much experience as I could before I was returned to the capital, to the Queen.

Before I was given to the gods.

A shiver tiptoed down my spine—uncertainty, along with a bite of desolation. I tamped it down, refusing to give life to it. Dwelling on what was to come and could not be changed served no purpose.

Besides, Ian had Ascended two years ago, and based on the monthly letters I received from him, he was the same. The only difference was that instead of spinning tales with his voice, he did so with words in each letter. Just last month, he wrote about two children, a brother and sister, who swam to the bottom of the Stroud Sea, befriending the water folk.

I smiled as I lifted the champagne flute, having no idea where he came up with those things. As far as I knew, it was impossible to swim to the bottom of the Stroud Sea, and there was no such thing as water folk.

Shortly after his Ascension, on the orders of the Queen and King, he'd married Lady Claudeya.

Ian never spoke of his wife.

Was he happy at all in his marriage? The curve of my lips faded as my gaze dropped to the fizzing, pinkish drink. I wasn't sure, but they'd barely known each other before marrying. How was that long enough when you'd presumably spend the rest of your life with a person?

And the Ascended lived for a very, very long time.

It was still odd for me to think of Ian as an Ascended. He wasn't a second son, but because I was the Maiden, the Queen had petitioned the gods for a rare exception to the natural order, and they had allowed him to Ascend. I wouldn't face what Ian had, marriage to a stranger, to another Ascended, one who was sure to covet beauty above all else, because attractiveness was seen as godlike.

And even though I was the Maiden, the Chosen, I would never be viewed as godlike. According to the Duke, I wasn't beautiful.

I was a *tragedy.*

Without realizing it, my fingers brushed the scratchy lace of the left side of the mask. I jerked my hand away.

A man I recognized as a guard rose from a table, turning to a woman wearing a white mask like I was. He extended a hand to her, speaking words too low for me to hear, but she answered with a nod and a smile before placing her hand in his. She rose, the skirt of her lilac-hued gown falling like liquid around her legs as he led her from the room toward the only two doors accessible by guests, one at either end of interconnecting chambers. The right went outside. The left door led upstairs, to more private rooms where Britta had said all manner of things occurred.

The guard took the masked woman to the left.

He'd asked. She'd said yes. Whatever it was they did upstairs, it would be welcomed and chosen by both, regardless of whether it lasted a few hours or a lifetime.

My attention lingered on the door long after it had closed. Was that another reason I had come here tonight? To…to experience pleasure with someone of my choosing?

I could if I wanted to. I'd overheard conversations between the Ladies in Wait, who weren't expected to remain untouched. According to them, there were…many things a woman could do that brought pleasure while retaining their purity.

Purity?

I hated that word, the meaning behind it. As if my virginity determined my goodness, my innocence, and its presence or lack thereof was somehow more important than the hundred choices I made every day.

There was even a part of me that wondered what the gods would do if I went to them no longer an actual maiden. Would they overlook everything else I did or didn't do simply because I was no longer a virgin?

I wasn't sure, but I hoped that wasn't the case. Not because I planned to have sex now or next week or…ever, but because I wanted to be able to make that choice.

Though, I wasn't quite sure how I'd find myself in a situation where that option would even arise. But I imagine there'd be willing participants who'd want to do the things I'd heard the Ladies in Wait speaking about here at the Red Pearl.

A nervous flutter beat in my chest as I forced myself to take another sip of the champagne. The sweet bubbles tickled the back of my throat, easing some of the sudden dryness in my mouth.

Truth be told, tonight had been a spur-of-the-moment decision. Most nights, I couldn't fall asleep until it was nearly dawn. When I did, I almost wished I hadn't. Three times this week alone, I woke from a nightmare, with my screams ringing in my ears. And when they came like this, in clusters, they felt like a harbinger. An instinct much like the ability to sense pain, screaming out a warning.

Drawing in a shallow breath, I glanced back to where I'd been looking before. The woman in red was no longer on the table. Instead, she was in the lap of the merchant who'd asked what would happen if two men won. He was inspecting his cards, but his hand was where hers had been heading earlier, delved deep between her thighs.

Oh, my.

Biting down on my lip, I pulled away from where I stood before my entire face caught on fire. I drifted into the next space that was separated by a partial wall, where another round of games was being played.

There were more guards here, some I even recognized as belonging to the Royal Guard, soldiers just like those who worked the Rise but who protected the Ascended instead. This was why the Ascended also had personal guards. People had tried to kidnap members of the Court before for ransom. No one was usually hurt too seriously in those situations, but there had been other attempts that stemmed from far different, more violent reasons.

Standing near a leafy potted plant that sported tiny, red buds, I was unsure of what to do from there. I could join another card game or strike up a conversation with any of the numerous people who lingered around the tables, but I wasn't all that good at making small talk with strangers. There was no doubt in my mind that I'd blurt out something bizarre or ask a random question that would make little sense to the conversation. So that was off the table. Maybe I should head back to my chambers. The hour had to be growing late and—

A strange awareness swept over me, starting as a tingling sensation along the back of my neck and intensifying with every passing second.

It felt like…like I was being watched.

Scanning the room, I didn't see anyone paying much attention to me, but I expected to find someone standing near. That was how potent the feeling was. Unease blossomed in the pit of my stomach. I started to turn toward the entrance when the soft, drawn-out notes of some sort of string instrument drew my attention to the left, my gaze landing on the gauzy, blood-red curtains that swayed gently from the movement of others in the establishment.

I stilled, listening to the rise and fall of the tempo that was soon joined by the heavy thump of a drum. I forgot about the feeling of being watched. I forgot about a lot of things. The music was…it was like nothing I'd heard before. It was deeper, thicker. Slowing, and then speeding up. It was…sensual. What had Britta, the servant, said about the kind of dancing that took place at the Red Pearl? She'd lowered her voice when she spoke of it, and the other maid Britta had been speaking to had looked scandalized.

Making my way along the outskirts of the room, I neared the curtains, reaching out to part them—

"I don't think you want to go in there."

Startled, I turned at the sound of the voice. A woman stood behind me—one of the ladies who worked for the Red Pearl. I recognized her. Not because she'd been on the arm of a merchant or businessman when I first came in, but because she was utterly beautiful.

Her hair was a deep black, thickly curled, and her skin was a deep, rich brown. The red gown she wore was sleeveless, cut low across her chest, and the fabric clung to her body like liquid.

"I'm sorry?" I said, unsure what else to say as I lowered my hand. "Why wouldn't I? They're just dancing."

"Just dancing?" Her gaze drifted over my shoulder to the curtain. "Some say that to dance is to make love."

"I...I hadn't heard that." Slowly, I looked behind me. Through the curtains, I could make out the shapes of bodies churning in time with the music, their movements full of mesmerizing and fluid grace. Some danced alone, their curves and forms clearly outlined, while others...

I sucked in a sharp breath, my eyes swinging back to the woman before me.

Her red-painted lips curved into a smile. "This is your first time here, isn't it?"

I opened my mouth to deny that statement but could feel the heat spreading across every visible part of my face. That alone was telling. "Is it that obvious?"

She laughed, and the sound was throaty. "Not to most. But to me, yes. I've never seen you here before."

"How would you know if you had?" I touched my mask just to make sure it hadn't slipped.

"Your mask is fine." There was a strange, knowing glint to her eyes, which were a mix of gold and brown. Not exactly hazel. The gold was far too bright and warm for that. They reminded me of another who had eyes the color of deep citrine. "I know a face, whether it's half-hidden or not, and yours is one I haven't seen here before. This is your first time."

Truly, I had no idea how to respond to that.

"And it's the Red Pearl's first time also." She leaned in, her voice lowering. "As we've never had the Maiden walk through the doors."

A wave of shock rolled through me as my grip tightened on the slippery champagne glass. "I don't know what you mean. I'm a second daughter—"

"You are *like* a second daughter, but not in the way you intend," she cut in, lightly touching my cloaked arm. "It's okay. There is nothing to fear. Your secret is safe with me."

I stared at her for what felt like an entire minute before I recovered the use of my tongue. "If that were true, why would that kind of secret be safe?"

"Why would it not be?" she returned. "What would I have to gain by telling anyone?"

"You'd earn the favor of the Duke and Duchess." My heart thumped.

Her smile faded as her stare hardened. "I have no need of a favor from an Ascended."

The way she said that, it was as if I'd suggested that she was courting favor with a pile of mud. I almost believed her, but no one who lived within the kingdom would waste the chance to earn an Ascended's esteem unless they…

Unless they didn't recognize Queen Ileana and King Jalara as the true, rightful rulers. Unless they supported he who called himself Prince Casteel, the true heir to the kingdom.

Except he was no prince or heir. He was nothing more than a remnant of Atlantia, the corrupt and twisted kingdom that had fallen at the end of the War of Two Kings. A monster who had wreaked havoc and caused bloodshed, the embodiment of pure evil.

He was the Dark One.

And yet there were those who supported him and his claim. Descenters who had been a part of riots and the disappearances of many Ascended. In the past, the Descenters only caused discord through small rallies and protests, and even then, that had been few and far between due to the punishment that was meted out to those who were suspected to be Descenters. The trials couldn't even be called that. No second chances. No long-term imprisonment. Death was swift and final.

But things had changed of late.

Many believed the Descenters had been responsible for the mysterious deaths of high-ranking Royal Guards. Several in Carsodonia, the capital, had inexplicably fallen from the Rise. Two had been killed with arrows through the back of their heads in Pensdurth, a smaller city on the coast of the Stroud Sea, near the capital. Others had simply vanished while in the smaller villages, never to be seen or heard from again.

Only a few months ago, a violent uprising had ended in bloodshed in Three Rivers, a teeming trade city beyond the Blood Forest. Goldcrest Manor, the Royal Seat in Three Rivers, had been burned, razed to the ground, along with the Temples. Duke Everton had died in the fire, along with many servants and guards. It was only by some miracle that the Duchess of Three Rivers had escaped.

The Descenters weren't just Atlantians who were hidden among the people of Solis. Some of the Dark One's followers didn't even have a drop of Atlantian blood in them.

My gaze sharpened and zeroed in on the beautiful woman. Could she be a Descenter? I couldn't fathom how anyone could support the fallen kingdom, no matter how hard their lives were or how unhappy they may be. Not when the Atlantians and the Dark One were responsible for the mist, for what festered inside of it. For what most likely had ended Finley's life—had taken countless more lives, including my mother's and father's, and had left my body riddled with the reminder of the horror that thrived inside the mist.

Pushing aside my suspicions for the moment, I opened myself up to sense if there was some great pain inside her, something that went beyond the physical and stemmed from either grief or bitterness. The kind of pain that made people do horrible things to try and alleviate the anguish.

There was no hint of that radiating from her.

But that didn't mean she wasn't a Descenter.

The woman's head tilted. "As I said, you have nothing to worry about when it comes to me. Him? That's another story."

"Him?" I repeated.

She moved to the side as the main door opened, and a sudden gust of cool air announced the arrival of more patrons. A man walked in, and behind him was an older gentleman with sandy blond hair and a weathered face, colored by the sun—

My eyes widened as disbelief thundered through me. It was Vikter Wardwell. What was he doing at the Red Pearl?

An image of the women with the short gowns and partially exposed breasts came to mind, and I thought about why I was here. My eyes widened.

Oh, gods.

I didn't want to think about the purpose for his visit any longer. Vikter was a seasoned member of the Royal Guard, a man well into his fourth decade of life, but he was more than that to me. The dagger strapped to my thigh had been a gift from him, and it was he who broke with custom and made sure I not only knew how to use it, but also how to wield a sword, strike a target unseen with an arrow, and even when weaponless, how to take down a man twice my size.

Vikter was like a father to me.

He was also my personal guard and had been since I'd first arrived in Masadonia. He wasn't my only guard, though. He shared duties with Rylan Keal, who'd replaced Hannes after he'd passed in his sleep a little less than a year ago. It had been an unexpected loss as Hannes had been in his early thirties and in prime health. The Healers believed it to have been some unknown ailment of the heart. Still, it was hard to imagine how one could go to sleep healthy and whole and never wake up again.

Rylan didn't know I was as well trained as I was, but he knew I could handle a dagger. He wasn't aware of where Vikter and I all too often disappeared to outside the castle. He was kind and often relaxed, but we weren't nearly as close as Vikter and I were. If it had been Rylan here, I could've easily slipped away.

"Dammit," I swore, turning sideways as I reached back and pulled the hood of my cloak up over my head. My hair was a rather noticeable shade of burnt copper, but even with it hidden now and my entire face obscured, Vikter would recognize me.

He had a sixth sense that only belonged to parents and made itself known when their child was up to no good.

Glancing back toward the entrance, my stomach dropped as I saw him sit at one of the tables facing the door—the only exit.

The gods hated me.

Truly, they did, because there was no doubt in my mind that Vikter would see me. He wouldn't report me, but I'd rather crawl into a hole full of roaches and spiders than attempt to explain to him, of all people, why I was at the Red Pearl. And there would be lectures. Not the speeches and punishments the Duke loved to deliver, but the kind that crawled under your skin and made you feel terrible for days.

Mainly because you had been caught doing something you deserved reprimand for.

And, frankly, I didn't want to see Vikter's face when he discovered that I realized he was here. I stole another peek and—

Oh, gods, a woman knelt beside him, a hand on his leg!

I needed to scrub my eyes.

"That's Sariah," the woman explained. "As soon as he arrives, she's at his side. I do believe she carries a torch for him."

Slowly, I looked at the woman beside me. "He comes here often?"

One side of her lips curved up. "Often enough to know what happens beyond the red curtain and—"

"That's enough," I cut her off. I now needed to scrub my brain. "I don't need to hear any more."

Her laugh was soft. "You have the look of one who is in need of a hiding place. And, yes, in the Red Pearl, that is an easily recognizable look." She deftly took my champagne glass. "Upstairs, there are currently unoccupied rooms. Try the sixth door on the left. You will find sanctuary there. I'll come for you when it's safe."

Suspicion rose as I met her gaze, but I let her take my arm and lead me toward the left. "Why would you help me?"

She opened the door. "Because everyone should be able to live a little, even for a few hours."

My mouth dropped open as she parroted what I'd thought to myself minutes ago. Stunned, I stood there.

Giving me a wink, she closed the door.

Her figuring out who I was couldn't be a coincidence. Repeating back to me what I'd been thinking earlier? There was no way. A rough laugh escaped my lips. The woman may be a Descenter, or at the very least, she wasn't a fan of the Ascended. But she might also be a Seer.

I didn't think there were any of them left.

And I *still* couldn't believe that Vikter was here—that he came here often enough that one of the ladies in red liked him. I wasn't sure why I was so surprised. It wasn't like Royal Guards were forbidden from seeking pleasure or even marrying. Many were quite…promiscuous since their lives were rife with danger and often far too short. It was just that Vikter had a wife who'd passed long before I even met him, dying in childbirth along with the babe. He still loved his Camilia as much as he had when she lived and breathed.

But what could be found here had nothing to do with love, did it? And everyone got lonely, no matter if their heart belonged to someone they could no longer have or not.

A little saddened by that, I turned around in the narrow stairwell lit by oil wall sconces. I exhaled heavily. "What have I gotten myself into?"

Only the gods knew, and there was no turning back now.

I slipped my hand inside the cloak, keeping it close to the hilt of the dagger as I climbed the steps to the second floor. The hallway was wider and surprisingly quiet. I didn't know what I expected, but I'd thought I would hear...sounds.

Shaking my head, I counted until I reached the sixth door on the left. I tried the handle and found it unlocked. I started to open the door but stopped. What was I doing? Anyone or anything could be waiting beyond this door. That woman downstairs—

The sound of a male chuckle filled the hallway as the door beside me opened. Panicked, I quickly backed into the room in front of me, closing the door behind me.

Heart pounding, I looked around. There were no lamps, just a tree of candles on a mantel. A settee sat in front of an empty fireplace. Without even looking behind me, I knew the only other piece of furniture had to be a bed. I drew in a deep breath, catching the scent of the candles. Cinnamon? But there was something else, something that reminded me of dark spices and pine. I started to turn—

An arm curled around my waist, pulling me back against a very hard, very male body.

"This," a deep voice whispered, "is unexpected."

Chapter 2

Caught off guard, I looked up. A mistake that Vikter had taught me never to make. I should've gone for my dagger, but instead, I stood there as the arm around my waist tightened, and his hand settled at my hip.

"But it's a welcome surprise," he continued, sliding his arm away.

Snapping out of my stupor, I whirled to face him, the hood of the cloak remaining in place as my hand went for the dagger. I looked up...and then up some more.

Oh, my gods.

I froze, utter shock rippling through me, shorting out all common sense when I saw his face in the soft glow of the candlelight.

I knew who he was, even though I'd never spoken with him.

Hawke Flynn.

Everyone in Castle Teerman knew when the Rise Guard arrived from Carsodonia, the capital, a few months ago. I'd been no different.

I wanted to lie to myself and say that it was due to his striking height, placing him nearly a foot taller than me. Or it was because he moved with the same inherent, predatory grace and fluidity that belonged to the large, gray cave cats that normally roamed the Wastelands but that I had seen once in the Queen's palace as a child. The fearsome, wild animal had been caged, and the way it continuously prowled back and forth in the too-small enclosure had equally fascinated and horrified me. I'd seen Hawke pacing in the same manner on more than one occasion, as if he too were caged. It could've been the sense of authority that seemed to bleed from his pores even though he couldn't be much older than I was—maybe the same age as my brother or a year or two older. Or perhaps it was his skill with the sword. One morning while I stood beside the Duchess on one of the many balconies at Castle Teerman, overlooking the training yard below, she'd told me Hawke had come from the capital with glowing recommendations and was well on his way to becoming one of the youngest Royal Guards. Her gaze had been fixed on Hawke's sweat-slick arms.

So had mine.

Since his arrival, I'd found myself hidden in the shadowy alcoves more than a few times, watching him train with the other guards. Other than the weekly City Council sessions held in the Great Hall, it was the only time I saw him.

My interest could simply be because Hawke was…well, he was beautiful.

It wasn't often that could be said about a male, but I could think of no better word to describe him. He had dark, thick hair that curled at the nape of his neck and often fell forward, brushing equally dark brows. The planes and angles of his face made me yearn for some talent with a brush or a pen. His cheekbones were high and wide, nose surprisingly straight for a guard. Many of them had suffered at least one broken nose. His square jaw was firm, and his mouth well formed. The few times I'd seen him smile, the right side of his lip curved up, and a deep dimple appeared. If he had a matching one in his left cheek, I didn't know. But his eyes were by far his most captivating feature.

They reminded me of cool honey, a striking color I'd never seen before, and he had this way of looking at you that left you feeling stripped bare. I knew this because I felt his stare during the Councils held in the Great Hall, even though he'd never seen my face or even my eyes before. I was sure his regard was due to the fact that I was the first Maiden in centuries. People always stared when I was in public, whether they were guards, Lords and Ladies in Wait, or commoners.

His stare could also just be a product of my imagination, driven by my small, hidden desire that he was as curious about me as I was of him.

Perhaps it was all those reasons why he caught my interest, but there was another one that I was a little embarrassed to even acknowledge.

I'd purposely reached out with my senses when I saw him. I knew it was wrong to do when there was no good reason. Nothing to justify the invasion. And I had no excuse other than wondering what often made him pace like a caged cave cat.

Hawke was *always* in pain.

Not the physical kind. It was deeper than that, feeling like chips of sharp ice against my skin. It was raw and it felt never-ending. But the anguish that seemed to follow him like a shadow never overwhelmed him. If I hadn't prodded, I never would have felt it. Somehow, he kept that kind of agony in check, and I knew of no one else who could do that.

Not even the Ascended.

Only because I never felt *anything* from them, although I knew they felt physical pain. The fact that I never had to worry about picking up residual pain from them should make me seek out their presence, but instead, it gave me the creeps.

"I wasn't expecting you tonight," Hawke spoke. He was giving me that half-smile of his now, the one that showed no teeth, made the dimple in his right cheek appear, but never quite reached his eyes. "It's only been a few days, sweetling."

Sweetling?

I opened my mouth and then clamped it shut as realization rose. I blinked. He thought I was someone else! Someone he'd obviously met here before. I glanced down at my cloak—the borrowed garment. It was rather distinctive, a pale blue with an edging of white fur.

Britta.

Did he think I was Britta?

She and I were about the same height, a little under average, and the cloak hid the shape of my body, which was not nearly as thin as hers. No matter how active I was, I could not achieve the willowy frame of Duchess Teerman or some of the other Ladies.

Inexplicably, there was a little part of me, the same bit that was hidden, that was…disappointed, and maybe even a little envious of the pretty maid.

My gaze swept over Hawke. He wore the black tunic and breeches that all guards wore under their armor. Had he come straight here after his shift? I gave the room a quick once-over. There was a small table beside the settee, where two glasses sat. Hawke hadn't been alone in here before I arrived. Could he have been with another? Behind Hawke, the bed was made and didn't appear as if anyone had...slept in it.

What should I do? Turn and run? That would be odd. He'd be sure to ask Britta about it, but as long as I returned the cloak and mask without her knowing, I would be in the clear.

Except Vikter was most likely still downstairs, and the woman was, too—

My gods, she had to be a Seer. Instinct told me she had known this room was occupied. She'd sent me here on purpose. Had she known that Hawke was here and likely to mistake me for Britta?

It seemed too unreal to believe.

"Did Pence tell you I was here?" he asked.

My breath caught as my heart started pounding like a hammer against my ribs. I thought Pence was a guard on the Rise, one around Hawke's age. A blond, if I remembered correctly, but I hadn't seen him downstairs. I shook my head.

"Have you been watching for me, then? Following me?" he asked, tsking softly under his breath. "We'll have to talk about that, won't we?"

There was an odd threat to his voice, one that gave me the impression that he was not all that pleased by the idea of Britta following him.

"But not tonight, it seems. You're strangely quiet," he observed. From what I knew of Britta, she was rarely ever demure.

But the moment I spoke, he'd know I wasn't the maid, and I...I wasn't ready for him to discover that. I wasn't sure what I was ready for. My hand was no longer on the dagger, and I didn't know what that meant. All I knew was that my heart was still racing.

"We don't have to talk." He reached for the hem of his tunic, and before I could take another breath, he pulled it over his head, tossing it aside.

My lips parted and my eyes widened. I'd seen a man's chest before, but I'd never seen his. The muscles that flexed and bunched under the thinner shirts the guards trained in were now on display. He was broad of shoulder and chest, all lean muscles defined by years of intense training. There was a fine dusting of hair under his navel that disappeared behind his breeches. My gaze dipped even lower, and heat returned, a different kind that didn't just flush my skin but also invaded my blood.

Even in the candlelight, I could see how tight his breeches were, how they gloved his body, leaving very little to the imagination.

And I had a vast imagination thanks to the Ladies' frequent tendency to overshare, and *my* frequent tendency to listen in on conversations.

A strange curling sensation hit my lower stomach. It wasn't unpleasant. Not at all. It was warm and tingling, reminding me of my first sip of bubbly champagne.

Hawke stepped toward me, and my muscles tensed to run, but I held myself still by sheer will. I knew I should've stepped away. I should've spoken and revealed that I wasn't Britta. I should've left immediately. The way he prowled toward me, his long legs eating up the distance between us, told me his intent, even if he hadn't removed his tunic. And while I had little—all right, absolutely *no* experience—I inherently knew that if he reached me, he would touch me. He may do even more. He might kiss me.

And that was forbidden.

I was the Maiden, the Chosen. Not to mention, he thought I was another woman, and he'd obviously been in this room with someone else before I got here. That didn't mean he'd *been* with someone, but he could've.

I still didn't move or speak.

I waited, my heart beating so fast I felt faint. Tiny tremors racked my hands and legs.

And I never trembled.

What are you doing? whispered the reasonable, sane voice in my head.

Living, I whispered back.

And being incredibly stupid, the voice countered.

I was, but again, I stood there.

Senses hyperaware, I watched as Hawke stopped in front of me and lifted his hands, gripping the back of the hood with one. For a moment, I thought he might pull it back, and the charade would be over, but that wasn't what he did. The hood only slipped back a couple of inches.

"I don't know what kind of game you're about tonight." His deep voice was husky. "But I'm willing to find out."

His other arm came around my waist. A gasp left me as he hauled me to his chest. This was nothing like the brief embraces I'd received from Vikter. I'd never been held by a man like this. There wasn't an inch between his chest and mine. The contact was a jolt to my senses.

He lifted me up onto the tips of my toes, then clear off my feet. His strength was staggering since I wasn't exactly light. Stunned, my hands landed on his shoulders. The heat of his hard skin seemed to burn through my gloves and the cloak and thin white gown I usually slept in.

His head slanted, and I felt the warmth of his breath on my lips. A tight tremor of anticipation coiled its way down my spine at the same moment my stomach dipped with uncertainty. There was no time for the two warring emotions to battle. He pivoted and strode forward with the same kind of feline grace I'd seen from him before. In a matter of a few stuttering heartbeats, he was guiding us down, his grip strong but careful, as if he were aware of his strength. He came down over me, his hand still behind my head, his weight a shock as he pressed me into the bed, and then his mouth was on mine.

Hawke kissed me.

There was nothing sweet or soft, like I'd imagined a kiss to be. It was hard and overwhelming, claiming, and when I sucked in a sharp breath, he took advantage, deepening the kiss. His tongue touched mine, startling me. Panic flared in the pit of my stomach, but so did something else, something far more powerful, a pleasure I hadn't experienced before. He tasted of the golden liquor I'd once snuck, and I felt that stroke of his tongue in every part of me. It was in the shivers that erupted all over my skin, in the inexplicable heaviness in my chest, in that curling, tightening sensation below my navel and even lower still where there was a sudden, throbbing pulse between my legs. I shuddered, my fingers digging into his flesh, and I suddenly wished I hadn't worn gloves because I wanted to feel his skin, and I doubted I'd be in any shape to concentrate on what he was feeling. His head tilted, and I felt the brush of his oddly sharp—

Without warning, he broke the kiss and lifted his head. "Who are you?"

Thoughts oddly slow and skin humming, I blinked open my eyes. Dark hair fell forward onto his forehead. His features were shadowed in the soft, flickering light, but I thought his lips looked as swollen as mine felt.

Hawke acted too fast for me to track the movement, tugging my hood back, exposing my masked face. His brows lifted as the haze cleared from my thoughts. My heart jumped around in my chest for a whole different reason, even though my lips still tingled from the kiss.

My first kiss.

Hawke's golden-eyed gaze rose to my head, and he shifted his hand out from behind my neck. I tensed as he picked up a strand of my hair, drawing it out so it shone a deep auburn in the candlelight. His head tilted to the left.

"You are most definitely not who I thought you were," he murmured.

"How did you know?" I blurted out.

"Because the last time I kissed the owner of this cloak, she damn near sucked my tongue down her throat."

"Oh," I whispered. Was I supposed to have done that? It didn't sound like it would be something enjoyable.

He stared down at me, gaze assessing as he remained with half his body atop mine. One of his legs was thrust between mine, and I had no idea exactly when that had happened. "Have you been kissed before?"

My face caught fire. Oh, gods, was it that obvious? "I have!"

One side of his lips kicked up. "Do you always lie?"

"No!" I immediately lied.

"Liar," he murmured, his tone almost teasing.

Embarrassment flooded my system, suffocating the shivery pleasure as if I'd been doused in cold, winter sleet. I pushed at his bare chest. "You should get off."

"I was planning to."

The way he said it made my eyes narrow.

Hawke laughed, and it was…it was the first time I'd heard him do so. When I saw him in the Hall, he was quiet and stoic like most guards, and I'd only seen that half-grin of his while he trained. But never a laugh. And with the anguish I knew lingered below the surface, I wasn't quite sure that he ever laughed.

But he had now, and it sounded real, deep, and nice, and it rumbled through me, all the way to the tips of my toes. I was slow to realize that this was the most I'd heard him speak. He had a slight accent, an almost musical lilt to his tone. I couldn't quite place it, but I'd only ever been to the capital and here, and it was not often that many spoke to me or around me if they knew I was present. The accent could be quite common for all I knew.

"You really should move," I told him, even though I liked the weight of him.

"I'm quite comfortable where I am," he added.

"Well, I'm not."

"Will you tell me who you are, Princess?"

"Princess?" I repeated. There were no Princesses or Princes in the entire kingdom beyond the Dark One, who called himself such. Not since Atlantia had ruled.

"You are quite demanding." He lifted one shoulder in a shrug. "I imagine a Princess to be demanding."

"I am not demanding," I stated. "Get off me."

He arched a brow. "Really?"

"Telling you to move is not being demanding."

"We'll have to disagree on that." He paused. "Princess."

My lips twitched in wry humor, but I managed to stifle the smile. "You shouldn't call me that."

"Then what should I call you? A name, perhaps?"

"I'm...I'm no one," I told him.

"No One? What a strange name. Do girls with a name like that often make a habit of wearing other people's clothing?"

"I'm not a girl," I snapped.

"I would sure hope not." He paused, lips curling down at the corners. "How old are you?"

"Old enough to be in here, if that's what you're worried about."

"In other words, old enough to be masquerading as someone else, allowing others to believe you're another person and then allowing them to kiss—"

"I get what you're saying," I cut him off. "Yes, I'm old enough for all those things."

One eyebrow rose. "I'll tell you who I am, although I have a feeling you already know. I'm Hawke Flynn."

"Hi," I said, feeling foolish for doing so.

The dimple in his right cheek deepened. "This is the part where you tell me your name."

My lips nor my tongue moved.

"Then I'll have to keep calling you Princess." His eyes were much warmer now, and I wanted to see if the pain had eased but managed to resist. I thought that perhaps his pain had gone away. If so...

"The least you can do is tell me why you didn't stop me," he said before I could give in to the curiosity and reach out with my senses.

I had no idea how I could answer that when I didn't fully understand it myself.

One side of his lips quirked up. "I'm sure it's more than my disarming good looks."

I wrinkled my nose. "Of course."

Another short, surprised-sounding laugh left him. "I think you just insulted me."

Chagrined, I winced. "That's not what I meant—"

"You've wounded me, Princess."

"I highly doubt that. You have to be more than well aware of your appearance."

"I am. It has led to quite a few people making questionable life choices."

"Then why did you say you were insulted—?" Realizing he was teasing me and feeling foolish for not seeing that right away, I pushed at his chest once more. "You're still lying on me."

"I know."

I took a breath. "It's quite rude of you to continue doing so when I've made it clear that I would like for you to move."

"It's quite rude of you to barge into my room dressed as—"

"Your lover?"

He raised a brow. "I wouldn't call her that."

"What would you call her?"

Hawke appeared to mull that over while still sprawled halfway across me. "A...good friend."

Part of me was relieved that he hadn't referred to her as something derogatory like I'd overheard other men do before when speaking of women they'd been intimate with, but a good friend? "I didn't know friends behaved this way."

"I'm willing to wager you don't know much about these sorts of things."

The truth in his statement was hard to ignore. "And you wager all of this on just one kiss?"

"Just one kiss? Princess, you can learn a wealth of things from just one kiss."

Staring at him, I couldn't help but feel...very inexperienced. The only thing I could tell from his kiss was what it had made me feel. Like he was seeking to possess me.

"Why didn't you stop me?" His gaze swept over the mask and then lower, to where I realized the cloak had parted, exposing the too-thin gown and its rather daring neckline. Honestly, I didn't know what I'd been thinking when I slipped on the garment. It was almost like I'd subconsciously been preparing myself for...something. My stomach tumbled. More likely, the gown was false bravado.

Hawke's gaze found mine. "I think I'm beginning to understand."

"Does that mean you're going to get up so I can move?"

Why haven't you made him get up? whispered that stupid, very reasonable, and very logical voice. That was a great question. I knew how to use a man's weight against them. More importantly, I had my dagger and access to it. But I hadn't gone for it, nor had I truly made an attempt to put space between us. What did that mean? I...I supposed I felt safe. At least, at the moment. I may know very little about Hawke, but he wasn't a stranger, at least he didn't feel that way to me, and I wasn't afraid of him.

Hawke shook his head. "I have a theory."

"I'm waiting with bated breath for this."

That dimple in his right cheek appeared once more. "I think you came to this very room with a purpose in mind."

He was right about that, but I doubted he would be right about the actual reason.

"It's why you didn't speak or attempt to correct my assumption of who you were. Perhaps the cloak you borrowed was also a very calculated decision," he continued. "You came here because you want something from me."

I started to deny what he suggested, but no words rose to the tip of my tongue. Silence wasn't a denial or agreement, but my stomach dipped again.

He shifted ever so slightly, his hand coming to rest against my right cheek, his fingers splayed out. "I'm right, aren't I, Princess?"

Heart skipping all over the place, I tried to swallow, but my throat had dried. "Maybe...maybe I came here for...for conversation."

"To talk?" His brows rose. "About what?"

"Lots of things," I said.

His expression smoothed out. "Like?"

My mind was uselessly empty for several seconds, and then I blurted out the first thing that came to mind. "Why did you choose to work on the Rise?"

"You came here tonight to ask that?"

Not a single thing about his tone or his look said he believed me, but I nodded while I added that this was yet another example of how I was really bad at making conversation with people.

He was quiet and then said, "I joined the Rise for the same reason most do."

"And what is that?" I asked, even though I knew most of the reasons.

"My father was a farmer, and that was not the life for me. There aren't many other opportunities offered than joining the Royal Army and protecting the Rise, Princess."

"You're right."

His eyes narrowed as surprise flickered across his features. "What do you mean by that?"

"I mean, there aren't many chances for children to become something other than what their parents were."

"You mean there aren't many chances for children to improve their stations in life, to do better than those who came before them?"

I nodded as best I could. "The...the natural order of things doesn't exactly allow that. A farmer's son is a farmer or they—"

"They choose to become a guard, where they risk their lives for stable pay that they most likely won't live long enough to enjoy?" he finished. "Doesn't sound much like an option, does it?"

"No," I admitted, but I had already thought that. There were jobs Hawke could've strived for. Trader and hunter, but they too were hazardous, as they required going outside the Rise frequently. It just wasn't as dangerous as joining the Royal Army and going to the Rise. Was the source of his anguish due to what he'd seen as a guard? "There may not be many choices, but I still think—no, I know—that joining the guard requires a certain level of innate strength and courage."

"You think that of all the guards? That they are courageous?"

"I do."

"Not all guards are good men, Princess."

My eyes narrowed. "I know that. Bravery and strength do not equal goodness."

"We can agree on that." His gaze dropped to my mouth, and my chest felt inexplicably tight.

"You said your father was a farmer. Is he…has he gone to the gods?"

Something crept across his face, gone too quickly for me to decipher. "No. He is alive and well. Yours?"

I gave a small shake of my head. "My father—both of my parents are gone."

"I'm sorry to hear that," he said, and it sounded genuine. "The loss of a parent or a family member lingers long after they're gone, the pain lessening but never fading. Years later, you'll still find yourself thinking that you'd do anything to get them back."

He was right, and I thought that this was perhaps the source of the pain he felt. "You sound like you know firsthand."

"I do."

I thought of Finley. Had Hawke known him well? Most of the guards were close, developing a bond thicker than blood, but even if he hadn't known Finley, there were surely others he knew that had been lost. "I'm sorry," I said. "I'm sorry for whoever it is that you've lost. Death is…"

Death was constant.

And I saw a lot of it. I wasn't supposed to, as sheltered as I was, but I saw death all too frequently.

His head tilted, sending a tumble of dark locks over his forehead. "Death is like an old friend who pays a visit, sometimes when it's least expected and other times when you're waiting for her. It's neither the first nor the last time she'll pay a visit, but that doesn't make any death less harsh or unforgiving."

Sadness threatened to take up residence in my chest, crowding out the warmth. "That it is."

He dipped his head suddenly, his lips nearing mine. "I doubt the need for conversation led you to this room. You didn't come here to talk about sad things that cannot be changed, Princess."

I knew why I came here tonight, and Hawke was right, yet again. It wasn't to talk. I came here to live. To experience. To choose. To be anyone other than who I was. None of those things included talking.

But I'd had my first kiss tonight. I could stop there or tonight could be a night of many firsts, all of my choosing.

Was I…? Was I really considering this, whatever this was? Gods,

I truly was. Tiny tremors rocked me. Could he feel them? They piled in my stomach, forming little knots of anticipation and fear.

I was the Maiden. The Chosen. My earlier convictions about what the gods concerned themselves with weakened. Would they find me unworthy? Panic didn't seize me like it should. Instead, a spark of hope did, and that unsettled me more than anything. The tiny glimmer of hope felt traitorous and wholly concerning, given that being deemed unworthy resulted in one of the most serious consequences.

If I were to be found unworthy, I'd face certain death.

I'd be exiled from the kingdom.

Chapter 3

As far as I knew, there had only been one person who'd been found unworthy upon Ascension. Their name had been erased from our histories, as well as any piece of information about who they were and whatever deeds had caused his or her exile. They'd been forbidden to live among mortals, and without family, support, or protection, faced certain death. Even the villages and the farmers with their small Rises and guards suffered staggering mortality rates.

While my Ascension was different from the others, I could still be found unworthy, and I imagined my punishment would be just as grave, but I didn't have the mental capacity to deal with that.

No.

That was a lie.

I didn't *want* to deal with that. I should, but I wasn't leaving the room. I wasn't stopping Hawke. I'd already made up my mind even if I didn't understand why he was still here, with me.

Dampening my lower lip with my tongue, I felt dizzy and even a little faint, and I never felt *faint*. Those impossibly thick lashes lowered, and his gaze was so intent on my mouth that it was like a caress. I shivered.

Those eyes of his seemed even brighter than before as his finger traced the outline of my mask, all the way to where the satin ribbon disappeared under the fall of my hair. "May I remove this?"

Unable to speak, I shook my head no.

Hawke halted for a moment, and then the half-smile appeared—no dimple this time, though. He trailed his finger away from the mask, then ran it along the line of my jaw and down my throat, to where the cloak was fastened. "How about this?"

I nodded.

His fingers were deft, and he brushed the cloak aside and then trailed just one fingertip along the neckline, following the rapid rise and fall of the swell of my breast. A riot of sensations followed his finger, so many I couldn't make sense of them all.

"What do you want from me?" he asked, toying with the small bow between my breasts. "Tell me, and I'll make it so."

"Why?" I blurted out. "Why would you...do this? You don't know me, and you thought I was someone else."

A flicker of amusement crossed his striking features. "I have nowhere to be at the moment, and I'm intrigued."

My brows lifted. "Because you have nowhere to be at the moment?"

"Would you rather I wax poetic about how I'm charmed by your beauty, even though I can only see half your face? Which, by the way, from what I can see is pleasing. Would you rather I tell you I'm captivated by your eyes? They are a pretty shade of green from what I can tell."

I started to frown. "Well, no. I don't want you to lie."

"None of those things were a lie." He tugged on the bow as he dipped his head, brushing his lips over mine. The soft contact sent a wave of awareness through me. "I told you the truth, Princess. I'm intrigued by you, and it's fairly rare anyone intrigues me."

"So?"

"So," he repeated with a chuckle as his lips glided along my jaw. "You've changed my evening. I'd planned to return to my quarters. Maybe get a good, albeit boring, night of sleep, but I have a suspicion that tonight will be anything but boring if I spend it with you."

I drew in a shallow breath, weirdly flattered, and yet still confused by his motivations. I wished someone was here to ask, but even if they were, that would be weird—and awkward.

The two glasses by the settee appeared in my mind. "Were you...were you with someone before me?"

His head lifted and stared down at me. "That's a random question."

"There are two glasses by the settee," I pointed out.

"It's also a random, *personal* question asked by someone whose name I don't even know."

My cheeks warmed. He had a point.

He was quiet for so long that doubt crept in. Maybe I shouldn't care if he had been with someone else this evening, but I did, and if that told me anything, it screamed that this was a mistake. I was in over my head. I knew nothing about him, of what was—

"I was with someone," he answered, and disappointment swelled. "A friend who is not like the owner of the cloak. One I hadn't seen in a while. We were catching up, in private."

The dismay eased, and I decided that he must be telling the truth. He didn't have to lie to have me when he could have any number of others who would be eager to *intrigue* him.

"So, Princess, will you tell me what you want from me?"

I took another uneven breath. "Anything?"

"Anything." He moved his hand then, cupping my breast as he ran his thumb across the center.

It was such a light touch, but I gasped as bolts of pleasure darted through me. My body reacted on its own, arching into his touch.

"I'm waiting," he said, swiping his thumb once more and scattering my already disjointed thoughts. "Tell me what you enjoy, so I can make you love it."

"I…" I bit down on my lip. "I don't know."

Hawke's gaze flew to mine, and such a long moment passed that I began to wonder if I'd said the wrong thing. "I'll tell you what I want." His thumb moved in slow, tight circles across a most sensitive part. "I want you to remove your mask."

"I…" A sharp, pulsing thrill rippled through my body, quickly followed by my heady wonder. What I felt… I'd never felt anything like it before. Sharp and sweet, a different type of anguish. "Why?"

"Because I want to see you."

"You can see me now."

"No, Princess," he said, lowering his head until his lips brushed the neckline of my gown. "I want to really see you when I do this without your gown between you and my mouth."

Before I could ask what he meant, I felt the wet, warm glide of his tongue through the thin, silken gown. I gasped, shocked by the act and by the rush of liquid heat it brought forth, but then his gaze lifted to mine as his mouth closed over the tip of my breast. He sucked deep and long, and the gasp turned to a cry that would surely embarrass me later.

"Remove your mask." His head lifted as he slid a hand over my hip. "Please."

He wouldn't recognize me if I did. Hawke would never know who I was with or without the mask, but...

If I removed the facial covering, would he say what the Duke often did? That I was both a masterpiece and a tragedy? And when he felt the uneven slices of skin scattered along my stomach and thighs, would he jerk his hand away in horror?

My skin chilled.

I hadn't thought this through.

At all.

The wonderful, exhilarating heat dimmed. Hawke wasn't an Ascended, but he was like them in appearance, nearly flawless. I had never been ashamed of the scars before. Not when they were proof of the horror I'd survived. But if he—

Hawke's hand slid down my outer right thigh to where the dress parted and stopped, right over the hilt of the dagger. "What the...?"

Before I could even take another breath, he'd unsheathed the blade, his fingers coming precariously close to one of the scars. I sat up, but he was faster, rocking backward.

The candlelight glinted off the red blade. "Bloodstone and wolven bone."

"Give that back," I demanded, scrambling to my knees.

His gaze shifted from the dagger to me. "This is a unique weapon."

"I know." My hair fell forward, over my shoulders.

"The kind that's not inexpensive," he continued. "Why are you in possession of this, Princess?"

"It was a gift." Which was true. "And I'm not foolish enough to come to a place like this unarmed."

He stared at me for a moment and then focused on the dagger again. "Carrying a weapon and having no idea how to use it doesn't make one wise."

Irritation flared to life just as hotly as the desire he'd elicited from me mere moments ago. "What makes you think I don't know how to use it? Because I'm female?"

"You can't be surprised that I would be shocked. Learning how to use a dagger isn't exactly common for females in Solis."

"You're right." And he was. It wasn't socially appropriate for females to know how to wield a weapon or be able to defend themselves, something that always bothered me. If my mother had known how to defend herself, she might still be here. "But I do know how to use it."

The right side of his lips curved up. "Now, I'm truly intrigued."

He moved unbelievably fast, thrusting the dagger blade down into the bed. I gasped, wondering what the owners of the Red Pearl would think of that, but then he pounced. He took me back down to the mattress, his weight covering me once more, and he pressed into me in a way that caused all the interesting parts to meet. His mouth lined up with mine—

A fist pounded on the door, silencing whatever he was about to ask. "Hawke?" A male voice rang out. "You in there?"

He stiffened above me, his warm breath against my lips as he closed his eyes.

"It's Kieran." The man called out a name I didn't recognize.

"As if I didn't know that already," Hawke muttered under his breath, and a small giggle left me. His eyes opened, and that half-grin appeared.

"Hawke?" Kieran pounded some more.

"I think you should answer him," I whispered.

"Dammit," he cursed. Looking over his shoulder, he called out, "I'm thoroughly, happily busy at the moment."

"Sorry to hear that," Kieran replied as Hawke refocused on me. Kieran knocked again. "But the interruption is unavoidable."

"The only unavoidable thing I see is your soon-to-be broken hand if you pound on that door one more time," Hawke warned, and my eyes widened. "What, Princess?" His voice lowered. "I told you I was really intrigued."

"Then I must risk a broken hand," Kieran answered.

A growl of frustration rumbled from deep within Hawke's throat, the sound strangely animalistic. Goosebumps pimpled my skin.

"The…envoy has arrived," Kieran added through the door.

Shadows crept across Hawke's face. His lips moved as if he

murmured something, but the sound was too low for me to hear.

A chill chased away some of the heat. "An…envoy?"

He nodded. "The supplies we've been waiting for," he explained. "I need to go."

I nodded in return, understanding that he had to leave as I reached between us, grasping the edge of the cloak.

For a long moment, Hawke didn't move, but then he shifted off me, standing. He called out to Kieran as he grabbed his tunic off the floor. I yanked the forgotten dagger out of the mattress, quickly sheathing it as he pulled the tunic over his head and shrugged a baldric over his shoulders, securing the belt at his waist. There were two sheaths at his sides for weapons—weapons I hadn't been aware of until now.

He picked up two short swords from the chest near the door, and I thought that maybe I needed to be better aware of my surroundings the next time I barged into a room.

His blades were honed to a wicked, deadly point, intended for close-contact fighting, and each side was serrated, designed to cut through flesh and muscle.

I knew how to use them, too, but I kept that to myself.

"I'll come back as soon as I can." He sheathed the swords flat to his sides. "I swear."

I nodded once more.

Hawke stared at me. "Tell me that you'll wait for me, Princess."

My heart skipped over itself. "I will."

Turning, he walked to the door and then stopped. He faced me. "I look forward to returning."

I said nothing as he left the room, opening the door only wide enough for him to slip through. When the door clicked into place behind him, I let go of the breath I had been holding and looked down at the front of my gown. The area of my breast was still damp, the white material nearly transparent. My cheeks flushed hotly as I scooted off the bed and stood on surprisingly weak knees.

My gaze lifted to the door, and I closed my eyes, unsure if I was disappointed or relieved by the interruption. Truthfully, it was a mixture of both, because I'd lied to Hawke.

I wouldn't be here when he returned.

"What did you do last night?"

The question snapped my attention from the biscuit I was currently devouring to the Lady in Wait who sat across from me.

Tawny Lyon was the second daughter of a successful merchant, given to the Royal Court at the age of thirteen during the Rite. Tall and lithe, with rich brown skin and beautiful brown eyes, she was absolutely enviable. Some of the Ladies and Lords in Wait were assigned tasks outside of preparation to join the Court after Ascension, and since we were the same age, she had been assigned as my companion shortly after her Rite. Her duty ranged from keeping me company to assisting me with my bath or to dress if I required it.

Tawny was one of the few people who could make me laugh over the silliest things. Actually, she was one of the few people who were even allowed to speak to me. She was the closest thing I had to a friend, and I cared for her deeply.

I believed she cared for me too, or at the very least, liked me, but she was required to be with me unless I dismissed her for the day. If she hadn't been given the task of being my companion, we never would've spoken. That fact was not a reflection upon her as a person, but because she would be like all the rest, either forbidden to socialize with me or wary of my presence.

The knowledge often sat heavy in my chest, another chunk of ice, but even though I knew our friendship was rooted in duty, I trusted her.

At least, to a certain degree.

She knew I was trained, but she didn't know the things I sometimes assisted Vikter with, and she had no knowledge of my gifts. I kept those things to myself because sharing that information would either put others or her in harm's way.

"I was here." Wiping buttery crumbs from my fingers, I gestured to the rather sparse chamber. We were in the small anteroom that opened up to the bedroom. There were only two chairs by the fireplace, a wardrobe and a chest, a bed, one nightstand, and a heavy fur rug under our feet. Others had more…creature comforts. Tawny had a beautiful chaise in her room and a pile of plush floor coverings, and I knew some of the other Ladies and Lords in Wait had vanities or desks, walls lined with bookshelves, and even electricity.

Over the years, those items had been stripped from my chamber for one infraction or another.

"You were not in your room," Tawny said. A simple topknot was trying—and failing—to keep the mass of brown and gold curls swept back from her face. More than a few had snuck free to rest against her cheeks. "I checked on you shortly after midnight, and you weren't here."

My heart skipped a beat. Had something occurred where the Duke or Duchess had sent Tawny for me? If so, Tawny wouldn't be able to lie, but I imagined if that had happened, I would already know.

I would have already been summoned to the Duke's private office.

"Why were you checking on me?" I asked.

"I thought I heard your door opening and closing, so I decided to investigate, but no one was here." She paused. "No one. Including you."

There was no way she'd heard me return. I'd used the old servants' access, and while that door was as creaky as a bag of bones, her room was on the other side of where my bed sat. That door was one of the reasons I'd never asked to be moved to the newer, renovated parts of the stronghold. Through there, I could access nearly any part of the castle and could come and go without being seen.

It more than compensated for the lack of electricity and the constant, chilly draft that seemed to always make its way in around the windows no matter how sunny the day was.

My palms dampened as I glanced at the closed hallway door. Had someone been looking for me? Again, I would know by now, so it was likely Tawny thought she'd heard something.

Knowing Tawny as I did, I knew she wouldn't let this go if I didn't give her something. "I couldn't sleep last night."

"Nightmares?"

I nodded, feeling a little guilty for the sympathy that crept into her eyes.

"You've been having a lot of them lately." She leaned back in the chair. "Are you sure you don't want to try one of the sleeping drafts the Healer made for you?"

"Yes. I don't like the idea of—"

"Being knocked out senseless?" she finished for me. "It's really not that bad, Poppy. You rest very deeply, and honestly, with as little sleep as you manage, I think it would be good to at least try."

The mere idea of taking something that would put me in such a deep sleep that it would take an army marching through my chamber to wake me made me sweat. I would be rendered completely helpless, and that was something I would never allow to happen.

"So, what did you do?" A pause. "Or should I ask, where did you go?" Her eyes narrowed as I became enraptured in the fine trim of the napkin. "You snuck out, didn't you?"

In that moment, Tawny proved that she knew me just as well as I knew her. "I don't know why you'd think that."

"Because you don't have a history of doing that?" She laughed when I glanced up at her. "Come on, tell me what you did. I'm sure it's more exciting than what I was doing, which was listening to Mistress Cambria prattle on about how inappropriate this Lady or Lord in Wait is. I pled a viciously upset stomach just to be able to excuse myself."

I giggled, knowing that Tawny would've done just that. "The Mistresses are a lot to handle."

"That is being too kind," she remarked.

Grinning, I picked up the cup of creamed coffee. The Mistresses were servants of the Duchess, who helped her run the household but also kept track of the Ladies in Wait. Mistress Cambria was a dragon of a woman that scared even me.

"I did sneak out," I admitted.

"Where did you go without me?"

"I think you might be upset when you hear where."

"Most likely."

I peeked up at her. "The Red Pearl."

Her eyes widened to the size of the saucers scattered across the trolley between us. "Are you serious?"

I nodded.

"I can't..." She appeared to take a deep breath. "How?"

"I borrowed one of the maid's cloaks, and I used that mask I found."

"You...you devious little thief."

"I returned the cloak this morning, so I don't think you can call me a thief."

"Who cares if you returned it." She tipped forward. "What was it like?"

"Interesting," I said, and when she begged for more details, I told her what I'd seen. She was enthralled, hanging on every word I said as if I were sharing with her the actual ritual that completed the Ascension.

"I can't believe you didn't take me with you." She fell back in her chair with a pout, but then sprang forward once more. "Did you see anyone there you recognized? Loren claims she goes there nearly every other evening."

Loren, another Lady in Wait, claimed many things. "I didn't see her, but..." I trailed off, unsure if I should tell her about Hawke.

I'd left no more than ten minutes after Hawke had, relieved to find that Vikter was also nowhere to be seen. Neither was the strange woman who knew more than she should. I'd done everything in my power not to think about what had happened in that room with him.

Which meant, I failed the moment I returned to my bed. I'd lain there until exhaustion claimed me, replaying everything he'd said...everything he'd done. I'd woken with the strangest frustration, an ache in my chest and lower belly.

"But what?" she asked.

I wanted to tell her. Gods, did I ever want to share what'd happened with Hawke with someone. I had a hundred questions bursting to be let out, but last night was different. I'd crossed a big line, and while I didn't feel like I had debased myself or done anything truly wrong, I knew that my guardians wouldn't agree. Neither would the Priests and Priestesses. Going to the Red Pearl was one thing. Sharing myself in any form with another was a totally different matter. That knowledge could be a weapon.

I trusted Tawny, but as I acknowledged before, only to a certain degree.

And even though the mere thought of Hawke made my stomach tighten into dozens of little coils, it wasn't something that would ever happen again. When I saw him during the City Council sessions, he wouldn't know that it had been me he'd called *Princess*. He'd have no idea that he'd been my first kiss.

What we'd done...it belonged to just me.

It had to stay that way.

I exhaled slowly, ignoring the sudden scratchy lump in my throat. "But many were wearing masks. She could've been there, and I wouldn't have known. Anyone could've been."

"If you ever go to the Red Pearl without me again, I will cut holes in the bottoms of your shoes," she warned, toying with the white beads dotting the neckline of her rose-colored gown.

A shocked laugh left me. "Wow."

She giggled.

"Honestly, I'm glad you didn't go with me." When she frowned, I quickly added, "I really shouldn't have gone there myself."

"Yes, going to the Red Pearl is forbidden, and I'm sure it's as forbidden as you being trained to use a dagger or a sword as a guard on the Rise."

That was something I hadn't been able to hide from Tawny, and she had never shared, which was one of the reasons I knew I could trust her with most things. "Yes, but—"

"Just like that one time you snuck out to view a fighting ring. Or when you convinced me to bathe in the lake—"

"That was your idea," I corrected, and her willingness to aid me in doing forbidden things was the other reason she held almost all of my trust. "And it was also your idea to do it without clothing."

"Who bathes in their clothes?" she asked, widening her eyes innocently. "And that was a mutual idea, thank you very much. I think we should do that again and soon before it gets too cold to even walk outside. But I could spend all morning listing things that you've done that are either forbidden by the Duke and Duchess or prohibited for the Maiden to do, and up until now, nothing has happened. The gods haven't appeared and deemed you unworthy."

"That's true," I acknowledged as I smoothed a crease from the skirt of my gown.

"Of course, it is." She plucked up a small, round powdery pastry and popped it into her mouth. Somehow, she didn't get a single dusting of sugar on her. Meanwhile, if I so much as breathed in the direction of those pastries, I ended up with a fine coating of white powder in places that made no sense. "So, when do we go back?"

"I...I don't think I should."

"You don't want to?"

I opened my mouth, then closed it and tried not to fall down that rabbit hole. The problem was that I wanted to go back.

When I was lying in bed and hadn't been obsessively rewinding the time spent with Hawke, reliving the razor-edged yearning and thrill his kiss had dragged out of me, I'd wondered if he had come back like he promised, and if I had done the right thing by leaving.

Of course, in the eyes of my guardians and the gods, it had been the right thing, but had it been so for me? Should I have stayed and experienced infinitely more before there might not be any more chances?

My gaze lifted to the windows that faced the west portion of the Rise. The dark shapes of the guards patrolling the ledge were the only movement. Was Hawke out there? Why was I even wondering that?

Because there was more than just a small part of me that wished I'd stayed, and I knew it would be a long time before I stopped wondering about what would've happened if I'd waited. Would he have carried out whatever I'd wanted?

I didn't even know what that would've entailed. I had ideas. I had my imagination. I had other people's stories of their experiences, but they were not mine. They were just thin, transparent copies of the real thing.

And I knew if I returned, I would go back in hopes that he'd be there. That was why I shouldn't go back.

Looking at the open wardrobe, I saw first the white veil with its delicate gold chains, and a heaviness settled over me. I could already feel its substantial weight, even though the material was made out of the finest, lightest silk. When it was first slipped over my head at age eight, I'd panicked, but after ten years, I should've grown used to it by now.

While I no longer felt like I couldn't breathe or see while wearing it, it still felt heavy.

Hanging beside it was the only color in my wardrobe, a splash of red among a sea of white. It was a ceremonial gown tailored for the upcoming Rite. The dress had arrived the morning before, and I hadn't tried it on yet. It would be the first time I was allowed to attend—allowed to wear anything other than white and be seen without the veil. Of course, I would be masked, like everyone else.

The only reason I was allowed to attend this Rite when all the others had been forbidden, was because it would be the last Rite before my Ascension.

Whatever excitement I felt about the Rite was tempered by the fact that it would be the last.

Tawny rose and drifted to one of the windows. "The mist hasn't come in a while."

Tawny had a habit of jumping from topic to topic, but this switch was jarring. "What made you think of that?"

"I don't know." She tucked back a loose curl. "Actually, I do. I overheard Dafina and Loren talking last night," she said. "They claimed they heard from one of the Huntsmen that the mist has been gathering beyond the Blood Forest."

"I hadn't heard that." My stomach knotted as I remembered Finley, and I wished I hadn't eaten so many slices of bacon.

"I probably shouldn't have brought it up." She turned from the window. "It's just that...it has been decades since the mist even neared the capital. It's not something we'd have to worry about there."

No matter where we were, the mist was something to worry about. Just because it hadn't gotten close in decades didn't mean it wouldn't, but I didn't say that.

She pushed away from the window, coming back to the table to kneel next to where I sat. "Can I be honest with you for a moment?"

My brows rose. "Aren't you always?"

"Well, yes, but this...is different."

More than curious to know what she was thinking about, I nodded for her to go on.

Tawny drew in a deep breath. "I know our lives are different, as were our pasts, and as our futures will be, but you treat the Ascension as if it may very well be your death when it's the exact opposite. It's life. It's a new beginning. It is a Blessing—"

"You're starting to sound like the Duchess," I teased.

"But it's the truth." She reached over and clasped my hand. "In a few months, you won't be dead, Poppy. You'll be alive and no longer bound by these rules. You'll be in the capital."

"I'll have been given to the gods," I corrected her.

"And how amazing is that? You will experience something very few people do. I know... I know you fear that you won't return from them, but you're the Queen's favorite Maiden."

"I'm her only Maiden."

Her eyes rolled. "You know that's not why."

I did.

The Queen had done more for me than what was ever required of her, but that didn't change that my Ascension would be nothing like hers.

"And when you come back, Ascended, I will be right by your side. Just think of the mischief we can make." Tawny squeezed my hand, and I saw that she truly believed that would happen.

It could.

But it wasn't a certainty. I had no idea what it truly meant to be given to the gods. Although every small detail seemed to be documented about the history of the kingdom, there were a few things that weren't written about. I'd never been able to find anything about previous Maidens, and I'd asked Priestess Analia over a hundred times what it meant to be given to the gods, and the answer was always the same.

A Maiden doesn't question the gods' plans. She has faith in them without knowledge of them.

Maybe I truly wasn't worthy of being a Maiden, because I found it hard to have faith in anything without knowledge of it.

But Tawny did. As did Vikter and Rylan, and literally everyone else I knew. Even Ian.

None of them had been given to the gods, though.

I searched Tawny's eyes, looking for just the slightest hint of fear. "You're not afraid at all, are you?"

"Of the Ascension?" She rose, locking her fingers together in front of her. "Nervous? Yes. Afraid? No. I'm excited to begin a new chapter."

To begin a life that was her own, where she could wake up and eat whenever she pleased, spend her days however she wanted, and with whomever she desired instead of being my perpetual shadow.

Of course, she wasn't afraid. And while I didn't feel the same, I had not once taken into consideration what it meant for her.

For the most part, Tawny was always more than willing to take part in whatever adventure I conjured up, and often suggested some herself. But if the gods were watching, especially this close to the Ascension, they could find her unworthy for taking part. That wasn't something I'd just now thought about, but it hadn't struck me with such clarity before that my attitude towards the Ascension could ruin her eagerness.

Guilt surfaced, the taste of it sour in the back of my throat. "I'm so selfish."

Tawny blinked, bewildered. "What makes you say that?"

"I've most likely tarnished your excitement with all my doom and gloom," I told her. "I haven't really thought about how excited you must be."

"Well, when you put it that way," she said and then laughed, the sound soft and warm. "Honestly, Poppy, you haven't. How you feel about the Ascension hasn't affected how I feel."

"I'm relieved to hear that, but still, I should be more excited for you. That's what…"—I took a thin breath—"that's what friends do."

"Have you been excited for me? Happy?" she asked. "Even though you're worried for yourself?"

I nodded. "Of course."

"Then you have done what a friend does."

Maybe that was true, but I promised myself I would be better, starting with no longer risking her Ascension by involving her in my escapades. I could live with the dire consequences of being found unworthy because it would be my life and my own actions that led to it, but I wouldn't do that to Tawny.

I couldn't live with that.

After I took supper in my room later that day, Vikter knocked on my door. When I looked up at his face, golden and weathered by life on the Rise and years in the sun, I didn't think about knowing where he was the night before and the subsequent awkwardness. I saw his expression and knew something had occurred.

"What's happened?" I whispered.

"We've been summoned," he said, and my heart lurched in my chest. There were only two reasons why we'd be summoned. One would be the Duke, and the other was equally terrible, but for far different reasons. "There's a cursed."

Chapter 4

Without wasting one unnecessary second, we left my room and the Castle through the old servants' access. We then moved like ghosts through the city until we found ourselves standing before an old, battered door.

The white handkerchief tacked just below the handle was the only reason the home in the Lower Ward of Masadonia was distinguishable from the other squat, narrow houses stacked on top of one another.

Glancing over his shoulder to where two City Guards chatted under the yellow glow of a streetlamp, Vikter quickly pulled the handkerchief off the door and slipped it into a pocket inside his dark cloak. The small, white cloth was a symbol of the network of people who believed death, no matter how violent or destructive, deserved dignity.

It was also evidence of high treason and disloyalty to the Crown.

I'd accidentally discovered what Vikter took part in when I was fifteen. He'd left one of our training sessions in a hurry one morning, and sensing that something was going on based on the mental pain the messenger had been throwing off, I'd followed.

Obviously, Vikter hadn't been pleased. What he was doing was considered treasonous, and being caught wasn't the only danger. However, I'd always been disturbed by how these things were typically handled. I demanded he allow me to help. He had said no—repeated it probably a hundred times—but I had been relentless, and besides, I was uniquely suited to assist in such matters. Vikter knew what I could do, and his empathy for others had aided my desire to help.

We'd been doing this for about three years now.

We weren't the only ones. There were others. Some were guards. A few were citizens. I never met any. For all I knew, Hawke could be one.

My stomach dipped and then rolled before I shoved any thoughts of Hawke out of my mind.

Vikter quietly rapped his knuckles on the door and then returned his gloved hand to the hilt of his broadsword. A couple of seconds later, hinges creaked as the old battered door shuddered open, revealing the pale, round face, and red, puffy eyes of a woman. She might've been in her mid to late twenties, but the tense pinch to her brow and the lines bracketing her mouth made her appear decades older. The cause of her worn appearance had everything to do with the kind of pain that cut deeper than the physical and was caused by the smell wafting out of the building from behind her. Under the thick, cloying smoke of earthy incense, was the unmistakable sour and sickeningly sweet scent of rot and decay.

Of a curse.

"You're in need of aid?" Vikter spoke low.

The woman fiddled with the button on her wrinkled blouse, her weary gaze darting from Vikter to me.

I opened my senses to her. Soul-deep pain radiated from her in waves I couldn't see, but it was so heavy, it was almost a tangible entity surrounding her. I could *feel* it slicing through my cloak and clothing and scraping against my skin like rusty, icy nails. She felt like someone who was dying but hadn't suffered a single injury or disease. That was how raw and potent her pain was.

Fighting the urge to take a step back, I shuddered inside my heavy cloak. Every instinct in me demanded that I put distance between us, get as far away as possible. Her grief formed iron shackles around my ankles, weighing me down as it tightened around my neck. Emotion clogged my throat, tasting like...like bitter desperation and sour hopelessness.

I pulled back my senses, but I had opened myself up for too long. I was tuned into her anguish now.

"Who is that?" she rasped, her voice hoarse with the tears I knew had swelled her eyes.

"Someone who can help you," Vikter answered in a way I was all too familiar with. He used that calm tone whenever I was seconds away from acting out in anger and doing something entirely reckless—which, according to Vikter, was way too often. "Please. Allow us to enter."

Fingers stilling around the button below her throat, she gave a curt nod and then stepped back. I followed Vikter inside, scanning the dimly lit room, which turned out to be a combined kitchen and living space. There was no electricity in the home, only oil lamps and fat, waxy candles. That wasn't exactly surprising to see, even though electricity had been provided to the area of the Lower Ward, to light the streets and some of the businesses. Only the wealthy had it inside their homes, and they would not be found in the Lower Ward. They'd be closer to the center of Masadonia, near Castle Teerman and as far from the Rise as possible.

But here, the Rise loomed.

Drawing in a shallow breath, I tried not to focus on how the woman's grief painted the walls and floors an oily black. Her pain had gathered here, among the knick-knacks and clay plates, quilted blankets with frayed edges and tired furniture. Clasping my hands together under the cloak, I took another breath, this one deeper, and looked around.

A lantern sat on a wooden table, next to several sticks of burning incense. Surrounding the brick hearth were several chairs. I zeroed in on the closed door on the other side of the fireplace. My hooded head tilted as I squinted. On the mantel, closest to the door, was a narrow spike of a blade the color of burgundy in the low light.

Bloodstone.

This woman had been prepared to handle this herself, and with the way she felt, that would be disastrous.

"What is your name?" Vikter asked as he reached up to lower the hood of his cloak. He always did this. Showed his face to comfort family or friends, to put them at ease. A lock of blond hair fell across his forehead as he turned to the woman.

I did not reveal myself.

"A-Agnes," she answered, her throat working on a swallow. "I...I heard about the white handkerchief, but I...I wasn't sure if anyone would come. I wondered if it was some kind of myth or a trick."

"It's no trick." Vikter may be one of the deadliest guards in the entire city, if not the kingdom, but I knew when Agnes looked up into his blue eyes, all she saw was kindness. "Who is ill?"

Agnes swallowed once more, the skin around her eyes puckering as she briefly squeezed them shut. "My husband, Marlowe. He's a Huntsman for the Rise, and…and he returned home two days ago—" Her breath caught, and she exhaled heavily. "He'd been gone for months. I was so happy to see him. I'd missed him terribly, and with each day, I feared he'd perished on the road. But he came back."

My heart squeezed as if it had been caught in a fist. I thought of Finley. Had he been a Huntsman, a part of this group that involved Marlowe?

"He seemed a little under the weather at first, but that's not uncommon. His work is exhausting," she continued. "But he started…he started to show signs that night."

"That night?" Only a small note of alarm had crept into Vikter's tone, and my eyes widened with a whole cartload more dismay. "And you waited until now?"

"We hoped it was something else. A cold or the flu." Her hand fluttered back to the buttons. Threads were beginning to show along the wooden discs. "I…I didn't know until last night that it was something more. He didn't want me to know. Marlowe is a good man, you understand? He wasn't trying to hide it. H-he planned to take care of himself, but…"

"But the curse would not allow it," Vikter finished for her, and she nodded.

I glanced back at the door. The curse progressed differently for everyone. It took hold for some in a matter of hours, while for others, it could take a day or two. But I knew of no cases that went beyond three. It had to be only a matter of time before he succumbed, possibly hours…or minutes.

"It's okay," Vikter assured her, but it truly wasn't. "Where is he now?"

Pressing her other hand to her mouth, she jerked her chin toward the closed door. The sleeve of her blouse was stained with some dark substance. "It's still him." Her words were a little muffled. "He's…he's still in there. That's how he wants to go to the gods. As himself."

"Is there anyone else here?"

She shook her head, letting out another ragged breath.

"Have you said your goodbyes?" I asked.

The woman jerked at the sound of my voice, her eyes widening. My cloak was rather shapeless, so I imagined she was surprised to hear that I was female. A female would be the last thing anyone expected in situations like these.

"It's you," she whispered.

I stilled.

Vikter didn't. Out of the corner of my eye, I saw his hand return to the hilt of the sword.

Agnes moved suddenly, and Vikter went to unsheathe his weapon, but before he or I could react, she collapsed to her knees before me. Bowing her head, she folded her hands under her chin.

My eyes widened under the hood as I slowly looked at Vikter.

He arched a brow.

"They spoke of you," she whispered, rocking in short, jerky movements. My heart might've stopped. "They say you're the child of the gods."

I blinked once and then twice as tiny goosebumps pimpled my skin. My parents were flesh and blood. I was definitely not a child of the gods, but I knew many people of Solis saw the Maiden as such.

"Who has said this?" Vikter asked, shooting me a look that said this was something we'd be talking about later.

Agnes lifted tear-stained cheeks, shaking her head. "I don't want to get anyone in trouble. Please. They didn't speak to spread rumors or ill will. It's just that..." She trailed off, her gaze drifting toward me. Her voice dropped to barely a whisper. "They say you have the *gift*."

Someone had definitely been talking. A subtle shiver curled its way down my spine, but I ignored it as the woman's pain pulsed and flared. "I'm no one of importance."

Vikter inhaled noisily.

"Agnes. Please." Under the cloak, I tugged off my gloves, placing them into a pocket. I slipped my hand through the opening of the heavy folds, offering it to her as I stole a quick glance at Vikter.

His eyes narrowed on me.

I was *so* going to hear about this later, but whatever lecture I was bound to receive would be worth it.

Agnes's gaze dropped to my hand, and then slowly, she lifted her arm and placed her palm against mine. As she rose, I curled my fingers around her cool hand, and I thought of the golden, sparkling sand surrounding the Stroud Sea, of warmth and laughter. I saw my parents, their features no longer clear but lost to time, fuzzy and undefined. I felt the warm, damp breeze in my hair, the sand under my feet.

It was the last happy memory I had of my parents.

Agnes's arm trembled as she took a sudden, heavy breath. "What...?" She trailed off, her mouth going lax as her shoulders lowered. The suffocating anguish retracted, collapsing into itself like a matchstick house in a windstorm. Her dampened lashes blinked rapidly, and rosy color infused her cheeks.

I let go of her hand the moment the room felt more...open and light, fresher. There was still a sharp edge of pain lingering in the shadows, but it was now manageable for her.

For me.

"I don't—" Agnes placed a hand to her breast, giving a little shake of her head. Her brow pinched as she stared at her right hand. Almost tentatively, she returned her gaze to me. "I feel like I can breathe again." Understanding crept across her face, quickly followed by the gleam of awe in her eyes. "The *gift*."

I slipped my hand back under my cloak, conscious of the ball of tension brewing inside me.

Agnes trembled. For a moment, I was afraid that she would drop to the floor again, but she didn't. "Thank you. Thank you so much. My gods, thank—"

"There's nothing you need to thank me for," I cut her off. "Have you said your goodbyes?" I asked once more. Time was getting away from us, time we didn't have.

Tears glimmered as she nodded, but the grief didn't seize as it did before. What I'd done wouldn't last. The pain would resurface. Hopefully, by then, she would be able to process it. If not, the grief would always linger, a ghost that would haunt every happy moment in her life until it became all she knew.

"We will see him now," Vikter announced. "It would be best if you remained out here."

Closing her eyes, Agnes nodded.

Vikter touched my arm as he turned, and I followed. My gaze landed on the settee closest to the hearth as Vikter reached the door.

A floppy-headed stuffed doll with yellow hair made of yarn lay partially hidden behind the thin cushion. Tiny goosebumps broke out across my skin as unease balled in the pit of my stomach.

"Will you...?" Agnes called out. "Will you ease his passing?"

"Of course," I said, turning back to Vikter. I placed a hand on his back and waited for him to dip his head. I kept my voice low as I said, "There is a child here."

Vikter halted with his hand on the door, and I tilted my head toward the settee. His gaze followed. I couldn't sense people, only their pain once I saw them. If a child was here, he or she must be hidden away, and possibly completely unaware of what was happening.

But then why hadn't Agnes admitted to the child being here?

The unease expanded, and the worst-case scenario played out in my mind. "I will handle this. You handle *that*."

Vikter hesitated, his blue eyes wary as they lifted to the door.

"I can take care of myself." I reminded him of what he already knew. The fact that I could defend myself rested solely on his shoulders.

A heavy sigh rattled from him as he muttered, "That doesn't mean you always have to." He stepped back, though, facing Agnes. "Would it be too much trouble to ask for something warm to drink?"

"Oh, no. Of course, not," Agnes answered. "I could make up some tea or coffee."

"Do you perhaps have hot cocoa?" Vikter asked, and I smirked. While that was something a parent may have on hand and could be seen as him searching for additional evidence of a child, it was also Vikter's greatest weakness.

"I do." Agnes cleared her throat, and I heard the sound of a cupboard opening.

Vikter nodded at me, and I stepped forward, placing my hand on the door and pushing it open.

If I hadn't been prepared for the too-sweet and the bitter-sour stench, it would've knocked me over. My gag reflex threatened to be triggered as my gaze adapted to the candlelit bedroom. I would just have to...not breathe as often.

Sounded like a solid plan.

I swept the room with a quick glance. Except for the bed, a tall wardrobe, and two rickety-looking end tables, the room was bare.

More incense burned in here, but it couldn't beat back the smell. My attention returned to the bed, to the form lying impossibly still in the center of it. Stepping inside, I closed the door behind me and started forward, slipping my right hand back into the cloak, to my right thigh. My fingers curled over the always-cold hilt of my dagger as I focused on the man. Or what was left of him.

He was young, that much I could tell, with light brown hair and broad shoulders that trembled. His skin had taken on a gray pallor, and his cheeks were sunken as if his stomach hadn't been full in weeks. Dark shadows blossomed under eyelids that spasmed every couple of seconds. The color of his lips was more blue than pink. Taking a deep breath, I opened myself up once more.

He was in great pain, both physical and emotional. It wasn't the same as Agnes's, but no less potent or heavy. In here, the anguish left no room for light, and it went beyond suffocating. It choked and clawed in the knowledge that there was no way out of this.

A tremor coursed through me as I forced myself to sit beside him. Unsheathing the dagger, I kept it hidden under my cloak as I lifted my left hand and carefully pulled the sheet down. His chest was bare, and the shivers increased as the cooler air of the room reached his waxy skin. My gaze traveled down the length of his concave stomach.

I saw the wound he'd hidden from his wife.

It was above his right hip, four ragged tears in his skin. Two, side by side, an inch or so above two identical wounds.

He'd been bitten.

One who didn't know better would think some sort of wild animal had gotten ahold of him, but this wasn't the wound of an animal. It seeped blood and something darker, oilier. Faint, reddish-blue lines radiated out from the bite, spreading across his lower stomach and disappearing under the sheet.

A ravaged moan drew my gaze upward. His lips peeled back, revealing just how close he was to a fate worse than death. His gums bled, streaking his teeth.

Teeth that were already changing.

Two on top, two on the bottom—his canines—had already elongated. I looked to where his hand rested next to my leg. His nails had also lengthened, becoming more animalistic than mortal. Within an hour, both his teeth and nails would harden and sharpen. They'd be able to cut and chew through skin and muscle.

He would become one of *them*.

A Craven.

Driven by an insatiable hunger for blood, he would slaughter everyone in sight. And if anyone were to survive his attack, they would eventually become just like him.

Well, not everyone.

I hadn't.

But he was becoming what existed outside the Rise, what lived inside the thick, unnatural mist—the foulness that the fallen Kingdom of Atlantia had cursed these lands with. Some four hundred years after the War of Two Kings had ended, they were still a plague.

The Craven were creations of the Atlantians, the product of their poisonous kiss, which acted like an infection, turning innocent men, women, and children into starved creatures whose body and mind became twisted and decayed by ceaseless hunger.

Even though the majority of Atlantians had been hunted into extinction, many still existed, and there only needed to be one Atlantian alive for there to be a dozen Craven, if not more. They weren't completely mindless. They could be controlled, but only by the Dark One.

And this poor man had fought back and escaped, but he must have known what the bite meant. From birth, we all knew. It was a part of the kingdom's blood-soaked history. He was cursed, and there was nothing that could be done. Had he come back to say goodbye to his wife? To a child? Had he thought he would be different? Blessed by the gods?

Chosen?

It didn't matter.

Sighing, I replaced the sheet, leaving his upper chest bare. Trying not to breathe too deeply, I set my palm on his skin. His flesh…it felt all wrong, like cold leather. I concentrated on the beaches of Carsodonia, the capital, and the dazzling blue waters of the Stroud. I remembered the clouds, how fat and fluffy they were. How they looked like peace must feel. And I thought of the Queen's Gardens outside of Castle Teerman, where I could simply be and not think or feel anything, where everything, including my own mind, was quiet.

I thought of the warmth those too-brief moments with Hawke had brought forth.

Marlowe's shivers subsided, and the twitching behind his eyes slowed. The puckered skin at the corners of his eyes smoothed out.

"Marlowe?" I said, ignoring the dull pain that started to blossom behind my eyes. A headache would eventually come. One always did when I repeatedly opened myself or used my gift.

The chest under my hand rose deeply, and clumped lashes fluttered. His eyes opened, and I tensed. They were blue. Mostly. Bolts of red shot through the irises. Soon, there would be no blue left. Only the color of blood.

His dry lips parted. "Are you…are you Rhain? Have you come to take me at my end?"

He thought I was the God of the Common Man and Endings, a god of death.

"No. I'm not." Knowing that his pain would be eased long enough for this to be completed, I lifted my left hand and did the one thing I was expressly forbidden to do. Not just by the Duke and Duchess of Masadonia, or by the Queen, but also by the gods. I did what Hawke had asked in regard to the mask, but I'd refused. I pulled down my hood and then removed the white domino mask I wore just in case my cloak slipped, revealing my face.

I figured, or hoped, that the gods would make an exception in cases like this.

His crimson-laced gaze drifted over my features, starting where wisps of burnt copper hair curled against my forehead, then the right side of my face, followed by my left. His stare lingered there, over the evidence of what a Craven's claws could do. I wondered if he thought the same thing the Duke always did.

Such a shame.

Those three words seemed to be the Duke's favorite. That and: *you have disappointed me.*

"Who are you?" he rasped out.

"My name is Penellaphe, but my brother and a few others call me Poppy."

"Poppy?" he whispered.

I nodded. "It's a strange nickname, but my mother used to call me that. It sort of stuck."

Marlowe blinked slowly. "Why are…?" The corners of his mouth cracked, the new wounds seeping blood and darkness. "Why are you here?"

Forcing a smile, I tightened my grip on the hilt of the dagger and did another thing that should end with me being hauled to the Temple but hadn't yet because this wasn't the first time I'd revealed myself to the dying. "I am the Maiden."

His chest rose with a sharp inhale, and he closed his eyes. A tremor coursed through him. "You're the Chosen, *'born in the shroud of the gods, protected even inside the womb, veiled from birth.'"*

That was me.

"You…you are here for me." His eyes opened, and I noticed the red had spread until only a hint of blue remained. "You will…give me dignity."

I nodded.

Anyone cursed by a Craven's bite did not die in their beds quietly and as peacefully as possible. They were not afforded that kindness or sympathy. Instead, they were generally dragged to the town square to be burned alive in front of a mass of citizens. It didn't matter that most became cursed either protecting those who cheered their horrific demise or working to better the kingdom.

Marlowe's gaze shifted to the closed door behind me. "She's…she's a good woman."

"She said you're a good man."

Those eerie eyes tracked back to me. "I won't be a—" His upper lip curled, revealing one deadly sharp tooth. "I won't be a good man much longer."

"No, you won't be."

"I…I tried to do it myself, but…"

"It's okay." Slowly, I pulled the dagger out from under my cloak. The glow of the nearby candle glittered off the deep red blade.

Marlowe eyed the dagger. "Bloodstone."

Before any signs of the curse, a mortal could be killed in any number of ways, but once there were signs, only fire and bloodstone could kill the cursed. Only bloodstone or wood sharpened into a stake from the Blood Forest could kill a fully turned Craven.

"I just…I just wanted to say goodbye." He shuddered. "That was all."

"I understand," I told him, even though I wished he hadn't returned here, but I didn't have to agree with his actions to understand them. His pain was starting to return, rising in sharp pulses and then ebbing. "Are you ready, Marlowe?"

His gaze shifted to the closed door once more, and then his eyes closed. He nodded.

Chest heavy, and unsure if it was my grief or his that weighed me down, I shifted ever so slightly. There were two ways to kill a Craven or someone cursed as long as you had a bloodstone blade or wood from a Blood Forest tree. Penetrate the heart or destroy the brain. The former wasn't immediate. It could take minutes to bleed out, and it was painful...and messy.

Placing my left hand against his too-cold cheek, I leaned over him—

"I wasn't...I wasn't the only one," he whispered.

My heart stopped. "What?"

"Ridley...he was...he was bitten, too." A wheezing breath left him. "He wanted to say goodbye to his father. I don't...know if he took care of himself or not."

If this Ridley had waited until the curse began to show signs, there was no way he would've been able to do it. Whatever was in the blood of the Craven—of an Atlantian—triggered some sort of primal survival instinct.

Gods.

"Where does his father live?"

"Two blocks over. Third home. Blue...I think blue shutters, but Ridley...he lives in the dorms with...the others."

Good gods, this could be bad.

"You've done the right thing," I told him, wishing he'd done it sooner. "Thank you."

Marlowe grimaced, and his eyes opened once more. There was no more blue. He was close. Seconds. "I don't have—"

I struck as fast as the black vipers that hid in the valleys that led to the Temples. The tip of the dagger sank into the soft spot at the base of his skull. Angled frontward and between the vertebrae, the blade pierced deep, severing the brain stem.

Marlowe jerked.

That was all. He'd taken his last breath before he even knew it. Death was as instantaneous as it could be.

I eased the blade out as I rose from the bed. Marlowe's eyes were closed. That...that was one small blessing. Agnes would not see how close he'd come to turning into a nightmare.

"May Rhain escort you to paradise," I whispered, wiping the

blood from my dagger on a small towel that had been draped over the end table. "And may you find eternal peace with those who have passed before you."

Turning from the bed, I sheathed the dagger and then replaced my mask and lifted my hood, tugging it over my head.

Ridley.

I started for the door.

If Ridley were still alive, he had to be within minutes of turning. It was nighttime, and if he was in that dorm where others who were off duty slept....

I shuddered.

No matter how well trained they were, they were as vulnerable as anyone else while asleep. Concern for a certain guard from the Rise surfaced, and fear pierced my chest and stomach.

A massacre could be minutes away from happening.

Worse yet, the curse would spread, and I more than anyone knew how quickly it could ravage a city until nothing but blood pooled in the streets.

Chapter 5

We left Agnes in the bedroom, her husband's limp hand pressed to her chest as she carefully brushed his hair back from his face.

It was an image I wouldn't forget for a very long time.

But I couldn't dwell on it then. I'd learned from Vikter that there was a daughter, but luckily, she was staying with friends, having been told that her father was ill. Vikter saw no reason to not believe Agnes. I was relieved to know that my worst fear hadn't come true. That the child hadn't also been cursed. Once someone had been cursed, a bite from them would pass on the curse, and even though Marlowe hadn't fully turned, he would've been prone to uncontrollable rages and thirst from the moment he'd been bitten.

But now I stood outside another tiny home, in the shadows of the narrow, dirt-packed alley, listening to another tragedy. The moment I'd shared with Vikter what Marlowe had told me, we'd gone straight for the father's house since it was closer than the dorms. I was beyond glad I couldn't see the man because I could hear the heartbreak in his voice as he told Vikter what had happened, and the ache in my head was now throbbing. If I saw the poor father, I would've wanted to somehow ease his pain. The old man knew precisely why Vikter was there when he asked if he'd seen his son.

Ridley hadn't been able to take care of himself.

However, his father had.

He'd shown Vikter where he'd buried Ridley in the backyard,

under a pear tree. He'd ended his son's life the day before.

I was still thinking about that as Vikter and I left the Lower Ward, using the heavily wooded area outside the Citadel to avoid any City Guards. Many years ago, animals such as deer and wild boar had been plentiful in Wisher's Grove, but only the smallest critters and large, predatory birds remained after years of hunting. The Grove now served more or less as a border between the haves and have-nots, the thick tree line all but erasing the cramped living arrangements for the vast majority of Masadonia from those who lived in homes triple the size of the one Agnes now mourned in. A part of the Grove, closer to the center of the city, had been cleared, creating a park where fairs and celebrations were held, people often rode their horses, sold goods, and picnicked on warmer days. The Grove ran right into the inner walls of Castle Teerman. Literally.

Very few traveled the Grove, believing it to be haunted by any who'd died there. Or were they haunted by the spirits of guards? Or was it the spirits of hunted animals that roamed between the trees? I wasn't sure. There were so many different versions. Either way, it worked for us because we could easily slip out of the Queen's Gardens and into the Grove without being seen as long as we kept an eye on the patrolling guards. From the Grove, one could go anywhere.

"We need to discuss what happened in that house," Vikter announced as we navigated the forest floor with only a sliver of moonlight to guide us. "People have been talking about you."

I knew this was coming.

"And you using your gift back there didn't help matters," he added, keeping his voice low even though it was unlikely we'd be overheard by anything other than a raccoon or an opossum. "You all but confirmed who you were."

"If people are talking, they haven't said anything," I replied. "And I had to do something. That woman's pain was...it was unbearable for her. She needed a break."

"And it became unbearable for you, too?" he surmised. When I didn't say anything, he added, "Your head hurts now?"

"It's nothing," I dismissed.

"Nothing," he growled. "I understand why you want to help. I respect that. But it's a risk, Poppy. No one has said anything yet. Maybe they feel indebted to you, but that could change, and you need to be more careful."

"I am careful," I said. Even though I couldn't see his expression as he too had lifted his hood to cover his face, I knew he sent me a look of disbelief. I grinned, but it quickly faded. "I know what the risks are—"

"And you're prepared to face the consequences if the Duke ever discovers what you're doing?" he challenged.

My stomach dipped as I toyed with a loose thread from my cloak. "I am."

Vikter cursed under his breath. In any other situation, I would've giggled. "You're as brave as any guard on the Rise."

Taking that as a huge compliment, I smiled. "Well, thank you."

"And just as foolish as any new recruit."

My smile turned upside down. "I take my thank you back."

"I never should've allowed you to begin doing this." He caught a low-hanging branch, moving it aside. "You going out among the people poses too much of a risk of discovery."

Dipping under the branch, I looked back at him. "You didn't allow me," I reminded him. "You just couldn't stop me."

He stopped, catching my arm and turning me so I faced him. "I understand why you want to help. You couldn't when your mother and father lay dying."

I flinched. "It has nothing to do with them."

"That's not true, and you know it. You're trying to make up for what you were unable to do as a child." His voice dropped so low, I could barely hear him over the breeze stirring the leaves above us. "But it's more than that."

"And what is that?"

"I think you want to be caught."

"What? You really think that?" I took a step back, pulling free of his hold. "You know what the Duke would do if he ever found out."

"Trust me, I know. It's not likely I'll forget any of those times I had to help you walk back to your room." His voice hardened, and heat blasted my cheeks.

I hated that.

Hated the way I felt for something someone had done to me. Absolutely *hated* the heavy shame that threatened to choke me.

"You take too many risks, Poppy, even knowing it's not just the Duke or even the Queen you'd have to answer to," he continued. "Sometimes, I wonder if you want to be found unworthy."

Irritation flared to life, and there was a part of me that recognized it was because Vikter was scraping at old wounds and getting too close to a hidden truth I didn't want to delve into and uncover. "Whether I'm caught or not, wouldn't the gods already know what I do? There would be no reason for me to take additional risks when nothing is hidden from them."

"There is no reason for you to take any risks at all."

"Then why have you spent the last five or so years training me?" I demanded.

"Because I know why you need to feel like you can defend yourself," he shot back. "After what you suffered, what you have to live with, I can understand the need to take your protection into your own hands. But if I had known that it would lead to you putting yourself in situations where you risked exposure, I never would've trained you."

"Well, it's too late for that change of heart."

"That it is." He sighed. "And way to avoid what I just said."

"Avoid what?" I asked, pretending ignorance.

"You know exactly what I'm talking about."

Shaking my head, I turned and started walking. "I don't help those people because I want the gods to find me unworthy. I didn't help Agnes because I hoped she would tell someone, and it would get out. I help them because it's already a tragedy that doesn't need to be compounded upon by being forced to watch their loved ones be burned to death." I stepped over a fallen tree limb, my headache worsening. However, it had nothing to do with my gift and everything to do with the conversation. "Sorry to ruin your theory, but I'm not a sadist."

"No," he said from behind me. "You're not. You're just afraid."

Whipping around, I gaped at him. "Afraid?"

"Of your Ascension. Yes. You're afraid. There's no shame in admitting that." He came forward, stopping in front of me. "At least, not to me."

But to others, like my guardians or the Priests, it wouldn't be something I could ever admit. They would see that fear as being sacrilegious, as if the only reason I'd have to be afraid would be due to something horrible and not the fact I had no idea what would happen to me upon my Ascension.

If I were to live.

Or die.

I closed my eyes.

"I understand," Vikter repeated. "You have no idea what will happen. I get it. I do, but Poppy, whether you take these unnecessary risks on purpose or not, regardless of if you're afraid or not, the end result will not change. All you will do is incur the Duke's wrath. That is all."

I opened my eyes and saw nothing but darkness.

"Because no matter what you do, you're not going to be found unworthy," Vikter said. "You will Ascend."

Vikter's words kept me up for most of the night, and I ended up skipping our normal morning training session held in one of the old rooms in the all-but-abandoned part of the castle. Unsurprisingly, Vikter hadn't knocked on the old servants' door.

If that wasn't evidence enough of how well he knew me, I didn't know what would be.

I wasn't mad at him. Honestly, I could be annoyed and irritated with him every other day, but I was never mad at him. I didn't think he felt that I was. He just…he'd hit a raw nerve last night, and he was aware of that.

I was afraid of my Ascension. I knew that. Vikter knew that. Who wouldn't be? Although Tawny believed that I would return as an Ascended, no one could be sure. Ian wasn't like me. There'd been no rules imposed on him when we'd been in the capital or while we grew up here. He'd Ascended because he was the brother of the Maiden, the Chosen, and because the Queen had petitioned for the exception.

So, yes, I was afraid.

But was I purposely pushing the envelope and happy-dancing over the line in hopes of being found unworthy and stripped of my status?

That was…that would be incredibly irrational.

I could be quite irrational.

Like when I saw a spider, I behaved as if it were the size of a horse with the cold calculation of an assassin. That was irrational. But being found unworthy meant exile, and that was also a death sentence. If I were afraid of dying upon Ascension, then getting myself exiled didn't exactly improve the situation.

And I was afraid of dying, but my wariness of the Ascension was more than that.

It wasn't my choice.

I had been born into this, in the same way that all the second sons and daughters were. Even though none of them seemed to dread their future, it wasn't their choice either.

I hadn't been lying or trying to cover up a hidden agenda when I helped Agnes or exposed myself to Marlowe. I did that because I could—because it was *my* choice. I trained to use a sword and bow because it was *my* choice. But was there another motive behind sneaking off to watch fights or swimming naked? Visiting gambling dens or lurking in parts of the castle forbidden to me and listening in on conversations that I wasn't supposed to hear? Or when I left my chambers without Vikter or Rylan just so I could spy on the balls held in the Great Hall and people-watch in Wisher's Grove? What about the Red Pearl? Letting Hawke kiss me? Touch me? All of those things that I'd done, I did because they were *my* choice, but...

But could it also be what Vikter had suggested?

What if, deep down, I wasn't just trying to live and experience everything I could before my Ascension? What if I was, on some kind of unconscious level, trying to ensure that the Ascension never happened?

These thoughts troubled me throughout the day, and for once, I wasn't all that restless in my confinement. At least not until the sun began to set. Having dismissed Tawny hours before supper since there was no reason for her to sit around while I did nothing but morosely stare out the windows, I finally got annoyed with myself and yanked open the door.

Only to find Rylan lounging across the hall.

I drew up short.

"Going somewhere, Pen?" he asked.

Pen.

Rylan was the only one who called me that. I liked it. I let go of the door, and it slowly inched back, bumping my shoulder. "I don't know."

He grinned at me as he ran a hand over his light brown hair. "It's time, isn't it?"

Glancing behind me to the windows, I saw that it was dusk. Surprise flickered through me. I'd wasted an entire day in self-reflection.

Priestess Analia would be thrilled to hear that, but not the reasons. Either way, I wanted to punch myself in the face.

But it *was* time. I nodded and started to step out—

"I think you're forgetting something," he said, tapping a finger on his bearded cheek.

My veil.

Good gods, I'd almost walked out into the hall without it or a hood. Other than my guardians—the Duke and Duchess—and Tawny, only Vikter and Rylan were allowed to see me without my veil. Well, the Queen and King could, and Ian was permitted, but obviously, they weren't here. If anyone else had been in the hall, they would've possibly fallen over in a dead faint.

"I'll be right back!"

His grin increased as I whipped around and hurried back into the room, slipping the veil over my head. It took a little more than a couple of minutes to clasp all the little chains so it was secured in place. Tawny was so much faster at it than I was.

I started back out—

"Shoes, Pen. You should put some shoes on."

Looking down at myself, I let out a very unladylike groan. "Gods! One moment."

Rylan chuckled.

Totally scatterbrained, I toed on my well-worn shoes, which were nothing more than satin and a thin leather sole, and then reopened the door.

"Having a bad day?" Rylan mused as he joined me in my room.

"Having a weird day," I countered, heading for the old servants' access. "A forgetful one."

"It must be for you to not realize the time."

Rylan was right. Unless something was going on, both he and Vikter were always ready for me just before dusk.

Our pace was quick as we hurried down the narrow, dusty staircase. It emptied out into an area beside the kitchen, and while we took the old access to avoid being seen as much as possible, it wasn't completely avoidable. Kitchen servants stopped mid-step as Rylan and I passed them, their brown garb and white caps making them nearly indistinguishable from one another. I heard a basket of potatoes hit the floor and the harsh, biting reprimand. Out of the corner of my eye, I saw blurred faces bow their heads as if they were praying.

I swallowed a groan while Rylan did what he always did and pretended that there was nothing off about their behavior.

You're the child of the gods.

Agnes's words came back to me. The only reason they thought that was because of the veil and the paintings and various artworks representing the Maiden.

That and how often it was that they didn't see me.

We started toward the banquet hall. From there, we could enter the foyer and be able to access the Queen's Garden. There'd be more servants, but there really wasn't any other way to access it from within the castle that didn't require scaling a wall. We made it halfway past the long table when one of the many doors on either side opened behind us.

"Maiden."

A wave of goosebumps spread over my skin in revulsion. I recognized that voice, and I wanted to keep walking—to pretend I'd suddenly lost my hearing.

But Rylan had stopped.

If I kept walking, it wouldn't end well for me.

Inhaling deeply, I turned to face Lord Brandole Mazeen. I didn't see what I was sure most saw, a dark-haired man who appeared to be in his mid-twenties, handsome and tall. I saw a bully.

I saw a cruel man who had long ago forgotten what it was like to be mortal.

Unlike with the Duke, who seemed to despise me without cause, I knew precisely why Lord Mazeen found such glee in harassing me.

Ian.

And it all stemmed from the vainest, most inconsequential thing possible. A year before my brother Ascended, he'd bested Lord Mazeen at a game of cards, to which the Lord had ungraciously accused Ian of cheating. I, who probably shouldn't have even been present for the game, had laughed. Mainly because the Lord was utterly terrible at poker. From that moment on, the Lord had sought to irritate both Ian and me whenever he got the chance. It only got worse once Ian Ascended, and the Lord began to...assist the Duke with his *lessons.*

Clasping my hands together, I said nothing as he strode toward me, his long legs encased in black breeches. He wore a black dress shirt, and the darkness of his clothing created a striking contrast against his pale skin and lips the color of ripe berries. His eyes...

I didn't like to look into them. They seemed fathomless and empty.

Like all Ascended, they were such a dark black that the pupils weren't visible. I wondered what his eye color had been before he Ascended or if he even remembered. The Lord may only appear to be in his second decade of life, but I knew he'd Ascended after the War of Two Kings, along with the Duke and Duchess. He was hundreds of years old.

Lord Mazeen gave a tight, close-lipped smile when I didn't respond. "I'm surprised to see you here."

"She's taking her evening walk," Rylan replied, tone flat. "As she is allowed."

Eyes like shards of obsidian narrowed on the guard. "I didn't ask the question of you."

"I'm taking my walk," I stepped in, answering before Rylan said another word.

That unnerving, fathomless gaze shifted to me. "You're going to the garden?" One side of his lips quirked when surprise flickered through me. "Isn't that where you always go at this time of day?"

I did.

And it was more than a little disconcerting that the Lord was aware of that.

I nodded.

"She must be on her way now," Rylan interjected. "As you know, the Maiden must not linger."

In other words, I wasn't allowed to interact, not even with the Ascended. The Lord knew that.

But he disregarded it. "The Maiden also must be respectful. I wish to speak with her, and I'm sure the Duke would be most disappointed to learn that she was unwilling to do so."

My spine straightened as a wave of anger swept through me so swiftly, I *almost* reached for the dagger strapped to my thigh. The reaction shocked me in a way. What would I have done with it if I hadn't stopped? Stabbed him? I almost laughed.

But none of this was funny.

His thinly veiled threat of speaking to the Duke had been effective. The Lord had backed both Rylan and me into a corner because even though I was not supposed to interact, the Duke didn't hold Lord Mazeen to the same rules as others. If I walked away, I would be punished. So would Rylan. And while my punishment wasn't something to take lightly, it would be nothing compared to what Rylan would face.

He could be removed from the Royal Guard, and the Duke would ensure that it was known that he had fallen out of the Duke's favor. Rylan would soon be unemployed and therefore dishonored. It wouldn't be the same as being exiled, but his life would become measurably more difficult.

I squared my shoulders. "I would love nothing more than to speak with you."

A look of smugness settled on his handsome features, and I wanted nothing more than to kick him in the face. "Come." He reached out, curling his arm over my shoulders. "I wish to speak in private."

Rylan stepped forward—

"It's okay," I told him, although it really wasn't. Looking over at him, I willed him to listen. "Truly, it is fine."

Rylan's jaw hardened as he stared at the Lord, and I could tell he wasn't remotely happy about this, but he nodded curtly. "I'll be right here."

"Yes, you will," the Lord replied.

Gods.

Not all Ascended were like the Lord, who wielded his power and station like a poison-tipped sword, but Lord Mazeen wasn't even the worst example.

He steered me to the left, nearly causing a servant to drop the basket she carried. He seemed completely unaware of her as he strode forward. Whatever hope I had that he planned to speak to me a few steps away ended quickly as he took us into one of the shadowy alcoves between the doors.

I should've known.

He swept aside thick, white curtains and all but pulled me into the narrow space where the only source of light was a small sconce above a thickly cushioned chaise. I had no idea what the purpose of these half-hidden rooms was, but on more than one occasion, I'd found myself trapped in them.

I stepped back, a little surprised that the Lord allowed it. He watched me, the smirk returning as I positioned myself so I was close to one of the curtains. He sat on the chaise, stretching out his legs as he folded his arms across his chest.

Heart thumping, I chose my words carefully. "I really cannot linger. If someone were to see me, I would be in trouble with Priestess Analia."

"And what would happen if the good Priestess of the Temples were to hear you were lingering?" he asked, his body appearing loose and relaxed, but I knew better.

Appearances could be deceiving. The Ascended were fast when they wanted to be. I'd seen them move in a manner that made them nothing more than a blur.

"Would she report such misbehavior to the Duke?" he continued. "I do so enjoy his lessons."

Disgust was a weed taking root inside me. Of course, he enjoyed the Duke's *lessons*. "I'm not sure what she would do."

"It might be worth discovering," he mused idly. "At least, for me."

My fingers curled inward. "I don't wish to displease the Duke or the Priestess."

His lashes lowered. "I'm sure you would not."

A sharp, stinging pain radiated out from where my nails dug into my palms. "What is it that you wish to speak to me about?"

"You didn't ask your question appropriately."

Searching for restraint and calm, I was grateful for the veil. If he could see my face in its entirety, he'd know exactly what I was feeling.

Which was red-hot, burning *hatred*.

I didn't know why the Lord found such great entertainment in harassing me. Why he found such enjoyment in making me uncomfortable, but he'd been this way the last several years. He was worse toward the servants, though. I'd heard the whispered warnings to new staff. Avoid gaining his attention or his displeasure. No matter what, there was a limit to how far he could go with me. With the servants, I didn't believe he felt there was even a line to cross.

I lifted my chin. "What would you like to discuss with me, *Lord*

Mazeen?"

A hint of a cold smile appeared. "I realized it had been a while since I last saw you."

It had been sixteen days since he'd last cornered me. So, not long enough.

"I've missed you," he added.

Doubtful.

"My Lord, I must be on my way—" I sucked in a sharp breath as he rose. One second, he was stretched out on the chaise. The next, he was directly in front of me.

"I'm insulted," he said. "I told you I missed you, and your only response was to say you must leave? You wound me."

The fact that he'd said nearly the same words Hawke had uttered no more than two nights ago didn't go unnoticed. Neither did the vastly different reactions I had to them. While Hawke had come across teasing, Lord Mazeen spoke the words as a warning. I wasn't charmed. I was revolted.

"It wasn't my intention," I forced out.

"You sure?" he asked, and I felt his finger against my jaw before I even saw him move his hand. "I have the distinct impression that was exactly your intent."

"It wasn't." I leaned back—

He curled his fingers around my chin, holding my head in place. When I took my next breath, I thought his fingers smelled like...a flower, musky and sweet. "You should try to be more convincing if you wish me to believe that."

"I'm sorry if I'm not as convincing as I should be." It took great effort to keep my voice steady. "You shouldn't be touching me."

He smirked as he trailed his cool thumb along my lower lip. The sensation of thousands of tiny insects skittering over my skin followed. "And why is that?"

The Lord knew exactly why.

"I'm the Maiden," I said, nonetheless.

"That you are." He trailed his fingers down my chin over the scratchy lace that covered my throat. His hand continued, brushing over my collarbone.

My palm practically burned with the need to feel the hilt of the dagger against it, and my muscles tensed with the knowledge and skill to react—to make him stop. A tremor coursed through me as I fought the desire to fight back. It wouldn't be worth what would happen. I kept telling myself that as his fingers slid down the center of my gown. It wasn't just the fear of punishment. If I showed what I was capable of, the Duke would learn that I had been trained, and I doubted it would take any large leap of logic to determine that Vikter was responsible. Yet again, whatever I faced would be nothing compared to what Vikter would.

But I could only tolerate so much.

I took a step back, putting distance between us.

Lord Mazeen tilted his head and then chuckled softly. Instinct sparked, and I moved to step out from the curtain, but I hadn't been fast enough. He caught me by the hip and turned me. There wasn't even a second to react as his arm clamped around my waist, and he hauled me back against him. His other hand remained where it was, between my breasts. The contact of his body against mine, the *feel* of it, sent a wave of revulsion through me.

"Do you remember your last lesson?" His breath was icy against my skin just below the veil. "I can't imagine you've forgotten."

I hadn't forgotten a single one.

"You didn't make a sound, and I know it had to hurt." His grip tightened on my waist, and even in my all-too-limited knowledge of things, I knew what I felt against me. "Admittedly, you've impressed."

"Thrilled to hear that," I gritted out.

"Ah, there it is," he murmured. "There's that tone unbecoming of the Maiden. The very same one that has gotten you into trouble a time or two—or a dozen. I was wondering when it would make an appearance. I'm sure you also remember what happened the last time it came out."

Of course, I remembered that, too.

My temper had gotten the best of me. I'd snapped back at the Duke, and he'd struck me hard enough that I'd lost consciousness. I came to, only to feel like I'd been run over by a horse and finding the Duke and the Lord sprawled out on the settee, both appearing to have drunk a bottle's worth of whiskey while I lay on the floor. For days, I'd felt like I'd come down with the flu. I imagine I had a bit of a concussion.

Still, seeing the shock widen the Duke's otherwise emotionless gaze had been worth it.

"Perhaps I will go to the Duke myself," he mused. "Tell him how disrespectful you've been."

Fury boiled my blood as I stared at the gray stones of the wall. "Let me go, Lord Mazeen."

"You didn't ask nicely enough." His hips pressed against me, and my skin flushed with rage. "You didn't say please."

There would be no way I'd say please. Consequences be damned, I'd had enough. I was not his toy. I was the Maiden, and while he was incredibly faster and stronger, I knew I could hurt him. I had the element of surprise on my side, and my legs were free. I widened my stance as I felt something damp and wet against my jaw—

A scream tore through the alcove, startling the Lord enough that he loosened his hold. I tore free and spun to face him, my chest heaving as I slipped my hand through the slit in my gown, to the hilt of the dagger.

The Lord muttered something under his breath as the screams came again, high-pitched, and full of terror.

Taking advantage of the distraction, I darted out from behind the curtain instead of unsheathing the dagger and slicing off what I was sure was the Lord's most prized possession.

The Lord threw aside the curtains as he stormed out, but the screams were bringing others rushing into the banquet hall. Servants. Royal Guards. There was nothing more Lord Mazeen could do now. Through the veil, my gaze met his. I knew it. His nostrils flared. He knew it.

The screams came again, ringing out from one of the nearby rooms, drawing my attention. Two doors down, the door was open.

Rylan was at my side. "Pen—"

I skirted his reach and headed toward the sound. What happened in that alcove with the Lord fell to the wayside as my fingers curled around the handle of my dagger. Screams were never a good sign.

A woman rushed out—the servant who'd been carrying the basket. Her face leached of all color as her hand opened and closed against her throat. She backed away, shaking her head.

I reached the room at the same time Rylan did and looked inside.

I saw her immediately.

She was lying on an ivory-colored settee, her pale blue gown wrinkled and bunched around her waist. One arm dangled limply off the side, her skin the shade of chalk. I didn't have to open my senses to know she felt no pain.

That she'd never feel anything again.

I lifted my gaze. Her head rested against a pillow, neck twisted at an unnatural angle and—

"You shouldn't see this." Rylan grabbed me, and this time, I didn't move out of his reach. I didn't stop him as he turned me away, but I already saw.

I saw the deep puncture wounds.

Chapter 6

Rylan promptly escorted me right back to my room while Lord Mazeen stood in the doorway, flanked by several others, his gaze fixed on the dead girl. I wanted to push him aside and close the door. Even if it weren't for the state of her undress, with so much flesh exposed, it was a lack of dignity tossed aside for morbid curiosity.

She was a person, and while what was left behind was nothing more than a shell, she was someone's daughter, sister, friend. More than anything else, people would talk about how she was found, with the skirt of her gown shoved up, and the bodice gathered at the waist. No one else needed to bear witness.

I hadn't been given a chance, though.

And now Castle Teerman was on virtual lockdown as each and every space in the one hundred plus rooms was searched for either the culprit or more victims.

Pacing in front of the fireplace, Tawny worried the tiny pearl buttons of her bodice. "It was a Craven," she said, the deep violet gown swishing about her legs. "It had to be a Craven."

I glanced over at Rylan, who leaned against the wall, arms crossed. Normally, he didn't stay inside my room, but tonight was different. Vikter was assisting with the search, but I imagined he'd be back soon.

With my veil removed, Rylan's gaze met mine. He'd seen that girl. "Do you think it was a Craven?"

Rylan said nothing.

"What else could it have been?" Tawny turned to where I sat in the chair. "You said yourself she was bit—"

"I said it *looked* like a bite, but it...it didn't look like a Craven bite," I told her.

"I know you've seen what a Craven can do." She sat across from me, her fingers still twisting the pearl just as Agnes had done to the button on her blouse. "But how can you be sure?"

"The Craven have four elongated canines," I explained, and she nodded. This was common knowledge. "But she only had two marks, as if..."

"As if two sharp fangs had penetrated her throat," Rylan finished. Tawny's head whipped in his direction.

"What if it was a cursed? Someone who hadn't fully turned yet?" she asked.

"Then it would look like either normal teeth marks or a bite from a Craven," Rylan answered, shaking his head as he stared out the window toward the Rise. "I've never seen anything like that."

I had to agree with him. "She...she was pale, and it wasn't just the shroud of death. It was like she had no blood in her, and even if it were a two-fanged Craven—" My nose scrunched. "It would've been...messier and not so precise. She looked like..."

"Looked like what?"

My gaze dropped to my hands as the image of the woman reappeared. She'd been with someone, willing or not, and as far as I knew, Craven weren't interested in anything but blood. "It just looked like someone had been in that room with her."

Tawny sat back. "If it wasn't a Craven, then who would do something like that?"

There were many people in and out of the castle—servants, guards, visitors...the Ascended. But that didn't make sense either. "That wound appeared to be right over her jugular. There should've been blood everywhere, and I didn't even see a drop of it."

"That...that is more than just a little strange."

I nodded. "And her neck was clearly broken. I know of no Craven that would do that."

Tawny folded her arms around herself. "And I don't want to know of any person capable of that."

Neither did I, but we all knew that people were capable of all manner of atrocities, and so were the Ascended. After all, they too had been mortal at one time, and the capability for cruelty seemed to be one of the few traits some carried over.

My thoughts wandered to Lord Mazeen. He was cruel, a bully, and based on our latest interaction, I suspected that he could be much worse. But was he capable of what was done? I shuddered. Even if he were, why would he do it, and how? I didn't have an answer for that.

There was only one thing I could think of that could do that, but it seemed too unreal to believe.

"Did you…did you recognize her?" Tawny asked softly.

"I didn't, but I have to think she was a Lady in Wait or perhaps a visitor based on her gown," I told her.

Tawny nodded silently, returning to twisting the pearl on her bodice. Silence crept into the space, and Vikter arrived not long after, stepping into the room to speak quietly to Rylan. I scooted to the edge of my seat when he stepped away from Rylan, sighing as he sat on the edge of the chest that rested at the foot of my bed.

"Every inch of this castle was searched, and we found no other victims or Craven," he said, leaning forward. "Commander Jansen believes the grounds are safe." He paused, squinting as he lifted his gaze. "Relatively speaking, that is."

"Did you…did you see her?" I asked, and he nodded. "Do you think it was a Craven attack?"

"I've never seen anything like that," he replied, repeating what Rylan had said.

"What would that even mean?"

"I don't know," he stated, rubbing his hand against his forehead.

My attention zeroed in on him, noting how he massaged the skin above his brow and how he'd squinted when he looked to where we sat near the oil lamps. Sometimes, Vikter got headaches. Not like the ones I got after opening up my senses or using my gifts too much, but far more severe, where light and sound made him nauseous and his head pulse.

I opened up my senses and immediately felt the sharp pounding ache behind my eyes. I quickly severed the connection, and it was like visualizing a cord connecting me to him being snipped in two. The last thing I wanted was to end up with another throbbing headache keeping me up.

"If it wasn't a Craven, then are there any suspects?" Tawny asked.

"The Duke believes it was the work of a Descenter."

"What?" I demanded as I rose.

"Here? In the castle?" Tawny cried.

"That is what he believes." Vikter lifted his head as I walked over to him, his gaze wary.

"And what do you believe?" Rylan asked from where he still stood by the door. "Because I'm unsure how a Descenter could've managed to inflict wounds like that without leaving blood."

"Agreed," Vikter murmured, watching me. "There would be no way to clean something like that up, especially not when the victim had been seen less than an hour before."

"So, why would the Duke insist it was a Descenter?" Tawny queried. "He's not unintelligent. He would have to realize that, too."

I casually placed my hand on the back of Vikter's neck as I reached for a small fur quilt. His skin was warm and dry as I thought of the beaches and my mother's laugh. I knew his pain was eased the moment he took a deep, shuddering breath.

"I'm unsure why the Duke believes this, but he must have his reasons." Vikter's gaze was grateful as I slipped my hand away and walked back to the chair, placing the throw in my lap.

Tawny looked over at me and then took a deep breath before she refocused on Vikter. "Do you know who she was?"

Sitting straight, he was definitely more clear-eyed when he spoke again. "She was identified by one of the servants. The victim's name was Malessa Axton."

The name was unfamiliar to me, but Tawny whispered, "Oh."

I twisted toward her. "Did you know her?"

"Not well. I mean, I know *of* her." She gave a small shake of her head, sending several curls free from her twist. "I think she came to Court around the same time as I did, but she was often with one of the Ladies who lives on Radiant Row. I think it's Lady Isherwood," she added.

Radiant Row was the nickname given to the row of homes closest to the castle and to Wishers' Grove park. Many of the opulent houses were owned by the Ascended.

"She was so young." Tawny lowered her hand to her lap. "And she had so much to look forward to."

I reached out with my senses and found that her sadness echoed my own. It wasn't the deep pain of loss that came when it was someone you knew, but the sorrow that accompanied any death, especially such a senseless one.

Rylan asked Vikter to step outside. After a few moments, Tawny excused herself to return to her room. I managed to stop myself from touching her. I knew if I did, I would take her pain, even though I'd done it before without her realizing. I ended up at the window, staring at the steady glow of the torches beyond the Rise when Vikter reentered.

"Thank you," he said as he joined me by the window. "The ache in my head was starting to get the best of me."

"Glad I could help."

"You didn't have to. I have the powder the Healer made for me."

"I know, but I'm sure my gift brought you much faster relief without the dizziness and sleepiness," I said. Those were only two of the many side effects that brownish-white powder often caused.

"That is true." Vikter fell quiet for several moments, and I knew his thoughts were as troubled as mine.

I had a hard time believing that it had been a Descenter, even though I imagined something like an ice pick could've made those wounds. However, the possibility of stabbing someone in the jugular and not getting blood everywhere seemed very unlikely, but even more baffling was the motive. What did creating those types of wounds indicate that was of any benefit to their cause? Because the only thing I knew that could make those kinds of wounds went against everything the Descenters believed in.

"Rylan spoke to me."

I looked over at Vikter with raised brows. "Yes?"

His sea-colored gaze flickered over my face. "Rylan told me about Lord Mazeen."

My stomach sank as I looked away. It wasn't as if I had forgotten my run-in with the Lord, but it simply wasn't the most concerning or traumatic thing to have happened in the last couple of hours. "Did he do anything, Poppy?" he asked.

A suffocating, stinging heat crept into my face, and I pressed my cheek to the windowpane. I didn't want to think about this. I never did. Nausea churned, and there was this…weird embarrassment that made my skin feel sticky and dirty. I didn't understand why I felt that way. I knew I'd done nothing to gain the Lord's attention, and even if I had, he was still in the wrong. But when I thought about how he felt entitled to touch me, I wanted to scratch at my own skin.

And I didn't want to think about how I'd been grateful for the servant's screams, having no idea what the cause had been.

I pushed all of that aside so it could later come to the forefront, most likely when I was trying to sleep. "He did nothing other than be an annoyance."

"Truthfully?"

I nodded, although that seemed a little too far from the truth, but I was okay with lying. What could Vikter do with the truth? Nothing. He was smart enough to know that.

A muscle throbbed in his jaw. "He needs to leave you alone."

"Agreed, but I'm able to handle him."

Kind of.

I didn't really want to think about how close I came to doing something utterly unforgivable. If I had unsheathed my dagger and used it, there would have been no hope for me. But, gods, I wouldn't have felt a drop of guilt over it.

"You shouldn't have to," Vikter replied. "And he should know better."

"He should, and I think he does, but I don't believe he cares," I admitted, turning so I rested against the ledge of the window. "You know I saw her in that room. I saw how she was…left. It made me think that she was with someone, either willingly or not."

He nodded. "The Healer who looked at her body believed there had been some level of physical relations before her death, but he didn't find any signs that she had been fighting. No dried blood or skin under her nails, but no one can be sure."

I pressed my lips together. "I was thinking that it wouldn't make sense for a Descenter to leave wounds like that, even if they were able to do it without it being…messy. What kind of message does that even send? Because the only thing that can do what was done to her is…"

Vikter's gaze met mine. "An Atlantian."

Relieved that he said it and not me, I nodded. "The Duke has to know that. Anyone who saw those wounds would have to think that and question why a Descenter would mimic something that could easily be attributed to an Atlantian."

"That's why I don't think it was a Descenter," he said, and pressure clamped down on my chest. "I think it was an Atlantian."

A Descenter moving freely through Castle Teerman was concerning, but the possibility of an Atlantian being able to gain access without anyone being the wiser was something truly terrifying.

I wanted to find something that would provide some sort of evidence that Vikter and I were being paranoid, so at the crack of dawn, when the castle was at its quietest, and Rylan guarded the room outside, I snuck down to the main floor and past the eerily quiet kitchen.

Once the sun rose, I didn't have to worry about running into Lord Mazeen or any Ascended.

Entering the banquet hall, I headed to the left, to the second door, where I often met with Priestess Analia for my weekly lessons. As I stepped inside, I glanced across the dimly lit hall to the room where Malessa had been found.

The door was closed.

Tearing my gaze from it, I quietly shut the door and hurried over to the bare wooden chair, spying the book I never foresaw myself reading of my own volition.

Mainly because it seemed as if I'd read *The History of The War of Two Kings and the Kingdom of Solis* about a million times. I carried it over to the lone window and quickly cracked it open, holding it in the faint beam of sunlight. I carefully thumbed through the thin pages, knowing if I were to tear one, Priestess Analia would be most displeased. I found the section I was looking for. It was only a handful of paragraphs that described what Atlantians looked like, their traits, and what they were capable of.

Unfortunately, all it did was confirm what I already knew.

I'd never actually seen an Atlantian—at least, I didn't think I had, and that was the problem. Atlantians looked *like* mortals. Even the extinct wolven, who had once lived alongside the Atlantians in Atlantia, could easily be mistaken for mortals, even though they had never been. The Atlantians' ability to blend in with the populace they were known to subjugate and hunt made them deadly, expert predators. One could walk right past me, and I wouldn't know.

Neither would the Ascended. For some reason, the gods hadn't taken any of that into consideration when they initiated the Blessing.

Scanning the paragraphs, one word stood out, causing my stomach to dip. *Fangs.* Although I knew what it would say, I read the sentences anyway.

Between year 19 and 21, those of blooded Atlantian descent leave the vulnerable state of immaturity, wherein the ill-spirits in their blood become active. Noted during this period is a disturbing increase in strength, and the ability to recover from most mortal wounds as they continue to mature. It is also to be noted that before the War of Two Kings and the extinction of the wolven, a bonding ritual was performed between an Atlantian of a certain class and a wolven. Not much is known about this bond, but it is believed that the wolven in question was duty-bound to protect the Atlantian.

For a true Atlantian, two upper canines will form fangs, becoming elongated and sharpened, but they will not be overly noticeable to the untrained eye.

I thought of the two puncture wounds on Malessa's neck. An Atlantian's fangs may not be as overgrown and noticeable as a Craven's, but the Duke could order the mouths of everyone in the castle to be checked.

Admittedly, that would be invasive.

I kept reading.

Upon the appearance of fangs, the next phase of their maturity begins, wherein they begin to thirst. As long as their unnatural demands are met, their aging slows dramatically. It is believed that a year to mortals is equivalent to three decades to an Atlantian. The oldest known Atlantian was Cillian Da'Lahon, who saw 2,702 calendar years before his death.

Meaning that an Atlantian could appear to be in their twenties, but in reality, they would be over a hundred years old, possibly even closer to two hundred or more. But they still aged, unlike the Ascended, those Blessed by the gods, who stopped at whatever age they were when they received the Blessing. Only the oldest of the Ascended appeared older than someone in their thirties, and they *could* live for an eternity.

However, both the Atlantians and Ascended still lived an unfathomable amount of time, the closest thing to immortality—to the gods.

I couldn't even fathom living that long. I gave a little shake of my head and kept reading.

At this time, the Atlantians are capable of passing on the ill-spirits in their blood to mortals, creating a violent and destructive creature known as a Craven, who share some of the physical traits of their creators. This curse is passed through a poisonous kiss…

A poisonous kiss wasn't referencing two lips coming into contact with one another. The Atlantians did what the Craven did, albeit not as…messily. Atlantians bit and drank the blood of mortals, something they had to do to survive.

Their enormous lifespans, strength, and healing abilities all stemmed from feeding off mortals, their primary food source. I shuddered.

It had to be an Atlantian that had bit and fed from Malessa, which explained how there was no apparent bloodshed, and why she had looked so incredibly pale.

What it didn't explain was why the Atlantian had then snapped her neck, effectively killing her before the curse could spread. Why wouldn't the Atlantian allow her to turn? Then again, the bite wasn't exactly in a place that could easily be hidden. The bite itself was the warning to all who saw it.

An Atlantian was deep within our midst.

Closing the book, I carefully placed it back on the stool, thinking about how my Ascension would occur on my nineteenth birthday and how the Atlantians reached a certain majority around that age. It wasn't exactly surprising. After all, our gods had been their gods at one time.

But the gods no longer supported the Atlantians.

Making my way out of the room, I started for the kitchens when my gaze landed on the room Malessa had been found in. I needed to go back to my chambers before the staff became active, but that wasn't what I did.

I crossed the space and went to the door, finding it unlocked when I turned the handle. Before I could really think about what I was doing and where I was, I slipped inside, grateful that the wall sconces cast a soft glow throughout the room.

The settee was gone, the space bare. Accent chairs remained, as did the round coffee table with some sort of floral arrangement neatly placed in the center. I crept forward, unsure of what I was even looking for, and wondering if I'd even know if I found it.

Other than the missing furniture, nothing seemed out of place, but the room felt oddly cold, as if a window had been open, but there were no windows on this side of the banquet hall.

What had Malessa been doing in here? Reading a book or waiting for one of the other Ladies in Wait or perhaps Lady Isherwood? Or had she snuck in here to meet with someone she trusted? Had she been blindsided by the attack?

A shiver danced down my spine. I wasn't sure what was worse—being betrayed or blindsided.

Actually, I did know. Being betrayed would be worse.

I stepped forward, stopping short as I glanced down. Something was behind the leg of one of the chairs. Bending down, I reached under the chair and picked up the object. My head tilted as I ran a thumb over the smooth, soft white surface.

It was…a petal.

My brows knitted as the scent reached me. Jasmine. For some reason, my stomach roiled, which was odd. I normally liked the smell.

Rising, I looked to the vase and found the source. Several white lilies were spaced throughout the arrangement. No jasmine. Frowning, I looked down at the petal. Where did this come from? I shook my head as I walked over to the bouquet, placing the petal in with the rest of the flowers as I gave the room one last look. There was no blood on the cream carpet, something that would've definitely stained if it had spilled.

I had no idea what I was doing. If evidence had been found, it had been removed, and even if it hadn't been, I didn't have experience in this. I just wanted to be able to do something or to find anything that would put our worst fears to rest.

But there was nothing to be done or found here other than what was most likely reality, and what did I believe about truth? That it often could be terrifying, yes. But with truth came power.

And I was never one to hide from the truth.

I'd made it back to my room that morning without any issues and ended up remaining in it the entire day, which wasn't exactly all that different from any other day.

Tawny had stopped by briefly, until one of the Mistresses summoned her. No one was sequestered, but I thought that the attack would at least slow down the preparations for the Rite.

Obviously, that was a silly thought. I doubted the Earth shaking would get in the way of the Rite.

I spent a lot of time thinking about what had happened to Malessa. And the more I thought about why the Duke would lie about the attacker being a Descenter, the more it started to make sense. Just like Phillips, the guard from the Rise, hadn't wanted to talk about Finley's death to stop panic and fear from taking root and spreading.

But it didn't explain why the Duke wasn't being honest with the Royal Guard. If there was an Atlantian among us, the guards needed to be prepared.

Because while the Ascended were powerful and strong, the Atlantians were too, if not more.

Shortly before dusk, Rylan knocked on my door. "You want to try for the garden? I thought I would ask."

"I don't know." I glanced at the windows. "You think it will be okay?"

Rylan nodded. "I do."

I really could use the fresh air and time away from my own thoughts. It just seemed... I wasn't sure. As if it weren't even twenty-four hours after Malessa had been killed, yet it was like any other evening.

"You don't have to stay in here," Rylan said, and I glanced back to him. "Not unless that's what you want to do. What happened last night, with the poor girl and with the Lord, has nothing to do with what you find joy in."

A small smile tugged at my lips. "And you're probably tired of standing in the hall."

Rylan chuckled. "Possibly."

I grinned as I stepped back. "Let me get my veil."

It took only a few minutes for me to don the headdress and become ready. This time, there were no interruptions as we made our way to the garden. However, there were servants who did the stop-and-stare thing, but as I continued down the path of one of my favorite places on the grounds of the castle, my worries and obsessive thoughts slipped away like they always did. While I was in the sprawling garden, my mind calmed, and everything and anything ceased to nibble away at me.

I wasn't thinking about Malessa and the Atlantian who'd gained access to the castle. I wasn't haunted by the image of Agnes holding her husband's limp hand or what had happened in the Red Pearl with Hawke. I wasn't even thinking about the upcoming Ascension and what Vikter had said. In the Queen's Garden, I was simply...*present* instead of being caught up in the past or the future full of what-ifs.

I wasn't sure why the gardens were called what they were. As far as I knew, it had been a very long time since the Queen had been to Masadonia, but I guessed the Duke and Duchess had named it after her as some sort of homage.

Never once while I lived with the Queen had I seen her step foot in the lush gardens of the palace.

I glanced over at Rylan. Normally, the only threat he may face was an unexpected rain shower, but tonight, he was more alert than I'd ever seen him in the garden. His gaze continuously scanned the numerous pathways. I used to think these trips bored him, but never once had he complained. Vikter, on the other hand, would've grumbled about literally anything else we could've been doing.

Come to think of it, Rylan might actually enjoy these outings, and not just because he wasn't standing in the hall outside my room.

A cool wind whipped through the garden, stirring the many leaves and lifting the edge of my veil. I wished I could remove the headdress. It was transparent enough for me to see, but it did make traveling at dusk and beyond in low-lit places a bit difficult.

I made my way past a large water fountain that featured a marble and limestone statue of a veiled Maiden. Water poured endlessly from the pitcher she held, the sound reminding me of the rolling waves, crashing in and out of the coves of the Stroud Sea. Many coins shimmered under the water, a token to the gods in hopes that whatever the wisher wanted would be granted.

I neared the outer most parts, which fed into a small but thick outcropping of jacaranda trees that camouflaged the inner walls that kept Castle Teerman separated from the rest of the city. The trees were tall, reaching over fifty feet, and in Masadonia, bold, lavender-colored, trumpet-shaped flowers blossomed all year round. Only during the coldest months, when snow threatened, did the leaves fall, blanketing the ground in a sea of purple. They were breathtaking, but I appreciated them not just for their beauty but also for what they provided.

The jacaranda trees hid the crumbling section of the wall that Vikter and I often used to leave the grounds unseen in order to access Wisher's Grove.

I stopped in front of the mass of intertwined vines that crawled up and over interlocking wooden trellises as wide as the jacaranda trees were tall. Glancing up at the rapidly darkening sky, I then fixed my gaze ahead.

Rylan came to stand behind me. "We made it in time."

The corners of my lips tilted up before my grin faded. "We did tonight."

Only a few moments passed, and then the sun conceded defeat to the moon. The last rays of sunlight pulled away from the vines. Hundreds of buds scattered over the vines trembled and then slowly peeled open, revealing lush petals the shade of a starless midnight.

Night-blooming roses.

Closing my eyes, I inhaled the faintly sweet aroma. They were at their most fragrant upon opening and then again at dawn.

"They are quite beautiful," Rylan commented. "They remind me—" His words ended in a strangled grunt.

Eyes flying open, I spun around, and a scream of horror knotted in my throat as Rylan staggered backward, an arrow protruding from his chest. A look of disbelief marked his features as he lifted his chin.

"Run," he gasped, blood trickling from the corner of his lips. "*Run.*"

Chapter 7

"Rylan!" I rushed to his side, throwing an arm around him as his legs crumpled. His weight was too much, and when he fell, I went down with him, my knees cracking as they hit the pathway. The impact didn't register as I pressed my hands around Rylan's wound, trying to stanch the flow of blood. I opened my senses to him, expecting to feel pain. "Rylan—"

Whatever words I was about to say died on my tongue, tasting of ash.

I...I felt *nothing*, and that wasn't right. He'd have to be in so much pain, and I could help that. I could take his pain, but I felt *nothing*, and when I looked at his face, I didn't want to see what I saw. His eyes were open, gaze fixed yet unseeing on the sky above. I shook my head, but under my hands, his chest didn't move.

"No," I whispered, blood turning to ice and slush. "Rylan!"

There was no answer, no response. Underneath him, a pool of blood spread across the walkway, seeping into the symbols etched into the stone. A circle with an arrow piercing the center. Infinity. Power. The Royal Crest. I pressed down on his chest, my trembling hands soaked with blood, refusing to believe—

A footstep echoed like thunder behind me.

I twisted at the waist. A man stood a few feet from me, a bow at his side. A hooded cloak shielded his face.

"You're going to do as I say, Maiden," the man spoke in a voice that sounded like churning gravel. "And then, no one will be hurt."

"No one?" I gasped.

"Well, no one *else* will be hurt," he amended.

I stared up at the man, and...and Rylan's chest *still* didn't move under my palms. In the back of my mind, I knew it would never rise again. He'd been dead before he even hit the ground. He was *gone*.

Pain, so sharp and so real, cut through me. Something hot hit my veins and poured into my chest, filling up the empty space. My hands stopped trembling. The grip of panic and shock lessened, replaced by rage.

"Stand," he ordered.

I rose carefully, aware of how my gown, tacky with Rylan's blood, stuck to the knees of my thin leggings underneath. My heart slowed as my hand slipped into the slit along the gown's side. Was this the same person who'd killed Malessa? If so, he was an Atlantian, and I'd have to be quick if I had any hope.

"We're going to walk out of here," he said. "You're not going to make a sound, and you're not going to give me any trouble, are you, Maiden?"

My fingers closed around the smooth, cool handle of the dagger. I shook my head no.

"Good." He took a step toward me. "I don't want to have to hurt you, but if you give me any reason, I will not hesitate."

I remained completely still, the heat of my fury building in me, brimming to the surface. Rylan had died because of me. That was his duty as my personal guard, but he was dead because this man thought he could take me. Malessa had possibly been assaulted and then murdered, and for what?

If he was an Atlantian or a Descenter, he wouldn't use me for ransom. I'd be used to send a message, just like the three Ascended who had been kidnapped from Three Rivers. They were returned in *pieces*.

At the moment, I didn't care what the man's agenda was. All that mattered was that he'd killed Rylan, who found the night-blooming roses just as beautiful as I did. And he might've been the one to kill Malessa, leaving her body on display in such a careless, disrespectful way.

"This is good," he cajoled. "You're behaving. That's smart of you. Keep being smart, and this will be painless for you." He reached for me—

Unsheathing the dagger, I shot forward, dipping under his arm.

"What the—?"

I sprung up behind him, fisting the back of the man's cloak. I thrust the dagger into his back, aiming where Vikter had taught me.

The heart.

Even caught off guard, he was quick, lurching to the side, but he wasn't fast enough to avoid the dagger altogether. Hot blood gushed as the blade sank deep into his side, missing his heart by mere centimeters.

He yelped in pain, the sound reminding me of a dog. Jerking the dagger out, a vastly different sound tore from his throat. A rumbling growl that raised the tiny hairs on my body and kicked my instinct into overdrive.

That was such an…*inhuman* sound.

My grip on the dagger tightened as I moved to shove it deep into his back once more. He swung around, and I didn't see his fist until pain exploded along my jaw and at the corner of my mouth, affecting my aim. I tasted something metallic. Blood. The dagger sliced into his side, cutting deep, but not deep enough.

"*Bitch*," he grunted, slamming his fist into the side of my head this time.

The blow was sudden, stunning. Staggering back, lights danced across my eyes as the corners of my vision turned dark. I almost went down, managing to stay on my feet by sheer will alone. If I fell, I knew I wasn't getting back up. Vikter had also taught me that.

Blinking rapidly, I tried to clear the lights from my vision as the man whirled on me. The hood of his cloak had fallen back. He was young, probably only a handful of years older than I, and his dark hair was shaggy. He pressed his hand to his side. Blood seeped out between his fingers. It was coming out of him fast. I must've hit something vital.

Good.

His lips peeled back in a feral snarl as his gaze lifted to mine. Even in the moonlight, I could see his eyes. They were the color of frosted water. A pale, luminous blue.

"You will pay for that," he growled, voice even more abrasive, as if his throat were filling with pebbles.

I braced myself, instinct telling me that if I ran, he would give chase like any predator would. And if I got close again, my aim had better not be off. "Take one more step toward me, and I won't miss your heart a third time."

He laughed, and a chill swept through me. It sounded too deep, too *changed*. "I'm going to enjoy tearing your skin off your weak, fragile bones. I don't care what he has planned for you. I will bathe in your blood and feast on your entrails."

Fear threatened to take root, but I couldn't cave to it. "That sounds delightful."

"Oh, it will be." He smiled then, teeth smeared with blood, and he took a step toward me. "Your screams—"

A sharp, piercing whistle came from somewhere deep in the trees, silencing him. He stopped, his nostrils flaring. The sound came again, and he seemed to vibrate with rage. The skin around his mouth went white as he took a step back.

My grip was steady on the dagger, but a tremor started in my legs as I watched him, refusing to blink.

He picked up the fallen bow, wincing as he straightened. His gaze met mine once more. "I'll be seeing you again real soon."

"Can't wait," I gritted out.

He smirked. "I promise I'll make damn sure that smart mouth of yours is rewarded."

I doubted it was the kind of reward I'd be eager to receive.

Backing up until he was beyond the roses, he spun around and loped off, quickly disappearing in the heavy shadows that gathered under the trees. I stayed where I stood, breaths coming out in short, quick bursts, ready in case this was some trick where he waited for me to turn my back. I wasn't sure how long I stood there, but the tremors had spread to my hand by the time I realized that he wasn't coming back.

Slowly, I lowered the dagger, my gaze snagging on the spattering of blood where he'd stood. Another short breath left me as I lifted my gaze to the roses. Drops of blood glimmered on the onyx-hued petals.

A shudder racked me from head to toe.

I forced my body to turn around.

Rylan remained where he'd fallen, arms lax at his sides and eyes dull. I opened my mouth to speak, but there were no words, and I had no idea what I would've said anyway.

I looked down at my dagger, and I felt a scream building in my throat, clawing at me.

Get it together. Get it together.

I had to find someone to help Rylan. He shouldn't lay out here like this, and they couldn't see me with a bloodied dagger. They couldn't know that I'd fought the attacker off. My lips trembled as I pressed them together.

Get it together.

Then, like a switch had been thrown, the shaking stopped, and my heart slowed. I still couldn't take in a deep enough breath, but I walked forward, dipping down and wiping the blade on Rylan's breeches. "I'm sorry," I whispered, my actions causing guilt to make my skin crawl, but it had to be done. Head and face throbbing, I sheathed the dagger. "I'm going to get someone for you."

There was no answer. There never would be.

I started walking the path without realizing what I was doing. A numbness had invaded my body, seeping in through my pores and settling in my muscles. The lights from the castle windows guided me forward as I edged around the water fountain, coming to a sudden stop. Footsteps sounded ahead of me. My hand slipped to the dagger, fingers curled around—

"Maiden? We heard shouting," a voice called out. It was a Royal Guard who'd often kept watch over the Ladies and Lords in Wait. His eyes widened upon seeing me. "Is that—good gods, what happened to you?"

I went to answer, but I couldn't get my tongue to form words. Another guard cursed, and then there was a taller form with golden hair brushing past the two guards, his weathered face stoic. *Vikter.* His gaze swept over me, lingering on my knees and hands, and then the unveiled part of my face.

"Are you hurt?" He grasped my shoulders, his grip gentle, and his voice even more so. "Poppy, are you injured?"

"It's Rylan. He's…" I stared up at Vikter, suddenly stopping as what Hawke had said about death surfacing without warning. It was something I'd already known, but it still managed to shock me.

Death is like an old friend who pays a visit, sometimes when it's least expected and other times when you're waiting for her.

Death had indeed paid an unexpected visit.

"How did this happen?" Duchess Teerman demanded. The jeweled flower securing her brown hair glittered under the chandelier as she paced the room usually reserved for greeting guests. "How did someone get into the garden and come that close to taking her?"

Probably the same way someone got into the castle and killed the Lady in Wait the day before.

"The others are scouting the inner wall as we speak," Vikter said instead. He stood behind where I sat perched on the edge of the velvet settee, half afraid that I would get blood on the golden cushions. "But I imagine the culprit came through the section that has been damaged by the jacaranda trees."

The very same section Vikter and I used to leave the castle grounds unnoticed.

The Duchess's dark eyes flashed with anger. "I want them all torn down," she ordered.

I gasped.

"Sorry, my lady," the Healer murmured, dabbing a damp cloth under my lip and then handing the material to Tawny, who provided him with a clean one. She'd been summoned as soon as I'd been placed in the sitting room.

"It's fine," I assured the silver-haired man. What had caused the reaction wasn't what the Healer had been doing. Granted, the astringent stung, but it was what Duchess Teerman had demanded. "Those trees have been here for hundreds of years—

"And they have lived a long, healthy life." The Duchess turned to me. "You have not, Penellaphe." She strode toward me, the skirt of her crimson gown gathering around her ankles, reminding me of the blood that had pooled around Rylan. I wanted to pull away but didn't wish to cause offense. "If this man had not been scared off, he would've taken you, and the last thing you would've been worried about is those trees."

She had a point there.

Only Vikter knew what had happened—that I had managed to

wound the man before he'd been signaled off. While the details couldn't be shared because we'd run the risk of exposure, Vikter would notify the Healers in the city to keep an eye out for anyone wounded in such a manner.

But the trees...

They may have caused the deterioration of the wall, but it had been like that for as long as I could remember. There was no doubt in my mind that the Duke and Duchess knew about the wall and simply hadn't ordered it repaired.

"How badly is she injured?" she asked the Healer.

"Superficial wounds, Your Grace. She'll have a few bruises and some discomfort, but nothing lasting." The old Healer's long, dark coat hung from his stooped shoulders as he rose on stiff, creaking joints. "You're incredibly lucky, young Maiden."

I wasn't lucky.

I had been prepared.

And that was why I sat here only with an aching temple and a sore lip. But I nodded. "Thank you for your assistance."

"Can you give her something for the pain?" the Duchess asked.

"Yes. Of course." He shuffled over to where his leather satchel sat on a small table. "I have the perfect thing." Rooting around until he found what he was looking for, he revealed a vial of pinkish-white powder. "This will help with any pain but will also make her drowsy. It has a wee bit of a sedating effect."

I had absolutely no intention of taking whatever was in that vial, but it was handed over to Tawny, who slipped it into the pocket of her gown.

Once the Healer had left, the Duchess turned to where I still sat. "Let me see your face."

Exhaling wearily, I reached for the chains, but Tawny moved to my side. "Allow me," she murmured.

I started to stop her, but my gaze caught on my hands. They'd been wiped as soon as I was placed in the sitting room, but blood had made its way under my nails, and flakes of it still dotted my fingers.

Was Rylan's body still in the courtyard by the roses?

Malessa's body had been in that room for hours and then removed. I wondered if she had been returned to her family, or if her body had been burned out of precaution.

Tawny unhooked the veil, carefully removing it so it didn't tangle in the strands of hair that had escaped the knot I'd gathered it into that morning.

Duchess Teerman knelt before me, her cool fingers grazing the skin around my lips and then my right temple. "What were you doing out in the garden?"

"I was looking at the roses. I do so nearly every night." I glanced up. "Rylan always goes with me. He didn't—" I cleared my throat. "He didn't even see the attacker. The arrow struck him in the chest before he was even aware that anyone was there."

Her bottomless eyes searched mine. "It sounds like he wasn't as alert as he should have been. He never should've been caught off guard."

"Rylan was very skilled," I said. "The man was hidden—"

"Your guard was so skilled that he was felled by an arrow?" she asked softly. "Was this man part ghost that he made no sound? Gave no warning?"

My back stiffened as I thought of the sound the man had made and how it hadn't resembled anything human. "Rylan was alert, Your Grace—"

"What have I told you?" Her delicately arched brows lifted.

Struggling for patience, I took a shallow breath. "Rylan was alert, *Jacinda*," I amended, using her first name. She sporadically required this, and I never knew when she would want me to use the name or not. "The man...he was quiet, and Rylan—"

"Was unprepared," Vikter finished for me.

My head cranked around so fast it sent a flare of pain across my temple. Disbelief seized me.

Vikter's blue eyes met mine. "He enjoyed your evening strolls in the garden. He never thought there would be a threat, and unfortunately, became too complacent. Last night should've changed that."

Last night *had* changed that. Rylan had been scanning the grounds constantly. My shoulders slumped, and then my brain switched gears. *Ian.* "Please don't say anything to my brother." My gaze swung between the Duchess and Vikter. "I don't want him to worry, and he will even though I'm fine."

"I will need to inform the Queen of what has happened, Penellaphe. You know this," she replied. "And I cannot control who she tells. If she feels Ian needs to know, she will tell him."

I sank further into myself.

Her cool fingertips touched my cheek, my left one. I turned back to her. "Do you understand how important you are, Penellaphe? You are the Maiden. You were *Chosen* by the gods. Ascensions of hundreds of Ladies and Lords in Wait, all across the kingdom, are all tied to yours. It will be the largest Ascension since the first Blessing. Rylan and all the Royal Guards know what is at stake if something were to happen to you."

I liked the Duchess. She was kind, nothing like her husband, and for a tiny moment there, I thought she was actually worried about me as a person, but it was what I signified that concerned her the most. What would be lost if something were to happen to me. It wasn't just my life, but the future of hundreds of those who were about to Ascend.

The worst part was the twinge of sadness when I should've known better.

"If the Descenters were to somehow stop that Ascension, it would be their greatest triumph." She rose, smoothing her hands over her gown. "It would be such a cruel strike against our Queen and King and the gods."

"You...you think he was a Descenter, then?" Tawny asked. "That he wasn't trying to take her for ransom?"

"The arrow used on Rylan was marked," Vikter answered. "It carried the Dark One's promise."

His promise.

Air lodged in my throat as my gaze swung to Tawny's. I knew what that meant.

From Blood and Ash
We Shall Rise.

It was his promise to his people and his supporters, to those scattered across the kingdom, that they would rise once more. A promise that had been scrawled across vandalized storefronts in every city and had been carved into the stone shell of what had remained of Goldcrest Manor.

"I must be blunt with you," the Duchess said, glancing toward Tawny. "And I trust that what I'm about to say won't become whispers on the lips of others."

"Of course," Tawny promised as I nodded.

"There is...reason to believe that the assailant from last night was an Atlantian," she said, and Tawny sucked in a sharp breath. I had no reaction to the news since Vikter and I had already suspected as much. "It's not news we want spread widely. The kind of panic that could cause...well, it would do none of us any favors."

I glanced at Vikter and found him watching the Duchess closely. "You think that was who came for me tonight? The same man responsible for Malessa's death?"

"I cannot say if it was the same man, but we do believe the one responsible for the disgraceful treatment of our Lady in Wait was a part of a group that visited yesterday," she explained, walking toward the credenza along the back wall. She poured herself a clear drink from the glass decanter. "After the castle was checked for any persons who didn't belong, we believed that the perpetrator had left, and that the act was to show how easy it was for them to gain access. We believed that the immediate threat had passed."

She took a sip of her drink, her lips twitching as she swallowed. "Obviously, we were wrong. They may no longer be in the castle, but they are in the city." She faced me, her already alabaster skin even paler. "The Dark One has come for you, Penellaphe."

I shuddered as my heart skipped a beat.

"We will protect you," she continued. "But I would not be surprised if once the King and Queen learn of what has happened, they take drastic steps to ensure your safety. They could summon you to the capital."

Chapter 8

"I don't think the man I saw in the garden was the Dark One," I said to Vikter as we made our way from the sitting room, passing under the large, white banners embossed with the Royal Crest in gold. He was escorting Tawny and me back to my room. "When he said he was basically going to feast on my body parts, he referenced someone else, saying he didn't care what he had planned. If the Dark One is behind this, I imagine the one with the plans would be him."

"I suspect whoever was in the garden was a Descenter," Vikter admitted, hand on the hilt of his short sword as he scanned the wide hall as if Descenters lurked behind the potted lilies and statues.

Several Ladies in Wait stood together, their voices quieting as we passed. A few placed their hands over their mouths. If they hadn't heard what had happened, they now knew something else had occurred based on the amount of blood that stained my gown.

"We should've gone the old way," I muttered. It was rare that any of them ever saw me, and to see me like this would be the gossip of the week.

"Ignore them." Tawny shifted so she blocked most of me from view as we crossed the hall. She still carried with her the white vial that she knew I had no plans to use.

"It may be good for them to see." Vikter decided after a moment. "What happened last night and just now could serve as a timely reminder that we are in a time of unrest. We all should be on guard.

No one is truly safe."

A shiver tiptoed its way down my spine. The numbness was still there, and all of this felt surreal until I thought of Rylan. My chest ached worse than my bruised jaw and temple. "When will...when will Rylan be put to rest?"

"Most likely in the morning." Vikter glanced down at me. "You know you cannot go."

The Ascended, as well as the Lords and Ladies in Wait, were not expected to attend the funeral of a guard. In fact, it was simply not done. "He was my personal guard, and he was...he was a friend. I don't care what's done and not done. I didn't attend Hannes' funeral because of protocol, and I wanted to be there." The guilt from that still ate at me, usually at three in the morning when I couldn't sleep. "I want to be there for Rylan."

Tawny appeared as if she wished to argue the point but knew better. Vikter simply sighed. "You know His Grace will not approve."

"He rarely approves of anything. This can be another thing he can add to his ever-growing list that contains all the ways I've disappointed him."

"Poppy," Vikter warned, his jaw tightening, reminding me of our argument last night. "You may continue to act as if angering the Duke is no big deal, but you know that will not lessen the weight of his anger."

Did I ever, but that knowledge didn't change anything. I was more than willing to deal with whatever consequences arose, just as I was when it came to me aiding those who'd been infected by the Craven. "I don't care. Rylan died right in front of me, and there was nothing I could do. I wiped—" My voice cracked. "I wiped my blade on his clothing."

Vikter stopped as we entered the foyer, placing his hand on my shoulder. "You did all that you could." He squeezed gently. "You did what you needed to do. You're not responsible for his death. He was doing his duty, Poppy. The same as if I were to die defending you."

My heart stopped. "Don't say that. Don't you ever say that. You won't die."

"But I will die someday. I may get lucky, and the god Rhain will come for me in my sleep, but it may be by the sword or by the arrow." His eyes met mine, even through the veil, and a knot lodged in my throat. "No matter how or when it happens, it will not be your fault, Poppy. And you will not waste one moment on guilt."

Tears blurred his features. I couldn't even think of something happening to Vikter. Losing Hannes and now Rylan, both who weren't nearly as close to me as Vikter, was hard enough. Other than Tawny, Vikter was the only person in my life who knew what kept me up at night and why I needed to feel like I could protect myself. He knew more than my own brother did. It would be like losing my parents all over again, but worse, because the memories of my mother and father, their faces and the sound of their voices, had faded with the passing of time. They were forever captured in the past, mere ghosts of who they once were, and Vikter was in the now, bright and in vivid detail.

"Tell me you understand that." His voice had softened.

I didn't, but I nodded nonetheless because that was what he needed to see.

"Rylan was a good man." His voice thickened, and for a moment, grief filled his gaze, proving that he wasn't unaffected by Rylan's death. He was just too skilled to show it. "I know it didn't sound like I thought so when we were with Her Grace. I stand by what I said. Rylan grew too complacent, but that can happen to the best of us. He was a good guard, and he cared for you. He would not want you to feel guilt." He squeezed my shoulder once more. "Come. You need to clean up."

The moment we reached my room, Vikter checked the space, assuring that the access to the old servants' stairs was locked. It was more than just a little unsettling to think that he felt the need to check my suite, but I figured he was operating on the better-safe-than-sorry mindset.

Before he left us, I recalled a part of what the Duchess had said. "The group the Duchess spoke about... Do you know who they are?"

"I wasn't aware of any group." Vikter glanced at where Tawny was carrying an armful of fresh towels into the bathing chamber. He often spoke openly in front of her, but this...all of this felt different. "But I'm not kept up to date on the comings and goings, so it's not exactly surprising."

"So, the Duke was just trying to avoid panic," I surmised.

"The Duchess has always been more forthcoming, but I imagine that he probably told the Commander the truth." His jaw hardened. "I should've been told immediately."

He should've been, and it didn't matter that he'd already suspected the truth.

"Try to get some rest." He placed his hand on my shoulder. "I'll be right outside if you need anything."

I nodded.

A hot bath was quickly drawn, placed near the fireplace, and then Tawny took the soiled gown. I never wanted to see it again. I sank into the steaming water and set about scrubbing my hands and arms until they were pink with heat and friction. Without any warning, the image of Rylan appeared in my mind, the look of shock on his face as he stared down at his chest.

Squeezing my eyes shut, I lowered myself more and let the water slip over my head. I stayed there until my lungs burned and I no longer saw Rylan's face. Only then did I allow myself to resurface. There I stayed, bruised knees tucked to my chest, until my skin puckered, and the water began to cool.

I rose from the soaking tub, pulling on a thick robe that Tawny had left on a nearby stool and padded on bare feet across the fire-warmed stone to the lone mirror. Using my palm to wipe away a bit of steam, I stared into my green eyes. My father had passed that color onto Ian and me. Our mother had brown eyes. I remembered that. The Queen had told me once that except for my eyes, I was a replica of my mother when she was my age. I had her strong brow and her oval-shaped face, angular cheekbones, and full mouth.

I tilted my cheek. The faintly red and bruised skin along my temple and the corner of my mouth were barely noticeable. Whatever the Healer had rubbed onto the skin had greatly sped up the healing process.

It had to be the same mixture I'd used to heal the welts that too often marked my back.

I pushed that thought from my head as I looked at my left cheek. That too had healed but had left a mark behind.

I didn't look at the scars often, but I did now. I studied the jagged streak of skin, a pink paler than my skin tone, that started below the hairline and sliced across my temple, narrowly missing my left eye. The healed injury ended by my nose. Another shorter wound was higher up, cutting across my forehead and through my eyebrow.

I lifted my damp fingers, pressing them to the longer scar. I'd always thought that my eyes and mouth seemed too large for my face, but the Queen had said that my mother had been considered a great beauty.

Whenever Queen Ileana spoke of my mother, she did so with pained fondness. They'd been close, and I knew she regretted granting my mother the one thing she'd ever asked her for.

Permission to refuse the Ascension.

My mother had been a Lady in Wait, given to the Court during her Rite, but my father had not been a Lord. She had chosen my father over the Blessing of the gods, and that kind of love…it was, well, I didn't have any experience with that. Probably never would, and I doubted most people did, no matter what their futures held. What my mom had done was unheard of. She'd been the first and the last to ever do so.

Queen Ileana had said more than once that if my mother had Ascended, she might've survived that night, but that night may have never come. I wouldn't be standing here. Neither would Ian. She wouldn't have married our father, and if she had Ascended, she would bear no children.

The Queen's beliefs were irrelevant.

But when the mist had come for us that night, if my parents had known how to defend themselves, both might still be alive. It was why I was standing here instead of the captive of a man determined to take down the Ascended and more than willing to shed blood to do so. If Malessa had known how to defend herself, her outcome may have still been the same, but she would've at least had a chance.

My gaze once more met my reflection's. The Dark One would not take me. That was a vow I would kill for and die to uphold.

I lowered my hand and then slowly turned from the mirror. I changed into a gown, leaving a lamp burning beside the door and crawled into bed. It couldn't have been more than twenty minutes before a soft knock sounded on the adjoining door, and Tawny's voice called out.

I rolled toward the entrance. "I'm awake."

Tawny eased inside, shutting the door behind her. "I…I couldn't sleep."

"I haven't even tried yet," I admitted.

"I can go back to my room if you're tired," she offered.

"You know I won't be falling asleep anytime soon." I patted the spot beside me.

Hurrying across the short distance, she snatched the edge of the blanket and slipped under it. Shifting onto her side, she faced me. "I keep thinking about everything, and I wasn't even there. I can't imagine what's going on in your head." She paused. "Actually, probably something that involves bloody vengeance."

I grinned despite all that had happened. "That's not entirely untrue."

"This is my shocked face," she replied, and then her smile faded. "I keep thinking about how unreal all of this feels. First with Malessa, and now Rylan. I saw him just after supper. He was alive and well. I'd passed Malessa yesterday morning. She was smiling and looked happy, carrying a bouquet of flowers. It's like...I can't process that they're gone. There one moment and not the next, without any warning."

Tawny was one of the few who hadn't been intimately touched by death. Her parents and her older brother and sister were alive. Other than Hannes, no one she knew well or saw often had died.

But even though I was too familiar with it, the death was still a shock, and like Hawke had also said, no less harsh or unforgiving.

I swallowed. "I don't know what it was like for Malessa." What I did know was that it had to be terrifying, though saying that wouldn't help matters. "But for Rylan, it was quick. Twenty or thirty seconds," I said. "And then he was gone. There wasn't a lot of pain, and what he did feel, it was over quickly."

She inhaled deeply, closing her eyes. "I liked him. He wasn't as stern as Vikter or as standoffish as Hannes and the rest. You could talk to him."

"I know," I whispered around the burn in my throat.

Tawny was silent for several moments and then said, "The Dark One." Her eyes opened. "He seemed more like a..."

"A myth?"

She nodded. "It's not like I didn't believe he was real. It's just that he's talked about like he's the bogeyman." She snuggled down, tucking the blanket to her chin. "What if that was the Dark One in the garden, and you managed to wound him?"

"That would be...pretty amazing, and I would brag until the end of time to you and Vikter. But, like I said, I don't think it was."

"Thank the gods you knew what to do." She reached across the bed, finding my hand and squeezing it. "If not..."

"I know." In moments like this, it was hard to remember that duty bound us together, created our bond. I squeezed her hand back. "I'm just glad you weren't with me."

"I would like to say I wished I was there so you didn't have to face that alone, but in truth, I'm glad I wasn't," she admitted. "I would've been nothing more than a shrieking distraction."

"Not true. I've shown you how to use a dagger—"

"Being shown the basics of how to use a blade and then using it on another living, breathing person are two very different things." She pulled her hand back. "I would've definitely stood there and screamed. I'm not ashamed to admit that, and my screams probably would've brought the guards' attention sooner."

"You would've defended yourself." I totally believed that. "I've seen how vicious you get when there is only one sweet cake left."

The skin around her eyes crinkled as she laughed. "But that is a sweet cake. I would push the Duchess off a balcony to get to the last one."

A short laugh burst from me.

Another quick grin appeared and then faded as she toyed with a loose thread on the blanket. "Do you think the King and Queen will summon you to the capital?"

Muscles tensed along my shoulders. "I don't know."

That wasn't true.

If they thought I was no longer safe in Masadonia, they would demand I return to the capital, almost a year ahead of my Ascension.

But that wasn't what caused the coldness in my chest to seep into every part of me. The Duchess had proven earlier that ensuring the Ascension wasn't thwarted was the greatest concern. There was one way to ensure that.

The Queen could petition the gods to move up the Ascension.

Shortly after dawn, when the sun shone brighter than I remembered for a morning so close to winter, I stood beside Vikter. We were at the foot of the Undying Hills and below the Temples of Rhahar, the Eternal God, and Ione, the Goddess of Rebirth. The Temples loomed above us, each constructed from the blackest stone from the Far East and both as large as Castle Teerman, casting half the valley into shadows but not where we stood. It was as if the gods were shining light down on us.

We were silent as we watched Rylan Keal's linen-wrapped body be lifted onto the pyre.

Vikter had been resigned when I joined him, not prepared to train but dressed in white and veiled. He knew he wasn't going to talk me out of this and said nothing as we walked to where funerals for all those who resided in Masadonia were held. While my presence had drawn many shocked glances, no one had demanded to know why I was present as we made the trek to the pyre. And even if they had said anything, it wouldn't have changed my decision. I owed it to Rylan to be here.

Surrounded by members of the Royal Guard and the guards from the Rise, we stood near the back of the small crowd. I didn't want to get closer out of respect for the guards. Rylan was my personal guard, he was a friend, but he was their brother, and his death affected them differently.

As the white-robed High Priest spoke of Rylan's strength and bravery, of the glory he would find in the company of the gods, of the eternal life that awaited him, the icy ache in my chest grew.

Rylan looked so small on the pyre, as if he'd shrunken in size as the Priest sprinkled oil and salt over the body. A sweet scent filled the air.

The Commander of the Royal Guard, Griffith Jansen, stepped forward, the white mantle draped from his shoulders rippling in the breeze as he carried forth the lone torch. Commander Jansen turned in our direction and waited. It took me a moment to realize why.

Vikter.

As the one who had worked the closest with Rylan, he would be given the task of lighting the pyre. He started to step forward, but stopped, his gaze swinging to me. It was clear he didn't want to leave my side, not even when I was surrounded by dozens of guards, and it was highly unlikely that anything would occur.

Oh gods, it struck me then that my presence interfered with his desire or need to pay his respects. I didn't for one second think that was why he'd initially resisted the idea of me coming the night before, but I hadn't even considered how it would impact him.

Feeling like a selfish brat, I started to tell him that I would be safe while he paid his respects.

"I have her," a deep voice said from behind me, one that shouldn't be familiar but was.

My stomach dipped as if I were standing on a ledge, while at the same time, my heart sped up. I didn't even need to turn around to know whom it was.

Hawke Flynn.

Oh, gods.

After everything that had happened, I had almost forgotten about Hawke. *Almost* being the keyword, because this morning, I had woken, wishing I had waited for him to come back to the Red Pearl.

To possibly be taken and used in whatever terrible manner my enemies deemed, or to be killed before I had the chance to experience all the things that people only whispered about seemed all too frightening a reality.

Vikter's steely blue-gray gaze shifted over my shoulder. A long, tense moment passed as several guards looked on. "Do you?"

"With my sword and with my life," Hawke replied, coming to stand at my shoulder.

The dipping motion returned to my stomach in response to his promise, even though I knew that was what all guards said, no matter if they were from the Rise or if they protected the Ascended.

"The Commander tells me you're one of the best on the Rise." Vikter's jaw hardened as he spoke quietly so only Hawke and I could hear him. "Said that he hasn't seen your level of skill with a bow or sword in too many years."

"I'm good at what I do."

"And what is that?" Vikter challenged.

"Killing."

The simple, short answer from lips that had felt as soft as they had firm, was a shock. But the one word didn't frighten me. I had quite the opposite reaction, and that probably should've disturbed me. Or, at the very least, concerned me.

"She is the future of this kingdom," Vikter warned, and I squirmed in a strange mix of embarrassment and fondness. He'd said what everyone from the Duchess to the Queen would say, but I knew he spoke those words because of *who* I was and not what I represented. "That is who you stand beside."

"I know who I stand beside," Hawke answered.

A hysterical giggle climbed its way up my throat. He honestly had no idea who he stood next to. By the grace of the gods, I was able to stop that laugh.

"She is safe with me," Hawke added.

I was.

And I wasn't.

Vikter looked at me, and all I could do was nod. I couldn't speak. If I did, Hawke might recognize my voice, and then…gods, I couldn't even begin to fathom what would occur.

With one last look of warning in Hawke's direction, Vikter pivoted on his heel and stalked toward the guard who held the torch. My heart hadn't slowed as I dared one quick peek in Hawke's direction.

I immediately wished I hadn't.

In the bright, early morning sun, with blue-black hair swept back from his face, his features were harder, harsher, and somehow all the more beautiful. The line of his lips was firm. No hint of a dimple to be seen. He had on the same black uniform he had worn the night at the Red Pearl, except now he also wore the leather and iron armor of the Rise, his broadsword at his side, the bloodstone blade a deep ruby.

Why had he stepped forward to watch over me? There were Royal Guards present. Dozens of them who should've done so. My gaze swept the crowd, and I realized that none of them looked long in my direction, and I wondered if it was because it was so rare that they ever saw me, or if they feared punishment by the Duke or the gods for even looking at me.

Their duty dictated that they give their life for someone who it would be considered a grave disrespect to look upon too long or approach without permission. The disturbing irony in that sat heavily on my shoulders.

But Hawke was different.

There was no way that he knew it had been me at the Red Pearl. He'd never heard me speak before, and I doubted my jaw and mouth were *that* recognizable.

The Duchess had said he came from the capital with glowing recommendations and would likely become one of the youngest Royal Guards. If that was what Hawke wanted, stepping up like this would surely help. After all, there was a sudden, unexpected opening in the

Royal Guard now.

And wasn't that a dark assumption to make?

A muscle flexed along his jaw, momentarily fascinating. Then I remembered why I was here, and that was not to ogle Hawke from behind my veil. I shifted my gaze to where Vikter approached the pyre.

Drawing in a shallow breath, I wanted to look away, to close my eyes when he lowered the torch. I didn't. I watched as the flames licked along the tinder and the sound of crackling wood filled the quiet. My insides twisted as the fire ignited in a rush, spreading over Rylan's body as Vikter dropped to one knee before the pyre, bowing his head.

"You do him a great honor by being here," Hawke spoke quietly, but his words startled me. My head swung in his direction. He was staring down at me with eyes so bright, they looked like the gods had polished the amber themselves and placed them there. "You do us all a great honor by being here."

I opened my mouth to tell him that Rylan and all of them were owed far more than the honor of my presence, but I stopped myself. I couldn't risk it.

Hawke's gaze flicked over my lower jaw, lingering on the corner of my mouth, where I knew the skin was inflamed. "You were hurt." It wasn't a question but a statement uttered in a hard-as-granite tone. "You can be assured that will never happen again."

Chapter 9

Sweat dampened my skin as I dipped down and spun, the long, thick braid of hair whipping around me. I kicked out, and my bare foot connected with the side of Vikter's shin. Caught off guard, he staggered to the side as I shot up beside him. He started to strike back but froze. His gaze dropped to where I held the dagger to his throat.

The corners of his lips turned down.

I smiled. "I win."

"It's not about winning, Poppy."

"It's not?" I lowered the dagger, stepping back.

"It's about surviving."

"Isn't that winning, though?"

He shot me a sidelong glance as he dragged his arm over his forehead. "I suppose you can look at it that way, but it's never a game."

"I know that." I sheathed the dagger at my thigh. Dressed in a pair of thick leggings and an old tunic of Vikter's, I walked across the stone floor toward an old, wooden table. I picked up the glass of water and took a long drink. If I could dress like this all day, every day, I'd be a happy girl. "But if it were a game, I still would've won."

"You only got the upper hand twice, Poppy."

"Yes, but both of those times, I would've sliced your neck. You got the upper hand three times, but they would've been nothing more than flesh wounds."

"Flesh wounds?" He barked out a short, rare laugh. "Only you would think disembowelment a paltry flesh wound. You're such a poor loser."

"I thought this wasn't a game?"

He scoffed.

Grinning, I shrugged as I faced him. Dust danced in the sunlight that poured through the open windows. The glass had long since been removed, and the room was either drafty and near frigid in the winter, or unbearably hot in the summer. But no one ever checked for us here, so the extreme temperature variances were more than manageable.

It was the morning after Rylan's funeral, too early for much of the castle to be moving about. Nearly all the staff and the stronghold's inhabitants followed the schedule of the Ascended, and the servants, as well as the Duke and Duchess, believed that I was still abed. Only Tawny knew where I was. Rylan hadn't even known, as Vikter always had morning duties with me.

"How is your head feeling?" he asked.

"Fine."

He arched a fair brow. "Are you telling the truth?"

A faint, bluish-purple bruise over my temple was all that remained. The skin around my mouth was no longer red. There was a superficial cut along the inside of my cheek that any amount of salt seemed to find its way into, but other than that, I *was* fine. Not that I would admit it, but Vikter suggesting I take it easy and rest yesterday probably had a lot to do with that.

After Rylan's funeral, I'd spent the day in my chambers, reading one of the books Tawny had brought to me. It was a tale of two lovers, star-crossed yet fated. The title had fallen in the Things Penellaphe is Forbidden to Read pile, which was pretty much everything that didn't involve some sort of educational material or the teachings of the gods. I'd finished the novel last evening, and I wondered if Tawny could bring me another. It was doubtful. Preparation for the upcoming Rite was consuming much of her spare time. Whenever Tawny couldn't bring a book for me to read, I would simply sneak into the Atheneum and help myself. Plus, with the attempted kidnapping and what had happened to Malessa, I didn't want her out there roaming around.

Which meant I also shouldn't be roaming around unguarded, but the Atheneum wasn't too far. Just a few blocks beyond the castle and easily accessible through the Grove. Disguised, no one would know that I was the Maiden, but it still felt too risky and dumb to do something like that so quickly after the attack.

"It hurt a little last night, but not since I woke up." I paused. "The man had a weak punch."

Vikter snorted as he approached me, sliding his short sword into its scabbard. "Did you sleep well?"

I considered lying. "Do I look like I haven't slept?"

He stopped in front of me. "You rarely ever sleep well. I imagine what happened with Rylan has exacerbated your already poor sleeping patterns."

"Aw, are you worried about me?" I teased. "You're such a good father."

His expression turned bland. "Stop deflecting, Poppy."

"Why? I'm so good at it."

"But you're actually not."

Rolling my eyes, I sighed. "It took a while to fall asleep, but I haven't had a nightmare in a while."

Vikter's gaze searched mine as if trying to determine whether I was lying—and the man probably could. I wasn't lying…exactly. I hadn't had a night terror since I went to the Red Pearl, and I wasn't sure why that was.

Perhaps falling asleep thinking about what had happened in the Red Pearl had somehow switched the gears of my brain away from past trauma. If so, I wasn't going to look a gift horse in the mouth.

"Who do you think will replace Rylan?" I changed the subject before he could continue down that road of questioning.

"I'm not sure, but I assume it will be decided fairly soon."

My mind immediately went to Hawke, even though he couldn't possibly be in the running, not when there were so many others from the Rise who'd been here longer. But the question sort of toppled out of me anyway. "Do you think it would be the one who came from the capital recently? The guard who stood by my side at the funeral?"

Who assured me that I wouldn't be hurt again?

"You're talking about Hawke?" Vikter asked, securing his other sword.

"Oh, is that his name?"

He lifted his gaze to mine. "You're a terrible liar."

"Am not!" I frowned. "What am I supposedly lying about?"

"You didn't know his name?"

Praying that my flushing cheeks didn't give me away, I folded my arms over my chest. "Why would I?"

"Every woman in this city knows his name."

"What does that have to do with anything?"

His lips twitched as if he were fighting a smile. "He's a very handsome young man, or so I've been told, and there's nothing wrong with you taking notice of him." He glanced away. "As long as that is all you do."

My cheeks did flush hotly then because I had done far more than simply take notice of Hawke. "When exactly would I have had a chance to do anything other than take notice, which is, might I remind you, strictly forbidden?"

Vikter laughed once more, and my frown increased. "When has something being forbidden ever stopped you?"

"*That* is different," I said, wondering if the gods would strike me down for so blatantly lying. "And when would I even have a chance to do something like that?"

"I'm actually glad you brought that up. Your little adventures will need to come to an end."

My stomach jumped. "I have no idea what you're talking about."

He ignored that. "I haven't said much in the past about you and Tawny sneaking off, but after what happened in the garden, that has to end."

I snapped my mouth shut.

"Did you think I didn't know?" His smile was slow and smug. "I'm watching even when you think I'm not."

"Well, that is…creepy." I didn't even want to know if he knew that I'd been to the Red Pearl.

"Creepy or not, just remember what I said the next time you think of sneaking out in the middle of the night." Before I could respond, he said, "And regarding Hawke, I would say that his age would make him becoming your personal guard doubtful."

"But?" My heart started thumping, and I was barely aware of Vikter taking the glass from me.

"But he is exceptionally skilled, more so than many of the Royal Guards now. I wasn't stroking his ego yesterday when I said that. He came here, held in high regard by the capital, and he appears to be close to Commander Jansen." He finished off my glass of water. "I wouldn't be all that surprised if he *was* promoted over others."

Now my heart was slamming itself against my ribs. "But...but to become *my* personal guard? Surely, someone who is more familiar with the city would be a better fit."

"Actually, someone new and less likely to be complacent would be the best," he said. "He would see things differently than many of us who've been here for years or longer. See weaknesses and threats we may overlook out of monotony. And he showed yesterday that he has no problem stepping up while everyone else stood by."

All of that made sense, but...but he couldn't become my personal Royal Guard. If he did, I'd have to speak to him eventually, and if I did that, he'd recognize me at some point.

And then what?

If he was close to the Commander and determined to rise through the ranks, he would be sure to report me. After all, the highest-ranking guards who had a chance of living to see a well-funded retirement, were the Royal Guards who protected the Duke and Duchess of Masadonia.

During the day, when the sun was high, the Great Hall, where the weekly City Councils and grand celebrations were held, was one of the most beautiful rooms in the entire castle.

Windows taller than most of the homes in the city were spaced every twenty feet or so, allowing the warm, bright sun to drench the polished white limestone walls and floors. The windows offered views of the gardens to the left and the Temples atop the Undying Hills.

Heavy white tapestries hung the length of the windows and in between them. The golden Royal Crest embossed the center of each banner. Creamy white pillars adorned with flecks of gold and silver were spaced throughout the long, wide chamber. White and purple jasmine flowers climbed out of silver urns, perfuming the air with their sweet, earthy scent.

The hand-painted ceiling was the true masterpiece of the Great

Hall. Above, all the gods could be seen watching over us. Ione and Rhahar. The flaming redheaded Aios, the Goddess of Love, Fertility, and Beauty. Saion, the dark-skinned God of the Sky and the Soil—he was Earth, Wind, and Water. Beside him was Theon, the God of Accord and War, and his twin Lailah, the Goddess of Peace and Vengeance. The dark-haired Goddess of the Hunt, Bele, armed with her bow. There was Perus, the pale, white-haired God of the Rite and Prosperity. Beside him was Rhain, the God of the Common Man and Endings. And then there was my namesake, Penellaphe, the Goddess of Wisdom, Loyalty, and Duty—which I found highly ironic. All their faces were captured in striking, vivid detail—all but Nyktos, the King of all the gods, who had made the first Blessing. His face and form were nothing but brilliant silvery moonlight.

But as I stood on the raised dais to the left of the seated Duchess, there was no sunlight pouring in through the windows, only the dark night. Several sconces and oil lamps placed to provide as much light as possible cast a golden glow throughout the Hall.

The gods did not walk in the sun.

So, neither did the Ascended.

How had Ian adapted to that? If it was a sunny day, he could be found outside, scribbling in one of his journals, recording whatever stories his mind had drummed up. Did he now write in the moonlight? I would know sooner rather than later if I was summoned back to the capital.

Anxiety bloomed, and I pushed that thought aside before the unease could spread. I scanned the throng of people who had filled up the Great Hall, pretending that I wasn't searching for one face in particular, and failing miserably.

I knew Hawke was here. He always was, but I hadn't seen him yet.

Full of nervous energy, I unclasped and then wrung my hands as someone—a banker—continued to heap praise upon the Teermans.

"You all right?" Vikter bent his head, keeping his voice low enough so only I would hear him.

I turned just the slightest to the left and nodded. "Why do you ask?"

"Because you've been fidgeting like you have spiders in your gown since the beginning of this," he answered.

Spiders in my gown?

If I had spiders in my gown, I wouldn't be fidgeting. I'd be screaming and stripping down to nothing. I wouldn't care at all who witnessed it.

I wasn't sure exactly what had me so incredibly restless. Well, there were myriad things, considering everything that had happened recently, but it felt like...more than that.

It had started after I'd left Vikter, a brief headache I attributed to the punch and possibly overdoing it during training. Not that I would admit that, but after lunch, it had faded, only to be replaced by a wealth of nervous energy. It reminded me of the blend of coffee beans Ian had shipped from the capital. Tawny and I had only drunk half a cup, and neither of us could sit still for the entire day afterward.

Making a more conscious effort to remain still, my gaze shifted to the left, to the gardens, where I'd found such peace before. My chest ached. I hadn't gone to the gardens last night or at any time today. The area hadn't been forbidden to me, but I knew if I stepped foot outside, I would be surrounded by guards.

I couldn't even imagine how the upcoming Rite would go.

But I didn't think I could ever go back to the gardens, no matter how much I loved them and the roses therein. Even now, just looking at the shadowy outline of the garden through the windows brought forth an image of Rylan's blank stare.

Drawing in a shallow breath, I pulled my attention from the garden to the front of the Hall. Members of the Court, those who had Ascended, stood the closest, flanking the dais. Behind them were the Ladies and Lords in Wait. Royal Guards stood among them, their shoulders bearing white mantles with the Royal Crest. Merchants and businessmen, villagers and laborers crowded the hall, all there to petition the Court for one thing or another, air their grievances, or curry favor with His or Her Grace.

Plenty of the faces that stared up at us were wide-eyed and slack-jawed with awe. For some, this was the first time they'd seen the brown-haired beauty, Duchess Teerman, or the coolly handsome Duke, whose hair was so blond it was almost white. For many, this was the first time they'd been as close as they were to an Ascended.

They looked like they were in the presence of the gods themselves, and in a way, I guessed they were. The Ascended were descendants of the gods, by blood, if not by birth.

And then there was...me.

Nearly none of the commoners who stood in the Great Hall had ever seen the Maiden before. For that alone, I was subjected to many curious, quick glances. I imagined that word of Malessa's death and my attempted abduction had also traveled widely by now, and I was sure that had aided in the curiosity and the buzz of anxious energy that seemed to permeate the Hall.

Except for Tawny. She looked half-asleep as she stood there, and I bit down on the inside of my cheek when she smothered a yawn. We'd been here for nearly two hours already, and I wondered if the Teermans' asses ached as much as my feet were beginning to.

Probably not.

Both looked mighty comfortable. The Duchess was dressed in yellow silk, and even I could admit that the Duke cut a rather dashing figure in his black trousers and tailcoat.

He always reminded me of the pale snake I'd once stumbled upon near the beach as a little girl. Beautiful to look upon, but its bite dangerous and often deadly.

Swallowing a sigh as the banker began to speak of their great leadership, I started to look toward the Temples—

I saw him.

Hawke.

A strange, funny little hitch took up residence in my chest at the sight of him. He stood between two pillars, arms folded across his broad chest. Like yesterday, there was no teasing half-grin on his face, and his features would've been considered severe if it weren't for the unruly strands of midnight-hued hair tumbling over his forehead, softening his expression.

A tingling sense of awareness swept down my spine, spreading tiny bumps all over my skin. Hawke's gaze was lifted to the dais, to where I stood, and even from across the hall and from behind the veil, I swore our gazes connected. Air whooshed from my lungs, and the entire Hall seemed to fade away, going silent as we stared at one another.

My heart thumped heavily as my hands spasmed open and then closed. He was staring at me, but so were a lot of others. Even the Ascended often stared.

I was a curiosity, a sideshow put on display once a week to serve as a reminder that the gods could actively intervene in births and in lives.

But my legs still felt strange, and my pulse fluttered as if I'd spent the last hour practicing different combat techniques with Vikter.

Magnus, a steward to the Duke, announced the next to speak, drawing my attention. "Mr. and Mrs. Tulis have requested a word, Your Graces."

Dressed in simple but clean clothing, the fair-headed couple stepped out from a grouping of those waiting toward the back. The husband had his arm around his shorter wife's shoulders, keeping her tucked close to his side. Hair pulled back from her bloodless face, the woman wore no jewels but held a small swaddled bundle in her arms. The bundle stirred as they approached the dais, little arms and legs stretching the pale blue blanket. Their gazes were fixed to the floor, heads bowed slightly. They didn't look up, not until the Duchess gave them permission to do so.

"You may speak," she said, her voice hauntingly feminine and endlessly soft. She sounded like someone who'd never raised their voice or hand in anger. Neither were untrue, and for what had to be the hundredth time, I wondered exactly what she and the Duke had in common. I couldn't remember the last time I'd even seen them touch one another—not as if that was necessary for the Ascended to marry.

Unlike others, Mr. and Mrs. Tulis clearly shared a wealth of feelings for one another. It was the way Mr. Tulis held his wife close, and in the way she lifted her gaze, first to him and then to the Duchess.

"Thank you." The wife's nervous gaze darted to the male Royal. "Your Grace."

Duke Teerman tilted his head in acknowledgement. "It is our pleasure," he told her. "What can we do for you and your family?"

"We are here to present our son," she explained, turning so the bundle faced the dais. The little face was creased and ruddy as he blinked large eyes.

The Duchess leaned forward, hands remaining clasped in her lap. "He is darling. What is his name?"

"Tobias," the father answered. "He takes after my wife, as cute as a button, if I dare say so myself, Your Grace."

My lips curled into a grin.

"That he is." The Duchess nodded. "I do hope all is well with you and the babe?"

"It is. I'm perfectly healthy, just like him, and he's been a joy, a true blessing." Mrs. Tulis straightened, holding the baby close to her breast. "We love him very much."

"Is he your first son?" the Duke asked.

Mr. Tulis's Adam's apple bobbed with a swallow. "No, Your Grace, he isn't. He's our third son."

The Duchess clapped her hands together. "Then Tobias is a true blessing, one who will receive the honor of serving the gods."

"That's why we're here, Your Grace." The man slipped his arm from around his wife. "Our first son—our dear Jamie—he…he passed no more than three months ago." Mr. Tulis cleared his throat. "It was a sickness of the blood, the Healers told us. It came on real quick, you see. One day, he was fine, chasing around and getting into all kinds of trouble. And then the following morning, he didn't wake up. He lingered for a few days, but he left us."

"I'm incredibly sorry to hear that." Sorrow filled the Duchess's voice as she settled back in her seat. "And what of the second son?"

"We lost him to the same sickness that took Jamie." The mother began to tremble. "No more than a year into his life."

They'd lost two sons? My heart was already aching for them. Even with the loss I'd experienced in my life, I couldn't even begin to understand the kind of anguish a parent must suffer when they lose a child, let alone two. If I felt it, I knew I would want to do something about it, and I couldn't. Not here. I locked down my gift.

"That is truly a tragedy. I hope you find solace in the knowledge that your dear Jamie is with the gods, along with your second born."

"We do. It's what's gotten us through his loss." Mrs. Tulis gently rocked the baby. "We come today to hope, to ask…." She trailed off, seeming unable to finish.

It was her husband who took over for her. "We came here today to ask that our son not be considered for the Rite when he comes of age."

A rolling gasp echoed through the chamber, coming from all sides at once.

Mr. Tulis's shoulders stiffened, but he forged ahead. "I know that it's a lot to ask of you and the gods. He is our third son, but we lost our first two, and my wife, as much as she desires more babes, the Healers said she shouldn't have more. He is our only remaining child. He will be our last."

"But he is still your third son," the Duke responded, and my chest hollowed. "Whether your first thrived or not doesn't change that your second son and now your third are fated to serve the gods."

"But we have no other child, Your Grace." Mrs. Tulis's lower lip trembled as her chest rose and fell rapidly. "If I were to get pregnant, I could die. We—"

"I understand that." The tone of the Duke's voice didn't change. "And you do understand that while we've been given great power and authority by the gods, the issue of the Rite is not something we can change."

"But you can speak with the gods." Mr. Tulis moved to step closer but drew up short when several Royal Guards shifted forward.

A low murmur rose from the audience. I glanced to where Hawke stood. He was watching what I believed to be the Tulises' third tragedy play out before us, his jaw as hard as the limestone around us. Did he have a second or third brother or sister who'd been given over to the Rite? One who may go on to serve the Court and receive the Blessing from the gods, and another he would never be able to see again?

"You can speak with the gods on our behalf. Couldn't you?" Mr. Tulis asked, his voice rough like sand. "We are good people."

"Please." Tears rolled down the mother's face, and my fingers itched to reach out and touch her, to ease her pain even if for a little while. "We beg of you to at least try. We know the gods are merciful. We have prayed to Aios and Nyktos every morning and every night for this gift. All we ask is that—"

"What you ask cannot be granted. Tobias is your third son, and this is the natural order of things," the Duchess stated. A piercing sob left the woman. "I know it's hard, and it hurts now, but your son is a gift to the gods, not a gift from them. That is why we would never ask that of them."

Why not? What harm could there be in asking? Surely, there were enough in service to the gods that one boy would not upset the natural order of things.

And besides, some exceptions had been made in the past. My brother was proof of that.

Many in the audience appeared rooted in shock as if they could not believe the audacity of what was being asked. There were others, though, whose faces were soaked in sympathy and marked with anger. Their stares were fixed on the dais—on Duke and Duchess

Teerman—and on me.

"Please. I beg of you. I beg." The father dropped to his knees, his hands folded as if in prayer.

I gasped, my chest squeezing. I wasn't sure how it happened or why, but my control over my gift snapped, and my senses opened. I sucked in a sharp breath as grief poured into me in icy waves. The potency shook my knees, and I could barely breathe around it.

A moment later, I felt Vikter's hand on my back, and I knew he was prepared to grab me in case I went to them. It took everything in me to stand there and do nothing.

Tearing my gaze away from Mr. Tulis, I forced out deep, even breaths. My wide eyes roamed the crowd as I pictured a wall in my mind, one as great as the Rise, so tall and thick that no one's pain could breach it. That had always worked in the past, and it worked now. The claws of sorrow loosened their grip, but—

My gaze snagged on a blond man. He stood several rows back, his chin bowed, and much of his face obscured by the curtain of hair that fell forward. I felt...*something* burning through the wall I'd built, but it didn't quite feel like anguish. It felt hot, like physical pain, but this was...it was bitter-tasting in the back of my throat as if I'd swallowed acid. He had to be in pain, but...

Unnerved, I closed my eyes and rebuilt the wall until all I felt was the pounding of my heart. After a few seconds, I was able to take a deeper, stronger breath, and finally, the strange sensation disappeared. I opened my eyes as the father pleaded.

"*Please.* We love our son," he cried. "We want to raise him to be a good man, to—"

"He will be raised in the Temples of Rhahar and Ione, where he will be cared for while in service to the gods as it has been done since the first Blessing." The Duke's voice brooked no argument, and the woman's sobs deepened. "Through us, the gods protect each and every one of you from the horrors outside the Rise. From what comes in the mist. And all we must do is provide them with service. Are you willing to anger the gods to keep a child at home, to grow old or possibly sicken and die?"

Mr. Tulis shook his head, his face draining of all color. "No, Your Grace, we would not want to risk that, but he's our son—

"That is what you ask, though." The Duke cut him off. "In one month from his birth, you will give him to the High Priests, and you will be honored to do so."

Unable to look at the tear-stricken faces any longer, I closed my eyes once more and wished I could somehow drown out the sounds of their heartbreak. However, even if I could, I wouldn't forget them. And, truthfully, I needed to hear their pain. I needed to bear witness to it and remember. Serving the gods in the Temples was an honor, but this was still a loss.

"Cease the tears," the Duchess implored. "You know that this is right and what the gods have requested."

But this didn't feel right. What harm would come in asking for one child to remain at home with his parents? To grow, to live, and to become a useful member of society? Neither the Duke nor the Duchess would bend to grant such a simple favor. How could anyone mortal be unmoved by the mother's pleas, her cries, and her husband's desolate hopelessness?

But I already knew the answer to that.

The Ascended were no longer mortal.

Chapter 10

I smothered a yawn as Tawny helped secure my veil in place, feeling like I hadn't gotten a moment of rest.

My mind wouldn't shut down last night. I couldn't stop thinking about Malessa and Rylan, the threat of the Dark One, and what had happened with the Tulis family. The utter hopelessness that had drenched the mother's face as her husband had led her from the chamber haunted me, as did the audience parting and giving them a wide berth. It was as if their request had left the Tulises with an infectious taint. As they left, cradling their infant, their heartbreak had projected, becoming a tangible, lingering entity.

But that wasn't the only part of this that preyed upon my mind.

The look that had settled over Hawke's face as he watched the broken couple also kept resurfacing. Anger had hardened his jaw and pressed his lips into a firm, unyielding line. And he wasn't the only one in attendance who'd borne what could easily be construed as the mark of resentment. I thought of the blond man I'd seen and what I'd felt from him. It had to be some form of pain, as that was the only thing I could feel from others. But it had reminded me of the anger that had settled into Hawke's features and in others.

Men and women of different classes who didn't look upon the Tulises with distaste, but had instead stared at the dais, unable to hide their displeasure and bitterness. Had some of them handed over third sons and daughters to the Priests, or would they soon be watching their second sons and daughters go to Court after their Rite.

Had the Duke and Duchess noticed those stares? I doubted they did, but I was sure the Royal Guards had.

As Vikter had said, this was a time of unrest, and it was spreading. I didn't think all could be blamed on the Descenters. Some of the fault could be laid at the feet of the *natural order of things*—to the Rite, which was beginning to feel unnatural when extenuating circumstances such as the Tulises' plight were ignored.

Could it be changed? The way things were done? That was another thing that had kept me awake. Surely, the gods had enough sons and daughters to serve them. They had the entire kingdom, and maybe it could become a case-by-case basis when it came to those who served the gods at the time of their Rite. Many parents were honored to have their children do so, and for some, a lifetime in servitude to the gods was a far better life than the one they would've had if they remained at home. Could I change the order of things once I returned to the capital, before I Ascended? Did I have that kind of power? Surely I had more than the Ladies and Lords in Wait, as I was the Maiden. I could speak to the Queen on behalf of the Tulises, and if I ended up returning from the gods as one of the Ascended, I could continue petitioning for change.

I could at least try, which was more than the Duke and Duchess were willing to do. That was what I'd decided before I'd finally drifted off to sleep, only to wake a few hours later to meet with Vikter.

"You sound like you need a nap," Tawny commented as she secured the final chain of the veil.

"If only I could do just that." I sighed.

"I have no idea how you can't nap during the day." She stepped to my side, tucking the ends of the veil so the length fell down the center of my back. "Give me any comfy chair and—"

"You'll be out cold in minutes. It makes me so jealous." I slipped my feet into white slippers with all-too-thin soles. "Once the sun comes up, I can't sleep."

"That's because you can't stand to be idle," she responded. "And sleeping requires a certain amount of idleness, which is something I excel at."

I laughed. "We all have to be good at something."

She shot me a look just before a sharp rap sounded, and then Vikter's voice rang out. Heading for the hall door, I groaned even though I had expected his arrival. I was due to meet with Priestess Analia for prayers, but in reality, the time was generally spent with the Priestess criticizing everything from my posture to the wrinkles in my gown.

"If you want to make a run for it, I'll tell Vikter you jumped out the window," Tawny offered.

I snorted. "That would only buy me a five-second lead time."

"True." Tawny reached the door before me, all but throwing it open. The moment I saw Vikter's face, I tensed. Deep grooves of tension bracketed his mouth.

"What happened?" I asked.

"You've been summoned to meet with the Duke and Duchess," he announced, and knots of dread formed.

Tawny sent me a quick, nervous glance. "What for?"

"I believe it has to do with who will replace Rylan," he said, and instead of feeling relief like I knew Tawny did given how her shoulders loosened, my unease grew.

"Do you know who?" I followed him out into the hall.

He shook his head, sending a lock of sandy blond hair across his forehead. "I haven't been told."

That wasn't exactly uncommon, but I would think that since Vikter would be working closely with whoever replaced Rylan, he'd be one of the first to know.

"What about Priestess Analia?" I asked, ignoring the raised brows that Tawny directed at me as she fell into step beside me. And, yes, I was surprised that I was asking since jumping out a window would almost be preferable to spending an afternoon listening to all the things that were wrong with me. But a bad, anxious feeling had taken root in my stomach.

"She's been advised there will be no session this week," Vikter answered. "I'm sure you're disappointed to hear that."

Tawny stifled a giggle as I stuck my tongue out at Vikter's back. We made our way to the end of the otherwise vacant wing of the castle and headed to the narrow hallway that accessed the main staircase. The wide stone steps fed into a large foyer where servants dusted statues of Penellaphe and Rhain. The eight-foot-tall, limestone statues stood in the center of the circular space and were cleaned every afternoon. How there could even be a speck of dust or dirt on any part of the statue was beyond me.

The foyer led to the front of the castle, where the Great Hall, sitting rooms, and atrium were located. However, Vikter led us to the right of the statues, through the archway adorned with lush, green garland. The large banquet table designed to seat dozens was cleared of all except for the golden vase in the center, containing several long-stemmed, night-blooming roses. Air catching in my throat, my gaze latched on to the roses as we skirted the table, walking toward one of the doors to the right that had been left ajar. The sight of the flowers, the scent....

I could practically smell the blood.

Tawny lightly touched my shoulder, drawing my attention. I exhaled, forcing a smile. Her worried gaze lingered as Vikter opened the door to one of the Teermans' many office spaces in the castle, this one used for less intimate meetings. My gaze swept the room, and my heart stopped.

It wasn't because the Duke sat behind his black-painted desk, his pale head bent as he scoured whatever paper he held in his hand. Nor was it because the Duchess stood to the right of his desk, speaking with Commander Jansen. What caused the reaction was the dark-haired young man standing beside the Commander, dressed in black and armored in leather and iron.

My lips parted as my heart tumbled all the way to the pit of my stomach while Tawny came to a sudden stop, blinking rapidly as if she'd just walked into the room to find one of the gods. Slowly, she looked over at me, and the corners of her lips turned up. She looked curious and amused, and I was sure if she could see my face, I likely looked like I was five seconds from bolting from the room.

In that moment, I really wished I'd told her about Hawke and the Red Pearl.

I couldn't think of another reason why Hawke would be here with the Commander, but I desperately clung to the hope that Vikter had been wrong, and it had nothing to do with Rylan's replacement. But what other reason could there be?

A sudden new fear took root. What if Hawke had discovered that it was me at the Red Pearl? Oh, my gods. That seemed improbable, but wasn't Hawke becoming my guard just as unlikely? My heart seemed to restart and was now in a race with itself.

The Duke looked up from his paper, his coolly handsome face giving me no indication of what was about to occur. "Please, close the door, Vikter."

The stately room stood out in too-vivid detail as Vikter moved to obey the request. The Royal Crest painted in gold on a white marble wall behind the Duke was blinding, and the bare walls were in stark contrast to the black chair rails that ran along the length and width of the room. There was only one chair besides the one the Duke sat in. That was a plush, cream-colored wingback chair that the Duchess usually occupied. The only other seating options were polished limestone benches placed in three neat rows.

The room was as cold as the Duke, but it was far better than the chamber he usually preferred. The one I'd been summoned to far too often.

"Thank you." Teerman nodded at Vikter, his smile close-lipped as he lowered the paper to the desk. His black, fathomless eyes flicked to where I stood, just inside the door. His mouth tightened as he motioned me forward. "Please sit, Penellaphe."

Legs oddly numb, I forced myself to cross the short distance, wholly aware of Hawke's gaze tracking my every step. I didn't need to look to know that he watched. His gaze was always that intense. I sat on the edge of the middle bench, folding my hands in my lap. Tawny took the bench behind me, while Vikter moved to stand to my right so he stood between me and the Commander and Hawke.

"I hope you're feeling well, Penellaphe?" the Duchess said as she sat in the chair beside the desk.

Hoping that I was only asked simple yes and no questions, I nodded.

"I'm relieved to hear that. I was worried that attending the City Council so soon after your attack would be too much," she said.

For once, I was beyond grateful for the veil. Because if my face were visible, there'd be no hiding how ridiculous that concern was. I'd been bruised. Not seriously injured or shot through the chest with an arrow, as Rylan had. I would be fine—I *was* fine. Rylan would never be okay.

"What happened in the garden is why we're all here," the Duke took over, and muscles all along my neck and back began to tense. "With the death of..." His fair brow pinched as disbelief whirled through me. "What was his name?" he asked of the Duchess, whose forehead creased. "The guard?"

"Rylan Keal, Your Grace," Vikter answered before I blurted out his name.

The Duke snapped his fingers. "Ah, yes. Ryan. With Ryan's death, you are down one guard."

My hands curled into fists. Rylan. His name was *Rylan*. Not Ryan. No one corrected him.

"Again," the Duke added after a pause, a faint twist of his lips forming a mockery of a smile. "Two guards lost in one year. I hope this isn't becoming a habit."

He said it as if it were somehow my fault.

"Anyway, with the upcoming Rite, and as you draw closer to your Ascension, Vikter cannot be expected to be the only one keeping a close watch on you," Teerman continued. "We need to replace Ryan."

I bit the inside of my cheek.

"Which, as I am sure you realize now, explains why Commander Jansen and Guard Flynn are here."

I might've stopped breathing.

"Guard Flynn will take Ryan's place, effective immediately," the Duke said, confirming what I had already guessed the moment I walked into the room. But hearing him say it aloud was an entirely different thing. "I'm sure this is surprising, as he's new to our city and quite young for a member of the Royal Guard."

I was wondering exactly that. The Duke sounded like he too was questioning it.

"There are several Rise Guards in line to be promoted, and bringing on Hawke is no slight to them." The Duke sat back, crossing one leg over the other. "But the Commander has assured us that Hawke is better suited to this task."

I couldn't believe this was happening.

"Guard Flynn may be new to the city, but that isn't a weakness. He's able to look at possible threats with fresh eyes," Commander Jansen spoke up then, nearly parroting what Vikter had said before. "Any number of guards would've overlooked the potential of a breach occurring in the Queen's Gardens. Not due to lack of skill—"

"Debatable," murmured the Duke.

The Commander wisely continued without acknowledging the comment. "But because there is a false sense of security and complacency that often comes with being within one city for too long. Hawke does not have such familiarity."

"He also has recent experience with the dangers outside the

Rise," the Duchess spoke, and my gaze sharpened on her. "Your Ascension is a little less than a year from now, but even if you're summoned sooner than expected or at the time of your Ascension, having someone with that kind of experience is invaluable. We won't have to pull from our Huntsmen to ensure that your travel to the capital is as safe as possible. The Descenters and the Dark One are not the only things to fear out there, as you know."

I did know.

And what she said made sense. There were fewer Huntsmen, and not many guards were suited for travel outside the Rise. Those who were had to excel at...

Killing.

Wasn't that what Hawke had said he was really good at?

"The possibility of you being summoned to the capital unexpectedly played a role in my decision," Jansen stated. "We plan trips outside the Rise at least six months in advance, and there could be a chance that when and if the Queen requests your presence in the capital, we'd have to wait for the Huntsmen to return. With Hawke being assigned to you, we would be able, for the most part, to avoid that situation."

The gods hated me.

And that wasn't exactly surprising considering all the things I regularly did that were forbidden. Maybe they had been watching, and this was my punishment. Because how in the world did the Commander not think a single Rise Guard was better suited or qualified?

Was Hawke *that* good?

My head moved then without any command from my brain. I looked to where Hawke stood and found his gaze fixed on me. A shiver curled its way down my spine. He inclined his head in acknowledgement, and I swore there was a faint glimmer to his amber eyes as if he were amused by all of this. But surely that had to be my paranoia.

"As a member of the Maiden's personal Royal Guard, it is likely that a situation may occur where you will see her unveiled." The Duchess's tone was soft, even a little sympathetic, and then it struck me. I knew what would occur now. "It can be distracting, seeing someone's face for the first time, especially a Chosen, and that could interfere with your ability to protect her. That is why the gods allow this breach."

For some reason, I had been so caught up in fear of being discovered that I'd forgotten what had happened when Rylan was brought in to work with Vikter.

"Commander Jansen, if you will, please step outside," the Duke said, and my wide gaze shot to him. There was a smile on his face, one that was wholly pleased and not at all forced and brittle.

I didn't even realize the Commander had left until the click of the door closing behind him jolted me.

"You are about to bear witness to what only a select few have seen, an unveiled Maiden," Teerman announced to Hawke, but his gaze was centered on me, to where my hands trembled in my lap. A real smile appeared on his face, turning my stomach. "Penellaphe, please, reveal yourself."

Chapter 11

There had been a handful of times in my life where reality felt more like a dream.

The night I'd heard my mother's screams and my father's shouts to run was one of them. Everything had felt hazy, as if I was there but somehow disconnected from my body. My parents being slaughtered was far more serious and traumatizing than what was happening right now. Still, I was on the brink of possibly being discovered. And if Hawke told the Duke where I'd been…

My mouth dried as a fist clenched deep in my chest.

Perhaps there was some truth to what Vikter had said about me wanting to be found unworthy. But even if that were true, I would want to be as far away from the Duke as possible if and when that occurred.

Hawke hadn't seen my full face the night at the Red Pearl, but he'd seen enough that it could trigger recognition. At some point, he was bound to figure it out. Probably after he heard me speak. However, I hadn't considered that moment occurring here in front of the Duke and Duchess.

"Penellaphe." The Duke's tone carried a thread of warning. I was taking too long. "We do not have all day."

"Give her a moment, Dorian." The Duchess turned to her husband. "You know why she hesitates. We have time."

I was *not* hesitating for the reason they believed—why the Duke smiled with such relish. Of course, I was uncomfortable baring my face, my *scars* in front of Hawke. Truthfully, though, that was the least of my concerns at the moment, but the Duke was probably internally screaming with twisted joy.

The man absolutely loathed me.

Dorian Teerman pretended that he didn't, that he thought I was this miracle-born, a Chosen, just like his wife believed. But I knew better. The time spent in his other *office* proved exactly how he felt about me.

I wasn't sure what it was about me that he hated, but there had to be something. As far as I knew, he was at least somewhat decent toward the Ladies and Lords in Wait. But me? He loved nothing more than discovering something that made me uncomfortable, only to then exploit it. And if I really wanted to make his day, I'd give him something to be disappointed in, a reason to continue his *lessons*.

Face burning as if on fire—from anger and frustration more than embarrassment—I reached for the clasps along the chains at the same moment Tawny rose, nearly tearing them apart as I unhooked them. The veil loosened, and before it could fall, Tawny caught the sides and helped ease the headdress off.

Cool air kissed my cheeks and the nape of my neck. I stared straight at the Duke. I wasn't sure what he saw in my face, but his smile faded, and his eyes turned to shards of obsidian. His jaw clenched, and I knew I shouldn't, but I couldn't stop myself...

I smiled.

It was just a hint of a grin, one that probably wasn't noticeable to anyone but the Duke, but he saw it. I knew he did.

I was sure I'd pay for it later, but at that moment, I didn't care.

Someone shifted to my right, ending my epic stare-off with the Duke, and reminding me that we weren't the only two in the room. He wasn't the only one looking at me.

The right side of my face was visible to Hawke, the side that the Duke often said was beautiful. The side I imagined matched my mother's.

Drawing in a shallow breath, I turned my head until I completely faced Hawke. No side profiles. No hiding or mask that covered the two scars. My hair was secured in a braid and then wrapped in a knot, so it too provided no curtain. He saw everything that had been bared at the Red Pearl and then some. He saw the scars. I braced myself. Just like the Duke knew I would, because deep down, whether Teerman knew why or not, Hawke's reaction would affect me.

It would hurt more than it should.

But I'd be damned if I let it show.

Lifting my chin, I waited for the look of shock or revulsion, or even worse, pity. I expected nothing less. Beauty was highly coveted and worshipped, flawlessness even more.

Because beauty was considered godlike.

Hawke's golden gaze roamed my face, his stare so potent that it felt like a caress along the scars, my cheeks, and then my lips. A shiver danced across my shoulders as his eyes came back to mine. Our gazes locked. Held. The air seemed to be sucked from the room, and I felt flushed, as if I'd been sitting out in the sun for too long.

I didn't know what I saw as I stared back at him, but there was no shock etched into his expression, no revulsion, and especially no pity. His face wasn't empty, exactly. There was *something* there, in his eyes and in the set of his mouth, but I had no idea what it was.

But then the Duke spoke, his tone deceptively pleasant. "She's truly unique, isn't she?"

I stiffened.

"Half of her face is a masterpiece," the Duke murmured, and my skin flashed cold and then hot as my stomach twisted. "The other half a nightmare."

A tremor coursed down my arms, but I kept my chin high and resisted the urge to pick up something, *anything*, and throw it at the Duke's face.

The Duchess spoke, though saying what, I wasn't sure. Hawke's gaze remained fastened on mine as he stepped forward. "Both halves are as beautiful as the whole."

My lips parted on a sharp inhale. I couldn't even look to see what the Duke's reaction was, though I was sure it was nothing short of cataclysmic.

Hawke placed a hand on the hilt of his broadsword and bowed slightly, his gaze never once leaving mine. "With my sword and with my life, I vow to keep you safe, Penellaphe," he spoke, voice deep and smooth, reminding me of rich, decadent chocolate. "From this moment until the last moment, I am yours."

Closing my bedroom door behind me, I leaned against it and exhaled raggedly. He'd said my name when he took his vow as my guard. Not what I was but *who* I was, and that was...

That wasn't the way it was supposed to be.

With my sword and with my life, I vow to keep you safe, Maiden, the Chosen. From this moment, until the last moment, I am yours.

That was how Vikter had sworn his oath, as did Hannes and then Rylan.

Had the Commander not informed Hawke of the correct words? I couldn't imagine he'd forget. The look on the Duke's face once Hawke had straightened could've set fire to wet grass.

Tawny spun to face me, the pale blue gown she wore swishing around her feet. "Hawke Flynn is your guard, Poppy."

"I know."

"Poppy!" she repeated my name, practically shouting it. "That!"—she pointed to the hall—"is your guard."

My heart toppled over itself. "Keep your voice down." I peeled away from the door and took her hand, pulling her farther into the chamber. "He's probably standing outside—"

"As your personal guard," she stated for the third time.

"I *know*." Heart thumping, I pulled her toward the window.

"And I know that this is going to sound terrible, but I have to say it. I can't contain it." Her eyes were wide with excitement. "It's a vast improvement."

"Tawny," I replied, slipping my hand free of hers.

"I know. I recognize that it was terrible, but I had to say it." She pressed her hand to her chest as she glanced back to the door. "He's quite...exciting to look at."

Indeed.

"And he's clearly interested in moving up in the ranks."

Her brows knitted as she turned back to me. "Why would you say that?"

I stared at her, wondering if she'd paid any attention to what the Duke had said. "Have you ever heard of a Royal Guard that young?"

Tawny's nose scrunched.

"No. You haven't. That's what befriending the Commander of the Royal Guard will do for you," I pointed out, heart thumping. "I cannot believe that there was no other Royal Guard just as qualified."

She opened her mouth, closed it, and then her eyes narrowed. "You're having a very strange, unexpected reaction."

I crossed my arms. "I don't know what you mean."

"You don't? You've watched him train in the yard—"

"I have not!" I totally had.

Tawny cocked her head to the side. "I've been with you on more than one occasion as you watched the guards train from the balcony, and you weren't watching just any guard. You were watching *him*."

I snapped my mouth shut.

"You seem almost angry about him being named your guard, and unless there's something you haven't told me, then I have no idea why."

There was a lot that I hadn't told her.

The suspicion in her gaze grew as she studied me. "What haven't you told me? Has he said something to you before?"

"When would I have had a chance for him to speak to me?" I asked weakly.

"As much as you creep around this castle, I'm sure there is a lot you overhear that doesn't actually require you speaking to someone," she pointed out and then stepped forward. Her voice lowered. "Did you overhear him say something bad?"

I shook my head.

"Poppy...."

The last thing I wanted was for her to think Hawke had done something wrong. That was why I blurted out what I did. Or maybe it was because I had to say something. "I kissed him."

Her lips parted. "What?"

"Or he kissed me," I corrected. "Well, we kissed each other. There was mutual kiss—"

"I get it!" she shrieked and then took a visible deep breath. "When did this happen? How did this happen? And why am I now just hearing about this?"

I plopped down in one of the wingback chairs by the fireplace. "It was...it was the night I went to the Red Pearl."

"I knew it." Tawny stomped her slippered foot. "I knew

something else had happened. You were acting too weird—too worried about being in trouble. Oh! I want to throw something at you. I can't believe you haven't said anything. I would be screaming this from the top of the castle."

"You'd be screaming it because you could. Nothing would happen to you. But me?"

"I know. I know. It's forbidden and all that." She hurried over to the other chair and sat, leaning toward me. "But I'm your friend. You're supposed to tell your friends these kinds of things."

Friend.

I wanted so very badly to believe that we were—that we'd be that if she weren't bound to me. "I'm sorry I didn't say anything. It's just that...I've done a lot of things I shouldn't do, but this...this is different. I thought if I didn't say anything, it would, I don't know..."

"Go away? That the gods wouldn't know?" Tawny shook her head. "If the gods know now, they knew then, Poppy."

"I know," I whispered, feeling terrible, but I couldn't tell her why I'd kept it to myself. I didn't want to hurt her, and I sensed that this would. I wouldn't need my touch to know that.

"I'll forgive you for not telling me if you tell me what happened in very, very graphic detail," she said.

I cracked a grin, and then I did just that. Well, almost that. As I slowly unhooked my veil and draped it across my lap, I told her how I'd come about to be in the room with him and how he thought I was Britta. I told her how he offered to do whatever I wanted once he realized that I wasn't her, and that he'd asked me to wait for him to return. But I didn't tell her how he'd kissed me *elsewhere*.

Tawny stared at me with more awe than even Agnes had when she realized I was the Maiden. "Oh, my gods, Poppy."

I nodded slowly.

"I so wish you'd stayed."

"Tawny." I sighed.

"What? You can't say you don't wish you'd stayed. Not just a little bit."

I couldn't say that.

"I bet you wouldn't be a Maiden any longer if you had."

"Tawny!"

"What?" She laughed. "I'm kidding, but I bet you'd *barely* be a Maiden. Tell me, did you...enjoy it? The kissing?"

I bit down on my lip, almost wishing that I could lie. "Yes. I did."

"Then why are you so upset that he's your guard?"

"Why? Your hormones must be clouding your rational thought."

"My hormones are always clouding my rational thought, thank you very much."

I snorted. "He's going to recognize me. He has to once he hears me speak, right?"

"I imagine."

"What if he goes to the Duke and tells him that I was at the Red Pearl? That I…allowed him to kiss me?" And do more, but at this point, the kissing would be bad enough. "He has to be one of the youngest Royal Guards, if not *the* youngest. It's clear he's interested in advancement, and what better way to secure that than to gain the Duke's favor. You know how his favorite guards or staff are treated! They're practically treated better than those on the Court."

"I don't think he has an interest in gaining *His Grace's* favor," she argued. "He said you were beautiful."

"I'm sure he was just being kind."

She stared at me as if I'd admitted to snacking on dog hair. "First off, you are beautiful. You know that—"

"I'm not saying that to fish for compliments."

"I know, but I felt the overwhelming need to remind you of such." She gave me a quick, broad smile. "He didn't have to say anything in response to the Duke being a general ass."

My lips twitched.

"He could've just ignored it and proceeded on to the Royal Guard oath, which, by the way, he made sound like…*sex*."

"Yes," I admitted, thinking I wouldn't have realized that before the night in the Red Pearl. "Yes, he did."

"I almost needed to fan myself, just so you know. But back to the more important part of this development. Do you think he's already recognized you?"

"I don't know." I let my head fall back against the seat. "I wore a mask that night, and he didn't remove it, but I think I would recognize someone in or out of a mask."

She nodded. "I would like to think that I would, and I would definitely hope that a Royal Guard would."

"Then that means he chose not to say anything." He hadn't said anything as both Vikter and he had escorted us to my chambers.

"Although, he might not have recognized me. It was dimly lit in that room."

"If he didn't, then I imagine he will when you speak, as you said. It's not like you can be completely silent every time you're around him," she stated. "That would be suspicious."

"Obviously."

"And odd."

"Agreed." I toyed with the chains on the veil. "I don't know. Either he didn't, or he did and chose not to say anything. Maybe he's planning to lord it over my head or something."

Her brows slammed down. "You're an incredibly suspicious person."

I started to deny that but realized I couldn't. I wisely moved along. "He probably just didn't recognize me." A weird mixture of relief and disappointment mingled with a thrill of anticipation. "You know what?"

"What?"

"I don't know if I'm relieved or disappointed that he didn't recognize me. Or if I'm excited that he might have." Shaking my head, I laughed. "I just don't know, but it doesn't matter. What…what happened between us was one time only. It was just this…thing. It can't happen again."

"Sure," she murmured.

"Not that I'm even thinking he'd *want* to do any of that again, especially now that he knows it was me. If he does."

"Uh-huh."

"But what I'm trying to say is that it's not a thing to even consider. What he does with the knowledge is the only thing that matters," I finished with a nod.

Tawny looked as if she were seconds away from clapping. "You know what I think?"

"I'm half afraid to hear it."

Her brown eyes glimmered. "Things are about to get so much more exciting around here."

Chapter 12

Early afternoon, the following day, I sat in the airy, sun-drenched atrium with Tawny and not one but two Ladies in Wait, wondering how I'd ended up in this situation.

My trips outside my chambers were always well timed, especially when I came to the atrium, so no one but me would be in the room. When I arrived some thirty minutes ago, it was empty as usual.

That had changed within minutes of sitting down and picking at the tiny sandwiches Tawny had confiscated from another room. Loren and Dafina had arrived, and while I sat as I'd been groomed to do—hands clasped lightly in my lap, ankles crossed, and feet tucked behind the ivory hem of my gown—I shouldn't be in the room.

Not while the Ladies in Wait were present since they'd cozied up to the table Tawny and I had sat at. The situation could easily be construed as me interacting with them, which was one of the many things expressly forbidden by the Priests and Priestesses. Interaction was, in their words, too familiar.

I wasn't interacting, though. I imagined I was the picture of well-bred serenity. Or I could easily be mistaken for one of the statues of the veiled Maidens. I may appear calm on the outside, but internally, I was nothing more than an exhausted, frazzled ball of nerves. Some of it had to do with the lack of any restful sleep the night prior—well, to be honest, for the last several days. It was also partly due to the fact that I knew I was going to be blamed for Dafina's and Loren's presence. I didn't even know if I was allowed to be in the atrium. It had never been an issue before, and no one had ever spoken to me about it. However, no one other than a stray servant or guard had ever shown up in the atrium while I'd been here before. They weren't the only reasons I was a mess of anxious, restless energy, though.

The primary cause stood catty-corner from where I sat, hand braced on the hilt of his sword, amber-colored eyes constantly alert.

Hawke.

It was strange to glance over and see him standing there. And it wasn't just because it was usually Rylan who watched over these afternoon brunches Tawny and I sometimes took in the atrium. It was how different it was with Hawke being here. Normally, Rylan had stared out into the garden or spent the majority of the time speaking with one of the other Royal Guards who were nearby as he lingered just inside the entrance. Not Hawke. He found the one area in the room where he had a view of the entire brightly lit space and the gardens outside the atrium.

Luckily, the windows didn't face the roses.

Unluckily, I often found myself staring at the fountain of the veiled Maiden.

In just one day, it had become almost painfully evident how lax Rylan had gotten in terms of security. Granted, there hadn't been an attempt before, but he *had* softened. I hated even acknowledging that. It felt like a betrayal to do so, but that wasn't the only thing that made this brunch so very different from the ones before.

Another thing that made it so different was the appearance of the two Ladies in Wait. I suspected that this was the first time they'd even been in the atrium since they'd arrived at Castle Teerman after their Rites.

Dafina, a second daughter of a rich merchant, fluttered a silk, lilac-hued folding fan as if she were attempting to end the life of an insect only she could see. While late-morning sun poured in through the windows, the atrium was still cool, and I doubted Dafina had grown overheated between eating cucumber sandwiches and sipping tea.

Beside her, Loren, the second daughter of a successful trader, had all but given up on sewing the tiny crystals onto her mask that was to be worn during the upcoming Rite, and had fully committed herself to watching every move the dark-haired Royal Guard made. I was confident she knew just how many breaths Hawke took in a minute.

Deep down, I knew why I hadn't risen and left the room like I was supposed to, like I knew Tawny waited for me to do. I understood why I was so willing to risk censure for simply sitting and minding my own business.

I was *enthralled* by the antics of the two Ladies in Wait.

Loren had already done several things to catch Hawke's attention. She'd dropped her pouch of crystals—which Hawke had gallantly assisted her in retrieving—while she pretended to be engrossed with a blue-winged bird hopping along the branches of a tree close to the windows. That had provoked Dafina to feign a faint, due to what, I had no idea. Somehow, the neckline of her blue gown had slipped so far, I wondered how she managed not to fall out of it.

I couldn't fall out of my dress if it was on fire.

My gown was all flowing sleeves, tiny beads, and a bodice that nearly reached my neck. The material was far too thin and delicate for me to sheathe the dagger to my thigh. As soon as I could change into something else, the blade would be back where it belonged.

Ever the gentleman, Hawke had escorted Dafina to the chaise and had brought her a glass of mint water. Not to be outdone, Loren then swooned from a sudden, inexplicable headache that she'd quickly recovered from once Hawke had brandished a smile, the one that showed the dimple in his right cheek.

There'd been no headache, just as there'd been no faint. I'd opened up my senses out of curiosity and felt no pain or anguish from either of them other than a thread of sadness. I thought that it might be due to Malessa's death, even though neither spoke of her.

"You know what I heard?" Dafina snapped her fan as she dragged her teeth over her lower lip, glancing toward Hawke. "Someone,"—she drew out the word and then lowered her voice—"has been a rather frequent visitor of one of those..." Her gaze flicked to me. "One of those dens in the city."

"Dens?" Tawny asked, giving up pretending that they weren't there. Not that I could blame her. She was friends with them, and while the Ladies in Wait were well aware that they probably shouldn't be sitting with me, Tawny appeared just as entertained as I was by their antics.

Dafina sent her a meaningful look. "You know the kind, where men and women often go to play cards and *other* games."

Tawny's brows lifted. "You're talking about the Red Pearl?"

"I was trying to be discreet." Dafina sighed, her glance darting pointedly in my direction. "But, yes."

I almost laughed at Dafina's attempt to shield me from the knowledge of such a place. I wondered what she'd do if she knew I'd been there.

"And what have you heard he does at such a place?" Tawny nudged me with her foot under the table. "I imagine he's there to play cards, right? Or do you...?" Pressing a hand to her chest, she slumped in her chair and sighed. A curl slipped free from the elaborate twist that was trying—and failing—to contain her hair. "Or do you think he engages in other, more illicit...games?"

Tawny knew exactly what Hawke did at the Red Pearl.

I wanted to kick her...like a Maiden, of course.

"I'm sure playing cards is all he does." Loren arched a brow as she pressed her yellow and red fan against the deep blue of her dress. The contrast of the fan and gown was...atrocious and also interesting. My gaze dipped to her mask. Crystals of every color were already sewn into the material. I was sure it would look like a rainbow had vomited all over her face once she finished. "If that is all he does, then that would be a...disappointment."

"I imagine he does what everyone does when they go there," Tawny said, humor dripping like syrup from her words. "Finds someone to spend...quality time with." Her mischievous gaze slid to mine.

I was going to replace the sugars Tawny loved to dump into her coffee with coarse salt.

She knew I wouldn't chime in, that I couldn't. I wasn't allowed to speak to the Ladies, and I still hadn't spoken to Hawke or around him. And other than Hawke asking if I wished to do anything after supper last night, to which I had shaken my head no, he hadn't spoken to me either.

Like before, I wasn't sure if I was relieved or disappointed.

"You shouldn't suggest such things in current company," Dafina suggested.

Tawny choked on her tea, and behind the veil, my eyes rolled.

"I imagine if Miss Willa were alive today, she would've snared him in her web," Loren said, and my interest was piqued. Was she talking about *the* Willa Colyns? "And then wrote about him in her diary."

She was.

Miss Willa Colyns was a woman who'd lived in Masadonia some two hundred years ago. She'd apparently had a very…active love life. Miss Colyns had detailed her rather scandalous affairs quite explicitly in her journal, and it had been filed away in the city Atheneum as some sort of historical account. I made a mental note to ask Tawny to retrieve that journal for me.

"I heard that she only wrote about her most skilled…*partners*," Dafina whispered with a giggle. "So, if he made it onto those pages, you know what that means."

I *did* know what that meant.

Because of *him*.

My gaze drifted to where Hawke stood. The black breeches and tunic molded to his body like a second skin, and I couldn't blame Dafina or Loren for how their gazes seemed to find their way back to him every couple of minutes. He was tall, with lean muscle, and the sheathed sword at his waist, along with the one at his side, said he was prepared for more than just fainting ladies. The white mantle of the Royal Guard was a new addition, draped over the back of his shoulders.

But he also filled the air with a certain type of unquantifiable tension, as if the room were electrified. Anyone around him had to be aware of that.

My gaze drifted over his chest, and the memory of how hard it had felt, even without the armor, sent heat creeping into my cheeks. A newly familiar heaviness settled in my chest, making the silk of my dress feel coarse against my suddenly sensitive and flushed skin.

Maybe one of those stupid fans would be useful.

Swallowing a groan, I wanted to smack myself in the face. But since that wasn't exactly an option, I took a sip of my tea, trying to ease the inexplicable dryness in my throat, and focused on Dafina and Loren once more. They were talking about the Rite, their excitement a heady hum. The celebration was just a week away, on the night of the Harvest Moon.

Their excitement was infectious. With it being my first Rite, I would be there, masked and not in white. Most would have no idea that I was the Maiden. Well, the two guards who were sure to be with me at all times would probably give me away to those paying attention. Still, a thrill of anticipation-laced uncertainty curled its way through me as my gaze slowly ticked its way back to Hawke.

My stomach tumbled.

If he saw me in the mask, would he know I was the one who'd been in the room with him? Would that even matter? By the time of the Rite, he would have to know I was one and the same, wouldn't he? If he hadn't realized it already.

He stood with feet shoulder-width apart, his gaze on our little group. The sunlight almost seemed drawn to him, caressing his cheekbones and brow like a lover. His profile was flawless, the line of his jaw as chiseled as the statues that adorned the garden and the castle foyer.

"You know that it has to mean that he's near," Loren was saying. "Prince Casteel."

My head snapped in her direction in shock. I had no idea what she was talking about or how the subject had come up, but I couldn't believe she had actually spoken his name aloud. My lips parted. No one other than the Descenters would dare utter his actual name, and I doubted that any of them would even speak it in the castle. It was treasonous to call him a prince. He was the Dark One.

Dafina was frowning. "Because of the…" She glanced at me, her brows knitted. "Because of the attack?"

It was only then that I realized they must've been talking about the attempted kidnapping while I'd been…

Well, while I'd been doing exactly what they had been doing earlier—staring and thinking about Hawke.

"Besides that." Loren returned to threading a blood-red crystal to her mask. "I overheard Britta saying so this morning."

"The maid?" Dafina huffed.

"Yes, the maid." The dark-haired Lady in Wait lifted her chin. "They know everything."

Dafina laughed. "Everything?"

She nodded as she lowered her voice. "People speak about *anything* in front of them. No matter how intimate or private. It's almost like they are ghosts in a room. There is nothing they don't overhear."

Loren had a point. I'd seen it myself with the Duchess and the Duke.

"What did Britta say?" Tawny placed her cup on the table.

Loren's dark eyes flicked to me and then moved back to Tawny. "She said that Prince Casteel had been spotted in Three Rivers. That it was he who started the fire that took Duke Everton's life."

"How could anyone claim that?" Tawny demanded. "No one who has ever seen the Dark One will speak of what he looks like or has lived long enough to give any description of him."

"I don't know about that," argued Dafina. "I heard from Ramsey that he is bald and has pointy ears, and is pale, just like...you know what."

I resisted the urge to snort. Atlantians looked just like us.

"Ramsey? One of His Grace's stewards?" Tawny arched a brow. "I should've stated, how could anyone *credible* claim that?"

"Britta claims that the few who've seen Prince Casteel say he's actually quite handsome," Loren added.

"Oh, really?" mused Dafina.

Loren nodded as she knotted the crystal to her mask. "She said that was how he gained access to Goldcrest Manor." Her voice dropped. "That Duchess Everton developed a relationship of a physical nature with him without realizing who he was, and that was how he was able to move freely through the manor."

Britta sure talked a lot, didn't she?

"Nearly all of what she says turns out to be true." Loren shrugged as she worked an emerald-green crystal beside the red. "So, she could be right about Prince Casteel."

"You should really stop saying that name," Tawny advised. "If someone overhears you, you'll be sent to the Temples faster than you can say 'I knew better.'"

Loren's laugh was light. "I'm not worried. I'm not foolish enough to say such things where I can be overheard, and I doubt anyone present will say anything." Her gaze flicked to me, brief but knowing. She knew I couldn't say a word because I'd have to explain how I was even a part of the conversation.

Which, for the record, I wasn't.

I was just sitting here.

"What...what if he was actually here?" Loren gave a delicate shudder. "In the city now? What if that was how he gained access to Castle Teerman?" Her eyes lit up. "Befriended someone here or perhaps even poor Malessa."

"You don't sound all that concerned by the prospect." Tawny picked up her cup. "To be blunt, you sound excited."

"Excited? No. Intrigued? Possibly." She lowered the mask to her lap, sighing. "Some days are just so dreadfully dull."

The shock of her statement caused me to forget who I was and where I was. All that I managed to do was keep my voice low when I spoke. "So, a good old rebellion may liven things up for you? Dead men and women and children are a source of entertainment?"

Surprise flickered across both her and Dafina's faces. It was probably the first time either had ever heard me speak.

Loren swallowed. "I suppose I…I might've misspoken, Maiden. I apologize."

I said nothing.

"Please ignore Loren," pleaded Dafina. "Sometimes, she speaks without any thought and means nothing by it."

Loren nodded emphatically, but I didn't doubt that she'd meant exactly what she said. A rebellion would break up the monotony of her day, and she hadn't thought of the lives affected or lost because she simply hadn't cared to.

It happened then, once more without any warning, causing my body to jerk forward and my spine to stiffen. My gift reached out on its own, and before I even realized it was happening, that invisible link formed between Loren and me. A sensation came through the connection, a mixture that reminded me of fresh air on a warm day and then something acrid like bitter melon. I focused on the sensations as my heart thumped against my ribs. They felt like…excitement and fear as Loren stared at me as if she wished to say something additional.

But that couldn't be what I was picking up on from Loren. It didn't make any sense. Those emotions had to be coming from me, and somehow, influencing my gift.

Dafina grabbed her friend's arm. "Come, we should be on our way."

Not given much choice, Loren was hauled out of her seat and quickly escorted out of the room with Dafina whispering in her ear.

"I think you scared them," Tawny said.

Lifting a trembling hand, I took a quick sip of the sweet lemon drink. I had no idea what had just happened.

"Poppy." Tawny touched my arm lightly. "Are you okay?"

I nodded as I carefully placed the cup down. "Yes, I'm just…" How could I explain it? Tawny didn't know about the gift, but even if she did, I wasn't sure I could have put it into words, or be sure that anything had actually happened.

I looked over at her and opened my senses. Like at first with Dafina and Loren, all I felt was a twinge of sorrow. No deep pain or anything I shouldn't be feeling.

My heart slowed, and my body relaxed. I sat back, wondering if it was just stress causing my gift to behave so oddly.

Tawny stared at me, concern creeping into her expression.

"I'm okay," I told her, still keeping my voice low. "I just can't believe what Loren said."

"Neither can I, but she's always been…amused by the most morbid things. Like Dafina said, she means nothing by it."

I nodded, thinking that whether or not she meant anything by it didn't exactly matter. I took another sip of the drink, relieved to find that my hand wasn't trembling. Feeling measurably more normal, I chalked up the weirdness to stress and lack of sleep. My thoughts returned to the Dark One. He could be behind the attacks and might very well be after me, but none of that meant he was actually within the city. However, if he were…

Unease trickled through me as I thought about Goldcrest Manor. It wasn't impossible for something like that to happen here, especially considering an Atlantian and a Descenter had already infiltrated the castle grounds.

"What are you going to do?" Tawny whispered.

"About the Dark One possibly being in the city?" I replied, confused.

"What? No." She squeezed my arm. "About him."

"Him?" I glanced at Hawke.

"Yes. Him." Sighing, she let go of my arm. "Unless there's another guy you've made out with while your identity was concealed."

"Yes. There are many. They have an actual club," I replied dryly, and she rolled her eyes. "There's nothing for me to do."

"Have you even spoken to him?" She tapped her chin, glancing at him.

"No."

She tilted her head. "You do realize you will have to actually speak in front of him at some point."

"I'm speaking right now," I pointed out, even though I knew that wasn't what she'd meant.

Her eyes narrowed. "You're whispering, Poppy. *I* can barely hear you."

"You can hear me just fine," I told her.

She looked as if she wanted to kick me under the table again. "I have no idea how you haven't confronted him yet. I understand the risks involved, but I would have to know if he recognized me. And if he did, why hasn't he said anything?"

"It's not like I don't want to know." I glanced at Hawke. "But there's..."

I stiffened as Hawke's gaze connected with mine and held. He was looking straight at me, and even though I knew he couldn't see my eyes, it still felt like he could. There was no way he could hear Tawny and me, not from where he stood and with as quietly as I was speaking, but his stare was piercing as if he could see not only through me, but into me.

I tried to brush off the sensation, but the longer he held my gaze, the more the feeling increased. It had to be his eyes and their color. Such a strange, stunning golden hue. One could imagine all sorts of things while staring into those eyes.

He broke eye contact, pivoting toward the entryway. My breath left me in a ragged exhale, my heart hammering as if I were running across the Rise once more.

"That was...intense," Tawny murmured.

I blinked, giving a shake of my head as I turned to her. "What?"

"That." Her brows were lifted. "You and Hawke staring one another down. And no, I can't see your eyes, but I knew you two were engaged in a rather heated one on one there."

I could feel warmth creep into my cheeks. "He's just doing his job, and I...I just lost track of what I was saying."

Tawny lifted her brow. "Is that so?"

"Of course." I smoothed my hands over the lap of my dress.

"So, he was just making sure you're still alive and—"

"Breathing?" Hawke suggested, startling both of us. He stood a mere foot from where we sat, having moved with the stealth of a trained guard and the quiet of a ghost. "Since I am responsible for keeping her alive, making sure she's breathing would be a priority."

My shoulders stiffened. How much had he overheard?

Tawny made a poor attempt to smother her giggle with a napkin. "I'm relieved to hear that."

"If not, I'd be remiss in my duty, would I not?"

"Ah, yes, your duty." She lowered her napkin. "Between protecting Poppy with your life and limb and gathering spilled crystals, you're very busy."

"Don't forget assisting weak Ladies in Wait to the nearest chair before they faint," he suggested. Those strange, mesmerizing eyes glinted with a hint of mischief, and I was...as transfixed with him as I'd been with the Ladies in Wait. This was the Hawke I'd met in the Red Pearl. A well of pain hidden behind a teasing and charming personality. "I am a man of many talents."

"I'm sure you are," Tawny replied with a grin while I fought the urge to reach out with my senses.

His gaze flicked to her, and the dimple in his right cheek appeared. "Your faith in my skills warms my heart," he said, glancing at me. "Poppy?"

My eyes widened behind the veil as I clamped my mouth shut.

Tawny sighed. "It's her nickname. Only her friends call her that. And her brother."

"Ah, the one who lives in the capital?" he questioned, still looking at me.

I nodded.

"Poppy," he repeated in a way that made it sound as if my name was wrapped in chocolate and would roll off his tongue. "I like it."

I gave him a tight smile to match how the muscles in my lower stomach suddenly felt.

"Is there a threat of stray crystals we need to be aware of, or is there something you need, Hawke?" Tawny asked.

"There are many things I'm in need of," he replied as his gaze slid back to me. Tawny tipped forward as if she couldn't wait to hear what those things were. "But we'll need to discuss that later. You've been summoned by the Duke, Penellaphe. I'm to escort you to him at once."

Tawny grew so very still I wasn't sure if she took another breath. Ice drenched my insides. Summoned by the Duke so quickly after yesterday? I knew it wasn't for idle conversation. Did Lord Mazeen make good on his threat and go to the Duke? Or was it because of how I'd stared back at the Duke and smiled when I was unveiled? Had he found out that I had stabbed the man who attempted to kidnap me? While most would celebrate that I'd been able to thwart the abduction, Duke Teerman would focus solely on the fact that I'd been carrying a dagger. Could someone have seen me in here and already reported back to him? Had he found out about the Red Pearl? My stomach dropped as I stared up at Hawke. Had he said something?

Gods, the options were truly limitless, and none of them were good.

Stomach churning as if I'd swallowed spoiled milk, I managed to plaster a smile on my face as I rose from the chair.

"I'll await you in your chambers," Tawny said, and I nodded.

Hawke waited until I was past him before falling in step slightly behind me, a position that allowed him to react to threats from the front and back. I led us out into the hall, where shimmering white and gold tapestries hung from the walls, and servants in maroon gowns and tunics scurried, carrying out various tasks that kept the large household running.

He didn't lead me toward the banquet hall. He aimed for the staircase, and my stomach sank even further.

We crossed the foyer and had neared the foot of the wide stairs before he asked, "Are you all right?"

I nodded.

"Both you and your maid seemed disturbed by the summons."

"Tawny is not a maid," I blurted out and then immediately cursed up a storm in my mind. It was silly to have tried not to speak, but it would've been better for it to have occurred when we weren't in the foyer, surrounded by any number of people.

And I would've liked to have lasted at least an entire day.

I braced myself as I snuck a peek at him.

He stared, expression utterly unreadable. If he recognized my voice, he showed no sign whatsoever.

That strange mixture of disappointment and relief hit me once more as I stared straight ahead. Did he seriously not know it had been me in that room? Then again, should I be surprised? He'd believed that I'd been Britta at first and had no problem continuing on when he realized I wasn't her. Who knew how many random women he…

"Is she not?" he queried. "She may be a Lady in Wait, but I was advised that she was duty-bound to be your ladies' maid. Your companion."

"She is, but she's not..." I glanced over at him as the stone staircase curved. One hand rested on the hilt of the sword at his waist. "She's..." She was duty-bound to be my companion. "It doesn't matter. Nothing is wrong."

He looked over at me then—well, he looked down at me, even though I was a step higher than he was. He was still taller, which seemed unfair. One dark brow rose, his gaze questioning.

"What?" I asked, heart seizing as I lifted my foot but not high enough. I tripped. Hawke reacted fast, curving his hand above my elbow, steadying me. Embarrassment flooded my system as I muttered, "Thank you."

"No insincere thanks are required or needed. It is my duty to keep you safe." He paused. "Even from treacherous staircases."

I took a deep, even breath. "My gratitude was not insincere."

"My apologies then."

I didn't have to look at him to know he was grinning, and I'd bet that stupid dimple was gracing the world with its presence. He fell quiet then, and we reached the third-floor landing in silence. One hall led to the old wing—to my chambers and many of the household staff. To the left was the newer wing. Stomach full of tiny lead balls, I turned left. My mind was now so fixated on what awaited me that I wasn't all that focused on Hawke's apparent lack of recognition or what it meant if he did realize it was me and just wasn't saying anything.

Hawke reached the wide, wooden doors at the end of the hall, his arm brushing my shoulder as he opened one side. He waited until I had entered the narrow spiral staircase. Sunlight poured in through the numerous oval-shaped windows. "Watch your step. You trip and fall here, you're likely to take me out on your way down."

I huffed. "I won't trip."

"But you just did."

"That was a rarity."

"Well, then, I feel honored that I bore witness to it."

I was glad he couldn't see my face then, and not out of fear of recognition, but because I was sure my eyes were so wide they took up my entire upper face. He was speaking to me in a way no other guard did—besides Vikter. Not even Rylan had been so...familiar. It was as if we had known each other for years instead of hours...or days. Whatever. The comfortable way he was talking to me was disconcerting.

He eased past me, reaching the entryway to the fourth floor. "I've seen you before, you know."

My breath hitched, and only by the grace of the gods did I not trip again.

"I've seen you on the lower balconies." Holding open the door, he gestured for me to enter. "Watching me train."

Heat blasted my cheeks. That had not been what I'd expected him to say. "I wasn't watching you. I was—"

"Taking in the fresh air? Waiting for your lady's maid, who is not a maid?" Hawke caught my arm as I walked past him, stopping me. He lowered his head until his lips were mere inches from my veil-covered ear and whispered, "Perhaps I was mistaken, and it wasn't you."

Surrounded by the earthy, woodsy scent of him, my breath caught. We were nowhere near as close as we were the night of the Red Pearl, but if I tilted my head to the left just a few inches, his mouth would touch mine. The curling motion inside me returned, settling even lower in my stomach this time. "You are mistaken."

He let go of my arm, and when I looked up, I saw that the corner of his lips was tipped up. My heart was doing funny, strange things in my chest as I stepped into the airy hall, my pulse thrumming.

Two Royal Guards were stationed outside the private quarters of the Duke and Duchess. There were several rooms on this floor used for greeting various members of the house and Court. Both had their own spaces and suites that connected to bedchambers, but based on where the Royal Guards stood, I knew the Duke was in the main suite.

Unease returned, slithering through my veins. For a brief moment, I'd forgotten about why I could've been summoned.

"Penellaphe?" Hawke said from behind me.

Only then did I realize two things. One, I'd come to a complete standstill in the hall, and I was sure that seemed odd to him. And secondly, he had called me by my name twice now instead of *Maiden.* He wasn't Vikter. He wasn't Tawny. Both of whom only called me by my name when we were alone.

I knew I should correct his use of my given name, but I couldn't. I didn't want to, and that frightened me as much as what awaited me in the Duke's office.

Taking a deep breath, I clasped my hands together as I straightened my shoulders and started forward.

The Royal Guards avoided eye contact as they bowed upon our approach. The dark-skinned one stepped aside, his hand on the door. He started to open it.

For some reason, I looked back at Hawke. Why, I had no idea. "I'll wait for you here," he assured.

I nodded and then faced forward again, forcing one foot in front of the other, telling myself that I was getting worked up over nothing.

Stepping into the suite, the first thing I noticed was that the curtains had been drawn. The soft glow of several oil lamps seemed to be absorbed by the dark wood paneling and the furniture fashioned from mahogany and crimson-hued velvet. My gaze fell to the large desk and then the credenza behind it, where several crystal bottles of various sizes were full of amber liquor.

Then I saw him.

The Duke sat on the settee, one booted foot resting on the table before him, and a glass of liquor in his hand. Chills swept through me as he looked over at me with eyes so dark, the pupil was almost indistinguishable.

It made me think that when next I saw Ian, his eyes would no longer be green like mine. They'd be like the Duke's. Pitch-black. Bottomless. But would they be as chilling?

I suddenly realized that the Duke wasn't alone.

Across from him was Lord Mazeen, seated in an arrogant sprawl. He held no drink in his hands, but his fingers tapped idly on his bent knee. There was a smirk on his well-formed lips, and every instinct in me screamed that I needed to run because there was no fighting what was coming.

The door clicked shut behind me, causing me to jump a little. I hated the response, hoping that the Duke hadn't seen it, and knowing that he had when I saw him smile.

Teerman rose from the settee in one fluid, boneless movement. "Penellaphe, I am so incredibly disappointed in you."

Chapter 13

Cold to my very core, I drew in a short, measured breath as I watched him take a drink from his glass. I knew I had to choose my words carefully. It wouldn't change what was to come, but it could determine the severity. "I'm sorry to have disappointed you," I started. "I—"

"Do you even know what you have done that has disappointed me?"

Muscles in my shoulders stiffened, and my gaze darted from the silent Lord to the corner of the suite, where several, narrow pieces of reddish-brown wood were propped against a bookcase. They were fashioned from a tree that grew within the Blood Forest. When I looked back at Lord Mazeen, I saw that he was smiling. I was beginning to think that he had reported something back to the Duke, but if I was wrong about that, it would only add to my problems.

And Lord Mazeen knew this as he watched me. He gave no indication of the role he played in this. Even if his part was only to bear witness. He rarely spoke when he attended these lessons. While his silence would typically give me relief, it only heightened my anxiety now.

I forced the next words out even though they rolled off my tongue all wrong. "I don't, but I'm sure, whatever it is, I am at fault. You're never disappointed in me without cause."

That was so not true.

There seemed to be times when the way I walked or how I cut

my food at supper was a disappointment to the Duke. I was sure how many breaths I took in a minute could be of offense to him.

"You're right. I wouldn't be disappointed for no reason at all," he agreed. "But this time, I find myself blindsided by what I have been told."

My stomach turned over as sweat dotted my brow. Dear gods, had he learned of my time at the Red Pearl?

I'd feared that Hawke would say something, had obsessed and stressed over it. A part of me must not have wanted to believe it was possible, though, because the ripe feeling of betrayal tasted like spoiled food in the back of my throat. Hawke most likely had no idea what went down in this room, but he had to have known there would be consequences. Wouldn't he? He probably thought I'd receive nothing more than a stern lecture. After all, I was the Maiden, the Chosen.

I would receive a dressing down.

But I doubted Hawke had any idea that the Duke's lessons were not…normal.

Teerman took a step toward me, and all my muscles tensed up. "Remove your veil, Penellaphe."

I hesitated for only the span of a few heartbeats, even though it was not uncommon for the Duke or the Duchess to request such a thing while in their presence. They didn't like speaking to half a face. I couldn't blame them, but normally, the Duke made me keep it on when Lord Mazeen was present.

"You do not want to test my patience." His grip had tightened on his glass.

"I'm sorry. It's just that we…we are not alone, and the gods forbade me from showing my face," I said, knowing full well that I'd done this before, but in situations vastly different.

"The gods will not find fault in today's proceedings," the Duke interrupted.

Of course, not.

Willing my hands steady, I lifted them and undid the fine clasps of the veil near my ears. The headdress immediately loosened. Keeping my gaze lowered as I knew he preferred, I slipped it off, over where my hair had been bound in a simple knot at the nape of my neck. My exposed cheeks and brows prickled. Teerman came forward, taking the veil from me and placing it aside. I clasped my hands and waited. I hated doing so.

But I waited.

"Lift your eyes," he demanded softly, and I did just that. His ebony gaze slowly tracked over my features, inch by inch, missing nothing, not even the wisps of burnt copper hair that I could feel curling against my temple. His perusal lasted an eternity. "You grow more beautiful each time I see you."

"Thank you, Your Grace," I murmured, revulsion bubbling in my stomach. I knew what was coming next.

The tips of his fingers pressed into the skin under my chin, tilting my head to the left and then to the right.

He clucked his tongue. "Such a shame."

And there it was.

I said nothing as my focus shifted to the large oil painting of the Temples, where veiled women knelt before a being who was so bright, he rivaled the moon.

"What do you think, Bran?" he asked of the Lord.

"As you said, such a shame."

I didn't give a Craven's ass what Lord Mazeen thought.

"The other scars are easy to hide, but this?" The Duke sighed almost sympathetically. "There will come a time when there will be no veil to hide this unfortunate flaw."

I swallowed, resisting the urge to pull away when his fingers left my chin to trail down the two ragged indentations that started at my left temple and continued downward, skirting my eye to end just beside my nose.

"Do you know what that new guard of hers said?"

The Lord didn't speak, but I imagined he shook his head no.

"He said she was beautiful," the Duke answered. "Half of her is truly stunning." There was a pause. "You look so much like your mother."

My gaze flew to his in shock. He knew my mother? He'd never—not once—mentioned that before. "You knew her?"

His eyes met mine, and it was hard to stare into the never-ending darkness. "I did. She was…special."

Before I could even question that, he said, "You do realize that the guard wouldn't have said otherwise? Wouldn't have spoken the truth."

I flinched as my chest hollowed.

Having spotted the reaction, the Duke's smile returned. "I suppose it's some small blessing. The damage to your face could've been far worse."

The damage could've included a missing eye, or worse, death.

But I didn't say that.

My gaze shifted back to the painting, wondering how his words could still sting after all these years. When I was younger, they'd hurt. His words had cut deep. But the last couple of years, there'd been nothing but numb resignation. The scars were not something I could change. I knew that. But today, they sliced through me as they had when I was thirteen.

"You do have such pretty eyes." He removed his fingers from the scars and pressed one to my lower lip. "And a well-formed mouth." He paused, and I swore I could feel his gaze lower and linger. "Most will find your body pleasing."

Bile clogged my throat and crawled across my skin like thousands of spiders. Only by sheer will, was I able to hold myself completely still.

"For some men, those things will be enough." Teerman dragged his finger across my bottom lip before lowering his hand. "Priestess Analia came to see me this morning."

Wait. What?

My heart started to slow as confusion surfaced. The Priestess? What could she possibly have to say about me?

"Do you not have anything to add?" Teerman asked, raising one pale brow.

"No. I'm sorry." I shook my head. "I don't know what Priestess Analia would have to say. I last saw her a week ago, in the second-floor parlor, and all seemed fine."

"I'm sure it did since you only spent half an hour there before leaving unexpectedly," he said. "I was advised you didn't once pick up your embroidery set, nor did you engage in any conversation with the Priestesses."

Irritation flared, but I knew better than to cave to it. Besides, if this was what he was upset over, it was far better than what I'd feared. "My mind was occupied with my upcoming Rite," I lied. The real reason I didn't engage in their conversation was because the women spent the entire time speaking poorly of the Ladies in Wait and how they were not deserving of the gods' Blessing. "I must've been daydreaming."

"I'm sure you're very excited about the Rite, and if this had been just one situation, I would've easily overlooked your poor conduct."

He was lying. The Duke never overlooked *any* perceived poor conduct.

"But I've learned that you were just in the atrium," he continued, and my shoulders slumped.

"Yes. I was. I didn't know that I wasn't supposed to be," I said, and that wasn't a lie. "I don't go often, but—"

"Spending time in the atrium is not the issue, and you're smart enough to know that. Don't play coy with me."

I opened my mouth and then closed it.

"You were speaking with two of the Ladies in Wait," he continued. "You know that is not allowed."

Knowing this was coming, I remained silent. I just hadn't realized he would find out so quickly. Someone must have been watching. Perhaps his steward or one of the other Royal Guards.

"Do you have nothing to say?" he asked.

Dipping my chin, I stared at the floor. I could tell him the truth. That I hadn't said more than one sentence to the Ladies, and that this was, as far as I knew, the first time they'd visited the atrium. It wouldn't matter, though. The truth didn't work with the Duke.

"Such a demure Maiden," the Lord murmured.

I could practically feel my tongue sharpen, but I softened my words as much as I could. "I'm sorry. I should've left when they entered, but I didn't."

"And why not?"

"I was...curious. They were talking about the upcoming Rite," I told him, looking up.

"I'm not surprised to hear that. You were always an active child with a curious mind that flicked from one thing to the next, something I warned the Duchess you wouldn't grow out of easily," he continued, his features turning taut, a glint of anticipation forming in his eyes. "Priestess Analia also informed me that she fears your relationship with your lady's maid has become far too familiar."

My spine stiffened as he turned, straightening the veil he'd draped over a chair. The back of my skull tingled as I said, "Tawny has been a wonderful lady's maid, and if my kindness and gratefulness has been mistaken for anything else, then I apologize."

He slid a long look in my direction. "I know it may be hard to keep boundaries with someone you spend so much time with, but a Maiden does not seek intimacies of the heart or the mind with those who serve them, not even those who are to become members of the Court. You must never forget that you are not like them. You were Chosen by the gods at birth, and they are chosen at their Rite. You will never be equals. You will never be friends."

The words I forced past my lips scratched at my heart. "I understand."

Teerman took another drink.

How much had he already consumed? My heart rate tripled. Once, when I'd upset the Duke, his *lesson* had been carried out after he'd indulged in what I'd heard the guards call "*Red Ruin*," a liquor brewed in the Cliffs of Hoar. The Lord had been with him then.

That was the time he'd struck me, and it had taken several days before I'd been able to resume training with Vikter.

"I don't think you do." His tone hardened. "You were Chosen at birth, Penellaphe. Only one other has ever been Chosen by the gods. It was why the Dark One sent the Craven after your family. It was why your parents were slaughtered."

I flinched once more, my stomach hollowing.

"That hurts, doesn't it? But it's the truth. That should've been the only lesson you ever needed." Placing his glass on the table, he faced me while the Lord unfolded his legs. "But between your lack of awareness regarding overstepping boundaries, your lack of attention with Priestess Analia, your blatant disregard today for what is expected of you, and..."—he drew the word out, enjoying the moment—"the attitude you displayed yesterday toward me. What? You thought I wouldn't address your behavior while we discussed Ryan's replacement."

The air I inhaled did nothing to inflate my lungs. That wasn't his name.

"You stared back at me as if you wished to do me physical harm." He chuckled, amused by the idea that I could do such a thing. "The meeting would've ended vastly different if others had not been present, and we weren't there to discuss Hawke replacing Ryan—"

"*Rylan*," I snapped. "His name is Rylan. Not Ryan."

"There it is," Lord Mazeen echoed the words he'd spoken the night Malessa had been found. He chuckled. "Not so demure now."

I ignored him.

Teerman cocked his head. "You mean his name *was* Rylan?"

I sucked in air that seemed to go nowhere.

"And does it really matter? He was just a Royal Guard. He would've been honored that I even thought of him."

Now, I truly wanted to inflict physical harm.

"Either way, you just proved that I must double my attempts to strengthen my commitment to make you more than ready for your Ascension. Apparently, I've been too easy on you." The gleam in his eyes brightened. "Unfortunately, that means you require yet another lesson. Hopefully, it will be your last, but somehow, I doubt it."

My fingers spasmed where I twisted them. Anger rose so swiftly, I was surprised that I didn't breathe fire when I exhaled. That was the last thing Teerman hoped for. If he couldn't find a reason to give me a lesson, then he'd have a complete breakdown.

"Yes," I bit out the word, my control slipping. "Hopefully."

He cut me a sharp look and a long, tense moment passed. "I believe four lashes should suffice."

Before I could remind myself who I was, *what* Teerman was, fury burned through my blood, seizing control. Nothing he'd taken me to task for mattered. None of that had anything to do with the Descenters and the Dark One being behind my attempted abduction and Rylan's murder. The gods blessed the Ascended with near immortality and unfathomable strength, and they spent their time worrying about who I was speaking to? I couldn't stop myself. "Are you sure that's enough? I wouldn't want you to feel as if you haven't done enough."

His gaze hardened. "How does seven sound?"

Apprehension flickered through me, but I'd received ten before.

"I see that number agrees with you," he said. "What do you think, Bran?"

"I think that is sufficient." There was no mistaking the eagerness in his tone.

The Duke looked back to me. "You know where to go."

Holding my chin high, it took everything in me to walk past him and not lay him flat on his back. That was the worst part as I walked to the shiny, cleared surface of his desk. The Ascended were stronger than even the most skilled guard, but neither Teerman nor Mazeen had raised a hand in combat since the War of Two Kings. I could easily knock him flat on his back.

But then what?

There'd be more lessons, and word would make its way back to Queen Ileana. She'd be disappointed, genuinely so, and unlike the Duke, I cared about what the Queen thought and felt. Not because I was her favorite, but because it had been she who had taken care of me as a wounded, terrified child. Her hands had changed my bandages and held me when I screamed and cried for my mother and father. And it was Queen Ileana who had sat with me when I could not sleep, terrified of the dark. She'd done things no Queen needed to do. Without her caring for me as my own mother would have, I would've been lost in a way I doubted I could have ever recovered from.

I stopped in front of the desk, hands shaking with barely leashed rage. I believed in my heart of hearts that if Queen Ileana knew what the Duke did in this room, things would not end well for the Ascended.

Out of the corner of my eye, I saw the Lord lean forward as Teerman picked up the red, narrow cane, smoothing his hand down its length.

But the Queen wouldn't know.

Letters sent to the capital were always read, and I wouldn't see her until I returned. But then? Then, I would tell her *everything*.

Because if he did this to me, I was sure he did this to others, as well. Even if no one ever spoke of it.

He came to stand beside me, that glint of eagerness now a shine in his eyes. "You're not ready, Penellaphe. You should know better by this point."

Clamping my jaw shut, I looked away as I lifted my hands to the row of buttons. My fingers only trembled once and then stilled as I undid the bodice, all too aware that Mazeen had picked his seat with knowledge of what was to come. He had an unobstructed view.

The Duke remained at my side, watching as the bodice of my gown gaped, revealing the all-too-thin undergarment underneath. Both slipped down my shoulders until the clothing pooled at my waist. Cool air washed over my back and chest, and I wanted to stand there as if I was wholly unaffected by the entire ordeal. Wished I could be strong and brave and unmoved. I didn't want them to see how humiliating this was, how much it bothered me to be seen like this, and not by someone of my choosing—someone worthy.

But I couldn't.

Cheeks burning and eyes stinging, I folded an arm over my chest.

"This is for your own good," Teerman spoke, his voice going dark and rough as he walked behind me. "This is a necessary lesson, Penellaphe, to ensure that you take your preparations seriously and are committed to them so you do not dishonor the gods."

He almost sounded like he believed what he said, as if he weren't doing this simply because it excited him to inflict pain. But I knew better. I knew what Mazeen would do if he could, and I'd seen the look in the Duke's eyes. I saw it far too many times before when I made the mistake of looking. The kind of look that told me if I wasn't the Maiden, he would inflict a different kind of pain. Just like I knew Mazeen would. I couldn't suppress the shudder that followed that thought.

A moment later, I felt his hand on my bare shoulder, and everything in me recoiled. It wasn't just the touch of his too-cool skin against mine, but it was also what I didn't feel.

I felt *nothing*.

No faint trace of anguish that all people carried within them, no matter how long ago the source of the hurt that had inflicted its damage. There was no pain of any kind, and it was that way for every Ascended. While that should bring me some sort of relief that I wouldn't pick up on pain, it only left me with the feeling of crawling skin.

It was a reminder of how different the Ascended were from mortals, what the Blessing of the gods did.

"Brace yourself, Penellaphe."

I planted a palm on the desk.

The room was silent except for the sound of the Lord's deep breaths, and then I heard the soft whistle of the cane cutting through the air a second before it struck my lower back. My entire body jerked as fiery pain rippled across my skin. The first strike was always a shock, no matter how many times it had happened before or that I knew what was coming. Another strike landed across my shoulders, pushing out a rough burst of air as fire swept across them.

Five more.

Another blow landed, and my body trembled as I lifted my gaze. *I will not make a sound. I will not make a sound.* My hips knocked against the desk with the next hit.

The settee creaked as Lord Mazeen rose.

Skin burning, I bit down on my lip until I tasted blood. I stared through the haze of tears at the painting of the veiled worshippers, wondering how horrible the Atlantians must've been for men like the Duke of Masadonia and Lord Mazeen to receive the Blessing of Ascension from the gods.

Chapter 14

The gods had granted me one small favor when I left the Duke's suite. Hawke hadn't been waiting for me, and that had been a blessing. I had no idea how I could've hidden what had happened.

Instead, it was Vikter who stood silently by the two Royal Guards. Neither looked at me as I stepped into the hall, skin pale and covered in a sheen of cold sweat.

Did they know what had happened in the Duke's chamber? I hadn't made a sound, not even when Lord Mazeen had come to stand beside the desk and pulled my arm away from my chest to place it beside my other. Not even when the sixth and seventh blows had felt like lightning streaking across my back, and Mazeen had watched every lash absorbed by my body with eager eyes.

If the guards were aware, there was nothing I could do about that or the bitter bite of shame that somehow burned worse than my back.

But Vikter knew. The knowledge was in the deep lines bracketing his mouth as we walked toward the staircase, each step tugging at the inflamed skin. He waited until the stairwell door closed behind us and then stopped on the landing, concern settling into his light blue eyes as he stared down at me.

"How bad is it?"

My hands trembled as I pressed them against the skirt of my gown. "I'm fine. I just need to rest."

"Fine?" His sun-kissed cheeks mottled. "Your breathing is rapid, and you're walking as if each step is a challenge. You have no reason to pretend with me."

I truly didn't, but admitting how bad it was felt like I was giving Teerman what he wanted. "It could've been worse."

Vikter's nostrils flared. "It shouldn't happen at all."

I couldn't argue with that.

"Did he break your skin?" he demanded.

"No. There are just welts."

"Just welts." His laugh was harsh and without humor. "You speak as if they are nothing more than scratches. Why were you punished this time?"

"Does he need a reason?" My smile was tired and felt brittle, as if it would crack my entire face. "He was upset over my lack of commitment to my time spent with the Priestesses. And today, while I was in the atrium, two Ladies in Wait showed up. He was not pleased about that."

"How is that your fault?"

"Does it need to be my fault?"

Vikter stared at me, struck silent for a moment. "So, this is why he took the cane to you?"

I nodded, gaze falling to the nearest oval-shaped window. The sun had drifted away while I'd been in the suite, the stairwell not nearly as bright and airy as it had been. "And he didn't like my attitude during the meeting yesterday. It's not nearly the most minor offense he has punished me for."

"This is why I said you must be careful, Poppy. If he lashes you for being in a room while others walk in, what do you think he would do if he learned of your little adventures?"

"Or if he learned that I've been training like a guard for years?" My shoulders tightened, the movement pulling at my skin. "I'd be caned, of course. Probably more than seven lashes."

Vikter's golden skin paled.

"He may petition the Queen to find me unworthy. And maybe the gods already do," I continued. "But as you've said before, my Ascension will happen no matter what I do. You, though? What would happen to you, Vikter, if it were ever discovered that you've been training me?"

"It doesn't matter what they may or may not do." There wasn't a second of hesitation there. "The risk is worth it, knowing you can protect yourself. I would gladly take whatever punishment I received, and I wouldn't regret what I've done."

I lifted my chin, holding his gaze. "And being able to defend my home, those I care for, and my life is worth the risk of whatever may happen."

He was quiet for a moment and then his wintery blue eyes closed. He might've been thinking of a prayer for patience, something I'd known him to do many times before.

That brought another small smile to my lips. "I'm careful, Vikter."

"Being careful doesn't seem to matter." His eyes opened. "I welcome the idea of the Queen summoning you to the capital sooner rather than later."

I shivered as I started down the stairs. "Because then I couldn't be subjected to the Duke's *lessons*?"

"Exactly."

That was something to look forward to, especially since I planned on telling the Queen everything.

"Was he alone? I asked the guards, but they acted as if they had no idea who was in the room with him," he said.

They always knew who was in with the Duke. They just hadn't wanted Vikter to know, and I...I didn't either. "He was alone."

He didn't answer, and I wasn't sure if that meant he believed me or not. I decided it was time to change the subject. "How did you know where I was?"

Vikter moved only a step behind me. "Hawke sent one of the Duke's stewards for me. He was...concerned about you."

My heart skipped a beat. "Over what?"

"He said that both you and Tawny appeared distressed over the Duke's summons," Vikter explained. "He thought I could explain why."

"And did you?"

"I told him there was nothing to be worried about, and that I would remain as your escort for the rest of the day." Vikter's brow wrinkled as he casually took my arm, lending me his support. "He wasn't exactly receptive, so I had to remind him that I was higher-ranking than him."

My lips twitched at that. "I'm sure that went over well."

"As well as an avalanche."

We rounded the next floor, the knowledge that I was getting

closer to my bed keeping me going as I mulled over what Hawke had done. "He is…quite observant, isn't he? And intuitive."

"Yes." Vikter sighed, obviously thinking that wasn't a good thing. "Yes, he is."

Three dozen torches blazed beyond the Rise, their flames a beacon of light in the vast darkness, a promise of safety to the slumbering city.

I cast a longing look toward the bed, letting out a tired sigh as I twisted the ends of my braid. Nightmares from a different night had driven me from sleep, leaving my skin slick with a cold sweat and my heart thrumming like a rabbit caught in a snare.

Luckily, I hadn't woken Tawny with my screams. She'd been up late the past two nights. The first night, she'd spent a good part of the evening doing everything possible to make sure the welts healed, and last night, she'd been summoned by the Mistresses to assist with preparations for the Rite.

Tawny had used a concoction the Healers swore by and which the guards frequently used for their numerous injuries, rubbing the mixture of pine and sage-scented arnica and honey onto the inflamed skin of my back. It was the same stuff the Healer had used the night of the abduction. The ointment had cooled my skin and eased the ache almost immediately. Still, we knew from previous experience that it had to be applied nearly every other hour to achieve the desired effect.

And it had worked. By yesterday evening, there was only a twinge of discomfort, even though the skin was still pinker than normal.

I hadn't been making light of what had occurred when I told Vikter and then Tawny that it could've been worse. The welts would most likely be gone by the morning, and there'd be little if any pain. I was lucky I always healed quickly, and even luckier that Teerman hadn't been drinking Red Ruin the afternoon of my summons.

The Duke had known my mother. How? As far as I knew, she'd never been to Masadonia, so that had to mean that the Duke had met her in the capital. It was rare for the Ascended to travel, especially such a great distance, but they'd obviously met.

There had been such a strange look on Teerman's face when he spoke of her. Nostalgia mixed with...what? Anger, perhaps? Disappointment. Had whatever interactions he'd had with her caused the way he behaved toward me?

Or was I just looking for a reason for his treatment, as if there had to be something to explain his cruelty?

There wasn't a lot that I knew about life, but I knew that, sometimes, there was no reason. A person, whether Ascended or not, was who they were with no explanation.

Sighing, I shifted my weight from foot to foot. I'd been holed up in my room the last two days, mainly because rest ensured that the ointment worked as fast as possible, and also because I was avoiding, well...everyone.

But especially Hawke.

I hadn't seen him since I'd stepped into the Duke's private office, and knowing that he'd sensed that something was wrong left me with a gurgling feeling of anxiety and embarrassment, even though what Teerman had done wasn't my fault. I just didn't want Hawke to figure out that something was wrong, and he was observant enough to do so.

Granted, staying in my room for two days would probably also send up a red flag, but at least he hadn't borne witness to how carefully I had to move while my back healed.

I didn't want Hawke to see me as weak, even though as the Maiden, he would expect exactly that.

And maybe it had to do with the weird mix of relief and disappointment I felt every time he showed no recognition that he'd met me at the Pearl.

Dragging my gaze from the bed, I returned to watching the torches beyond the Rise. The fires were calm tonight, as they had been for several nights, but when the flames danced like mad spirits, driven by the winds of twilight? It meant the mist would not be far behind. And sweeping, terrible death followed the thick, white fog.

Absently, my hand slipped through the thin folds of the dressing gown to the bone handle of the dagger strapped to my thigh. My fingers curled around the cool hilt, reminding me that I would be ready if and when the Rise fell.

Just as I would be ready if the Dark One tried to come for me again.

My hand drifted from the handle to a few inches above my knee, brushing over the patch of uneven skin on my inner thigh. Hawke had come so incredibly close to touching the scar. What would he have done if he had? Would he have jerked his hand away? Or pretended as if he hadn't felt anything?

I pulled my hand away. I wasn't going to think about that. I curled my fingers into a fist as I cut off those thoughts. There was no reason to go down that road. Nothing good would come from doing so. It didn't matter if he recognized me or not if I was just one of many girls he'd kissed in dimly lit rooms. It also didn't matter if he had gone back to the Red Pearl like he'd promised—

I shook my head as if I could scatter my thoughts, but it didn't work. One thing I'd discovered over the last two days of near isolation was that I could continue telling myself it didn't matter, over and over, but it did.

Hawke had been my first kiss, even if he didn't know that.

Silvery moonlight seeped through the chamber as I crept silently toward the west windows. Placing my fingers on the cool glass, I counted the torches. Twelve on the Rise. Twenty-four below. All aflame.

Good.

That was good.

I pressed my forehead to the thin glass that did very little to keep the chill from finding its way into the castle. In the west, where Carsodonia was nestled between the Stroud Sea and the Willow Plains, there was no need for glass windows. Summer and spring were eternal there, where autumn and winter forever reigned here. It was one of the things I looked forward to when I returned to the capital. The warmth. The sunshine. The scent of salt and sea, and all the glittering bays and coves.

Tawny, who had never seen the beaches, would absolutely love them. A tired grin tugged at my lips. When she'd been summoned by one of the Mistresses, Tawny had sent me a look that said she might've been happier scrubbing the bathing chambers than spending the evening attempting to please the unappeasable.

I often felt the same when it was time to meet with the Priestess. I'd rather spend the evening plucking my own body hair from very sensitive areas than spend hours with that dragon of a woman.

Perhaps I needed to be better at hiding how I felt when it came to her and the other Priestesses.

I still couldn't believe she'd gone to the Duke, all because I didn't spend half of my day listening to her and the others complain about everyone else.

Wrapping my arms around myself, I wished for what felt like the hundredth time that my brother was still in Masadonia. Ian had nightmares too, and if he were still here right now, he'd distract me with silly, made-up tales.

Did he still have nightmares after his Ascension? If not, then wasn't that something else to look forward to?

My gaze traveled along the Rise, catching sight of a guard patrolling along the top of the wall.

I'd rather be out there than in here.

The Ascended would be shocked to hear such a thing, as would most others. To even think it—that I, the Maiden, the Chosen, who would go to the gods, would want to exchange places with a commoner, a guard, would be an affront to not only the Ascended but also to the gods themselves. All over the kingdom, people would do anything to be in the presence of the gods. I was...

I was privileged no matter what I suffered, but at least if I were out there, on the Rise, I could be doing something productive. I'd be protecting the city and all those who enabled me to have such a comfortable life. Instead, I was in here, reaching an all new height of self-pity when in reality, my Ascension would do more than protect one city.

It would ensure the entire future of the kingdom.

Wasn't that doing something?

I wasn't sure, and I wanted nothing more than to be able to close my eyes and find sleep, but I knew it wouldn't come. Not for hours.

On nights like this, when I knew sleep would evade me, I caved to the urge to sneak out and explore the silent and dark city until I found places that didn't sleep, spots like the Red Pearl. Unfortunately, that would be the height of stupidity after the attempted abduction. Even I wasn't that reckless and—

A flame beyond the Rise began to dance, snapping me forward. I pressed both palms to the window, staring at the fire and refusing to blink. "It's nothing," I told the empty room. "It's just a breeze—"

Another flash moved, and then another and another, the whole line of torches beyond the wall rippling wildly, spitting sparks as the wind picked up. I took a breath, but it seemed to go nowhere.

The one in the middle was the first to be snuffed, sending my heart slamming against my ribs. The others rapidly followed, pitching the land beyond the Rise into sudden darkness.

I took a step back from the window.

Dozens of fiery arrows shot into the air, arcing high above the Rise and then racing downward, slamming into the tinder-filled trenches. A wall of fire erupted, running the entire length of the Rise. The flames were no defense against the mist or what came with it.

The fire made what was in the fog visible.

Returning to the window, I threw the latch and flung it open. Cold air and a kind of unearthly silence poured into the chamber as I gripped the stone ledge and leaned out, squinting.

Smoke wafted up and weaved through the flames, spilling into the air and onto the ground.

Smoke didn't move like that.

Smoke didn't creep under the tinder, a thick, murky white against the black of night. Smoke didn't blanket flames, suffocating them until they were extinguished and all that remained was a heavy, unnatural mist.

The mist wasn't empty.

It was full of twisted shapes that had once been mortal.

Horns blared from all four corners of the Rise, shattering the tense quiet. Within seconds, what few lights had shone through windows went dark. A second call of warning went out, and the entire castle seemed to shudder.

Snapping into action, I grabbed the window and latched it into place before I spun around. I'd have roughly three minutes, possibly less, before all exits were sealed. I started forward—

A moment later, the adjoining door swung open, and Tawny burst in, her white nightgown flowing around her and the mass of brown and gold curls spilling over her shoulders.

"No." Tawny stumbled to a halt, the whites of her wide eyes a stark contrast to her brown skin. "No, Poppy."

Ignoring her, I raced over to the chest, throwing open the heavy lid and rooting around until I found the bow. Rising, I tossed it onto the bed.

"You cannot be planning to go out there," she exclaimed.

"I am."

"Poppy!"

"I will be fine." I situated the quiver along my spine.

"Fine?" She gaped at me as I turned to her. "I can't believe I have to point out the obvious, but here I am. You're the Maiden. The *Chosen*. You cannot go out there. If they don't kill you, His Grace will if he catches you."

"He won't catch me." I snatched up a black, hooded cloak and shrugged it on, securing it at my neck and breast. "The Duke will be hiding in his room behind a dozen Royal Guards if not more, right alongside the Duchess."

"The Royal Guards will come for you."

I retrieved the curved bow by the grip. "I'm positive Vikter left for the Rise the moment he heard the horns."

"And Hawke? Their duty is to protect you."

"Vikter knows I can protect myself, and Hawke won't even know I've left my room." I paused. "He doesn't know about the servants' entrance."

"You're injured, Poppy. Your back—"

"My back is almost completely healed. You know that."

"And what of the Dark One? What if this is a ploy—?"

"This is no ploy, Tawny. I saw them in the mist," I told her, and her face grayed. "And if the Dark One tries to come for me, I will be ready for him, too."

She followed me as I crossed the room. "Penellaphe Balfour, stop!"

Surprised, I spun around and found her standing right behind me. "I have less than two minutes, Tawny. I will be trapped in here—"

"Where it's safe," she reasoned.

I grasped her shoulder with my free hand. "If they breach the walls, they will take the city, and they will find a way into the castle. And then there will be no stopping them. That, I know. They got to my family. They got to me. I will not sit and wait for that to happen once more."

Her eyes frantically searched mine. "But you didn't have the Rise to protect you then."

That was true, but... "Nothing is infallible, Tawny. Not even the

Rise."

"And neither are you," she whispered, her lower lip trembling.

"I know."

She drew in a deep breath, her shoulder sagging under my hand. "All right. If anyone comes, I'll tell them you're ill with fright and have locked yourself in the bathing chamber."

I rolled my eyes. "Of course, you will." I let go of her shoulder. "There are several bloodstone daggers in the chest, and a sword under the pillows—"

"Please tell me your head is not resting above a sword every night," Tawny demanded, voice ringing with disbelief. "No wonder you have nightmares. Only the gods know what kind of bad luck using a sword as a pillow—"

"Tawny," I cut her off before she really got going. "If the castle is breached, use the weapons. You know how."

"I know." And she did only because I made her learn in secret, just like Vikter had taught me. "The head or the heart."

I nodded.

"Be safe, Poppy. Please. I will be so very disappointed if I'm assigned to serve the Duchess. Or, worse yet, given to the Temple in service to the gods. Not that it wouldn't be an honor to serve them," she tacked on, placing her hand over her heart. "But the whole celibacy thing…"

I cracked a grin. "I will return."

"You'd better, Poppy."

"I promise." Giving her a quick kiss on the cheek, I spun and headed for the old servants' door beside the bathing chamber. This was the whole reason I had all but begged and pleaded to be moved to this room in the older, far uglier portion of the castle. These pathways and accesses were no longer used, but they connected to nearly every room in the old part of the stronghold including the stone bridge that led directly to the southern portion of the Rise.

Old hinges creaked as I opened the door. The pathways allowed me to move undetected throughout the castle. Over the last years, I'd used them to meet with Vikter in one of the old, unused rooms for training, and it was also how I was able to slip out of the castle without being seen.

But, most importantly, the old stairs and halls could provide a quick escape if necessary.

"Poppy," Tawny called out, stopping me. "Your face."

Confusion rose for only a moment, and then I realized that my face was unveiled.

"Right." I lifted the heavy hood, tugging it into place before I slipped out into the narrow, winding staircase.

Stone slid against metal as thick, iron doors rattled and began their descent as I raced down the cracked, uneven stone steps. My slippers weren't the best footwear for such a thing, but there hadn't been time to ferret out the only boots I owned from their hiding place, tucked under the head of the bed. If the maids found them, they would be sure to talk, and eventually, whatever they said would make its way back to someone.

I had less than a minute to get out.

Dust and small rocks drifted from above as the castle continued to tremble. Moonlight broke through the cracked, dusty windows as I rounded the final set of steps, slipping over the bottom two and all but sliding out into the empty pantry. The movement caused nothing more than a dull flare of pain where the welts were healing.

Thrusting the bow into the folds of the cloak, I darted into the chaotic kitchen where servants clamored for access to the hidden safe rooms that doubled as food storage. Guards rushed for the main entrance, where the largest shield would be locking into place within seconds. No one paid me any mind as I ran for the back hall, where one of the iron doors was already halfway down.

Spitting out a curse that Vikter would've turned red at, and Rylan would've…he would've smiled at if he were still here, I picked up speed and then dipped. The silk and satin slippers aided in the descent. I slid under the door, nearly losing my balance as I skidded out into the night air. The heavy door groaned as it settled into place. I backed away and then turned, my lips curving into a broad smile Tawny would've found not only concerning but also disturbing.

I'd made it to the bridge.

Not wasting time, I raced across the narrow walk high above the houses and shops. I didn't dare look to my sides as there was no railing. One slip, and well…

What was in the mist would no longer be a concern.

Reaching the wider ledge of the Rise, I tossed the bow onto the top and then hoisted myself up. The healing skin of my back stretched, causing me to wince as the cloak and the gown parted, revealing nearly the entire length of my leg. I yearned for the thin breeches often worn under certain styles of gowns, but there hadn't been enough time.

I grasped the bow and started toward the western wall, arriving as the mist seemed to become a solid mass, carrying with it the scent of metal and decay. Ahead, archers waited in their nests of stone, like birds of prey, their bows and arrows steady. I knew not to get too close, as a guard from the Rise would surely notice and ask questions. And while Tawny had exaggerated the killing me part, I would face yet another *lesson* from the Duke.

I cast a quick look around. The city had gone completely quiet and dark, except for the Temples. Their flames were never extinguished. Tearing my gaze from them and the unsettled feeling they often roused, I searched for an empty battlement until I found one. If it were to be manned by a guard, someone would already be in it.

Keeping close to the shadows clinging to the walls, I eased inside the enclosure. My smile returned when I saw several quivers resting near the short ladder. Perfect. Bloodstone arrows, their shafts made of wood from the Blood Forest, were not easy to come by when you were a Maiden who wasn't supposed to have a need for them. Grabbing several of the quivers, I scurried up the ladder.

Partially hidden behind the stone wall, I set the quivers beside me and pulled out an arrow. A sound came then, raising the hairs all over my body.

It started as a low howl, reminding me of the wind during the coldest part of winter, but the moaning gave way to shrill shrieks. Goosebumps pimpled my skin, and my stomach twisted with nausea even as I nocked an arrow. I would never forget that sound. It haunted my dreams, forcing me awake, night after night.

Shouts erupted from the ground, a call to fire. Sucking in a breath of awe, I watched the sky light up with burning arrows. They ripped through the encroaching mist as fires sprang to life once more, all around the Rise, turning the night to silvery dusk.

Guards waited on foot in front of the Rise, their black armor making them nearly indistinguishable as I searched out the familiar white cape of a Royal Guard. There. I found pale blond hair and a weathered face the color of sand. My heart skipped a beat. Toward the center stood Vikter. I expected to see him where death now gathered, but a knot of fear still gathered in my breast. Vikter was the bravest man I knew.

What about Hawke? I had no idea if he was in the castle, stationed outside my door, believing I was inside, or on the Rise. Or, like Vikter, perhaps he was beyond it. The knot expanded, but I couldn't let it grab hold of me.

Keeping an eye on Vikter, I curled my fingers around the string, pulling back as he donned his helmet. Another volley of arrows went up, these reaching farther. When they cut through the mist, I heard the screams.

And then I saw them.

Their pale bodies a milky white, leached of all color, their faces sunken and hollow, eyes burning like fiery coal. Mouths opened wide, revealing two sets of jagged, serrated teeth. Their fingers were elongated into claws, and both their fangs and their claws could flay skin like the softest butter.

I had the scars to prove it.

They were what Marlowe and Ridley would've become if their lives hadn't been ended before it was too late.

They poured out of the mist, the source of my nightmares, the creatures sent by the Dark One over a decade ago to rob my brother and me of our parents in a blood-soaked massacre. They were the evil ones who'd nearly killed me before my sixth birthday, clawing and biting in a frenzy of bloodlust.

The Craven were here.

Chapter 15

And now, they swarmed the guards outside the Rise, crashing into them in a wave that knew no fear of death. Screams of pain and terror tore through the night, and my breath seized. In a matter of seconds, I lost sight of Vikter.

"No," I whispered, fingers trembling around the string. Where was he? He couldn't have fallen. Not that quickly. Not Vikter—

I found him, holding his ground as he cleaved his sword through the air, slicing off the head of a Craven as another launched itself at him. He spun, narrowly avoiding a swipe that would have torn through his breastplate.

There was no time for relief. My gaze shifted as an archer's bloodstone arrow slammed into the head of a Craven, knocking it backward. Dark, inky blood spewed out the back of its skull. I focused on another Craven, calming my breath until it was deep and slow like Vikter had taught me. Years of training steadied my hand, but so did experience. This wasn't the first time I had aided the guards on the Rise.

"Once your fingers take hold of the string, the world around you must cease to exist." Vikter's instructions echoed in my mind. *"It's just you, the pull of the string, and your aim. Nothing else matters."*

And that was all it could be.

Trusting my aim, I released an arrow. It flew through the air, striking a Craven in the heart. I nocked another before what was once someone's child or parent even hit the ground. I found another, a Craven who had a guard on its back, tearing at its armor. I let the bow string go, smiling when the projectile burst through the Craven's head. Loading the next arrow, I caught sight of Vikter, his sword slick with dark blood as he shoved it deep into a Craven's stomach and then drew it upward with a shout—

A Craven rushed Vikter from behind as he yanked the sword out. I pulled back the string. The bolt sliced through the air, catching the creature in the back of its patchy-haired skull. The thing fell forward, dead before it even hit the ground.

Vikter's head whipped around, and I swore he looked straight at me—knew who had sent down that arrow. And although I couldn't see his face, I knew he wore the expression he always did when he was proud yet irritated.

Grinning, I readied another arrow and…and for what felt like a small eternity, I lost myself to the killing, taking down one Craven after another. I went through two quivers before one of the Craven broke through the line of guards. Hitting the wall, its clawed hands dug into the stone, gaining purchase.

For the briefest heartbeat, I stood transfixed as it tore its hand free and then slammed it down again, higher, pulling itself up the wall.

"My gods," I whispered.

The Craven let out a screeching wail, tearing me out of my stupor. I took aim, firing the arrow directly down into its skull. The impact knocked it off the wall—

A shout to my right jerked my head around. An archer fell forward, bow slipping from his hands as a Craven gripped him by the shoulders, sinking its jagged teeth into the guard's neck.

Good gods, they had reached the top.

Spinning around, I nocked an arrow and quickly let it go. The arrow didn't deliver a fatal blow, but the impact knocked the Craven free from the guard, sending it back to the ground below. It wasn't the only one that fell. The guard tumbled backward into nothing but air. I swallowed a cry, telling myself that the man was already dead before the loud, fleshy smack caused me to briefly squeeze my eyes shut.

The Craven's minds may be rotted, but they had enough sense to go for the archers. Vikter had once said that the only thing that rivaled their thirst for blood was their survival instincts.

A high-pitched scream jolted me into action. To my right,

another Craven had reached the edge of the Rise, seizing an archer. The guard dropped his bow and embraced the Craven, pushing forward.

He fell to the ground outside the Rise, taking the Craven with him.

A round of fiery arrows lifted once more into the air, reaching high above the wall. They came down, striking mortal and monster alike. Over the sound of unearthly howls and screams, hooves pounded off cobblestone and dirt, but I still stared at where the archer had fallen, his body swarmed by Craven.

The guard had sacrificed himself. This unnamed, unknown man had chosen death over allowing the Craven to reach the other side of the Rise.

Blinking back sudden tears, I gave a wordless shake of my head as battle cries erupted, forcing me into motion. Rising just enough to see over the ledge, I looked over my shoulder as more guards on horseback spilled out from the gate, brandishing sickle blades. They split into two directions, attempting to seal off access to the Rise. As soon as they cleared the entrance, the gates closed behind them.

A Craven launched itself at a guard, powering through the air like a large jungle cat would. It slammed into the guard, throwing him from his horse. They hit the ground.

"Dammit," I hissed, taking aim at the Craven, who was now halfway up the Rise.

I caught him at the top of his patchy-haired skull, knocking him from the wall. I quickly nocked another arrow, searching out the Craven who were at the Rise. They were the clear threat.

It quickly became obvious that these Craven were different. They looked less…monstrous. Still, their appearance was nothing short of nightmare fodder, but their faces were less hollow, their bodies less shriveled. Were they newly turned? Possible.

The battle below was lessening, bodies falling on top of one another. Catching sight of Vikter as he thrust his sword through the head of a fallen Craven, I dropped down to one knee so I could peer over the wall. The cloak parted, exposing nearly the entire length of my leg from my calf to my thigh to the chilled air.

There was only a handful of Craven remaining, half of them feeding on and tearing into wounded guards, unaware of anything around them. I could see no more near the Rise. Setting an arrow against the bow, I took aim at one who had torn through armor and into the cavity of a stomach, exposing thick, ropey innards. Bile clogged my throat. The guard was already dead, but I couldn't let the Craven continue desecrating the fallen man.

Focusing on the blood-and-gore-smeared mouth, I sent the arrow flying straight into it. The contact snapped the Craven back. Whatever satisfaction I felt was tempered by sorrow. The mist had begun to dissipate, revealing the carnage left behind. So many had fallen tonight. Too many.

The stone cold under my bare knee, I reached for another arrow as I searched—

"You must be the goddess Bele or Lailah given mortal form," a deep voice said from behind me.

Sucking in a sharp breath, I spun around on my knee, the cape and gown whirling around my legs. My arrow locked and ready, I aimed at—

Hawke.

Oh, gods...

My stomach tumbled with relief and dismay as I stared down. He stood under a beam of moonlight as if the gods themselves had blessed him with eternal light. Inky blood dotted his broad, high cheekbones and the straight line of his jaw. His wide, expressive lips were parted as if he were only able to take the thinnest breath, and those strange, beautiful eyes seemed to almost glow in the moonlight.

He held his blood-soaked sword at his side. His leather had been clawed, showing how close he'd come to falling.

Hawke had been beyond the Rise, and like Vikter, as a Royal Guard, that wasn't required. But he went out there, nonetheless. Respect blossomed in my chest, warming me, and I reacted without thought, reaching out with my senses to see if he was injured.

I felt the barest hint of the anguish that lingered in him. The battle had eased it, giving him an outlet in the same way my touch would. Temporary, but still effective. He wasn't injured.

"You are..." His stare was intense and unblinking as he sheathed his sword at his side. "You're absolutely magnificent. Beautiful."

I jolted, shocked. He'd said that I was beautiful before once he saw my face, and he sounded like he'd meant it then. But now? He'd spoken words which too often meant nothing and too rarely meant everything. And he said them in such a manner that there was a tight, tense curling sensation low in my stomach even though he had no idea who he spoke to. My heavy hood remained in place.

I needed to get away.

I glanced behind him, searching for the easiest path to escape. I swallowed hard. Hawke may not have realized yet that I was the girl who'd been at the Red Pearl, but there was no way I could let him know it was me up here now. I had no idea what he would do if he realized I was the one on the Rise.

"The last thing I expected was to find a hooded lady with a talent for archery manning one of the battlements." The dimple made an appearance in his right cheek, and I felt the tug low in my stomach.

Why did he have to have such a...charming grin? It was the kind I knew numerous others had fallen prey to.

I doubted any of them regretted that fall.

I knew I didn't.

He extended his gloved hand. "May I be of assistance?"

Swallowing a snort, I lowered the bow, shifting it to one hand. I stayed silent in case he recognized my voice, motioning for him to back up. With an arch of one dark brow, he placed the offered hand over his heart and took a step back.

Hawke bowed.

He actually *bowed,* with such elaborate flourish that a laugh crept up my throat. I managed to squelch it as I placed the bow down on the lower ledge, propping it against the wall. Keeping my gaze on him, I scooted to the ladder and slowly climbed down, not giving him my back.

The sounds of fighting had all but ceased down below. I needed to get back to my room, but there was no way I could enter the castle the way I'd come out, not with Hawke here. That would rouse suspicion. I slipped the bow under my cloak, hooking it to my back. I flinched as it rested against the still-healing welts.

"You're a..." He trailed off, an odd look settling into his features. I couldn't decipher what it was. Suspicion? Bemusement? Something entirely different? His eyes narrowed.

Below, the heavy gates groaned as they reopened for the wounded and dead to be recovered. The Craven would be burned where they lay. I moved to exit the battlement—

Hawke smoothly blocked my path, and my heart turned over heavily as my hands tightened into fists. I forced my fingers to relax.

The playful light in his eyes had faded. "What are you doing up here?"

Whatever patience his curiosity had brought was gone. Brushing past him, I knew I would have to go to the ground and lose him in the crowd as people began to leave their homes to take stock of the losses.

I didn't make it far.

Hawke caught me by the arm. "I think—"

Instinct sparked, seizing control. I spun and twisted under the arm that held mine, ignoring the faint burn along my back. The shock flickering over his face brought a savage smile to my lips. Popping up behind him, I dipped low and kicked out, sweeping his legs out from under him. He dropped my arm to throw out his hands, stopping his fall.

His curse rang in my ears as I took off, racing out of the battlement and onto the inner ledge of the Rise. The closest stairs were several yards—

Something caught my cloak. The force spun me around and jerked me back against the wall. I started to pull away but didn't make it more than a few inches. Looking down, I saw a dagger embedded deep in the wall, catching my cloak. Stunned, my mouth dropped open.

Hawke stalked toward me, his chin lowered. "That wasn't very nice."

Well, he wasn't going to think this was very nice either.

I gripped the handle of the dagger, wrenching it free. Flipping it so I held it by the blade, I cocked my arm back—

"Don't," he warned, stopping.

I threw the dagger directly at his annoyingly handsome face. He spun, just as I knew he would—

He caught the dagger by the handle, plucking it out of the air like it was nothing, and that was…impressive. And I was jealous. No way could I have done that. I didn't even think Vikter could.

Eyes glittering like chips of gold, he tsked softly and started toward me once more.

Pushing off the wall, I started running again, seeing the stairs up ahead. If I could make it to them—

A dark form dropped down in front of me. My feet skidded, and I slipped, losing my balance. Damn slippers and their smooth, soft sole! I went down hard on my hip, swallowing the cry of pain as it lanced up my lower back. At least I hadn't landed *on* my back.

Hawke rose from a crouch, the dagger held at his hip. "Now that really wasn't nice at all."

How had he...? My gaze flicked to the narrow ridge of the wall above. He'd run along that? It couldn't be wider than a few inches.

He was insane.

"I'm aware that my hair is in need of a trim, but your aim is off," he said. "You should really work on that since I'm quite partial to my face."

My aim had been spot-on.

With a silent snarl, I waited until he was close enough, and then I kicked out, catching him in the lower leg. He grunted as I jumped to my feet, ignoring the ache of what was surely a bruised hip and rear. I whirled to the right, and he jumped to block me, but I darted to the left. He came right back at me, and I kicked out once more—

Hawke caught me by the ankle. I gasped, arms pinwheeling until I steadied myself. Wide-eyed, I stared at him. He raised his brows as his gaze traveled the length of my bare leg. "Scandalous," he murmured.

A growl of annoyance burst from me.

He laughed. "And such dainty little slippers. Satin and silk? They're as finely tailored as your leg. The kind of slipper no guard of the Rise would wear."

How astute of him.

"Unless they are being outfitted differently than I am." Hawke dropped my ankle, but before I could run, he caught my arm and yanked me forward. Suddenly, I was against him and on the tips of my toes.

Air seized in my lungs at the sudden contact. My breasts were flattened against the hard leather and iron of his stomach. The warmth of his body seemed to bleed through his armor, sinking through my cloak and the thin gown underneath. A flash of heat rolled through me as I dragged in a deep breath. Beyond the rot of Craven blood, he smelled of dark spice and lush smoke. A flush crept into my cheeks.

His nostrils flared, and as crazy as it sounded, the hue of his eyes seemed to deepen to a striking amber color. He lifted his other arm. "You know what I think—"

The blade pressing into the skin of his throat silenced him. His lips thinned as he stared down at me. He didn't move or release me, so I pressed the tip of the dagger in just enough. A bead of blood swelled just below his throat.

"Correction," he said, and then he laughed as the trickle of blood seeped down his neck. It wasn't a harsh laugh or a patronizing one. He sounded *amused*. "You're an absolutely stunning, murderous little creature." Pausing, he glanced down. "Nice weapon. Bloodstone and wolven bone. Very interesting…" His gaze flicked up. "*Princess.*"

Chapter 16

The dagger. Damn it. I'd forgotten that he'd seen the knife at the Red Pearl. Gods, how could I forget that? I jerked the blade away, but it was too late.

And it was also a mistake.

Hawke's other hand moved lightning-quick, catching the wrist of the hand that held the weapon. "You and I have so much to talk about."

"We have nothing to talk about," I snapped, irritated at myself for making not one, not two, but *three* incredibly foolish moves. And beyond frustrated with Hawke because he'd gained the upper hand.

"She speaks!" He widened his eyes in false shock and then dipped his chin, causing me to tense. "I thought you liked to talk, Princess." He paused. "Or is that only when you're at the Red Pearl?"

I said nothing to that.

"You're not going to pretend that you have no idea what I'm talking about, are you?" he asked. "That you're not her?"

I pulled on my arms. "Let me go."

"Oh, I don't think so." He turned sharply, and suddenly, my back and the bow were against the stone wall of the Rise. The contact sent a dull wave of fire over my healing back, but he pressed in, caging my body with his. There was barely an inch between us. "After all we shared? You throw a dagger at my face?"

"All we shared? It was a handful of minutes and a few kisses," I said, and the truth of that struck me with startling clarity. That *was* all we'd shared. Gods, I was so…*sheltered.* Because in my limited experience, it had become…so much more to me. The wake-up call that it was only a few kisses was utterly brutal.

"It was more than a few kisses." His voice dropped low. "If you've forgotten, I'm more than willing to remind you."

Tiny coils of tension formed in my stomach. Part of me wanted to be reminded of what I surely had not forgotten. Thank the gods, the smarter, logical part of me won out. "There was nothing worth remembering."

"Now you insult me after throwing a dagger at my face? You've wounded my tender feelings."

"Tender feelings?" I snorted. "Don't be overdramatic."

"Hard not to be when you threw a dagger at my *head* and then cut my neck," he shot back, his grip on me surprisingly gentle compared to the hardness of his tone.

"I knew you'd move out of the way."

"Did you? Is that why you tried to slice open my throat?" His golden eyes burned from beneath heavy, thick lashes.

"I *nicked* your skin," I corrected. "Because you had a hold of me and wouldn't let go. Obviously, you haven't learned anything from it."

"I've actually learned a lot, Princess. That's why your hands and your dagger aren't getting anywhere near my neck." His thumb slid over the inside of my wrist as a reminder, and my fingers spasmed around the handle of my weapon. "But if you let go of the dagger, there's a whole lot of me I'll let your hands get close to."

I choked on my next breath. Did he not realize who he was speaking to? Was the sound of my voice so common that he had no idea it was me? But if he hadn't figured it out yet, that meant I still had the advantage. A small one, but still. "How generous of you," I retorted.

"Once you get to know me, you'll find that I can be *quite* benevolent."

"I have no intention of getting to know you."

"So, you just make a habit of sneaking into the rooms of young men and seducing them before running off?"

"What?" I gasped. "Seducing men?"

"Isn't that what you did to me, Princess?" His thumb made another slow sweep along the inside of my wrist.

"You're ridiculous," I sputtered.

"What I am is *intrigued.*"

Groaning, I pulled at my arms, and he chuckled in response, eyes reminding me of pools of warm honey. "Why do you insist on holding me like this?"

"Well, besides what we went over already, which is the whole being partial to my face *and* my neck thing, you're also somewhere you're not supposed to be. I'm doing my job by detaining and questioning you."

"Do you typically question those on the Rise who you don't recognize like this?" I challenged. "What an odd method of interrogation."

"Only pretty ladies with shapely, bare legs." He leaned in, and when I took my next breath, my chest met his. "What are you doing up here during a Craven attack?"

"Enjoying a relaxing evening stroll," I snapped.

His lips curled up on one side, but there was no dimple. "What were you doing up here, Princess?" he repeated.

"What did it look like I was doing?"

"It looked like you were being incredibly foolish and reckless."

"Excuse me?" Disbelief thundered through me. "How reckless was I being when I killed Craven and—"

"Am I unaware of a new recruitment policy where half-dressed ladies in cloaks are now needed on the Rise?" he asked. "Are we that desperately in need of protection?"

Anger hit my blood like wildfire. "Desperate? Why would my presence on the Rise signal desperation when, as you've seen, I know how to use a bow? Oh, wait. Is it because I happen to have breasts?"

"I've known women with far less beautiful breasts that could cut a man down without so much as blinking an eye," he said. "But none of those women are here in Masadonia."

I would've liked to know where this group of rather amazing-sounding women lived—*wait.* Far less beautiful breasts?

"And you are incredibly skilled," he continued, snapping my attention back to him. "Not just with an arrow. Who taught you how to fight and use a dagger?"

Clamping my mouth shut, I refused to answer.

"I'm willing to bet it was the same person who gave you that blade." He paused. "Too bad whoever they are didn't teach you how to evade capture. Well, too bad for *you*, that is."

Anger flooded my system once more, overwhelming me. I thrust my knee up, aiming for a very sensitive part of him—the one that somehow made him more qualified than I was to fight.

Hawke sensed my move and shifted, blocking my knee with his thigh. "You're so incredibly violent." He paused. "I think I like it."

"Let me go!" I seethed.

"And be kicked or stabbed?" He shoved his leg between mine, preventing any future kicks. "We've already covered that, Princess. More than once."

I lifted my hips off the wall, attempting to throw him off, but all I accomplished was pressing a very sensitive part of my body against the hard length of his thigh. The friction created a sudden, jarring rush of heat that was so powerful, it was like being struck by lightning. Sucking in a startled breath, I stilled.

Hawke had done the same against me, his large body filling with tension. His chest rose and fell against mine. What...what was happening? I felt hot despite how far up we were and that we stood in the cold night air. My skin seemed to buzz as if fine currents of energy were dancing along my flesh, and hard, pounding heat had replaced the aching coldness in my body.

Several too-long moments stretched out between us and then he said, "I came back for you that night."

The noise from below was beginning to calm. At any moment, someone could come up here, but I *was* so incredibly reckless and foolish because I let my eyes drift shut as his words cycled through me.

He had come back.

"Just like I told you I would. I came back for you, and you weren't there," he continued. "You promised me, Princess."

A smidgen of guilt formed within me, and I wasn't sure if it was for lying to him, or the throwing the dagger at his face part. Probably both. "I...I couldn't."

"Couldn't?" His voice had dropped again, becoming lower, thicker. "I have a feeling that if there's something you want badly enough, nothing will stop you."

A harsh, bitter-sounding laugh escaped me. "You know nothing."

"Maybe." He'd let go of my arm, and before I knew what he was up to, his hand had slipped inside my hood. His cold fingers touched the unmarred skin of my right cheek. I gasped at the contact and started to draw back, but there was nowhere to go. "Maybe I know more than you realize."

A small measure of unease crawled across my skin.

Hawke bent his head, pressing his cheek to the left side of my hood. "Do you really think I have no idea who you are?"

Every muscle in my body tensed as my mouth dried.

"You have nothing to say to that?" He paused, and his voice was barely above a whisper when he said, "*Penellaphe?*"

Dammit.

I exhaled noisily, unsure if I was relieved or afraid that I no longer had to wonder if he knew. The confusion spiked my irritation into uncharted territories. "Are you just now figuring that out? If so, I'm concerned about you being one of my personal guards."

He chuckled deeply, the sound infuriatingly infectious. "I knew the moment you removed the veil."

My lips parted on a thin inhale. "Why...why didn't you say something then?"

"To you?" he asked. "Or to the Duke?"

"Either," I whispered.

"I wanted to see if you'd bring it up. Apparently, you were just going to pretend that you're not the same girl who frequents the Red Pearl."

"I don't frequent the Red Pearl," I corrected. "But I hear you do."

"Have you been asking about me? I'm flattered."

"I haven't."

"I'm not sure if I can believe you. You tell a lot of lies, Princess."

"Don't call me that," I demanded.

"I like it better than what I'm supposed to call you. *Maiden.* You have a name. It's not that."

"I didn't ask for what you liked," I said, even though I whole-heartedly agreed with his dislike of how I was supposed to be addressed.

"But you did ask why I didn't tell the Duke about your little explorations," he countered. "Why would I do that? I'm your guard. If I were to betray you, then you wouldn't trust me, and that would definitely make my job of keeping you safe much harder."

His very logical reasoning for not saying anything carried a bitter bite of disappointment, and I didn't even want to delve into why. "As you can see, I can keep myself safe."

"I see that." He drew back, brows furrowed, and then his eyes widened just a fraction as if he'd figured something out.

"Hawke!" a voice called out from the ground below, causing my heart to trip. "Everything okay up there?"

His gaze searched the darkness of my hood for a moment, and then he looked over his shoulder. "Everything is fine."

"You need to let me go," I whispered. "Someone is bound to come up here—"

"And catch you? Force you to reveal your identity?" Those amber eyes slid back to me. "Maybe that would be a good thing."

I sucked in a sharp breath. "You said you wouldn't betray me—"

"I said I *didn't* betray you, but that was before I knew you would do something like this."

Ice drenched my skin.

"My job would be so much easier if I didn't have to worry about you sneaking out to fight the Craven…or meet random men in places like the Red Pearl," he continued. "And who knows what else you do when all believe you're safely ensconced in your chambers."

"I—"

"I imagine that once I brought it to the Duke's and Duchess's attention, your penchant for arming yourself with a bow and climbing to the Rise would be one less thing I had to worry about."

My chest seized with panic, and I blurted out, "You have no idea what he'd do if you went to him. He'd—" I cut myself off.

"He'd what?"

Taking a slow, even breath, I lifted my chin. "It doesn't matter. Do what you feel you need to do."

Hawke stared down at me for so long it felt like a small eternity had passed and then he let go of me, stepping back. Cold air blew in between us. "You better hurry back to your chambers, Princess. We'll have to finish this conversation later."

Confusion held me in its grip for only a few moments, but then I snapped out of it. Easing away from the wall, I ran, and even though I didn't look back, I knew he didn't take his eyes off me.

Slipping through the old servants' access, I wasn't surprised when I found that Tawny was still in my chambers, even though it had taken me nearly an hour before the gates were lifted and I could sneak back in.

She gasped. "I thought you were never going to come back."

I closed the creaky door behind me and faced her, slowly reaching up to pull the hood down.

Tawny drew up short. "Are you...are you okay?" Her gaze searched mine, and I saw a faint tremor radiate through her. "Was it bad? The attack?"

Opening my mouth, I had no idea where to start, recalling all that had happened. I leaned against the door. My confrontation with Hawke still had my heart pounding. My mind was a confusing mess, and my stomach churned with the knowledge that the Craven had reached the top of the Rise.

"Poppy?" she whispered.

I decided to start with the most important. "There were a lot of them. Dozens."

Her chest moved as she took in a deep breath. "And?"

I wasn't sure if she really wanted to know, but to be in the dark was far more dangerous than fear of the truth. "And several of them reached the top of the Rise."

Tawny's eyes flew open. "Oh, my gods." She pressed a hand to her chest. "But the shields have lifted—"

"They were stopped, but a lot...a lot of guards died tonight." I peeled myself away from the door as I unbuttoned my cloak with chilled fingers. I went to the fireplace and stood there for several minutes, allowing the warmth to beat back some of the coldness. "There were just so many of them that they basically swarmed the front line. If there'd been more..."

"They would've breached the wall?"

"It's more than possible." Stepping away from the fire, I let my cloak fall in a messy puddle. I slipped off the bow, carefully placing it in the chest before I closed the lid. "They sent out the horsemen, but at least two Craven had already made it to the top of the Rise by then. If they wait like that again, it could be too late. But I don't think...I don't imagine they expected them to be able to do that."

Tawny sat down on the edge of the bed. "Did you...kill any of them?"

Toeing off my slippers, I looked over at her. "Of course."

"Good." Her gaze drifted to the window, to where the torches now burned brightly in the darkness. "There'll be a lot of black flags raised tomorrow."

There would be. Each house that had lost a son, a father, a husband, or friend would raise the flag in memoriam. Commander Jansen would visit each and every one of them over the next day or so. Many pyres would be lit.

And I feared that some of those who'd bravely faced down the Craven tonight would return to their homes or the dorms, *bitten*. It happened every time after an attack.

I plopped down on the bed, catching the scent of burnt wood in my hair. Before I could say anything else, there was a knock on the door.

"I'll get it." Tawny rose, and I didn't stop her, figuring it was Vikter or another Royal Guard checking on us. As she made her way over, I gripped the edge of my braid, quickly unraveling it as I heard Tawny open the door and say, "The Maiden is sleeping—"

"Doubtful."

Heart slamming against my ribs, I jumped up from the bed and spun around just as Hawke came through the door. My mouth dropped open, mirroring Tawny's expression.

Hawke kicked the door shut behind him. "It's time for that talk, Princess."

Chapter 17

The blood had been wiped from Hawke's face, and his dark hair was damp, curling against his temples and forehead. His broadsword was absent, but the two shorter swords were still attached to his waist. Standing in my chambers with his booted feet braced shoulder-width apart, and the curve of his jaw hard, Hawke reminded me so very much of Theon, the god of Accord and War.

He appeared no less dangerous than he had on the Rise.

And it was clear by the fiery burn of his amber gaze that he wasn't here to make peace.

He glanced over to where Tawny stood, struck as silent and still as I was. "Your services are no longer needed this evening."

Tawny's mouth dropped open.

Snapping out of my stupor, I had a very different reaction. "You don't have the authority to dismiss her!"

"I don't?" He raised a dark brow. "As your personal Royal Guard, I have the authority to remove any threats"

"Threats?" Tawny frowned. "I'm not a threat."

"You pose the threat of making up excuses or lying on behalf of Penellaphe. Just like you said she was asleep when I know for a fact that she was on the Rise," he countered, and Tawny snapped her mouth shut.

She turned to me. "I have a feeling I'm missing an important piece of information."

"I didn't get a chance to tell you," I explained. "And it wasn't that important."

Tawny lifted her brows.

Beside her, Hawke snorted. "I'm sure it was one of the most important things to have happened to you in a long time."

My eyes narrowed. "You have an over-inflated sense of involvement in my life if you really think that."

"I think I have a good grasp on just how much of a role I play in your life."

"Doubtful," I parroted back.

"I do wonder if you actually believe half the lies you tell."

Tawny's gaze snapped back and forth between us.

"I am not lying, thank you very much."

He smiled, showing off the dimple in his right cheek. "Whatever you need to tell yourself, Princess."

"Don't call me that!" I stomped my foot.

Hawke lifted an eyebrow. "Did that make you feel good?"

"Yes! Because the only other option is to kick you."

"So violent," he chuckled.

Oh, my gods.

My hands curled into fists. "You shouldn't be in here."

"I'm your personal guard," he replied. "I can be wherever I feel I am needed to keep you safe."

"And what do you think you need to protect me from in here?" I demanded, looking around. "An unruly bedpost I might stub my toe on? Oh, wait, are you worried I might faint? I know how good you are at handling such emergencies."

"You do look a little pale," he replied. "My ability to catch frail, delicate females may come in handy."

I sucked in a sharp breath.

"But as far as I can determine, other than a random abduction attempt, you, Princess, are the greatest threat to yourself."

"Well…" Tawny drew the word out, and when I shot her a look that should've sent her running from the room, she shrugged. "He kind of has a point there."

"You're absolutely no help."

"Penellaphe and I do need to speak," he said, his gaze never leaving mine. "I can assure you that she is safe with me, and I'm sure that whatever I'm about to discuss with her, she'll tell you all about it later."

Tawny crossed her arms. "Yes, she will, but that's not nearly as entertaining as witnessing it."

I sighed. "It's okay, Tawny. I'll see you in the morning."

She stared at me. "Seriously?"

"Seriously," I confirmed. "I have a feeling that if you don't leave, he's just going to stand there and drain precious air from my room—"

"While looking exceptionally handsome," he added. "You forgot to add that."

A short, light giggle left Tawny.

I ignored the comment. "And I would like to get some rest before the sun rises."

Tawny exhaled loudly. "Fine." She glanced over at Hawke. "*Princess.*"

"Oh, my gods," I muttered, a dull ache pulsing behind my eyes.

Hawke watched Tawny, waiting until she had slipped through the adjoining door before saying, "I like her."

"Good to know," I said. "What is it you wish to talk about that couldn't wait until the morning?"

His gaze slid back to me. "You have beautiful hair."

I blinked. My hair was unbound, and without seeing it, I knew it was a mess of crimped waves. I resisted the urge to touch it. "Is that what you wanted to talk about?"

"Not exactly." Then his gaze dipped and roamed slowly, starting at my shoulders, moving all the way down to the tips of my toes. His stare was heavy, almost like a touch, and a flush followed in its wake.

It was at that exact moment I remembered that not only was my face uncovered, but I was also wearing only a thin sleeping gown. I knew that with the light of the fire and the oil lamps behind me, very little of the shape of my body was hidden from Hawke. The flush deepened, became headier. I started for the robe lying at the foot of the bed.

Hawke's lips twisted into a knowing half-smile that sent a bolt of irritation streaking through me.

I stopped, meeting his gaze and holding it. Hawke might not have seen all the shadowy areas visible beneath the flimsy white gown, but he'd done more than just feel a few of them with his hands. There was a tiny part of me that thought about moving my hair to cover the left side of my face, but he'd seen the scars already, and I wasn't ashamed of them. I utterly *refused* to allow what the Duke had said about Hawke saying that I was beautiful to have any impact on me. Hiding my face or covering myself was rather pointless, but more importantly, I swore I saw a challenge in his gaze. As if he expected me to do both things.

I would not.

A long, tense moment passed. "Was that all you were wearing under the cloak?"

"That's none of your concern," I told him as I held my arms to my sides.

Something flickered across his face, reminding me of the look Vikter often gave me when I bested him, but it was gone too quickly for me to be sure. "Feels like it should be," he said.

The rasp of his voice caused a wave of goosebumps to break out over my skin. "That sounds like your problem, not mine."

He stared at me with that strange expression again. The one that made me think he was caught between amusement and curiosity. "You're…you're nothing like I expected."

The way he said that sounded so genuine that some of my irritation eased. "Was it my skill with an arrow or the blade? Or was it the fact that I took you to the ground?"

"*Barely* took me to the ground," he corrected. His chin dipped, and his lashes lowered, shielding his odd eyes. "All of those things. But you forgot to add in the Red Pearl. I never expected to find the Maiden there."

I snorted. "I imagine not."

His lashes lifted, and there was a wealth of questions in his stare. I didn't think there'd be any avoiding them this time around.

Suddenly too tired to stand there and argue, I walked over to one of the two chairs by the fire, all too aware of how the sides of my gown parted, revealing nearly the entire length of my leg.

And all too aware of how Hawke tracked every step.

"That was the first time I was in the Red Pearl." I sat, letting my hands fall to my lap. "And the reason I was on the second floor was because Vikter came in." I wrinkled my nose as I gave a little shudder. "He would've recognized me, mask or not. I went upstairs because a woman told me the room was empty." I still felt as if she had set me up, but that was neither here nor there at the moment. "I'm not telling you this because I feel like I need to explain myself, I'm just…telling the truth. I didn't know you were in the room."

He remained where he stood. "But you knew who I was," he said, and that wasn't a question.

"Of course." I shifted my gaze to the fire. "Your arrival had already stirred up quite a bit of...talk."

"Flattered," he murmured.

My lips twitched as I watched the flames curl and ripple over the thick logs of wood. "Why I decided to stay in the room isn't up for discussion."

"I know why you stayed in the room," he said.

"You do?"

"It makes sense now."

I thought back to that night and remembered what he had said. He'd seemed to sense that I was there to experience, to live. Now that he knew what I was, it would make sense.

But that still wasn't something I was willing to discuss. "What are you going to do about me being on the Rise?"

He didn't answer for a long moment, and then he walked to where I sat, his long-legged prowl full of fluid grace. "May I?" He gestured to the empty seat.

I nodded.

Sitting across from me, he leaned forward, resting his elbows on his bent knees. "It was Vikter who trained you, wasn't it?"

My pulse skipped, but I kept my face blank.

"It had to be him. You two are close, and he's been with you since you arrived in Masadonia."

"You've been asking questions."

"I'd be stupid not to learn everything I could about the person I'm duty-bound to die to protect."

He had a very good point there. "I'm not going to answer your question."

"Because you're afraid I'll go to the Duke, even though I didn't before?"

"You said out on the Rise that you should," I reminded him. "That it would make your job easier. I'm not going to bring anyone else down with me."

He inclined his head. "I said I *should*, not that I *would*."

"There's a difference?"

"You should know there is." His gaze flickered over my face. "What would His Grace do if I had gone to him?"

My fingers curled inward. "It doesn't matter."

"Then why did you say I had no idea what he'd do? You sounded as if you were going to say more but stopped yourself."

I looked away, staring at the fire. "I wasn't going to say anything."

Hawke was quiet for a long moment. "Both you and Tawny reacted strangely to his summons."

"We weren't expecting to hear from him." The lie rolled off my tongue.

There was another pause. "Why were you in your room for almost two days after being summoned by him?"

Sharp, biting pain radiated from where my nails dug into my palms. The flames were dying, flickering softly.

"What did he do to you?" Hawke asked, his voice too soft.

Suffocating shame crept up my throat, tasting acidic. "Why do you even care?"

"Why wouldn't I?" he asked, and again, he sounded unbelievably sincere.

My head turned before I realized what I was doing. He'd sat back, hands curled around the arms of the wingback chair. "You don't know me—"

"I bet I know you better than most."

Heat creeped into my cheeks. "That doesn't mean you know me, Hawke. Not enough to care."

"I know you're not like the other members of the Court."

"I'm not a member of the Court," I pointed out.

"You're the Maiden. You're viewed as a child of the gods by the commoners. They see you higher than an Ascended, but I know you're compassionate. That night at the Red Pearl, when we talked about death, you genuinely felt sympathy for any losses I'd experienced. It wasn't a forced nicety."

"How do you know?"

"I'm a good judge of people's words," he remarked. "You wouldn't speak out of fear of being discovered until I referred to Tawny as your maid. You defended her at the risk of exposing yourself." He paused. "And I saw you."

"Saw what?"

He tipped forward again, lowering his voice. "I saw you during the City Council. You didn't agree with the Duke and Duchess. I couldn't see your face, but I could tell you were uncomfortable. You felt bad for that family."

"So did Tawny."

"No offense to your friend, but she looked half-asleep throughout most of that. I doubt she even knew what was going on."

I couldn't exactly argue that point, but what he had seen was me briefly losing control of my gift. However, that didn't change the fact that I wasn't okay with what was happening to the Tulis family.

"And you know how to fight—and fight well. Not only that, you're obviously brave. There are many men—*trained* men— who wouldn't go out on the Rise during a Craven attack if they didn't have to. The Ascended could've gone out there, and they'd have a higher chance of surviving, yet they didn't. You did."

I shook my head. "Those things are just traits. They don't mean you know me well enough to care about what does and doesn't happen to me."

His eyes fixed on mine. "Would you care what happens to me?"

"Well, yes." My brows knitted in a frown. "I would—"

"But you don't know me."

I snapped my mouth shut. Dammit.

"You're a decent person, Princess." He sat back. "That's why you care."

"And you're not a decent person?"

Hawke lowered his gaze. "I'm many things. Decent is rarely one of them."

I had no idea how to respond to that little bit of honesty.

"You're not going to tell me what the Duke did, are you?" He sighed, his back bowing slightly in the chair. "You know, I'll find out one way or another."

I almost laughed. I was confident that was one thing no one would ever speak about. "If you think so."

"I know so," he replied, and a heartbeat passed. "It's weird, isn't it?"

"What is?"

His gaze met mine again, and I felt a hitch in my chest. I couldn't look away. I felt...ensnared. "How it feels like I've known you longer. You feel that, too."

I wanted to deny it, but he was right, and it was weird. I said none of that because I didn't want to acknowledge it. Doing so felt like a start down a road I couldn't travel. Knowing that caused a deep, twisting sensation in my chest, and I didn't want to acknowledge that either.

Because it felt a lot like disappointment. And didn't that mean I'd already begun to travel that road? I broke eye contact, my gaze falling to my hands.

"Why were you on the Rise?" he asked, changing the subject.

"Wasn't it obvious?"

"Your motivation wasn't. At least, tell me that. Tell me what drove you to go up there to fight them."

Easing open my fingers, I slipped two of them under the sleeve of my right arm. They skimmed my skin until the tips brushed over two jagged tears. There were others, along my stomach and my thighs.

It would be easy to lie, to come up with any number of reasons, but I wasn't sure if there was any harm in the truth. Was three instead of two knowing the truth somehow earth-shattering? I didn't think it was.

"The scar on my face. Do you know how I got it?"

"Your family was attacked by some Craven when you were a child," he answered. "Vikter..."

"He filled you in?" A faint, tired smile pulled at my lips. "It's not the only scar." When he said nothing, I slipped my hand out from under my sleeve. "When I was six, my parents decided to leave the capital for Niel Valley. They wanted a much quieter life, or so I'm told. I don't remember much from the trip other than my mother and father being incredibly tense throughout the whole thing. Ian and I were young and didn't know a lot about the Craven, so we weren't afraid of being out there or stopping at one of the smaller villages—a place I was told later hadn't seen a Craven attack in decades. There was just a short wall, like most of the smaller towns, and we were staying at the inn only for one night. The place smelled like cinnamon and cloves. I remember that."

I closed my eyes. "They came at night, in the mist. There was no time once they appeared. My father...he went out onto the street to try and fend them off while my mother hid us, but they came through the door and the windows before she could even step outside." The memory of my mother's screams forced my eyes open. I swallowed. "A woman—someone who was staying at the inn—was able to grab Ian and pull him into this hidden room, but I hadn't wanted to leave my mom and it just..." Dark and disjointed flashes of the night attempted to piece themselves together. Blood on the floor, the walls, running down my mother's arms. Losing my grip on her slippery hand, and then grabbing hands and snapping teeth. The claws... And then the soul-crushing, fiery pain until, finally, nothing. "I woke up days later, back in the capital. Queen Ileana was by my side. She told me what had happened. That our parents were gone."

"I'm sorry," Hawke said, and I nodded. "I truly am. It's a miracle you survived."

"The gods protected me. That's what the Queen told me. That I was Chosen. I came to learn later that it was one of the reasons the Queen had begged my mother and father not to leave the safety of the capital. That...that if the Dark One became aware of the Maiden being unprotected, he'd send the Craven after me. He wanted me dead then, but apparently, he wants me alive now." I laughed, and it hurt a little.

"What happened to your family is not your fault, and there could be any number of reasons for why they attacked that village." He dragged a hand through his hair, pushing the now-dry strands back from his forehead. "What else do you remember?"

"No one...no one in that inn knew how to fight. Not my parents, none of the women, or even the men. They all relied on the handful of guards." I rubbed my fingers together. "If my parents knew how to defend themselves, they could've survived. It might've been just a small chance, but one nonetheless."

Understanding flickered across Hawke's face. "And you want that chance."

I nodded. "I won't...I refuse to be helpless."

"No one should be."

Blowing out a little breath, I stilled my fingers. "You saw what happened tonight. They reached the top of the Rise. If one makes it over, more will follow. No Rise is impenetrable, and even if it were, mortals come back from outside the Rise cursed. It happens more than people realize. At any moment, that curse could spread in this city. If I'm going down—"

"You'll go down fighting," he finished for me.

I nodded.

"Like I said, you're very brave."

"I don't think it's bravery." I returned to staring at my hands. "I think it's…fear."

"Fear and bravery are often one and the same. It either makes you a warrior or a coward. The only difference is the person it resides inside."

My gaze lifted to him in stunned silence. It took me a moment to formulate a response. "You sound so many years older than what you appear."

"Only half of the time," he said. "You saved lives tonight, Princess."

I ignored the nickname. "But many died."

"Too many," he agreed. "The Craven are a never-ending plague."

Letting my head rest against the back of the chair, I wiggled my toes toward the fire. "As long as an Atlantian lives, there will be Craven."

"That is what they say," he said, and when I glanced back at him, a muscle flexed along his jaw as he stared at the dwindling fire. "You said that more come back from outside the Rise cursed than people realize. How do you know that?"

I opened my mouth. Dammit. How *would* I know that?

"I've heard rumors."

Shit.

His gaze slid to me. "It's not spoken about a lot, and when it is, it's only whispered."

Unease stirred. "You're going to need to be more detailed."

"I've heard that the child of the gods has helped those who are cursed," he said, and I tensed. "That she has aided them, given them death with dignity."

I didn't know if I should be relieved that was all he'd heard and that he hadn't brought up my gift. But the fact that he, someone who hadn't been in the city all that long, had heard such rumors wasn't exactly reassuring.

If Vikter found out that Hawke had heard such a thing, he would not be happy. Then again, I doubted if Vikter would allow me to assist him after the last time anyway.

"Who has said such things?" I asked.

"A few of the guards," he told me, and my stomach sank even further. "I didn't believe them at first, to be honest."

I schooled my features. "Well, you should've stuck with your initial reaction. They're mistaken if they think I would commit outright treason against the Crown."

His gaze flickered over my face. "Didn't I just tell you that I was a good judge of character?"

"So?"

"So, I know you're lying," he replied. I wondered what exactly made him believe that it was me the guards had been talking about. "And I understand why you would. Those men speak of you with such awe that before I even met you, I half expected you to be a child of the gods. They would never report you."

"That may be the case, but you heard them talking about it. Others could hear them, as well."

"Perhaps I should be clearer in what I said about hearing rumors. They were actually speaking to me," he clarified. "Since I too have helped those who are cursed die with dignity. I did so in the capital and do so here, as well."

My lips parted as my stomach steadied, but my heart flipped and flopped around like a fish out of water.

"Those who come back cursed have already given all for the kingdom. Being treated as anything other than the heroes they are, and being dragged in front of the public to be murdered is the last thing they or their families should have to go through."

I didn't know what to say as I stared at him. He was speaking my own thoughts, and I knew there were others out there who believed the same. Obviously. But to know that he was willing to risk high treason to do what was right...

"I've kept you up long enough."

I arched a brow. "That is all you have to say about me being on the Rise?"

"I ask only one thing of you." He rose, and I prepared for him to tell me to stay away from the Rise. I'd probably tell him I would. Of course, I wouldn't, and I didn't think he'd believe me. "The next time you go out, wear better shoes and thicker clothing. Those slippers are likely to be the death of you, and that dress...the death of me."

Chapter 18

Hawke hadn't reported my presence, but he did tell someone.

I discovered that when I woke up only a few hours after he'd left and went to see if Vikter was up for training. There wasn't a single part of me that was surprised to find him waiting for me and more than ready to get physical. I'd wanted to talk to him about what had happened with the Craven reaching the top of the Rise.

Vikter wanted to talk about what Hawke had told him. Apparently, after he'd left my room, he went straight to Vikter. I wasn't exactly mad about that. Mostly just annoyed with Hawke feeling the need to tell Vikter anything. But it confirmed that Hawke figured Vikter would be aware of my presence on the Rise, or at the very least, not surprised or angered by it.

Hawke had miscalculated the whole not-being-angered part.

Vikter frowned as he prowled around me, eyeing my stance. He was checking to make sure my legs were braced, and my feet were planted shoulder-width apart. "You shouldn't have been on the Rise."

"But I was."

"And you were caught." Vikter stopped in front of me. "What would you have done if it had been another guard who discovered you?"

"If it were anyone else, I wouldn't have been caught."

"This isn't a joke, Poppy."

"I didn't say anything funny," I said. "I'm being honest. Hawke is…he's fast, and he's very well trained."

"Which is why we're working on your hand-to-hand combat."

My lips thinned. "My hand-to-hand fighting skills aren't bad."

"If that was true, he wouldn't have caught you. Go," Vikter ordered.

Keeping my chin low, I threw a punch. He blocked with his forearm, and I pulled back, looking for an opening, though not finding one. So, I made one. I shifted as if to kick, and his arms dropped a fraction of an inch. My opening appeared, and I swung, slamming my fist into his stomach.

He grunted softly. "Nice move."

I dropped my arms, smiling. "It was, wasn't it?"

Vikter smirked, but it faded quickly. "I know you're probably tired of me saying this," he started, "but I'm going to say it again. You need to be more careful. And you're throwing punches with your arm instead of your core."

I *was* getting tired of hearing him say that. "I am careful, and I'm throwing a punch like you taught me."

"Your swings are weak. Limp. That's not how I taught you." He grabbed my arm, shaking it like a wet noodle. "You don't have a lot of upper body strength. Your strength is here." He placed his hand in front of my stomach. "You will inflict way more damage this way. When you throw a punch, your torso and hips should move with you."

I nodded and did what he said. I missed, but I could feel the difference in the swing. "Hawke isn't going to report me to His Grace."

"You really think that?" He blocked my next punch. "Better."

"If he was going to say anything, he would've gone straight to the Duke."

"There could be a hundred reasons why he hasn't said anything yet."

A few days ago, I would've agreed, but not anymore. Not after what he'd confessed the night prior. "I don't think he's going to, Vikter. I don't have anything to worry about, and neither do you. I didn't tell him you were the one who trained me."

"Poppy," he said. He said it in the same way he had when I asked if he thought I could hide a broadsword under my veil. I still believed I could. I just needed to position it right— "You don't know him."

"I know that." I crossed my arms as Vikter backed off. "But you don't know him either."

"You don't know what his motivations are—why he would keep quiet."

I knew what he'd said about the Red Pearl, and I was sure it also applied to the Rise. But it was more than that. The fact that Hawke was willing to risk being charged with high treason to help those who'd been cursed spoke volumes about who he was as a person. It didn't feel right sharing that with Vikter, though. There was a reason we didn't know the identities of others in the network.

So, I went with, "He said that if he had, he knew I wouldn't trust him, which would make his job harder. You have to admit, he has a point."

"He does, but that doesn't mean you shouldn't be careful." Vikter fell silent for a moment. "And I understand. I do."

"Understand what?"

"Like I said before, he's an attractive young man—"

"That has nothing to do with it."

"And you've been surrounded by old men like me."

"You're not all that old."

He blinked. "Thanks." A pause. "I think."

"It has nothing to do with how he looks. I'm not saying that I don't think he's attractive. I do, but that's not why I trust him." And that was the truth. My faith didn't stem from what he looked like. "I'm not that foolish."

"I'm not suggesting you are." He thrust a hand through his hair. "So, you trust him?"

"I...I told him why I needed to be out on that Rise. I told him about the night my family was attacked. You know how he responded? Even though he said at first that I shouldn't be out there, he listened to my reasons, and the only thing he said was that I needed to wear better shoes." I figured I'd keep the part about my gown to myself. "I trust him, Vikter. Is there a reason I shouldn't?"

Vikter sighed heavily as he looked away. "He hasn't given us any reason to doubt him. I know that. It's just that we don't know him, and you're important to me, Poppy. Not because you're the Maiden, but because you're...you."

A knot of emotion formed in my chest and fought its way up my throat. I didn't give him a chance to realize what I was doing. I launched myself at him, wrapping my arms around his waist and hugging him tightly. "Thank you," I murmured against his chest.

Vikter was as stiff as a guard on the Rise for their very first time, but then he put his hands on my back. And patted me.

I grinned.

"You know I'll never replace your father, nor would I ever try to, but you're like a daughter to me."

I hugged him tighter.

He patted me again. "I worry about you. Partly because it's my job, but mostly because it's you."

"You're important to me, too." My words were muffled against his chest. "Even though you think my punches are weak."

His chuckle was rough as he dropped his chin to the top of my head. "Your punches are weak when you're not doing them correctly." He pulled back, clasping my cheeks. "But, girl, your aim is deadly. Don't ever forget that."

"The gods have not failed us. The Ascended have not failed you." The Duke's voice carried from where he stood on the balcony of the castle wall that evening. Below him, a mass of people filled the open yard, and under the glow of oil lamps and torches, I could see several wore all black, the somber color of death. Among them were guards astride horses, keeping an eye on the nervous crowd.

I'd never known His Grace to address the people like this. He and the Duchess were never in front of so many, not even during the Councils or the Rite. I couldn't have been more surprised when both Vikter and Hawke arrived after supper to escort me to the balcony.

Then again, how many years had it been since such a significant movement of Craven reached the Rise?

Black flags had been raised over too many homes, and too many funeral pyres had been lit at dawn. The air was still choked with ash and incense.

"Because of the gods' Blessing," Teerman continued, "the Rise did not fall last night."

Standing back, next to Tawny, and flanked by Vikter and Hawke,

I wondered exactly how the gods' Blessing had kept the wall from falling. It had been the guards, men like the archer, who had chosen death over allowing the Craven to come over the top.

"They reached the top!" a man shouted. "They almost made it over the Rise. Are we safe?"

"When it happens again?" the Duchess answered, her soft voice silencing the murmurs. "Because it will happen again."

Behind the veil, my brows lifted. Over my right shoulder, I heard Hawke murmur dryly, "That will surely ease fears."

My lips twitched.

"The truth is not designed to ease fears," Vikter responded.

"Is that why we tell lies, then?" Hawke questioned, and I pressed my lips together.

Ever since they'd arrived to escort Tawny and me, they had been doing this. One of them would say something. Anything. The other would disagree, only for the one who'd spoken first to have the last word. It started with Hawke commenting that it was surprisingly warm this evening and that I should enjoy it, to which Vikter had followed up by stating that the temperatures would surely drop too rapidly for that. Hawke had proceeded to ask Vikter where he'd gained such prophetic knowledge of the weather.

In the span of an hour, it had only progressed from there as they attempted to out-snark each other.

Hawke was winning, by at least three comebacks.

Even after I had defended him to Vikter—and I hadn't been lying when I told him that I trusted Hawke—there was still a small part of me that couldn't believe what he'd said. He hadn't told me never to go on the Rise again. He hadn't demanded that I stay in my room, where it was theoretically *safer*. Instead, he'd listened to my reasons for why I needed to be out there and accepted them, only asking that I wear more suitable shoes.

And additional clothing.

The latter annoyed and excited me, which was altogether confusing. And was definitely not something that I'd shared with Vikter that morning.

My gaze slid to the Duchess as she stepped forward. "The gods didn't fail you," she repeated, placing her hands on the waist-high railing beside her husband. "We didn't fail you. But the gods *are* unhappy. That is why the Craven reached the top of the Rise."

A murmur of dismay swept through the crowd like a rainstorm.

"We have spoken to them. They are not pleased with recent events, here and in nearby cities," she said, scanning the paling and graying faces below. "They fear that the good people of Solis have begun to lose faith in their decisions and are turning to those who wish to see the future of this great kingdom compromised."

The whispers turned to outright cries of denouncement, startling the horses. The guardsmen quickly calmed the equines' nervous prancing.

"What did you all think would happen when those who support the Dark One and plot with him are standing among you right now?" the Duke asked. "As I speak, at this very moment, Descenters stare back at me, thrilled that the Craven took so many lives last night. In this very crowd, there are Descenters who pray for the day that the Dark One comes. Those who celebrated the massacre of Three Rivers and the fall of Goldcrest Manor. Look to your left and to your right, and you may see someone who helped conspire to abduct the Maiden."

I shifted uncomfortably as dozens and dozens of gazes landed on me. Then, one by one, as if the faces were dominos stacked side by side, they looked to each other as if seeing neighbors and familiar faces for the first time.

"The gods hear and know all. Even what's not spoken but resides in the heart," the Duke said, and my stomach twisted with unease. "What can any of us expect?" he repeated. "When those the gods have done all to protect, come before us, questioning the Rite?"

I tensed. Immediately, the image of Mr. and Mrs. Tulis formed in my mind. He hadn't said their names, but he might as well have screamed them from the top of Castle Teerman. I didn't see them in the crowd, but that didn't mean they weren't there.

"What can anyone expect when there are those who wish to see us dead?" Teerman asked, raising his hands. "When we are the gods given form and the only thing that stands between you and the Dark One and the curse his people have cast upon this land."

And yet, not a single Ascended—not the Duke or Duchess or any of the Lords or Ladies—had raised one hand to defend the Rise. All of them were faster and stronger than any guard. I imagined they could've taken down double the amount of Craven I had with a bow, and just like Hawke had said, they had a higher likelihood of surviving an attack.

"What do you think would've happened if the Craven had crested the Rise?" Teerman lowered his hands. "Many of you were born within these walls and have never experienced the horror of a Craven attack. Some of you know, though. You come from cities less guarded or were attacked on the roads. You know what would've happened if only a handful made it past our guards—if the gods had turned their backs on the people of Solis. It would've been the wholesale slaughter of hundreds. Your wives. Your children. Yourselves. Many of you would not be standing here." He paused, and the crowd swelled—

It happened again.

I felt my senses stretch out from me, and that wasn't too surprising. With a crowd like this, it was hard to keep myself locked down, but I didn't... I didn't just feel pain.

Something touched the back of my throat, reminding me of what I'd felt in the atrium with Loren.

Terror.

I *felt* terror swelling and rising, coming from so many different directions as my gaze skittered from face to face. Another sensation reached me. It was *hot* and acidic. It wasn't physical pain. It was anger. My heart started thumping. I wasn't feeling pain, but I...I had to be feeling something. It didn't make sense, but I could sense it pressing against my skin like a hot iron. My throat dried as I swallowed hard. People clasped their hands under their chins and prayed to the gods. I took a small step back. Others stared, their expressions hard—

Vikter's hand touch my shoulder as he murmured. "Are you all right?"

Yes?

No?

I wasn't sure.

Anxiety-spiked adrenaline flooded my system as icy ghost fingers danced along the back of my neck. Pressure clamped down on my chest. I wanted to run. I needed to get as far away from people as I could.

But I couldn't.

Closing my eyes, I focused on my breathing as I struggled to rebuild my mental walls. I kept breathing, in and out, as deeply and slowly as I could.

"And, if you're lucky, they'll go for your throat, and it will be a quick death," the Duke was saying. "Most of you will not be so fortunate. They'll tear into your flesh and tissue, feasting on your blood while you scream for the gods you've lost faith in."

"This is perhaps the least calming speech ever given after an attack," Hawke muttered under his breath.

His comment jarred me out of my spiral of panic, the utter dryness of his words cutting the cord that connected me to the people. My senses reeled back, and it was like a door slamming shut, locking.

I felt…I felt nothing but my pounding heart and the sheen of sweat on my forehead. What he had done did more than loosen the hold the public's fear had on me, it not only created a crack in its grip, it obliterated it. The feelings had vanished so quickly that I almost wondered if I had felt them at all. If it had just been my mind playing tricks on me as the faces before me became clear once more, a continuous onslaught of different shades of fear and panic—

My gaze sharpened as I took another look at the crowd, focusing on the faces that showed no emotion. Unnerved by their blank features, a trickle of unease curled its way down my spine. I focused on one of the men. He was younger, blond hair falling to his shoulders. He was too far away to make out his eye color, but he stared up at the Duke and Duchess, lips pressed firmly together, jaw a hard, broad line, while those who stood around him exchanged looks of terror.

I recognized him.

He'd been at the City Council. He'd had that same expression then, and that *thing* had happened—the weird flood of sensations I shouldn't be able to feel.

Or I didn't know I *could*.

I checked out the crowd once more, easily picking up on the ones like him. There were at least a dozen that I could see.

My gaze slid back to the blond man as I thought about what I'd felt when I'd been with Loren. What I'd felt from her made sense now, given what had occurred. She had been excited about the possibility of the Dark One being nearby, as disturbing as that was. And she would have reason to fear that I would say something. This man may not show emotion in his features, but if he hadn't agreed with what was being done to the Tulis family, it would come as no surprise that he'd feel anger now.

Maybe it was all in my head. Perhaps something was happening to my gift. Was it possibly evolving so I could feel other emotions besides pain? I didn't know, and I needed to find out, but I had to say something now just in case.

I turned my head to the right, toward Vikter. "Do you see him?" I whispered, describing the blond man.

"Yes." Vikter stepped closer.

"There are others like him." I faced the audience.

"I see them," he said. "Be alert, Hawke. There—"

"May be trouble?" Hawke cut him off. "I've been tracking the blond for twenty minutes. He's slowly working his way to the front. Three more have also inched closer."

My brows rose. He was so very observant.

"Are we safe?" Tawny asked, keeping her attention focused on the crowd.

"Always," Hawke murmured.

I nodded when her gaze briefly met mine, hoping she was reassured. My hand brushed my thigh. My dagger was sheathed under the white, floor-length tunic. The feel of the bone handle helped to ease whatever panic lingered.

The Duke was still mesmerizing the crowd with tales of gore and horror while I kept my focus on the blond man. He wore a dark cloak over his broad shoulders, and any number of weapons could be hidden underneath.

I knew that from personal experience.

"But we have spoken to the gods on your behalf." The Duchess's voice rang out. "We have told them that the people of Solis, especially those who live in Masadonia, are worthy. They haven't given up on you. We made sure of that."

Cheers rang out, the mood of the crowd shifting rapidly, but the blond man still showed no reaction.

"And we will honor their faith in the people of Solis by not shielding those you suspect of supporting the Dark One, who seek nothing but destruction and death," she said. "You will be rewarded greatly in this life and in the one beyond. That, we can promise you."

There was another round of cheers, and then someone yelled out, "We will honor them during the Rite!"

"We will!" the Duchess cried out, pushing back from the ledge. "What better way to show the gods our gratitude than to celebrate the

Rite?"

His and Her Grace stepped back from the balcony then, side by side, almost touching but not quite as they both lifted their hands on opposite sides of the bodies and began to wave—

"Lies!" a voice shouted from the crowd. It was the blond man. "*Liars.*"

Time seemed to stop. Everyone froze.

"You do nothing to protect us while you hide in your castles, behind your guards! You do nothing but steal children in the name of false gods!" he yelled. "Where are the third and fourth sons and daughters? Where are they really?"

Then there was a sound, a sharp intake of breath that came from everywhere, both inside and outside of me.

The blond man's cloak parted as he yanked out his hand. There was a shout—a scream of warning—from below. A guard astride a horse turned, but he wasn't fast enough. The blond man cocked back his arm and—

"Seize him!" shouted Commander Jansen.

The man threw something. It wasn't a dagger or a rock. It was too oddly shaped for that as it ripped through the air, headed straight toward the Duke of Masadonia. He moved incredibly fast, becoming almost nothing but a blur as Vikter shouldered me back. Hawke's arm folded around my waist, and he hauled me against him as the object flew past us, smacking into the wall. It thumped off the ground, and my gaze lowered to where it came to rest.

It was...it was a hand.

Vikter knelt, picking it up and rising, the line of his mouth tense. "What in the name of the gods?" he muttered.

But it wasn't just any hand. It was the clawed, grayish hand of a Craven.

I looked at the blond man. A Royal Guard had him on his knees, arms twisted behind his back. Blood smeared his mouth.

"From blood and ash," he yelled, even as the guard gripped the back of his head. "We will rise! From blood and ash, we will rise!" Over and over, he screamed the words, as even the guards dragged him through the crowd.

The Duke turned back to the crowd and *laughed*, the sound cold and dry. "And just like that, the gods have revealed at least one of you, haven't they?"

Chapter 19

Hawke quickly ushered Tawny and me back inside the castle, while Vikter moved to talk to the Commander.

"Where in the world did that man get a Craven's hand?" Tawny asked, the skin around her mouth tight as we walked past the Great Hall and under the banners.

"He could've been outside the Rise and cut it off one of those who was killed last night," Hawke answered.

"That's..." Tawny placed her hand to her chest. "I really have no words for that."

Neither did I, but the appendage might have been from a cursed who'd turned inside the Rise. I kept that to myself as we passed several servants. "I can't believe he said what he did about the children—the third and fourth sons and daughters."

"Neither can I," Tawny said.

What a terrible thing to claim. Those children, many who were adults by now, were in the Temples, serving the gods. While I didn't agree with there being no exceptions, insinuating that they were being stolen as if done for nefarious purposes was outrageous. There only needed to be a few words spoken for them to behave like an infection, tainting a person's mind. I didn't even want to imagine what the parents of those children were now thinking.

"I wouldn't be surprised if more people thought along those same lines," Hawke commented, and both Tawny and my heads swiveled in his direction. He walked beside me, only a step behind. He raised his brows. "None of those children have been seen."

"They've been seen by the Priests and Priestesses and the Ascended," Tawny corrected.

"But not by family." His gaze flickered over the statues as we headed toward the stairs. "Perhaps if people could see their children every so often, beliefs like that could easily be dismissed. Fears allayed."

He had a point, but...

"No one should make claims like that without any evidence," I argued. "All it does is cause unnecessary worry and panic—panic that the Descenters have created and then will exploit."

"Agreed." He glanced down. "Watch your step. Wouldn't want you to continue with your new habit, Princess."

"Tripping once isn't a habit," I shot back. "And if you agree, then why would you say you wouldn't be surprised if more felt the same way?"

"Because agreeing doesn't mean I don't understand why some would think that," he answered, and I snapped my mouth shut. "If the Ascended are truly concerned about those claims being believed, all they need to do is allow the children to be seen. I can't imagine that would interfere too badly with their servitude to the gods."

No.

I didn't think that would.

Glancing at Tawny, I saw her staring at Hawke as we strode down the second-floor hall, headed toward the older portion of the castle. "What do you think?" I asked.

Tawny blinked as she looked over at me. "I think you are both saying the same thing."

A half-grin formed on Hawke's face, and I didn't say anything as we climbed up the staircase. Hawke stopped us near Tawny's door. "If you don't mind, I need to speak to Penellaphe in private for a moment."

My brows lifted behind the veil while Tawny sent a poorly concealed glance between us as the corners of her lips tilted up. She then waited for me to signal whether it was fine or not.

"It's fine," I told her.

Tawny nodded and then opened her door, stopping long enough to say, "If you need me, knock." She paused. "*Princess.*"

I groaned.

Hawke chuckled. "I really do like her."

"I'm sure she'd love to hear that."

"Would you love to hear that I really like you?" he asked.

My heart skipped a beat, but I ignored the stupid organ. "Would you be sad if I said no?"

"I'd be devastated."

I snorted. "I'm sure." We reached my door. "What did you need to talk about?"

He motioned to the room, and figuring what he had to say was something he didn't want overheard, I went to open the door—

"I should enter first, Princess." He easily side-stepped me.

"Why?" I frowned at his back. "Do you think someone could be waiting for me?"

"If the Dark One came for you once, he'll come for you again."

A chill danced down my spine as Hawke entered the room. Two oil lamps had been left burning by the door and bed, and wood had been added to the fireplace, casting the room in a soft, warm glow. I didn't stare too long at the bed, which meant that I somehow ended up staring at Hawke's broad back as he scanned the room. The edges of his hair brushed the collar of his tunic, and those strands looked so...soft. I hadn't touched them that night at the Red Pearl, and I wished I had.

I needed help.

"Is it okay for me to enter?" I asked, clasping my hands together. "Or should I wait out here while you inspect under the bed for stray dust bunnies?"

Hawke looked over his shoulder. "It's not dust bunnies I'm worried about. Steps, on the other hand? Yes."

"Oh, my gods—"

"And the Dark One will keep coming until he has what he wants," he said, looking away. I shivered. "Your room should always be checked before you enter it."

I folded my arms over my chest, chilled despite the fire. I watched as he circled back to the door, quietly closing it.

Hawke faced me, one hand on the hilt of a short sword, and the flipping in my chest doubled. His face was so strikingly pieced together. From the wide set of his lips, the upward slant of his eyebrows, to the shadowy hollows under his high, broad cheekbones, he could've been the muse for the paintings that hung in the city's Atheneum.

"Are you all right?" Hawke asked.

"Yes. Why do you ask?"

"Something appeared to happen to you as the Duke addressed the people."

I made a mental note to remember exactly how observant Hawke was. "I was…" I started to say that I'd been fine, but I knew he wouldn't believe that. "I got a little dizzy. I guess I haven't eaten enough today."

His intense gaze tracked over what he could see of my face, and even with the veil, I felt unbearably exposed when he looked at me like he did then. "I hate this."

"Hate what?" I asked, confused.

Hawke didn't respond immediately. "I hate talking to the veil."

"Oh." Understanding rippled through me as I reached up and touched the length that hid my hair. "I imagine most people don't enjoy it."

"I can't imagine *you* do."

"I don't," I admitted and then glanced around the room as if I expected Priestess Analia to be hiding somewhere. "I mean, I'd prefer if people were able to see me."

He tilted his head to the side. "What does it feel like?"

Air hitched in my throat. No one…no one had ever asked me that before, and while I had a lot of thoughts and feelings about the veil, I wasn't sure how to put them into words even though I trusted Hawke.

Some things, once spoken, were given a life of their own.

I walked to one of the chairs and sat on the edge as I tried to figure out what to say. Suddenly, my brain sort of spit out the only thing that came to mind. "It feels suffocating."

Hawke drew closer. "Then why do you wear it?"

"I didn't realize I had a choice." I looked up at him.

"You have a choice now." He knelt in front of me. "It's just you and me, walls, and a pathetically inadequate supply of furniture."

My lips twitched.

"Do you wear your veil when you're with Tawny?" he asked.

I shook my head no.

"Then why are you wearing it now?"

"Because…I'm allowed to be without my veil with her."

"I was told that you were supposed to be veiled at all times, even with those approved to see you."

He was, of course, correct.

Hawke arched a brow.

I sighed. "I don't wear my veil when I'm in my room, and I don't expect anyone to come in other than Tawny. And I don't wear it then because I feel…more in control. I can make—"

"The choice not to wear it?" he finished for me.

Nodding, I was more than a little stunned that he'd nailed it.

"You have a choice now."

"I do." But it was hard to explain that the veil also served as a barrier. With it, I remembered what I was, and the importance of that. Without it, well, it was easy to want…to simply *want*.

His gaze searched the veil, and a long moment passed. He then nodded and rose slowly. "I'll be outside if you need anything."

A strange lump formed in my throat, making it impossible for me to speak. I remained where I was as he left the room, staring at the closed door once he was gone. I didn't move. I didn't remove the veil. Not for a long time.

Not until I no longer *wanted*.

The following evening, I stood outside the Duchess's receiving room on the second floor. It was at the opposite end of the hall from the Duke's, and I kept my back to his room. I didn't want to see it, let alone think about it.

Two Royal Guards stood outside Jacinda's room while Vikter waited beside me. I'd told him that morning what had really happened during the Duchess's and Duke's address to the people, and how I wasn't sure if I had actually felt something or not. He suggested that I speak with the Duchess, since the Priestess was unlikely to give me any useful information, and the Duchess, depending on her mood, was more likely to speak openly.

I just hoped she was in a talkative mood.

Neither Vikter nor I spoke in the presence of the other Royal Guards, but I knew he was concerned over what I shared. About what it could mean if it was my gift evolving, or if it was my mind.

"*It could just be the stress of everything that has happened,*" he'd said. "*It may be better to wait until you're sure it is your gift before alerting anyone.*"

I knew Vikter worried that if it was my mind, that it would somehow be held against me, but I didn't want to wait until it happened again. I'd rather know now if it was my gift or not so I could react better.

The door opened, and one of the Royal Guards stepped out. "Her Grace will see you now."

Vikter remained outside as planned since knowledge of my gift was supposed to be limited to the Duke and Duchess and the Temple clergy.

I broke so many rules, it was no wonder that Hawke had seemed surprised when I wouldn't remove my veil the night before. That's what I was thinking as I walked into the receiving room. I filed those thoughts away as I looked around.

I'd always liked this room with its ivory walls and light gray furnishings. There was something peaceful about it, and it was also warm and inviting despite there being no windows. It had to be all the dazzling chandeliers. My gaze found the Duchess seated at a small, circular table where she was drinking from a small cup. Garbed in a gown of the palest yellow, she reminded me of spring in the capital.

She looked up, a slight smile on her ageless face. "Come. Have a seat."

Walking forward, I took the chair across from her, noting the plate of pastries. All that was left were the items with nuts. The chocolate scones were probably the first to be devoured. The Duchess had the same weakness as Vikter.

"You wished to speak with me?" She placed the delicate, flowery cup on its matching saucer.

I nodded. "Yes. I know you're very busy, but I was hoping that you'd be able to help me with something."

Her head inclined, sending soft, russet-colored waves tumbling over her shoulder. "I must admit, you have me curious. I cannot remember the last time you came to me for assistance."

I could. It was when I'd asked for my chambers to be moved to the older part of the castle, something I was sure she still didn't quite understand. "I wanted to talk to you…" I drew in a deep breath. "I wanted to talk to you about my gift."

There was a slight widening of her pitch-black eyes. "I was not expecting that to be a topic. Has someone discovered your gift?"

"No, Your Grace. That's not at all what has happened."

Picking up the napkin from her lap, she wiped her fingers. "What, then? Please, do not keep me in suspense."

"I think something is happening with it," I told her. "There have been a few situations where I…I believe I felt something other than pain."

Slowly, she placed the napkin on the table. "You were using your gift? You know the gods have forbidden you to do so. Not until you have been found worthy of such a gift are you to use it."

"I know. I haven't," I lied easily. Probably a little too easily. "But, sometimes, it just happens. When I'm in a large crowd, I have trouble controlling it."

"Has this been discussed with the Priestess?"

Good gods, no. "It doesn't happen often. I swear, and it has only happened recently. I will double my efforts to control it, but when it happened earlier, I think I…I think I felt something other than pain."

The Duchess stared at me, unblinking for what felt like a small eternity, and then she rose from her seat. A little unnerved, I watched her go to the white cabinet against the wall. "What do you think you felt?"

"Anger," I answered. "During the City Council and last night, I felt anger." I wouldn't speak of Loren. I wouldn't do that to her. "It was that man who…"

"The Descenter?"

"Yes. At least, I think so," I amended. "I think I was feeling anger from him."

She poured a drink from a decanter. "Have you felt anything else that seems abnormal to you?"

"I…I think I've felt fear, too. When the Duke was speaking about the Craven attack. Terror is very similar to pain, but it feels different, and I thought that I might've felt something like…I don't know. Excitement? Or anticipation." I frowned. "Those two things are kind of the same thing, I suppose. In a way, at—"

"Do you feel anything now?" She turned to me, a glass of what I thought might be sherry in her hand.

I blinked from behind the veil. "You want me to use my gift on you?"

She nodded.

"I thought—"

"It doesn't matter what you thought," she interrupted, and I stiffened. "I want you to use your gift now and tell me what, if anything, you feel."

Despite finding her request more than strange, I did what she requested. I opened my senses, felt the cord stretch out between us, and...and connect with *nothing* but vast emptiness. A shiver danced over my skin.

"Do you feel anything, Penellaphe?"

Closing down the connection, I shook my head. "I don't feel anything, Your Grace."

The Duchess exhaled sharply through her nostrils, and then she downed her drink in one impressive gulp.

My eyes widened as my mind rapidly processed her reaction. It was almost as if she...expected me to feel something from her, but I'd never been able to. I didn't think I ever *would* be able to.

"Good," she breathed, her skirts swishing around her ankles as she turned back to the cabinet, placing the glass down.

"I was wondering if I was truly feeling something or..." I trailed off as she faced me.

"I believe your gift is...maturing," she said, coming toward me. The bright light above her glittered off the obsidian ring on her finger as she gripped the back of the chair. "It would make sense that it would be happening as you're nearing your Ascension."

"So this...is normal?"

She clucked her tongue off the roof of her mouth. For a moment, it appeared as if she were about to say something, but then she changed her mind. "Yes, I do believe so, but I...I would not speak to His Grace about this."

Tension crept into my shoulders at the thinly veiled warning. I was never sure if the Duchess knew about her husband's...predilections. I couldn't imagine how she could be completely blind to them, but there was a part of me that hoped she was. Because if she knew and did nothing to stop him, did it make her any better? Or was I even being fair to her? Just because she was an Ascended didn't mean she held power over her husband.

"It would…remind him of the first Maiden," she whispered.

Shocked, I stared up at her. I had not been expecting her to bring up the first Maiden, the one before me—the only other Maiden I knew of. "Did this…happen with the previous Maiden?"

"It did." Her knuckles started to turn white, and I nodded. There had only been two Maidens Chosen by the gods. "What do you know about the first Maiden?"

"Nothing," I admitted. "I don't know her name or even when she lived." Or what happened to her upon her Ascension.

Or why it mattered whether or not my developing gift reminded the Duke of her.

"There is a reason for that."

There was? Priestess Analia had never told me anything. She ignored any questions about her or my Ascension.

"We do not speak of the first Maiden, Penellaphe," she said. "It's not that we simply choose not to. It is that we cannot."

"The gods…forbade it?" I suspected.

She nodded as her stare seemed to penetrate my veil. "I will break the rule just once and pray that the gods forgive me, but I will tell you this in hopes that your future does not end the same as the first Maiden's did."

I had a really bad feeling about where this was going.

"We do not speak of her. Ever. Her name is not worthy of our lips nor the air we breathe. If it were possible, I'd have her name and her history scrubbed in its entirety." The chair cracked under Duchess Teerman's hand, startling me.

My heart nearly stopped in my chest. "Was she…found unworthy by the gods?"

"By some small miracle, she wasn't, but that doesn't mean she was worthy."

If she hadn't been found unworthy, then why was she never spoken about? Surely, she couldn't have been *that* bad if she hadn't been found unworthy.

"In the end, her worthiness didn't matter." Duchess Teerman lifted her fingers. The chair was warped, splintered. "Her actions put her on a path that ended with her death. The Dark One killed her."

Chapter 20

"'*After years of destruction that had decimated entire cities, leaving countrysides and villages in ruins, and ending hundreds of thousands of lives, the world was on the brink of chaos when, on the eve of the Battle of Broken Bones, Jalara Solis of Vodina Isles gathered his forces outside the city of Pompay, the last Atlantian stronghold.*'" I cleared my throat, wildly uncomfortable. Not only was that the longest sentence in the history of man, I always hated reading out loud, but especially when I had Hawke as an audience. I hadn't looked at him since I'd started reading. Still, I was almost positive that he was doing everything in his power to remain alert and not be bored into falling asleep while standing. "'*Which sat at the foot of the Skotos Mountains—*'"

"Skotos," Priestess Analia interrupted. "It's pronounced like Sko*tis*. You know how it's pronounced, Maiden. Do so correctly."

My fingers tightened around the leather binding. *The History of The War of Two Kings and the Kingdom of Solis* was well over a thousand pages, and every week, I was forced to read several chapters during my sessions with the Priestess. I'd probably read the entire tome aloud over a dozen times, and I swore that each time, the Priestess changed the way *Skotos* was pronounced.

I didn't say that. Instead, I took a deep, long breath and tried to ignore the almost overwhelming urge to throw the book at her face. It would do some damage. Probably break her nose. The image of her clasping her bloodied face brought forth a disturbing amount of glee.

I smothered a yawn as I concentrated on the text. Having been up most of the night thinking about what the Duchess had told me, I'd gotten little sleep.

And like I'd told Vikter, I'd gotten few answers. But it had been a relief to learn that what was happening wasn't something that my mind was conjuring up. My abilities were maturing, whatever that meant. The Duchess hadn't wanted to discuss it further. So, while I knew that what was happening was somewhat normal, I was also left with the knowledge that the first Maiden had done something that had put her on a path to interact with the Dark One, who'd killed her.

That wasn't exactly reassuring.

Neither was the knowledge that the first Maiden was somehow connected to the Duke. Was that why he treated me as he did? Perhaps it had nothing to do with my mother.

I drew in a shallow breath. "'*Which sat at the foot of the Skotis Mountains*—'"

"It's actually pronounced Skotos," came the interruption from the corner of the room.

My eyes widened behind the veil as I looked over to Hawke. His face was all but devoid of expression. I glanced at the Priestess, who sat across from me on an equally hard, cushion-less wooden stool.

I had no idea how old the Priestess was. Her face was bare of makeup and smooth, but I thought that she might be at the end of her third decade of life. There were no gray strands in her brown hair that was sharply pulled back and held in a bun at the nape of her neck, causing her face to remind me of the hawks that I sometimes saw perched up high in the Queen's Gardens. A shapeless red gown covered her from just under her neck, leaving only her hands visible.

I'd never seen the woman smile.

And she was definitely not smiling now as she looked over her shoulder at Hawke. "And how would you know?" Derision dripped from her tone like acid.

"My family originates from the farmlands not too far from Pompay, before the area was destroyed and became the Wastelands we know today," he explained. "My family and others from that area have always pronounced the mountain range as the Maiden first said." He paused. "The language and accent of those from the far west can be difficult…for some to master. The Maiden, however, appears to not fall into that group."

I was confident that my eyes were about to pop out of my face in response to the obvious insult. I bit down on my lip to stop myself from grinning.

Priestess Analia's already stiff shoulders jerked back as she stared at Hawke. I could practically see the steam coming out of her ears. "I did not realize I asked for your thoughts," she spoke, tone as withering as her stare.

"My apologies." He bowed his head in submission, but it was the poorest attempt at it because his amber eyes all but danced with amusement.

She nodded. "Apology—"

"I just didn't want the Maiden to sound uneducated if any discussion were to arise about the Skotos Mountains," he tacked on.

Oh, my gods…

"But I will remain quiet from here on out," Hawke said. "Please, continue, Maiden. You have such a lovely reading voice that even I find myself enthralled with the history of Solis."

I wanted to laugh. It was building in my throat, threatening to burst free, but I couldn't let it. My grip loosened on the edges of the book. "*Which sat at the foot of the Skotos Mountains, the gods had finally chosen a side.*" When the Priestess said nothing, I continued. "*Nyktos, the King of the gods, and his son Theon, the God of War, appeared before Jalara and his army. Having grown distrustful of the Atlantian people and their unnatural thirst for blood and power, they sought to aid in ending the cruelty and oppression that had reaped these lands under the rule of Atlantia.*" I took a breath.

"*Jalara Solis and his army were brave, but Nyktos, in his wisdom, saw that they could not defeat the Atlantians, who had risen to godlike strength through the bloodletting of innocents—*"

"They killed hundreds of thousands over the time of their reign. Bloodletting is a gentle description of what they actually did. They *bit* people," Priestess Analia elaborated, and when I looked up at her, there was a strange gleam to her dark brown eyes. "Drank their blood and became drunk with power—with strength and near immortality. And those they didn't kill became the pestilence we now know as the Craven. That is who our beloved King and Queen bravely took a stance against and were prepared to die to overthrow."

I nodded.

Her fingers were turning pink from how tightly she'd balled her hands where they rested in her lap. "Continue."

I didn't dare look at Hawke. "'*Unwilling to see the failure of Jalara of Vodina Isles, Nyktos gave the gods' first Blessing, sharing with Jalara and his army the blood of the gods.*" I shuddered. That was also another gentle term for drinking the blood of the gods. "*Emboldened with the strength and power, Jalara Of Vodina Isles and his army were able to defeat the Atlantians during the Battle of Broken Bones, therefore ending the reign of the corrupt and wretched kingdom.*'"

I started to turn the page, knowing the next chapter dealt with the Ascension of the Queen and the building of the first Rise.

"Why?" the Priestess demanded.

Confused, I looked over at her. "Why, what?"

"Why did you just shudder when you read the part about the Blessing?"

I hadn't realized my action had been so noticeable. "I…" I didn't know what to say that wouldn't irritate the Priestess and end with her running back to the Duke.

"You seemed disturbed," she pointed out, her tone softening. I knew better than to trust that. "What is it about the Blessing that would affect you so?"

"I'm not disturbed. The Blessing is an honor—"

"But you shuddered," she persisted. "Unless you find the act of the Blessing pleasurable, am I not to assume that it disturbs you?"

Pleasurable? My face flamed red-hot, and I was grateful for the veil. "It's just that…the Blessing seems to be similar to how the Atlantians became so powerful. They drank the blood of the innocent, and the Ascended drink the blood of the gods—"

"How dare you compare the Ascension to what the Atlantians have done?" The Priestess moved quickly, leaning forward and gripping my chin between her fingers. "It is not the same thing. Perhaps you've grown fond of the cane, and you purposely strive to disappoint not only me but also the Duke."

The moment her skin touched mine, I locked down my senses. I didn't want to know if she felt pain or anything else.

"I didn't say that it was," I said, seeing Hawke step forward. I swallowed. "Just that it reminded me of—"

"The fact that you think of those two things in the same thought greatly concerns me, Maiden. The Atlantians took what was not given. During the Ascension, the blood is offered freely by the gods." Her grip tightened, bordering on painful, and my gift stretched against my skin, almost as if it wanted to be used. "That is not something that I should have to explain to the future of the kingdom, to the legacy of the Ascended."

For as long as I could remember, everyone said that—even Vikter—and it grated on my nerves and sat like a boulder on my shoulders. "The future of the entire kingdom rests on me being given to the gods upon my nineteenth birthday?"

Her already thin lips became almost non-existent.

"What would happen if I didn't Ascend?" I demanded, thinking of the first Maiden. It hadn't sounded like she'd Ascended, and everyone was still here. "How would that stop the others from Ascending? Would the gods refuse to give their blood so freely—"

I sucked in a sharp gasp as the Priestess cocked her hand back. It wouldn't be the first time she had smacked me, but this time, the stinging blow didn't land.

Hawke had moved so fast that I hadn't seen him leave the corner. But now, he had the Priestess's wrist in his grasp. "Remove your fingers from the Maiden's chin. Now."

Priestess Analia's eyes had grown wide as she stared up at Hawke. "How dare you touch me?"

"How dare you lay a single finger on the Maiden?" His jaw flexed as he glared down at the woman. "Perhaps I was not clear enough for you. Remove your hand from the Maiden, or I will act upon your attempt to harm her. And I can assure you, me touching you will be the least of your concerns."

I might've stopped breathing as I watched them. No one had ever intervened during one of the Priestess's tirades. Tawny couldn't. If she did, she would face worse, and I'd never expect nor want that. Rylan had often turned in the other direction, as did Hannes. Even Vikter had never been so bold. He'd usually find a way to interrupt, to stop the situation from escalating. But I'd been slapped on more than one occasion in front of him, and there was nothing he could do.

But Hawke now stood between us, clearly prepared to follow through on his threat. And while I knew I would most likely pay for this later, as would he, I wanted to jump up and hug him. Not because he had protected me—I'd been slapped harder by stray branches while walking through Wisher's Grove. There was a far pettier reason. Seeing the Priestess's usual smugness vanish under the weight of shock and witnessing the way her mouth hung open and how her cheeks mottled with red was almost as satisfying as throwing the book in her face.

Vibrating with rage, she let go of my chin, and I leaned back. Hawke released her wrist, but he remained there. Her chest rose and fell under the gown as she placed both hands flat on her legs.

She turned her head to me. "The mere fact that you would even speak such a thing shows that you have no respect for the honor bestowed upon you. But when you go to the gods, you'll be treated with as much respect as you have shown today."

"What does that mean?" I asked.

"This session is over," she answered instead, rising from her seat. "I have too much to do with the Rite only two days away. I have no time to spend with someone as unworthy as you."

I saw Hawke's eyes narrow, and I stood, placing the book on the stool as I spoke before Hawke could. "I'm ready to return to my chambers," I said to him and then nodded at the Priestess. "Good day."

She didn't respond, and I started for the door, relieved when Hawke fell into step behind me. I waited until we were halfway across the banquet hall before speaking.

"You shouldn't have done that," I told him.

"I should've allowed her to hit you? In what world would that have been acceptable?"

"In a world where you end up punished for something that wouldn't even have hurt."

"I don't care if she hits like a baby mouse, this world is fucked up if anyone finds that acceptable."

Eyes widening, I stopped and looked at him. His eyes were like shards of amber, his jaw just as hard. "Is it worth losing your position over and being ostracized for?"

He glared down at me. "If you even have to ask that question, then you don't know me at all."

"I hardly know you at all," I whispered, irritated by the sting his words left behind.

"Well, now you know that I will never stand by and watch someone hit you or any person for no reason other than they feel they can," he shot back.

I started to tell him that he was being ridiculous and was missing the point, but he wasn't being ridiculous. This world we lived in *was* messed up, and the gods knew that wasn't the first time I'd thought that. But it had never hit me with such clarity before.

Silent, I turned from him and started walking. He was right beside me. Several moments passed. "It's not like I'm okay with how she treats me. It took everything in me not to throw the book at her."

"I wish you had."

I almost laughed. "If I had, she would've reported me. She'll probably report you."

"To the Duke? Let her." He shrugged. "I can't imagine that he's okay with her striking the Maiden."

I snorted. "You don't know the Duke."

"What do you mean?"

"He would probably applaud her," I said. "They share a lack of control when it comes to their tempers."

"He's hit you," Hawke stated. "Is that what she meant when she said that you'd grown fond of the cane?" He grabbed my arm, turning me to face him. "Has he used a cane on you?"

The disbelief and anger filling those golden eyes sent a wave of nausea through me. Oh, gods. Realizing what I'd basically just admitted, I felt the blood drain from my face and then rapidly flood back in. I pulled at my arm, and he let go. "I didn't say that."

He was staring straight ahead, his jaw flexing. "What were you saying?"

"J-just that the Duke is more likely to punish you than he is the Priestess. I have no idea what she meant by the cane," I continued in a rush. "She sometimes says things that make no sense."

Hawke glanced down at me, his lashes lowered. "I must've misread what you said then."

I nodded, relieved. "Yes. I just don't want you to get into trouble."

"And what about you?"

"I'll be fine," I was quick to say as I started walking again, aware of the darting glances passing servants sent our way. "The Duke will just...give me a lecture, make it a lesson, but you would face—"

"I'll face nothing," he said, and I wasn't so sure about that. "Is she always like that?"

I sighed. "Yes."

"The Priestess seems like a…" He paused, and I glanced over at him. His lips were pursed. "A bitch. I don't say that often, but I say it now. Proudly."

Nearly choking on my laugh, I looked away. "She…she is something, and she's always disappointed in my…commitment to being the Maiden."

"Exactly how are you supposed to prove you are?" he asked. "Better yet, what are you supposed to be committed to?"

I almost jumped on him in that moment and wrapped my arms around him. I didn't, because it would be grossly inappropriate. Instead, I gave him a sedate nod. "I'm not quite sure. It's not like I'm trying to run away or escape my Ascension."

"Would you?"

"Funny question," I muttered, my heart still thumping from what I'd almost exposed.

"It was a serious one."

My heart lurched in my chest as I stopped in the narrow, short hall and approached one of the windows that faced the courtyard. I stared up at Hawke, and everything about him said that it was, in fact, a genuine inquiry. "I can't believe you'd ask that."

"Why?" He came to stand behind me.

"Because I couldn't do that," I told him. "I wouldn't."

"It seems to me that this *honor* that has been bestowed upon you comes with very few benefits. You're not allowed to show your face or travel anywhere outside the castle grounds. You didn't even seem all that surprised when the Priestess moved to strike you. That leads me to believe it's something fairly common," he said, his brows dark slashes above his eyes. "You are not allowed to speak to most, and you are not to be spoken to. You're caged in your room most of the day, your freedom restricted. All the rights others have are privileges for you, rewards that seem impossible for you to earn."

I opened my mouth, but I didn't know what to say. He'd pointed out all that I didn't have, and made it so painfully clear. I looked away.

"So, I wouldn't be surprised if you did try to escape this *honor*," he finished.

"Would you stop me if I did?" I asked.

"Would Vikter?"

I frowned, not even sure I wanted to know why he'd asked that, but I answered honestly anyway. "I know Vikter cares about me. He's like…he's like I imagine my father would have been if he were still alive. And I'm like Vikter's daughter, who never got to take a breath. But he would stop me."

Hawke said nothing.

"So, would you?" I repeated.

"I think I would be too curious to find out exactly how you planned to escape to stop you."

I coughed out a short laugh. "You know, I actually believe that."

"Will she report you to the Duke?" he asked after a moment.

Pressure settled on my chest as I looked at him. He was staring out the window. "Why would you ask?"

"Will she?" he asked instead.

"Probably not," I said, lying all too easily. The Priestess probably went straight to the Duke. "She's too busy with the Rite. Everyone is." As the Duke would be, so I might get lucky and at least have a delay between now and when I would inevitably be summoned. Hopefully, that meant that Hawke would also get lucky. If he were removed from his post, it was unlikely that I would ever see him again.

The sadness that thought brought forth meant that it was far past time to change the subject. "I've never been to a Rite."

"And you've never snuck into one?"

I dipped my chin. "I'm offended that you'd even suggest such a thing."

He chuckled. "How bizarre that I could think that you, who has a history of misbehaving, would do such a thing."

I grinned at that.

"You haven't missed much, to be honest. There's a lot of talking, a bunch of tears, and too much drinking." His gaze slid to mine. "It's after the Rite where things can get...interesting. You know how it is."

"I don't know," I reminded him, even though I had an idea of what he spoke of. Tawny had told me that once the ritual of the Rite was completed, and the Mistresses and stewards took the new Ladies and Lords in Wait, and the Priests left with the third daughters and sons, the celebration changed. It became more...frantic and raw. Or at least that was what I'd interpreted from Tawny, but it seemed too bizarre to imagine the Ascended being involved in anything like that. They were always so...cold.

"But you know how easy it is to be yourself when you wear a mask." His voice was low as his gaze held mine. "How anything you want becomes achievable when you can pretend that no one knows who you are."

Warmth infused my cheeks. Yes, I did know that, and how *kind* of him to remind me. "You shouldn't bring that up."

His head tilted. "No one is close enough to overhear."

"That doesn't matter. You...we shouldn't talk about that."

"Ever?"

I started to say yes, but something stopped me. I pulled my gaze from his. Outside the window, the violet-hued butterfly bushes stirred softly in the breeze.

Hawke was quiet for several moments before asking, "Would you like to go back to your room?" he asked.

I shook my head. "Not particularly."

"Would you like to go out there instead?"

"You think it would be safe?"

"Between you and me, I would think so."

The corners of my lips lifted. I liked that he'd included me, acknowledging that I could hold my own. "I used to love the courtyard. It was the one place where, I don't know, my mind was quiet, and I could just be. I didn't think or worry...about anything. I found it so very peaceful."

"But not anymore?"

"No," I whispered. "Not anymore. It's strange how no one speaks of Rylan or Malessa. It's almost as if they never existed."

"Sometimes remembering those who died means facing your own mortality," he said.

"Do you think the Ascended are uncomfortable with the idea of death?"

"Even them," he answered. "They may be godlike, but they can be killed. They can die."

Neither of us spoke for several minutes as servants and others passed behind us. Several Ladies in Wait had stopped and pretended to take in the view of the garden while talking about the Rite, but I knew they were lingering near where we stood not because of the stunning flowers and lush greenery or because it was so rare for me to be seen, but because of the beautiful man who stood beside me. He seemed unaware of them, and even though I kept my gaze forward, I could feel his stare every couple of moments. Eventually, one of the Mistresses came along, shooing the Ladies away, and we were left alone once more.

"Are you excited about attending the Rite?"

"I am curious," I admitted. The Rite was only two days away.

"I'm curious to see you."

My lips parted on a soft inhale. I didn't dare look at him. If I did, I feared I'd do something incredibly stupid. Something that the first Maiden could've done that had made the Duchess feel that she was unworthy.

"You'll be unveiled."

"Yes." I also wouldn't be expected to wear the color white. It would almost be like going to the Red Pearl because I would be able to blend in, and no one would know who I was—*what* I was. "But I will be masked."

"I prefer that version of you," he said.

"The masked version of myself?" I asked, guessing that he was thinking of our time at the Red Pearl.

"Honest?" His voice sounded closer, and when I took another deep breath, the scent of leather and pine surrounded me. "I prefer the version of you that wears no mask or veil."

I opened my mouth, but as was becoming commonplace where Hawke was concerned, I didn't know what to say. It felt like I should discourage such statements, but those words wouldn't come to the surface either, just as they hadn't before.

So, I did the only thing I could think of. I changed the subject. "I remember you said your father was a farmer." I cleared my throat. "Do you have any other siblings? Any Lords in Wait in the family? A sister? Or..." I rambled on. "There's only Ian for me—I mean, I only have one brother. I'm excited to see him again. I miss him."

Hawke was quiet for so long that I had to look to make sure he was still there and still breathing. He was. He stared down at me, his amber eyes cool. "I had a brother."

"Had?" My senses stretched out, and I didn't even have a chance to control them. I opened myself up, and I locked my legs to stop myself from taking a step back. I didn't feel anything strange, but I felt Hawke's anguish, the bitterly cold pain that pelted my skin. It was sharper. This was where his pain stemmed from.

He'd lost a brother.

I reacted without thought to what he would think or to the fact that we were not alone. It was an uncontrollable urge, as if the gift itself had a hold of me.

I touched just his hand with mine and squeezed it in hopes that it would be construed as a gesture of sympathy. "I'm sorry," I said, and I thought of warm beaches and salty air. Those thoughts quickly changed to how I'd felt when Hawke had kissed me.

The taut lines of Hawke's expression smoothed out as he stared out the window. He blinked, not once but twice.

Lifting my fingers from his, I clasped my hands together, hoping that he hadn't realized that I'd done something. He stood there, though, as if he'd been struck immobile. I lifted my brows. "Are you okay?"

He blinked again. This time, he laughed softly. "Yes. It's...I just had the strangest feeling."

"Is that so?" I watched him closely.

Hawke nodded as he rubbed the palm of his hand over his chest. "I don't even know how to explain it."

Now I was starting to worry that I'd somehow done something other than relieve his pain. What, I wasn't sure, but if my gifts were evolving, anything was possible. I reached out with my senses once more, and all I felt in return was warmth. "Is it a bad feeling? Should we find a Healer?"

"No. Not at all." Hawke's laugh was stronger then, less uncertain. His eyes, now a warm honey, met mine. "My brother is not dead, by the way. So, no need for sympathy."

Now it was my turn to blink repeatedly. "Oh? I just thought..." I trailed off.

"Are you sure you wouldn't like to visit the garden?"

Thinking it was far past time for me to lock myself away before I did yet another reckless thing, I shook my head. "I think I would like to go back to my room now."

He hesitated for a moment but then nodded. Neither of us spoke as we made our way. Apparently, Hawke was trying to figure out why he felt...happier, lighter. And I was left wondering what exactly had happened to his brother to cause that kind of reaction, especially if his brother was still alive.

Chapter 21

It took less than twenty-four hours for me to, yet again, do something utterly reckless. This time, however, I may end up regretting it. Of all the ways I'd thought I might die, it had never occurred to me that it could happen while *borrowing* a book from the Atheneum.

There were far more dangerous things I'd done in my eighteen years of life, times where I would've been more likely to die in the process. Utter heaps of examples where even I had been a bit surprised that I'd walked away with my limbs and life intact. But here I was, one wrong step away from plummeting to my death, clutching the supposed diary of one Miss Willa Colyns, the book that Loren and Dafina had been talking about. Obviously, the book would most definitely be the type of reading material Priestess Analia would expressly forbid. And if I were caught with it in my possession, it would be yet another reason for her to believe that I wasn't respectful of my duty as the Maiden.

So, of course, I *had* to read it. I'd been so very bored all day.

I'd already read every book Tawny had snuck me at least three times, and I couldn't bring myself to read another too-familiar page even one more time. She had yet again been commandeered by the Duchess and the Mistresses, and I knew I might not even see her the following morning. So, I had another day of staring—uninterrupted except for my training with Vikter—at four stone walls. And the longer I stayed in my room with nothing to occupy my mind, the more I thought about what Hawke had said about all the rights that had been stripped away from me.

It wasn't like I didn't already know that, but it wasn't something that others appeared to even acknowledge. Maybe it was because they were with me constantly, so everything had become the norm. But to Hawke, who was new, none of this was normal.

And that was what led me to travel unaccompanied through Wisher's Grove to the Atheneum while Hawke stood outside my chamber door, thinking I was inside. Vikter was...well, I had no idea where he was. I had a feeling based on how tired and sad his eyes had looked this morning, that he'd been called upon the night before to take care of one of the cursed and hadn't invited me.

I also had a feeling that he wasn't going to involve me going forward, which irritated me. Of course, I planned to discuss that with him the first chance I got. I wouldn't be cut out when I could help people. And he would just have to deal with it.

But right now, I needed to focus on not dying, or worse yet, getting caught.

Cold night air whipped around me as I stood plastered against the stone wall, praying to any god that the foot-wide ledge I stood on wouldn't cave under my weight. I doubted when it was built that they had taken into consideration that, at some point, an entirely stupid Maiden would find herself standing on it.

How had this gone so terribly wrong?

Sneaking into the Atheneum hadn't been hard. With my shapeless black cloak, my trusty mask in place, and my face hidden under the hood, I doubted anyone on the streets of Masadonia had been able to tell if I was male or female, let alone the Maiden as I hurried down the alley toward the back entrance of the library. Moving along the grid of narrow halls and staircases without being seen was easy, too.

I knew how to be like a ghost when needed, quiet and still.

The problem started when I found the leather-bound journal of Miss Colyns. Instead of leaving and going back to the castle like I knew I should, I'd ducked inside an empty room.

I just...I had been going stir-crazy in that room and had dreaded going back. And the thickly cushioned settees called to me. The stocked liquor cabinet, something I found odd to discover in a library, confused me, however. But I'd sat by the large windows overlooking the city below and cracked open the worn book. My cheeks had been scalded by the end of the first page, having discovered what occurs when someone kisses one not on the mouth or on the breast like…like Hawke had done before he knew who I was, but some place *far* more intimate.

I couldn't stop reading, practically devouring the cream-hued pages.

Miss Willa Colyns lived a very…interesting life with many, many other…fascinating people. I had gotten to the part where she spoke of her brief fling with the King, which I could not even begin to picture, nor did I *want* to, when I heard voices outside the room—one in particular I'd never thought to hear in the Atheneum.

The Duke's.

Hearing his voice meant that I'd been so caught up in the diary, I hadn't even realized the sun had set.

I hadn't been summoned to meet with him the night before or today. With the preparations for the Rite, I'd been given a temporary reprieve, and I assumed Hawke had as well since he was still my guard. But that reprieve would come to a swift end if the Duke discovered me.

Which was why I was now perched on a ledge outside what turned out to be the Duke's personal room in the Atheneum. The only grace I'd been given was that the window I'd climbed out of wasn't the one facing the street but rather the one blocked by Wisher's Grove.

Only the hawks could see me…or witness my fall.

The sound of ice clinking against glass caused me to swallow a groan. He'd already been in the room for at least thirty minutes, and I was betting that he was on his second glass of whiskey. I had no idea what he was doing. With the Rite kicking off in just hours, I imagined he was busy meeting with the new Ladies and Lords in Wait, and the parents who would be giving their third sons and daughters to the Temples. But no, he was here, drinking whiskey by himse—

A knock on the door sounded. I closed my eyes, *lightly* banging the back of my head against the wall. Company? He was going to have visitors?

Maybe the gods had been watching me this whole time, and this was yet another punishment.

"Come in," he called out, and I heard the door clicking shut a few moments later. "You're late."

Oh, dear. I recognized that cold, flat tone. The Duke was not pleased.

"My apologies, Your Grace. I came as soon as I could," came the response. It was a male voice, one I didn't immediately recognize, which meant it could be any number of people. Ascended Lords. Stewards. Merchants. Guards.

"Not soon enough," the Duke replied, and I cringed for whoever was surely on the receiving end of a very disapproving stare. "I hope you have something for me. If so, that would go a long way to restoring my faith in you."

"I do, Your Grace. It took a while, as you know the man was not talkative."

"No, they never are once you get them out of the public eye where they can't cause a spectacle with their words," the Duke commented. "I'm guessing you had to be extremely convincing to get him to talk."

"Yes." There was a rough laugh and then, "He's not an Atlantian. That has been confirmed."

"Shame," the Duke said, and I frowned. Why would that be bad news?

"I've learned his name. Lev Barron, the first son of Alexander and Maggie Barron. He had two brothers, the second died of an…illness before his Rite, and the third was given to the Temples three years ago. He was not a known person of interest, and his behavior at the assembly wasn't expected."

They were talking about the Descenter—the one who'd thrown the Craven hand while the Duke and Duchess had spoken to the people after the attack.

"You've investigated his family?" the Duke asked.

"Yes. The father is deceased. The mother lives alone in the Lower Ward. She was useful in getting him to talk."

The Duke chuckled, and the sound turned my stomach. "What else have you learned?"

"I don't believe he was very connected within the community of Descenters. He claims that he has never met the Dark One nor believes him to be within the city."

A wealth of relief rose and spread through me even as the wind lifted the edges of my cloak.

"And you believed him?" the Duke asked.

"I gave him good reason not to lie," the man, who I assumed was one of the guards, answered. I thought about the man's mother. Had she been one of the reasons for him opening up?

If so, the knowledge sat heavy in the pit of my stomach. Descenters needed to be dealt with harshly, but I wasn't sure how I felt about family members being used to coerce information.

"And did he tell you anything about the claim he made? About the third sons and daughters?"

"All he would say was that he knew the truth—that they weren't servicing the gods, and that everyone would soon learn that."

"He didn't say what he believed to be the truth?"

I turned my head toward the window, all but holding my breath. I would love to know what he thought was happening.

"No, Your Grace. The only additional information I could glean from him was how he came to be in possession of a Craven's hand," he said, and that was, well…a good thing to know. "Apparently, he took it off the body of one of the guards who had become infected and returned to the city. He helped the family put the guard down after he'd changed."

"Death with dignity." The Duke scoffed, and my eyes widened. He…he knew about that? About us? "These bleeding hearts will be the death of the entire city one of these days."

That statement was a wee bit excessive, but I hadn't considered that there may be Descenters in the network.

"Did he happen to tell you who was involved with putting down the newly turned Craven?" he asked.

"No. He would not."

"That is also a shame. I would love to know who didn't contact us and why." The Duke sighed as if that were the worst possible thing to remain unanswered. "Do you have anything else to report?"

"No, Your Grace."

There wasn't an immediate response, but then the Duke asked, "Does the Descenter still breathe?"

"For now."

"Good." It sounded like he'd stood, and I hoped that meant he was leaving. *Please gods, let that mean he's leaving.* "I think I will visit with him myself."

My brows lifted.

Now *that* surprised me.

"As you wish." There was a beat of silence. "Will there be a trial that we need to prepare for?"

I almost laughed. Descenters weren't given an actual trial. They were put on public display while their charges were leveled against them. Execution quickly followed.

"There will be no need after my visit with him," the Duke said, and my mouth dropped open.

The meaning was clear. If there was no trial, that meant there'd be no public execution, and the only reason that would occur would be if the Descenter was already dead. That had happened before while they'd been imprisoned. Normally, it was believed to have been by their own hands or by an overzealous guard. But could it be that the Duke was meting out justice himself?

The same Ascended who I doubted had gotten a speck of blood on his hands since the War of Two Kings?

I shouldn't be surprised by that. He had a cruel streak and viciousness within him a mile wide, but he always kept that well hidden under a mask of civility. I also shouldn't be bothered by the idea of the Descenter being killed without the farce of a trial. They supported the Dark One, and even if some of them hadn't engaged in the riots and bloodshed, their words alone had sown the seeds that had caused blood to spill on more than one occasion.

But I…I was bothered by the idea of anyone being killed in a dark, dank cell, at the hands of an Ascended who was barely better than an Atlantian.

Finally, the door opened and closed, and there was nothing but silence. I waited, straining to hear any sound. I heard nothing. Wondering why the Duke had decided to have this meeting here and surprised by how aware of the network he was. I inched along the ledge toward the window. Clutching the journal to my chest with numb fingers, I neared the window—

There was a clicking sound from inside the room. I froze. Was that the door closing? Or was it locking? Oh, my gods, if it had been locked, I would have to bust through it—wait, the door could only be locked from the inside. Had someone else come into the room? Was it the Duke? There was no way he knew that I was out here unless he could suddenly see through walls. Who else—?

"You still out there, Princess?"

My lips parted as my eyes widened at the sound of *his* voice. Hawke. It was Hawke. In that room. I couldn't believe it.

"Or have you fallen to your death?" he continued. I briefly debated the merits of jumping. "I really hope that's not the case since I'm pretty positive that would reflect poorly on me since I assumed you were in your room." A pause. "*Behaving.* And not on a ledge, several dozen feet in the air, for reasons I can't even begin to fathom but am dying to learn."

"Dammit," I whispered, looking around as if I could find another escape route. Which was stupid. Unless I suddenly sprouted wings, the only exit point was through the window.

A heartbeat later, Hawke stuck his head out and looked up at me. The soft glow of the lamp glanced off his cheekbone as he raised a brow.

"Hi?" I squeaked.

He stared at me a moment. "Get inside."

I didn't move.

With a sigh so heavy it should've rattled the walls, he extended his hand toward me. "Now."

"You could say *please*," I muttered.

His eyes narrowed. "There are a whole lot of things I could say to you that you should be grateful I'm keeping to myself."

"Whatever," I grumbled. "Move back."

He waited, but when I didn't take his hand, he disappeared back into the room, grousing under his breath. "If you fall, you're going to be in so much trouble."

"If I fall, I'll be dead, so I'm not quite sure how I'd also be in trouble."

"Poppy," he snapped, and I couldn't help it. I grinned.

Had that been the first time he'd called me that? I thought so as I carefully inched across the ledge. Gripping the upper windowsill, I ducked down. Hawke was standing by the settee, but the moment he spotted me, he moved incredibly fast. Startled, I jerked back, but I didn't fall. He had an arm around my waist. A second later, I was inside the room, my feet on solid ground, and the journal stuck between his chest and mine. There was still a lot of full-body contact.

My stomach and legs were pressed against his, and when I drew in a breath, I could practically taste his dark spice and pine scent on my tongue. Before I could say a word, he reached up and fisted the back of my hood.

"Don't—" I started.

Too late.

He yanked it down. "A mask. This brings back old memories." His gaze roamed, flickering over the strands of hair that had escaped my braid and now fell against my cheeks.

I flushed as I tried to pull away. He didn't let go. "I understand you're probably upset—"

"Probably?" He laughed.

"All right. You're definitely upset," I amended. "But I can explain."

"I sure hope so, because I have so many questions," he said, golden eyes glimmering as he stared into mine. "Starting with, how did you get out of your room, and ending with why in the gods were you on the ledge?"

The last thing I wanted to tell him about was the old servants' entrance. I tried to put space between us. "You can let me go."

"I can, but I don't know if I should. You might do something even more reckless than climbing out onto a ledge that can't be more than a foot wide."

My eyes narrowed. "I didn't fall."

"As if that somehow makes this whole situation better?"

"I didn't say that. I'm just pointing out that I had the situation completely under control."

Hawke blinked, and then he laughed—he guffawed deeply, and the sound rumbled through me, eliciting a sharp wave of hot, tight shivers. Thankfully, he seemed unaware of the reaction. "You had the situation under control? I'd hate to see what happens when you don't."

I said nothing to that because I doubted whatever I would or could say would do me any favors. And neither did our proximity. Like on the Rise, the way he held me against him reminded me of our time at the Red Pearl, and that was something I didn't need help remembering. It was hard to think clearly when he held me this close. I wiggled, trying to slip free, but it resulted in our lower bodies being more in contact.

Hawke's arm tightened around me, and his hold felt like it had changed. As if he were no longer keeping me in place but...but holding me. *Embracing* me. My stomach dipped as I slowly lifted my gaze to his.

He stared down at me, the lines around his mouth taut as the silence stretched between us. I knew I should demand that he let me go. Better yet, I should make him. I knew how to escape a hold, but I...I didn't move. Not even when he lifted his other hand and placed his fingers just below the mask. Standing here, allowing this, was possibly the sweetest torture I'd ever put myself through. He hesitated, and I wondered if he was waiting to see what I'd do, what I would say. When I still did nothing, his eyes shifted to a fierce, burning amber. His fingers drifted from the mask and slowly traced the curve of my cheekbone. My skin hummed as his stare followed the path that his fingertips took. He glided them down my face and over my parted lips. I sucked in a sharp breath, my chest suddenly feeling too tight.

His chin dipped, and my breath caught as he lowered his head. Every muscle in my body seemed to tense with a heady mix of panic and anticipation. There was intent in the way his lashes lowered, and how he leaned in. He was going to kiss me. My heartbeat danced as his lips glided across my cheek, leaving a trail of fire in their wake. I knew what I should do, but I didn't. Maybe Hawke had been right when he'd said how I could have anything I wanted when, with a mask, I could pretend that no one knew who I was. He had to be.

Because my eyes closed, and I didn't move. Hawke had been my first kiss, but if he kissed me now, this...this would be our real first kiss. He knew who I was now. He'd seen me unveiled. He *knew*.

And I wanted this—wanted *him*.

Chapter 22

My heart was pounding so hard as his fingers drifted to my chin. He tilted my head back, and I felt like I was falling. His mouth moved to my ear, and his warm breath sent hot tingles through me.

"Poppy," he murmured, the word sounding rough, thick.

"Yes?" I whispered, barely recognizing my own voice.

His fingers slid down my throat. "How did you get out of the room without me seeing you?"

My eyes popped open. "What?"

"How did you leave your chambers?" he repeated.

It took me a moment to realize that he wasn't trying to kiss me. He was just trying to *distract* me. Feeling about seven different kinds of foolish, I cursed under my breath and pulled at his hold. This time, he let go.

Face flaming, I stepped back. I retreated several steps, lowering the journal as I dragged in a deep breath.

I was so incredibly...stupid.

Desperate to not let him see how close I'd come to letting him kiss me or the fact that I thought he was going to, I lifted my chin. The rawness was still there, though, and I felt no relief. "Maybe I walked right past you."

"No, you didn't. And I know you didn't climb out of a window. That would've been impossible," he replied. "So, how did you do it?

Frustration spiked as I turned back to the window, welcoming the cool air drifting in. I was perhaps foolish enough to get caught, but I was not stupid enough to realize that I could get away with not telling him. "There's an old servants' access to my chambers." My grip tightened on the journal. "From there, I can reach the main floor without being seen."

"Interesting. Where does it empty out on the main floor?"

I snorted as I turned back to him. "If you want to know that, you have to find out for yourself."

He lifted a brow. "All right."

Holding his stare, I couldn't help but acknowledge that there still wasn't any relief. There was just...gods, there was only disappointment that he hadn't kissed me. And if that was an indication of anything, it was that I needed to get control of myself.

"That's how you got onto the Rise without being seen," he stated, and I shrugged. "I'm assuming Vikter knows all about this. Did Rylan?"

"Does it matter?"

He cocked his head. "How many people know about this entrance?"

"Why do you ask?" I challenged.

Hawke took a step toward me. "Because it's a safety concern, Princess. In case you've forgotten, the Dark One wants you. A woman has already been killed, and there has already been one abduction attempt that we know of. Being able to move unseen through the castle, directly to your chambers, is the kind of knowledge he'd find valuable."

A shiver crept across my shoulders. "Some of the servants who've been at Castle Teerman for a long time know about it, but most don't. It's not a concern. The door locks from the inside. Someone would have to break down the door, and I'd be ready if that happened."

"I'm sure you would be," Hawke murmured.

"And I haven't forgotten what happened to Malessa or that someone tried to abduct me."

"You haven't? Then I guess you just didn't take any of that into consideration when you decided to go gallivanting through the city to the *library*."

"I didn't go *gallivanting* through anything. I went through Wisher's Grove and was on the street for less than a minute," I told him. "I also had my cloak up and this mask on. No one could even see a single inch of my face. I wasn't worried about being snatched, but I also came prepared, just in case."

"With your trusty little dagger?" The dimple reappeared.

"Yes, with my trusty little dagger," I snapped, about two seconds away from throwing the thing in his face. Again. "It hasn't failed me before."

"And that was how you escaped abduction the night Rylan was killed?" he surmised. "The man wasn't scared off by approaching guards."

I exhaled noisily. There was no point in lying about this now. "Yes. I cut him. More than once. He was wounded when he was called off. I hope he died."

"You are so violent," Hawke all but purred.

"You keep saying that, but I'm really not."

Hawke laughed again, the sound deep and real. "You really aren't all that self-aware."

"Whatever," I muttered. "How did you even realize I was gone?"

"I checked on you," he said, running a hand along the back of the settee. "I thought you might want company, and it seemed stupid for me to stand out in the hall bored out of my mind with you inside your room, most likely bored out of yours. Which, obviously, you were since you left."

What he said caught me off guard. "Did you really?"

His brows lifted.

"I mean, did you really check on me to ask if I…I wanted company?"

Hawke nodded. "Why would I lie about that?"

"I…" I didn't know how to explain that not even Vikter did that when he was on duty. My guards weren't allowed, as the Duke would see that as being too familiar. But no one checked on the old wing. Still, Vikter stayed outside, and I stayed inside, but Hawke was different. He'd shown that from the beginning. I shook my head. "It doesn't matter."

Hawke was quiet, and when I glanced over at him, I saw that he was closer, leaning against the settee. "How did you end up on the ledge?"

"Well, that's kind of a funny story…"

"I imagine it is. So, please, spare no details." He crossed his arms.

I sighed. "I came to find something to read, and I stopped inside this room. I…I didn't want to go back to mine yet, and I didn't realize that anything about this room was special." I eyed the liquor cabinet. That alone should have been a warning. "I was in here, and I heard the Duke outside in the hall. So, hiding on a ledge was a far better option than having him catch me here."

"And what would've happened if he had?"

I shrugged once more. "He didn't, and that's all that matters." I quickly moved on. "He had a meeting here with a guard from the prison. At least, I think that's who it was. They were talking about the Descenter who threw the Craven hand. The guard got the man to talk. He said that the Descenter didn't believe that the Dark One was in the city."

"That's good news."

Something about his tone snagged my attention. I glanced at him. "You don't believe him?"

"I don't think the Dark One has survived as long as he has by letting his whereabouts be widely known, even by his most fervent supporters," he responded.

Unfortunately, he had a point. "I think…I think the Duke is going to kill the Descenter himself."

He tilted his head slightly. "Does that bother you?"

"I don't know."

"I think you do, and you just don't want to say it."

It was so freaking irritating how correct he was…and how often. "I just don't like the idea of someone dying in a dungeon."

"Dying by public execution is better?"

I stared at him. "Not exactly, but at least then it's being done in a way that feels…"

"Feels like what?"

I inhaled heavily. "At least then it doesn't feel like it's something being hidden."

Hawke stared back at me, almost curiously. "Interesting."

The corners of my lips turned down. "What is?"

"You."

"Me?"

He nodded and then moved, his hand striking out. Before I even knew what he was doing, he had a hold of the book.

"Don't!" Unprepared, my fingers slipped over the leather

binding, and then it was free from my hand. He had it! Oh, my gods, he had the journal, and that was worse than falling to my death. If he saw what it was about—

"The Diary of Miss Willa Colyns?" His brows knitted as he turned it over. "Why does that name sound familiar?"

"Give it back." I reached for it, but Hawke danced away. "Give it back to me now!"

"I will if you read it for me. I'm sure this has to be more interesting than the history of the kingdom." He opened the book.

Maybe he couldn't read.

Please, let it be that he could not read.

The grin slowly slipped from his face.

Of course, he could read. Why was life so unfair?

His dark brows rose as he flipped through the pages. I knew what was on the first page. Miss Willa Colyns had been painfully detailed about the *intimate* kiss. "What interesting reading material."

My face was burning with the fire of a thousand suns, and I wondered how mad Hawke would get if I threw my dagger at his face.

Again.

The grin returned, and so did the dimple. "*Penellaphe.*" He said my name with so much shock, my eyes would've rolled if I weren't so incredibly mortified. "This is…just scandalous reading material for the Maiden."

"Shut up."

"Very naughty," he chided, shaking his head.

Annoyance hitting a record high, I lifted my chin. "There's nothing wrong with me reading about love."

"I didn't say there was." Hawke looked at me. "But I don't think what she is writing about has anything to do with love."

"Oh, so you're an expert on this now?"

"More so than you, I imagine."

I snapped my mouth shut. The truth in that statement stung, and I lashed out. "That's right. Your visits to the Red Pearl have been the talk of many servants and Ladies in Wait, so I suppose you do have a ton of experience."

"Someone sounds jealous."

"Jealous?" I laughed as I rolled my eyes. "As I said before, you have an overinflated sense of importance in my life."

He snorted as he returned to skimming through the book.

Irritated, I turned to the liquor cabinet. A short glass remained out. "Just because you have more experience with...what goes on at the Red Pearl, doesn't mean I don't know what love is."

"Have you ever been in love?" he asked. "Has one of the Duke's stewards caught your eye? One of the Lords? Or perhaps a brave guard?"

I shook my head. "I haven't been in love."

"Then how would you know?"

"I know my parents loved one another deeply." I toyed with the jeweled top of the decanter. "What about you? Have you been in love, Hawke?"

I hadn't expected an answer, so when he gave me one after a few moments, I was more than surprised. "Yes."

There was an odd twisting motion in my chest that I didn't quite understand as I looked over my shoulder at him, causing me to realize that the aching coldness had eased. I had no idea what it was about him that did that to me. It probably had to do with the fact that he irritated me. "Someone from your home?"

Do you still love her?

That was the second question bubbling to the surface, but by the grace of the gods, I managed to refrain from asking that question.

"She was." He was still looking down at the book. "It was a long time ago, though."

"A long time ago? When you were what? A child?" I asked, knowing that he couldn't be more than a handful of years older than I was, despite the way he made it sound as if it were an eternity ago.

He chuckled, and then his lips curved up in a small half-smile. The dimple made an appearance in his right cheek, causing the twisting motion inside me to increase. "How much of this have you read?"

"That's none of your business."

"Probably not, but I need to know if you got to this part." He cleared his throat.

Wait.

Was he going to read from it?

No.

Please, no.

"I only read the first chapter," I said in a rush. "And you look like you're in the middle of the book, so—"

"Good. Then this will be fresh and new to you. Let me see, where was I?" He dragged a finger over the page and then tapped the center. "Oh, yes. Here. '*Fulton had promised that when he was done with me that I wouldn't be able to walk straight for a day, and he was right.*' Huh. Impressive."

My eyes widened.

"'*The things the man did with his tongue and his fingers had only been surpassed by his shockingly large, decadently pulsing, and wickedly throbbing—*'" Hawke chuckled. "This woman has a knack for adverbs, doesn't she?"

"You can stop now."

"'*Manhood.*'"

"What?" I gasped.

"That's the end of that sentence," he explained, and when he glanced up, I immediately knew that whatever was about to come out of his mouth was going to burn me alive. "Oh, you may not know what she means by manhood. I do believe she's talking about his cock. Prick. Dick. His—"

"Oh, my gods," I whispered.

"His—apparently—extremely large, throbbing and pulsing—"

"I get it! I completely understand."

"Just wanted to make sure. Wouldn't want you to be too embarrassed to ask and think she was referencing his love for her or something."

"I hate you."

"No, you don't."

"And I'm about to stab you," I warned. "In a very violent manner."

Concern flickered across his face as he lowered the book. "Now that, I believe."

"Give me back the journal."

"But, of course." He offered it, and I snatched it out of his hand quickly, holding it to my chest. "All you had to do was ask."

"What?" My mouth dropped open. "I have been asking."

"Sorry." He didn't sound sorry at all. "I have selective hearing."

"You are… You are the worst."

"You got your words wrong." Striding past me, he patted the top of my head. I lashed out, narrowly missing him. "You meant, I'm the best."

"I got my words right."

"Come. I need to get you back before something other than your own foolishness puts you at risk." He stopped by the door. "And don't forget your book. I expect a summary of each chapter tomorrow."

He and I were never going to speak about this diary again.

But I did bring it with me when I followed him to the door. It was only when he reached for the handle that it struck me. "How did you know where I was?"

Hawke looked over his shoulder at me, a faint smile playing at his lips. "I have incredible tracking skills, Princess."

"I have incredible tracking skills," I muttered under my breath the following afternoon.

"What?" Tawny turned to me, frowning.

"Nothing. I'm just talking to myself," I said, taking a deep breath and pushing thoughts of Hawke out of my mind. "You look beautiful."

And that was true.

Tawny's hair was twisted up with a few tight curls framing her face. Her lips matched her mask and gown, a deep and vibrant shade of red. The thin, sleeveless dress hugged her lithe form. She wasn't just beautiful as she walked toward where I stood by the fireplace. She was confident and at ease with her body and herself, and I was in awe of her.

"Thank you." She straightened the material along her shoulder and then dropped her hand. "You look absolutely stunning, Poppy."

A flutter erupted in my chest and spread to my belly. "Do I?"

"Gods, yes. Have you not looked at yourself yet?"

I shook my head no.

Tawny stared at me. "So, you put on the dress—this absolutely beautiful, tailor-made dress—and haven't even looked at yourself? Not only that, you let me do your hair. I could've made it look like a nest for birds."

A nervous giggle left me. "I really hope you didn't."

She shook her head. "You are so...weird sometimes."

I was. Admittedly. But it was hard to explain why I hadn't looked at myself yet. It was so rare that I saw myself in anything other than white, and even when I dressed differently to sneak out, I didn't really look at myself. And this was still different because it was allowed. Because some who knew me would see me.

Hawke would see me.

The flutter turned into large birds of prey that began pecking away at my insides. I was so...nervous.

"Come on." Tawny caught my hand and dragged me into the bathing chamber where the only mirror was located. She marched me straight to where the nearly full-length mirror was propped against the corner. "Look."

I almost closed my eyes, as silly as that was, but I looked. I stared at my reflection, not quite sure I recognized myself, and it had nothing to do with the lack of veil and the red domino mask that had been delivered along with the gown.

"What do you think?" Tawny asked, her reflection appearing behind me.

What did I think? I felt...naked.

The gown was beautiful. No doubt there. The crimson gossamer sleeves, shaded just enough to hide the scars on my inner arms, were long and flowing, and had a delicate lace edge at the cuffs. The flimsy fabric was opaque at the breast and down to my thighs, the gown skimming my curves and shielding those areas. The skirt was loose, and a thicker band of gossamer created the illusion of tiers every few inches, but everything else was as translucent as a nightgown.

I really should've tried the dress on. It had been hanging in my wardrobe for long enough. I had no idea why I hadn't.

Lies.

I knew that if I tried it on, I probably would've sent it back.

Tawny had talked me into keeping most of my hair down. Only the sides were pulled back from my face, secured by tiny pins. The rest fell to the middle of my back in loose waves.

Hawke would see me in this dress.

"Maybe I could use my hair as a cloak?" I suggested, gathering the strands into two sections and pulling it over my shoulders.

"Oh my gods." Tawny laughed, shooing my hands away. She brushed the heavy waves back. "You can't see anything."

"I know, but..." I placed my cool hands against my flushed cheeks.

"You've never been allowed to wear anything like this," she finished for me. "I understand. It's okay to be nervous." She stepped back and dug around in the little bag she'd brought with her. "But you look beautiful, Poppy."

"Thank you," I murmured, glancing at my reflection. I did feel beautiful in this gown. Anyone would.

Tawny returned to my side, a pot in one hand, and a slim brush in the other. "Keep your lips parted and hold still."

I did as she ordered and held completely still as she painted my lips the same shade as my dress. When she was finished, she stepped aside. My lips were...bright.

I'd never worn paint on my lips or eyes before. Obviously, it wasn't allowed for me. Why? My skin was supposed to be as pure as my heart or something. I had no idea. Once, the Duchess had explained it to me, but I might've zoned out halfway through that conversation.

"Perfect," Tawny murmured, placing the pot and brush back into her bag. "You ready?"

No.

Not at all.

But I needed to be. The Rite would begin at dusk, and the sun was already setting.

Pulse pounding, I nodded. Tawny smiled at me, and I think I smiled back. Or at least I hoped I did as I followed her out into the main chamber. I felt a little dizzy as she reached for the door, opening it. Hawke would be out there with Vikter, and I wanted to turn back and run—to where, I had no idea. Maybe to the bed, where I could wrap the blanket around—

Vikter stood alone.

I looked up and down the hall, expecting to see Hawke, but the corridor was otherwise empty.

"You both look lovely," Vikter said. It was...weird seeing him in anything but black and without the white mantle of a Royal Guard. He was dressed for the Rite in a deep crimson, sleeveless tunic and breeches that matched.

"Thank you," Tawny said, curling her arm around mine as I murmured the same thing.

The corners of his lips turned up as he focused on me. "You sure you're ready, Poppy?"

"She is," Tawny answered, patting my arm.

"I am," I said, realizing that Vikter wouldn't move forward if I didn't say anything.

He nodded, and then the three of us started down the hall. Was Hawke not working tonight? I figured both of them would be on duty with me being at the Rite, but what if I'd assumed wrong? But he'd said he was…curious to see me. Didn't that mean that even if he wasn't on duty, he'd be here?

My heart thumped as we walked down the stairs to the second floor. It shouldn't matter if he was here or what he'd said. I wasn't dressed for him.

But where was he?

I told myself not to ask. I reminded myself over and over, but I blurted it out anyway. "Where's Hawke?"

"He had to meet with the Commander, I believe. He will meet us at the Rite."

Relief swept through me, and on its heels came the almost sweet thrill of anticipation. I exhaled roughly. If my question or reaction appeared odd to Vikter, he didn't show it. Tawny, on the other hand, squeezed my arm. I glanced at her.

She grinned, and if the mask hadn't covered her eyebrows, I knew one of them would be raised.

We made our way to the foyer, and there were many people—commoners and Ladies and Lords, both fully Ascended and those in Wait, and staff, all forming a sea of crimson. Cologne and perfumes mixed with the sounds of laughter and conversation.

It was…a lot to take in as we passed one of the statues. The first thing I did was lock down my gift, fortifying my walls. But my heart was still pounding as we entered the hall of banners. The archway of the Great Hall loomed ahead, brightly lit.

Air seemed to leak in and out of my lungs as we then entered the Great Hall.

Gods…

There were so many people. Hundreds stood before the raised dais, between the pillars, and in the windowed alcoves. Normally, I would be on the dais, removed from the throng, but not tonight. It still shocked me that the Duke and Duchess hadn't demanded that I join them, but there simply hadn't been any space. Not when there were at least half a dozen Temple clergy on the dais, including Priestess Analia, and just as many Royal Guards.

I looked around, trying to control my breathing. The white and gold banners usually hanging between the windows and behind the dais had been replaced by the deep crimson banners of the Rite, embossed with the Royal Crest. Deep red blossoms flowed from urns, variations of roses and other similarly hued flowers. Up by the dais there was a break in the color, a splash of white amongst the red. For once, it wasn't me who stood out. Dressed in white tunics and gowns, the second sons and daughters stood with their families. Behind them, the parents of the third sons and daughters crowded, their children in their arms. All of them, even the parents, bore wreaths of red roses and twine upon their heads.

"If I never see another rose, I will live happily," Tawny commented, following my gaze. "You have no idea how many thorns I had to pull out of my fingers while making those crowns."

"They're beautiful, though," I said as Vikter scanned the crowd that continued to file in.

Most paid us no mind as we walked among them. Only a few did a double-take when their gazes passed over us. Eyes rounded around their masks as they either recognized Tawny or Vikter, knowing that I had to be the one in between them. My cheeks heated, but there were so few of them that noticed. To everyone else, I was…just like them. For the most part, I was blending in. I was no one.

The pressure eased in my chest as my pulse slowed. Breathing became so much easier, and the mental walls blocking out my gift no longer felt as if they were seconds away from crumbling.

I wasn't the Maiden right now.

I was Poppy.

Briefly closing my eyes, muscles strung tight as a bow relaxed. This…*this* was what I'd been looking forward to—when I could just be Poppy.

And that made this moment, this night, a little magical.

Opening my eyes, I looked up at the dais again, ignoring the far left of the stage where the Priestess stood. I spotted the Duchess, speaking with one of the Royal Guards I recognized. I generally saw him outside the Duke's office. I scanned the dais, but I didn't see the Duke. I wondered where he was when one of the Priests joined the

Duchess and the Royal Guard. My gaze dropped to those before the dais, and my excitement dimmed as I thought of the Tulis family. They had to be up there with their son, preparing to say goodbye to yet another child. Tonight would not be a celebration for them, not—

"Maiden."

The hairs on the back of my neck rose as I looked over my shoulder, already knowing who I would see.

Lord Brandole Mazeen.

Chapter 23

Besides the Duke and the Dark One, he was the last person I wanted to see standing behind me. Like Vikter, his red tunic was sleeveless, and behind his mask, his pitch-black eyes seemed to glimmer. I managed to keep my voice level as I said, "My Lord."

A sardonic, tight-lipped grin twisted his mouth as his gaze flickered over me, lingering in a way that really made me wish that I were covered head to toe in a sack. Finally, he tore his gaze away and nodded at Tawny and Vikter. Then his attention settled back on me. "I hear that a certain Priestess is very unhappy with you."

The tension returned, sinking its rigid claws into my neck as I stared up at him.

The Lord stepped in close—too close for any level of propriety. "I do believe you're in for another lesson, my dear."

I inhaled sharply, almost overcome by some kind of thick, musky cologne. My gaze flew to his as his scent triggered a memory. He hadn't smelled of cologne the night he'd trapped me in an alcove—the night Malessa had been murdered.

He'd smelled of something else then—something sweet and musky.

Jasmine.

He'd smelled of jasmine.

My mind immediately went to the petal I'd found under the chair in the room Malessa had been found in. There hadn't been jasmine in that room, unless it had been replaced by the lilies, but hadn't Tawny—?

"Excuse me," Vikter stepped in, placing a hand on my arm. "We need to be—"

"No need to run off." Mazeen's gaze remained fixed on mine. "I'll be on my way now. Enjoy the Rite." And with that, he slipped around us and headed down the steps onto the main floor of the Great Hall.

"What was that about?" Vikter asked, his voice low.

"It's nothing." My thoughts raced as I turned back to Tawny. "You said you saw Malessa the day she died. That morning, correct?"

Tawny's lips pinched. "Yes. I did."

"Was she carrying a bouquet? Do you remember what kind of flowers it had?"

She blinked. "I…I don't know. I know they were white."

The petal in the room had been white, and it had definitely been jasmine. My stomach dipped.

Her gaze searched mine. "Why are you asking?"

"That's a good question," Vikter chimed in.

"I don't know…" I looked out over the mass of people, unable to find the Lord. I thought about how he'd stood in that doorway, staring and unmoving. He'd been there when Rylan had escorted me back to my chambers. And he'd come out of one of the rooms. Which one, I couldn't be sure, but what did any of that mean anyway?

He could've been with Malessa before she died, or it could be a coincidence, but an Atlantian had killed her. That much was clear. Nothing else could've made such a wound without getting blood everywhere.

"Poppy." Vikter touched my arm lightly as the Priest moved toward the center of the dais. "Is everything okay?"

I nodded. I would speak to him later about it, but I wasn't even sure what I was thinking.

"Where is the Duke?" Tawny whispered. "The Rite is starting."

And he still wasn't here. The Duchess kept pacing to her left where the dais could be accessed by the back entrance.

"We are gathered here tonight to honor the gods," the Priest spoke, hushing the crowd gathered on the floor below. "To honor the Rite."

"Excuse me," a soft voice came from behind us.

I turned the same time as Vikter, and another shock greeted me as I recognized the woman standing there.

It was Agnes.

Oh, my gods…

My eyes widened as she glanced nervously between Vikter and me. She was wearing red, like everyone else, a skirt and blouse dyed to match. She looked better than the last time I had seen her, but there were deep shadows under her eyes that told me that her grieving had not been easy.

"I'm sorry to interrupt," she said, keeping her gaze downcast. "I saw you…and I had to come over."

"It's okay." Vikter sent me a look. "Would you like to speak to me somewhere private?"

She nodded without looking up, and not for one second did I think she didn't realize who I was.

Vikter's gaze met mine. "I'll be right back."

"Actually, I would like to speak to her," Agnes said as the Priest launched into a prayer. "If it would be okay." Her gaze lifted briefly to mine. "It would only be for a moment."

Vikter started to deny her request, but people were beginning to pay attention, sending sharp looks of reprimand in our direction. "It's okay," I said quickly. "We can step outside."

Who is that? Tawny mouthed at me, and I forced a casual shrug. "I'll be here," she said.

Vikter quickly escorted Agnes out into the nearly empty corridor. There were a few stragglers as they hurried into the Hall. He led us to an alcove near one of the open archways that led out to the garden. "It's very unwise for you to approach us," he began almost immediately.

"I know. I'm sorry. I shouldn't have, but I…" She glanced at me, her eyes widening slightly. "I didn't think you'd be here."

"How did you know it was me?" I asked.

Vikter's head jerked in my direction, his mask doing very little to hide his disbelief. The fact that she'd identified me when she hadn't seen my face was worth the risks.

"I didn't until I heard that Ascended—I mean, the Lord—speaking to you," she said. "I wasn't expecting to see you here," she said again.

"Dammit," Vikter muttered under his breath.

Well, that was another thing I could hate Lord Mazeen for. Not that there needed to be another reason.

"What did you want to speak to her about?"

Agnes's throat worked on a swallow. "If I could speak to her in private—"

"That's not going to happen." The softness was gone from Vikter's tone. "At all."

Trepidation flickered across the woman's flushed face.

"It's not," I said. "Whatever you need to say to me can be said in front of Vikter."

She clasped her hands together. "You...I just...I wanted to thank you for what you did." She glanced around before continuing. "What you did for my husband and for me."

"There are no thanks needed," I assured her, wondering why she had wanted to speak to me alone about that.

Vikter was obviously wondering the same thing based on the way his eyes squinted.

"I know. You have been so kind. Both of you. I don't think—no, I *know* I wouldn't have been able to deal with it by myself. I just..." She trailed off, pressing her lips together.

A cheer rose inside, and I glanced toward the entrance. Names were being announced. Ladies and Lords in Wait, who would be handed over to the staff.

"You just what?" Vikter asked.

"It's just that..." Her chest rose with a heavy breath. "I heard about what happened to you—what's been happening here. That...that poor girl. And that someone tried to take you. There are rumors."

"What rumors?" Vikter demanded.

Agnes dampened her lips. "People have said that it was the Dark One coming for you."

That wasn't exactly news, but goosebumps still broke out over my skin.

"I don't know about that poor girl," Agnes continued. "I just...I didn't think you'd be here tonight. When I saw you, I felt that I needed to tell you what I've heard.

"Thank you," I said as another cheer erupted from inside. "I appreciate it."

Agnes briefly met my gaze. "I only want to make sure you're

safe."

"As do I." Vikter straightened to his full height.

She nodded. "Especially in crowds like this. There are so many people, and if he...he got in here once before, he could do it again. Others could, too."

"He got in here twice before," I corrected. "Or at least two who support him did."

Her mouth opened, but then she closed it.

"I think by now you've realized that I'm her personal Royal Guard," Vikter said, and Agnes nodded. "It is my sole duty to keep her safe. I appreciate your willingness to tell me what you've heard."

She nodded once more.

"We would be forever in your debt if you could tell us everything you know," he continued. "And I feel as if there is more that you're not sharing."

I looked sharply at Vikter.

"I'm not sure what you mean."

"You're not?" he asked softly.

She shook her head. "I've taken up too much of your time. I should be going." She started backing up. "I'm sorry. Just..." Her gaze met mine. "Be careful. Please."

Agnes turned, hurrying off toward the front of the castle. Vikter started after but stopped. "Dammit," he growled. "Where is Hawke?"

"I don't know." I looked around, my gaze snagging on one of the garden archways and to the darkness that lay beyond. "What do you think she wasn't telling us?"

"I'm not sure." He rubbed a hand through his hair. "It's only a feeling. Maybe I'm just being paranoid. Come on." He placed a hand on my back. "I'm sure it's nothing."

I wasn't so sure if he really believed that, but I let him guide me back into the Great Hall and to Tawny's side.

"Is everything okay?" she asked.

"Yes." Or at least, I hoped so. I had no idea what to make of what Agnes had said.

Tawny glanced at Vikter and then said, "They're almost done with the third sons and daughters."

I checked out the dais. "The Duke still hasn't arrived?"

"No," she whispered. "Odd, right?"

It was very odd. Had something happened when he went to see

the Descenter the night before? If so, then something would've been announced. Between the missing Duke, my suspicions concerning Lord Mazeen, and Agnes's unexpected presence, my mind was all over the place as the ceremony continued. Honest to the gods, it sounded like the Priest was speaking a different language. Maybe he was. I was unable to pay attention, and that was a shame because I'd always been curious about the—

The back of my neck tingled, and the strongest sense of awareness swept over me. I couldn't explain it, but I knew that when I looked over my shoulder, I would see him.

Hawke.

And I was right.

The next breath I took seemed to go nowhere as my gaze swept over the crimson-hued breeches and red tunic that showed just a hint of skin below his throat, as well as the carved line of his jaw and his lush lips. The curve of the red domino mask drew the eye to the rise of his cheekbones. A strand of dark hair tumbled over his forehead, brushing the stiff fabric.

He was...

Hawke looked like I imagined one of the gods waiting in the Temples appeared—striking and unattainable, alluring in a way that was a little frightening.

And I knew that he was looking at me just as intently as I was him. A wave of shivers followed his gaze as it tracked over me with such concentration that it felt like a caress. Every inch of my skin, what was exposed and what wasn't, became hyperaware. The flutter was back with a vengeance.

"Hi," I said, and immediately wished I'd kept my mouth shut.

One side of his lips kicked up, and that dimple of his made an appearance. "You look...lovely," he said, and my stomach dipped in the most pleasant way possible. He turned to Tawny. "As do you."

Tawny smiled. "Thank you."

He glanced at Vikter. "You, as well."

Vikter snorted, and I smiled while Tawny giggled. "You do look exceptionally handsome tonight," she said, and I swore Vikter's cheeks deepened in color as I turned back to the dais.

"Sorry for the delay," Hawke said as he came to stand behind me.

"Is everything okay?" I asked as I looked up at the dais. If Lord Mazeen knew about what had happened with Priestess Analia, then she'd definitely gone to the Duke as expected. I doubted she'd left out what Hawke had done.

"Of course," he replied. "I was pulled to assist with security sweeps. I didn't think it would take as long as it did."

I wanted to ask if anyone had said anything to him about what had happened with the Priestess. Still, if I said it in front of Vikter, he'd have questions, and I didn't want him to worry.

As those given to the Court and to the Temples were led out, the Duchess stepped off the dais, stopping to speak to the families and then some other Court members. Next to the dais, music began to play, and servants entered from the access doors, carrying trays of champagne. Ladies and Lords, along with those in Wait, broke into smaller groups. Merchants and other commoners joined them.

Vikter was eyeing the front before he turned to me. "I need to speak to the Commander," he said. When I nodded, he turned to Hawke.

"I have her," Hawke answered before Vikter could even speak, and that stupid, funny motion hit my stomach again.

Expecting Vikter to challenge the statement, I was surprised when he accepted the answer. Was he coming around to liking Hawke? Trusting him? Or did he just want to catch the Commander before he lost sight of him?

Probably the latter.

"Have I missed anything?" Hawke moved to my right, standing about a foot or so behind me.

"You haven't," Tawny answered. "Unless you were looking forward to a bunch of prayers and teary-eyed goodbyes."

"Not particularly," he commented dryly.

That reminded me. I looked at Tawny. "Did they call out the Tulis family?"

Her brow creased. "You know, I don't think they did."

Did that mean they hadn't come? If so, that would be considered treason. Guards would go to their home, the child would still be sent to serve the gods, and Mr. and Mrs. Tulis would most likely be imprisoned.

The only way they'd have a chance was if they left the city, but no one came in and out of the city without the Royals knowing. They'd have to be incredibly well connected to even attempt such a feat, and even if they did, where would they go? Word would be sent to all surrounding cities and towns to be on the lookout for them.

Knowing all of that, I still understood why they'd take the risk. It was their only child.

My attention shifted as the Duchess drew near, flanked by several Royal Guards who, like Vikter and Hawke, had swapped out their white mantles and typical black garb.

"Penellaphe," she said, her well-practiced smile in place.

"Your Grace," I murmured as demurely as possible.

She nodded at Tawny and Hawke, her gaze lingering on him for a few seconds. I bit down on the inside of my cheek to stop myself from smiling. "Are you enjoying the Rite?"

Considering I only saw a few minutes of it, I nodded. "Is His Grace not attending?"

"I believe he is running late," she answered smoothly, but the corners of her mouth tightened. She stepped closer, lowering her voice. "Remember who you are, Penellaphe. You are not to mingle or socialize."

"I know," I assured her.

Her dark eyes briefly met mine, and then she was on her way, like a jeweled hummingbird, buzzing from one group of people to the next. Laughter rang out from the floor, drawing my attention. I saw Loren and Dafina.

"I have a question," Hawke said.

I inclined my head. "Yes?"

"If you're not supposed to mingle or socialize, which are the same thing, by the way," he said, and I grinned, "what is the point of you being allowed to attend?"

My grin faded.

"That is actually a good question," Tawny remarked, hands lightly clasped in front of her.

"I'm not sure what the point is, to be honest," I admitted.

For several minutes, none of us spoke. I lost sight of the Duchess, and the Duke still hadn't appeared from what I could tell.

I sighed as I glanced at Tawny.

She really did look absolutely beautiful tonight, the red complementing the richness of her brown skin. I knew what she was so vividly focused on without following her gaze. Her expression could only be described as wistful as she watched couples pair off for some waltz I probably would never have been able to master even if

I'd been allowed. Her eyes tracked their movements fervently, and I knew for a fact that she knew every step of that dance. Why was she here and not out there with the rest of them?

Of course, I knew the answer.

It was because of me.

Guilt settled in my chest like a stone. "Tawny?"

She twisted toward me. "Yes?"

"You don't have to stand here beside me. You can go and have fun."

"What?" Her nose scrunched against the mask. "I'm having fun. Aren't you?"

"Of course, but you don't have to be right beside me. You should be out there." I gestured to the dancers and beyond, to where people huddled together in groups of three and four. "It's okay."

"I'm fine." She plastered on a bright smile, and my heart squeezed. "I'd rather be standing here with you than out there without you."

"You're the best," I said, wishing I could hug her. Instead, I reached between us and squeezed her arm. "You really are, but I don't need you to be my shadow tonight. I already have two of them."

Tawny's gaze flicked over my shoulder. "You really only have one. Vikter is still with the Commander."

"And one is all I need. Please." I squeezed her arm again. "Tawny, go. Please."

Her gaze searched mine, and I could tell that she was waffling. Before she could decide not to, I lied, "I'm actually feeling very tired. I didn't sleep all that well last night, so I don't plan to be down here for much longer."

"You're sure?"

I nodded.

Tawny's entire body practically vibrated with the effort required not to throw her arms around me, but she managed a subdued nod as I released her hand. She gave me one last long look and then headed down the steps, crossing the floor to where Dafina and Loren stood with three Lords in Wait.

I smiled, relieved. I hoped she let herself enjoy her night, and to ensure that, I knew I needed to leave. If I stayed down here for any amount of time, standing between the enormous, red geraniums, she would come back.

I felt Hawke step closer before he even spoke, and a shivery wave of warmth danced over my skin. I turned my head to the right, to where he stood no more than a few inches behind me.

"That was kind of you," he commented as he stared out over the floor.

"Not particularly. Why should she stand here and do nothing just because that's all I can do?"

"Is that really all you can do?"

"You were standing right here when Her Grace reminded me that I am not to mingle or—"

"Or fraternize."

"She said socialize," I corrected.

"But you don't have to stay here."

"I don't." I turned back to the floor, swallowing another sigh. I did have to leave. The idea of returning to my chambers held little appeal, but if I didn't, Tawny would return to my side. "I would like to go back to my room."

"You sure?"

No. "Of course."

"After you, Princess."

I turned, eyes narrowing as he stepped aside. "You need to stop calling me that."

"But I like it."

Brushing past him, I lifted the hem of my skirt as I stepped onto the slight rise. "But I don't."

"That's a lie."

I shook my head as I skirted around the groups of smiling, masked faces. None looked in my direction, most having thought twice about whether they'd seen the Duchess speak with me.

The air was much cooler outside the Great Hall, courtesy of the breeze coming through the open garden entrances. I spared only a quick glance out into the garden before I started down the hall.

"Where are you going?" Hawke asked.

Stopping, I turned to him in confusion. "Back to my rooms, as I..." I trailed off.

Hawke's amber eyes were assessing as they roamed over me, lingering where my hair lay draped over my shoulders. His gaze traveled over the tiny scalloped lace along the bodice of my gown. The neckline wasn't as low as I'd seen some of the Ladies in Wait wear, and just the upper swells of my breasts were visible, but that...that was a lot for me, considering my normal gowns had a neckline up to the throat.

"I was wrong earlier when I said you looked lovely," he said.

"What?"

"You look absolutely exquisite, Poppy. Beautiful," he said, giving a little shake of his head. "I just...I needed to tell you that."

His words brought forth such a sharp, swelling emotion that my control over my gift snapped, and my senses reached out before I could stop them. I didn't feel pain from him other than the hum of sadness. My gaze flew to his face. I felt...something else. Two separate emotions. One reminded me of lemon—tart against my tongue. The other sensation was heavier and...spicy, a bit smoky. I thought the first might be confusion or maybe uncertainty. As if he were unsure of something. The other...

Gods.

It took a few moments for my senses to zero in on what that was. It made me feel *hot* and...and *achy*. It felt like arousal.

"I have an idea," he said, slowly lifting that intense stare of his to mine.

"You do?" I felt strangely breathless as I wrangled my gift, closing it down.

He nodded. "It doesn't involve returning to your room."

Anticipation and excitement rose, but... "I'm confident that unless I remain at the Rite, I would be expected to return to my room."

"You're masked, as am I. You're not dressed like the Maiden. To use your own ideology from last night, no one will know who either of us is."

"Yes, but..."

"Unless you wish to go back to the room. Maybe you're so engrossed in that book—"

"I am not engrossed in that book." My cheeks flushed.

"I know you don't want to be cooped up in your chambers." When I opened my mouth, he added, "There's no reason to lie to me."

"I..." I couldn't lie. No one would believe me. "And where do you suggest that I go?"

"Where *we* go?" Light from the sconces glinted off the curve of his mask as he tilted his chin toward the garden.

My heart skipped at the same moment it twisted. "I don't know. It…"

"It used to be a place of refuge," he said. "Now, it's become a place of nightmares. But it can only stay that way if you let it."

"If I let it? How do I change the fact that Rylan died out there?"

"You don't."

I stared up at him. "I'm not following where you're going with this."

He stepped closer, dipping his chin. "You can't change what happened in there. Just like you can't change the fact that the courtyard used to give you peace. You just replace your last memory—a bad one—with a new one—a good one—and you keep doing that until the initial one no longer outweighs the replacement."

I opened my mouth, but then I really thought about what he'd said. My gaze traveled to the darkness beyond the door. What he'd said actually made sense. "You make it sound so easy."

"It's not. It's hard and uncomfortable, but it works." He extended his bare hand, and I looked down, staring at it as if a dangerous animal rested in his palm—a fluffy, cute one that I wanted to pet. "And you won't be alone. I'll be there with you, and not just watching over you."

I'll be there with you, and not just watching over you.

My startled gaze lifted to his face. His words struck a chord I tried to never touch. Gods, I couldn't even begin to know the number of times I'd felt alone since Ian had left, even though I rarely ever was by myself. But those around me the most were sometimes just there because they had to be. Even Tawny and Vikter. That acknowledgement didn't lessen how much I knew they cared for me and how much I cared for them, but it also didn't change that while they were with me, they were sometimes not *present*. Nor did it change the fact that I knew a lot of it was in my head. That small, very insecure part of myself that worried that our friendship would be non-existent if Tawny wasn't my lady's maid never really went away. I worried she'd be like Dafina and Loren and the other Ladies in Wait.

How did Hawke know that? Or *did* he know I felt that way? I wanted to ask, but again, it was something I didn't like to touch or talk about. Loneliness often brought with it a heavy, coarse blanket of shame, and a cloak constructed of embarrassment.

But with Hawke, even in the short time I'd known him, I didn't feel alone. Could it be simply his presence? When he was in a room, he seemed to become the center of it. Or was it more? I couldn't deny that I was attracted to him, forbidden or not.

And I didn't want to return to my room, left to confusing thoughts that I couldn't act upon. I didn't want to spend another night wishing I was living instead of actually doing it.

Was it wise, though, if I was right about what I'd felt from him? I could've been wrong, but if I wasn't? Did I have the willpower to remember what I was? I shouldn't even attempt to find out

But I…I wanted.

Drawing in a shallow breath, I reached for his hand but stopped. "If someone saw me…saw you—"

"Saw us? Holding hands? Dear gods, the scandal." Another quick grin surfaced, and this time, the dimple appeared. "No one is here." He glanced around the hall. "Unless you see people I can't."

"Yes, I see the spirits of those who've made bad life choices," I replied dryly.

He chuckled. "I doubt anyone will recognize us in the courtyard. Not with both of us masked, and just the moonlight and a few lamps to light the way." He wiggled his fingers. "Besides, I have a feeling anyone out there will be too busy to care."

My vast imagination filled in what could possibly cause others to be too busy to care.

"You're such a bad influence," I murmured as I placed my hand in his.

Hawke curled his fingers around mine. The weight and warmth of his hand was a pleasant shock. "Only the bad can be influenced, Princess."

Chapter 24

"That sounds like faulty logic to me," I told him.

He chuckled as he started toward the garden archway. "My logic is never faulty."

"I feel like that's not something one would be aware of if it was," I pointed out, smiling slightly.

Cold night air greeted us as we stepped outside, and my heart kicked up at the familiar, sweet scent of flowers and rich, damp soil.

My gaze bounced around a little wildly as I looked for something to be off, to be different than the last time I had been here. There had to be. Oil lanterns were spaced throughout the main pathway, but the sections that branched off were dark—the moonlight couldn't even penetrate them. My steps slowed as the soft breeze rattled the bushes and lifted strands of my hair.

Hawke spoke softly. "One of the last places I saw my brother was a favorite place of mine."

That snagged my attention, and I stopped scoping out every bunch of flowers we passed, looking for what, I had no idea. It was like I expected to see wilted petals dripping blood, or waited for the Duke to finally make his appearance. Hawke's earlier anguish over his brother had given me the impression that this was something he didn't want to discuss, so the topic surprised me.

"Back home, there are hidden caverns that very few people know about," he continued, his fingers still tightly woven with mine. "You have to walk pretty far in this one particular tunnel. It's tight and dark. Not a lot of people are willing to follow it to find what awaits at the end."

"But you and your brother did?"

"My brother, a friend of ours, and I did when we were young and had more bravery than common sense. But I'm glad we did because at the end of the tunnels, was this huge cavern filled with the bluest, bubbling, warm water I'd ever seen."

"Like a hot spring?" Hushed conversations drifted out from the areas full of shadows, quieting as we passed by.

"Yes, and no. The water back home... There's really no comparison."

"Where are—?" Glancing down a path where I heard soft sounds, I swallowed hard and quickly looked away. I became even more aware of the feeling of his hand against mine, the rough calluses on his palms, and the strength in his grip. I thought about that heavy, spicy, and smoky sensation I'd felt from him earlier. "Where...where are you from?"

"A little village I'm sure you've never heard of," he said, squeezing my hand. "We'd sneak off to the cavern every chance we got. The three of us. It was like our own little world, and at the time, there were a lot of things happening—things that were too adult and grown-up for us to understand then." His voice had taken on a far-off quality as if he were in a different space and time. "We needed that escape, where we could go and not worry about what could be stressing our parents, and fretting over all the whispered conversations we didn't quite understand. We knew enough to know they were a harbinger of something bad. It was our haven." He stopped and looked down at me. "Much like this garden was yours."

The veiled Maiden fountain was only a few feet from us, the sound of trickling water surrounding us. "I lost both of them," he said, his eyes shadowed, but his gaze no less powerful. "My brother when we were younger, and then my best friend a few years after that. The place that was once filled with happiness and adventure had turned into a graveyard of memories. I couldn't even think about going back there without them. It was like the place became haunted."

I didn't need to open my senses to know that the pain was festering in him, and it wasn't exactly a good idea to use my ability twice on him, especially when it was evolving. But through our connected hands, I dwelled on the all-too-shallow well of happy thoughts and let it briefly flow through him.

I felt his hand tremble slightly, and then I spoke, hoping to distract him. "I understand. I keep looking around, thinking that the garden should look different. Assuming there'd be a visible change to represent how it now feels to me."

Hawke cleared his throat. "But it is the same, isn't it?"

I nodded.

"It took me a very long time to work up the nerve to go back to the cavern. I felt that way, too. Like the water surely must've turned muddy in my absence, dirty and cold. But it wasn't. It was still as calm, blue, and warm as it always was."

"Did you replace the sad memories with happy ones?" I asked.

A half-smile appeared in the sliver of moonlight cutting across his face as he shook his head. The lines of his face had relaxed. "Haven't gotten a chance, but I plan to."

"I hope you do," I said, knowing that as a Royal Guard, it likely wouldn't be possible for many years to come. The breeze tossed a strand of hair across my shoulders and chest. "I'm sorry about your brother and friend."

"Thank you." He looked up to the star-blanketed sky and said, "I know it's not like what happened here, to Rylan, but I do understand how it feels."

I lowered my gaze to where his hand still held mine. My grip was loose and yet rigid, fingers sticking out instead of gripping. I wanted to curl the digits around his. "Sometimes, I think...I think it's a blessing that I was young when Ian and I lost our parents. My memories of them are faint, and because of that, there's this...I don't know, level of detachment? As wrong as this will sound, I'm lucky in a way. It makes dealing with their loss easier because it's almost as if they're not real. It's not like that for Ian. He has a lot more memories than I do."

"It's not wrong, Princess. I think it's just the way the mind and heart work," he said. "You haven't seen your brother at all since he left for the capital?"

I shook my head. "He writes as often as he can. Usually, once a month, but I haven't seen him since the morning he left." Pressing my lips together, I curled my fingers around his, and my stomach dipped a little. He wasn't holding my hand any longer. *We* were holding hands. To a lot of people, that would be nothing. Some would probably even find it silly, but it was huge to me, and I *cherished* it. "I miss him." I lifted my gaze, discovering that Hawke was looking down at me. "I'm sure you miss your brother, and I hope…I hope you see him again."

His head tilted slightly, and his mouth opened as if he were about to say something, but then it closed. A moment passed, and he lifted his other hand, catching a strand of my hair. I sucked in a startled, sharp breath as a wave of shivers followed the glide of his knuckles across the bare skin above my chest. Those shivers didn't stop there. They traveled down to below my breasts and lower.

Flushed, I dropped his hand and stepped back, turning away. My pulse thrumming, I clasped my fingers together. Was it normal to have such a strong response to a brush of the skin? I wasn't sure, but I couldn't imagine that it was. I took a few steps, searching for something to say. Anything.

"I…" I cleared my throat. "My favorite place in the garden is the night-blooming roses. There's a bench there," I rambled on. "I used to come out almost every night to see them open. They were my favorite flower, but now I have a hard time even looking at the ones cut and placed in bouquets."

"Do you want to go there now?" Hawke asked, no more than a foot behind me.

I thought about it, about the silky black petals and the deep violet blooms of the jacaranda trees…and the blood that had pooled on the pathway. The way it had filled the cracks in the stone reminded me of a different night. "I…I don't think so."

"Would you like to see my favorite place?"

I glanced over my shoulder as he came to stand by my side. "You have a favorite place?"

"Yes." He extended his hand once more. "Want to see?"

Knowing I shouldn't, but somehow unable to stop myself, I placed my hand in his. Hawke was quiet as he led me around the fountain and down the main path. It wasn't until he veered off to the left where the mild, sweet scent of lavender filled the air, that I knew where he was leading me.

The willow.

At the very edge of the southern side of the Queen's Garden was a large, several-hundred-year-old weeping willow. Its branches nearly reached the ground, creating a thick canopy. In the warmer months, tiny, white blossoms clung to the leaves.

"You're a fan of the weeping willow?" I asked as it came into view. Several lanterns hung from poles outside the willow, the flames still inside the glass enclosures.

He nodded. "Never saw one until I got here."

I wasn't surprised that he hadn't seen one in the capital. The trees, with their shallow roots, were known to break through the ground, but I wondered what village he'd lived in that had farming and caverns but no weeping willows. "Ian and I used to play inside. No one could see us."

"Play? Or do you mean hide?" he asked. "Because that's what I would've done."

I cracked a grin. "Well, yes. I would hide, and Ian would tag along like any good big brother." I looked up at him. "Have you gone under it? There're benches, but you can't see them now." I frowned. "Actually, anyone could be under there right now, and we wouldn't know."

"No one is under there."

My brows lifted above the mask. "How can you be sure?"

"I just am. Come on." He tugged on my hand as he strode forward. "Watch your step."

I wondered if his certainty had to do with his excellent tracking skills. I easily navigated the low, stone wall, trailing behind him as we passed one of the lanterns. Hawke reached out with his free hand, brushing aside several of the leafy branches. I stepped inside and, within a handful of seconds, we were pitched into almost complete darkness as the branches drifted back into place. The moonlight couldn't break through the heavy fall, and only the faintest glow from the nearby lanterns seeped into the willow.

I looked around, seeing only the outline of the trunk. "Gods, I forgot how dark it is in here at night."

"It feels like you're in a different world under here," he commented. "As if we've stepped through a veil and into an enchanted world."

I grinned, his words reminding me of Ian. "You should see it when it's warmer. The leaves bloom—oh! Or when it snows, and at dusk. The flakes dust the leaves and the ground, but not a lot makes it inside here. Then it really is like a different world."

"Maybe we'll see it."

"You think so?"

"Why not?" he asked, and I sensed his body angle toward mine. When he spoke next, I felt his breath against my forehead. "It will snow, will it not? We'll sneak off just before dusk and come out here."

Fully aware of how close he was standing now, I nervously dampened my lips. "But will we be here? The Queen could summon me to the capital before then," I said, acknowledging something I had tried not to think of.

"Possibly. If so, then I guess we'll have to find different adventures, won't we?" he said. "Or should I call them *mis*adventures?"

I laughed then. "I think it will be hard to sneak off anywhere in the capital, not with me...not with me being so close to the Ascension."

"You need to have more faith in me if you think I can't manage to find a way for us to sneak off. I can assure you that whatever I get us involved in won't end with you on a ledge." In the darkness, I thought I felt his fingertips caress my left cheek, but the touch was too soft and too brief to be sure. "We're out here on the night of the Rite, hidden inside a weeping willow."

"It didn't seem all that difficult."

"That's only because I was leading the way."

I laughed again. "Sure."

"Your doubt wounds me." His hand pulled on mine as he turned away. "You said there were benches in here? Wait. I see them."

I stared at the shadowy form of what I assumed was the back of his head. "How in the world do you see those benches?"

"You can't?"

"Uh, no." I squinted into the gloom.

"Then I must have better eyesight than you."

I rolled my eyes. "I think you're just saying you can see them, and we're probably a second away from tripping—"

"Here they are." Hawke stopped. Unbelievably, he sat down as if he could perfectly see the seats.

I was left staring, my mouth hanging open. Then I realized that it was quite possible he could see me gaping like a dying fish, so I closed my mouth. Maybe his eyesight was better than mine.

Or my eyesight was poorer than I realized.

"Would you like to sit?" he asked.

"I would, but unlike you, I can't see in the dark—" I gasped as he tugged on my hand, pulling me down. Before I knew it, I was sitting in his lap—his *lap*.

"Comfortable?" he asked, and he sounded like he was smiling.

I had no words. He was still holding my hand, and I was sitting in his lap, and all I could think about was that part in Willa Colyn's journal, where she described being in a man's lap. There had been less clothing—

"You can't be comfortable." One of his arms folded around my upper back, pulling my side against his chest. "There. That has to be much better."

It was.

And it wasn't.

"I don't want you getting too cold," he added, his breath warm against my temple. He was so much taller, even sitting as straight as I was, my head still didn't reach his chin. "I feel like that's an important part of my duty as your personal Royal Guard."

"Is that what you're doing right now? Protecting me from the cold by pulling me into your lap?"

"Exactly." His hand was against my side, the weight like a brand.

I stared at what I thought might be his throat. "This is incredibly inappropriate."

"More inappropriate than you reading a dirty journal?"

"*Yes*," I insisted, heat creeping into my face.

"No." His deep chuckle rumbled through me. "I can't even lie. This *is* inappropriate."

"Then why?"

"Why?" His chin grazed the top of my head. "Because I wanted to."

I blinked once and then twice. "And what if I didn't want to?"

Another chuckle sent an acute shiver through me. "Princess, I'm confident that if you didn't want me to do something, I'd be lying flat on my back with a dagger at my throat before I even took my next breath. Even if you can't see an inch in front of you."

Well...

"You have your dagger on you, don't you?"

I sighed. "I do."

"Knew it." He let go of my hand, and I let mine fall to my lap.

"No one can see us. No one is even aware that we're here. As far as anyone knows, you are in your room."

"This is still reckless for a multitude of reasons. If someone comes in here—"

"I'd hear them before they did," he said. Before I could voice that his hearing couldn't be as special as his sight, he added, "And if someone did, they'd have no idea who we are."

I drew my head back, putting space between my upper body and his. "Is this why you led me out here to this place?"

"What is *this*, Princess?"

"To be…inappropriate."

"And why would I do that?" he asked, his voice dropping low as his hand touched my arm.

"Why? I think it's pretty obvious, *Hawke*. I'm sitting in your lap. I doubt that's how you normally hold innocent conversations with people."

"Very rarely is anything I do innocent, Princess."

"Shocker," I muttered.

"So, you're suggesting I led you out here, instead of toward a private room with a *bed*"—he dragged the tips of his fingers down my right arm—"to engage in a particular type of inappropriate behavior?"

"That's exactly what I'm saying, though my room would've been a better option." My heart had already started pounding the moment my rear ended up in his lap. Now, it felt as if it were going to explode out of my chest.

"What if I said that isn't true?"

"I…" My stomach fluttered as his fingers found their way to my hip. "I wouldn't believe you."

"Then what if I said it didn't start off that way?" His thumb moved against my hip. "But then there was the moonlight and you, with your hair down, in this dress, and *then* the idea occurred to me that this would be the perfect location for some wildly inappropriate behavior."

"Then I…I would say that's more likely."

His hand glided over the thin, gauzy material of the gown. "So, there you have it."

"At least, you're honest." I bit down on my lip as the fluttering deepened. This was dangerous. Even if no one discovered us, it felt like tempting fate with the gods. A few stolen kisses—all right, a little more than a few stolen kisses—was possibly forgivable. But this?

Even those stolen kisses weren't forgivable, at least according to the Duke and Duchess—and the Queen. Then again, if the gods were to intervene, wouldn't they have done so already? I thought about what Tawny had once said about not being sure whether the rules imposed upon me were a decree from the gods.

And if I had interpreted what the Duchess had said about the first Maiden correctly, she'd done a lot of forbidden things.

She hadn't been found unworthy.

"Tell you what. I'll make you a deal."

"A deal?"

"If I do anything you don't like…" Hawke's hand slid down my thigh, causing my breath to catch. Through the dress, his hand closed over the dagger. "I give you permission to stab me."

"That would be excessive."

"I was hoping you'd give me just a measly flesh wound," he added. "But it'd be worth finding out."

I grinned. "You are such a bad influence."

"I think we've already established that only the bad can be influenced."

"And I think I already told you that your logic is faulty," I repeated, closing my eyes as his fingers followed the outline of the sheathed blade.

Another hot, tight shiver curled its way down my spine, and I had the sudden urge to squeeze my legs together. Somehow, I refrained.

I resisted him, despite knowing how I would've let him kiss me the night before.

"I'm the Maiden, Hawke," I reminded him—or myself, I wasn't sure.

"And I don't care."

My eyes flew open in shock. "I can't believe you just said that."

"I did. And I'll say it again. I don't care what you are." Hawke's hand slid off my back. A moment later, I felt his palm flatten against my cheek with unerring accuracy. "I care about who you are."

Oh.

Oh, gods.

My chest swelled so fast and full, it was a small miracle that I didn't float right out of his lap and into the willow. What he'd said…

It had to be the sweetest and most perfect thing anyone could say.

"Why?" I demanded, almost wishing he hadn't spoken those words. "Why would you say that?"

"Are you seriously asking me that?"

"Yes, I am. It doesn't make sense."

"You don't make sense."

I hit his shoulder—or chest. Some extremely hard part of him.

Hawke grunted. "Ouch."

I so did not hit him hard enough for that. "You're fine."

"I'm bruised."

"You're ridiculous," I retorted. "And it's you who makes no sense."

"I'm the one sitting here being honest. You're the one hitting me. How do I not make sense?"

"Because this whole thing makes no sense." Frustration rose swiftly through me, and I started to stand, but the hand on my hip stopped me. Or I let it stop me. I wasn't sure. And that was even more irritating. "You could be spending time with anyone, Hawke— any number of people you wouldn't have to hide in a willow tree to be with."

"And yet, I'm here with you. And before you even begin to think it's because of my duty to you, it's not. I could've just walked you back to your room and stayed out in the hall."

"That's my point. It makes no sense. You can have a slew of willing participants in…whatever this is. It would be easy," I said. Pretty Britta came to mind. I was sure he'd had her. "You can't have me. I'm…I'm un-have-able."

"I'm confident that's not even a word."

"That's not the point. I'm not allowed to do this. Any of this. I shouldn't have done what I did at the Red Pearl," I continued. "It doesn't matter if I want—"

"And you *do* want." His whisper danced over my cheek. "What you want is me."

My breath caught. "That doesn't matter."

"What you want should always matter."

A short, harsh laugh left me. "It doesn't, and that's another thing that isn't the point. You could—"

"I heard you the first time, Princess. You're right. I could find someone who would be easier." His fingers traced the line of my mask from my right ear and along my cheek. I had no idea how he could see. "Ladies or Lords in Wait, who aren't burdened by rules or limitations, who aren't Maidens I'm sworn to protect. There are a lot of ways I could occupy my time that don't include explaining in great detail why I'm choosing to be *where* I am, with *whom* I choose."

The corners of my lips started to turn down.

"The thing is," he went on, "none of them intrigue me. You do."

You intrigue me.

"It's really that simple for you?" I asked, wanting to believe him, and also not.

His forehead rested against mine, startling me. "Nothing is ever simple. And when it is, it's rarely ever worth it."

"Then why?"

"I'm beginning to believe that's your favorite question."

"Maybe." My lips twitched. "It's just that...gods, there are a lot of reasons why I don't understand how you can be this intrigued. You've seen me." My face heated, and I sincerely hoped he couldn't see it. I hated saying it, but it was a reality. "You've seen what I look like—"

"I have, and I think you already know what I think. I said it in front of you, in front of the Duke, and I told you outside the Great Hall—"

"I know what you said, and I'm not bringing up what I look like for you to shower me with compliments. It's just..." Gods, I wished I hadn't said anything. I shook my head. "Never mind. Forget I said that."

"I can't. I won't."

"Great," I muttered.

"You're just used to assholes like the Duke," he said, and what sounded like a low growl rumbled from him. "He may be an Ascended, but he's worthless."

My heart dropped. "You shouldn't say things like that, Hawke. You—"

"I'm not afraid to speak the truth. He may be powerful, but he's just a weak man, who proves his strength by attempting to humiliate those more powerful than he is. Someone like you, with your strength? It makes him feel incompetent—which he is. And your scars? They are a testament to your fortitude. They are proof of what you survived. They are evidence of why you are here when so many twice your age wouldn't be. They're not ugly. Far from it. They're beautiful, Poppy."

Poppy.

"That's the third time you've called me that," I said.

"Fourth," he corrected, and I blinked. "We're friends, aren't we? Only your friends and your brother call you that, and you may be the Maiden, and I'm a Royal Guard, but all things considered, I would hope that you and I are friends."

"We are." And we were.

His hand flattened against my cheek, and a sigh shuddered through him. "And I'm not...I'm not being a good friend or guard right now. I'm not..." His hand slid, and his fingers curled around the nape of my neck for a few seconds before he slipped his hand away. "I really should get you back to your room. It's getting late."

I exhaled raggedly. "It is."

He was going to take me back—to that room where I was the Maiden, the Chosen. Back to where I wasn't Poppy but a shadow of a person who wasn't allowed to experience, need, live, or *want*. I would no longer be who he saw.

"Hawke?" I whispered, my heart crashing like thunder. "Kiss me. Please."

Chapter 25

Hawke had gone so still against me that I wasn't sure if he even took a breath. My request had shocked him—shocked *me*.

I think *I* might've stopped breathing.

"Gods," he breathed, and one hand returned to my cheek. "You don't have to ask me twice, Princess, and you never have to beg."

Before I had a chance to respond, his lips brushed over mine. I gasped at the soft contact, and I swore I could feel his lips curve against mine in a smile. I wished I could see it because it seemed like a full grin, the kind that lifted both sides of his mouth and made both dimples appear, but then he moved his mouth along mine, painstakingly slow as if he were mapping out the curve of my lips with his. I held completely still, my heart feeling like a trapped butterfly as he retraced the path he'd just made. Tiny shivers hit every part of my body. I trembled as my hands curled into the front of his tunic, no doubt wrinkling the fine material.

This touch was barely a kiss, but gods, the gentleness, the sweetness of it shook me, rattled me to the core.

Then Hawke tilted his head, increasing the pressure, deepening the kiss. Suddenly, everything changed. This kiss—its rawness—left me breathless. Resulted in both of us gasping when we parted, our chests rising and falling quickly. I couldn't see his eyes in the dark, but I could feel his penetrating stare.

I wasn't thinking about what I was in those seconds. I wasn't thinking about what was forbidden and what was right. I wasn't thinking at all, truth be told, and I didn't know who moved first. Hawke? Me? Both of us at the very same moment? Our lips touched again, and this time, there was no hesitation. There was just want, so much of it, and a hundred other powerful, forbidden things that pounded through me. His lips scorched mine, heated my blood, and set fire to my senses. His hands moved to my shoulders, sliding down my arms. Hawke shuddered, and a sound emerged from the back of his throat, sort of like a half-growl, half-moan. It sent little shivers of pleasure and panic darting through me as he parted my lips. The hunger behind our kiss should've scared me—and maybe it did a little because it felt like too much and not nearly enough all at the same time. I moaned as his hands drifted down my sides. It felt like my body was sparking, igniting—

He gripped my waist, lifting me and settling me again so my knees fell to either side of his hips with *me* pressed against *him*. His breeches and my gown served as no real barrier. I could feel him, and I shuddered as a sharp, pulsing ache throbbed through me. His answering moan, another deep, rough sound, shattered whatever hesitancy I had. I placed my hands on his chest, marveling at the way his body jerked as I slid them up over his shoulders and then around his neck. I did then what I wished I'd done at the Red Pearl. I sank my fingers into his hair, and the strands were as soft as I'd thought they would be. No other part of him felt that way. He was all hard heat against me.

Hawke's arms moved around me, pulling me so tightly against him that there was barely any space between us. He kissed me again, kept kissing me, and I knew this was more than a kiss. It went beyond that, beyond how he felt and how he made me feel.

His words had touched the deepest part of me, and it was thrilling. I felt *alive*, like I was finally waking up.

And I never wanted it to stop.

Not with the rush of sensations flowing through me. I knew in the back of my mind that I'd lost control of my gift. My shields were wide open, and there was no way to tell if what I felt belonged to him or me or both of us.

Instinct took over, guiding my body—my hips to push and roll—and he shuddered again, catching my bottom lip between his. He grabbed fistfuls of the skirt of my gown, lifting until his hands touched my calves. A tremor went through me like lightning.

"Remember," he said against my lips as his palms glided up to the curve of my knees. "Anything you don't like, say the word, and I'll stop."

I nodded, seeking his mouth in the darkness. When I found him, I wondered how I'd made it this long without kissing him again.

I wondered how I could go on without doing it more.

That thought threatened to dampen the heat, but his hands were moving again, skimming over my skin and sending a rush of heated blood to every part of my body. I shifted forward until our hips were melded together. I moved. We moved. And I thought I whispered his name before I kissed him again, slipping my tongue between his lips, against his teeth—

Hawke jerked his head back, panting as he rested his forehead against mine. "Poppy," he said in a way that made my name sound like both a prayer and a curse.

"Yes?" My fingers opened and closed around the silky softness of his hair.

"That was the fifth time I've said your name, in case you're still keeping track."

I grinned. "I am."

"Good." He slipped his hands out from under my gown, and one of them found its way to my cheek. He traced the edge of my mask, surprising me yet again with his sight. "I don't think I was being honest a few moments ago."

"About what?" I loosened my grip on his hair, lowering my hands to his shoulders.

"About stopping," he admitted quietly, drawing his fingers down my cheek and over my jaw. "I would stop, but I don't think you would stop me."

"I'm not exactly understanding what you're saying." I let my eyes close. Despite being confused by his words and the fact that we weren't kissing, I liked the intimacy of how close we were, how his head rested against mine.

He drew the tips of his fingers down the side of my neck. "Do you want me to be blunt?"

"I always want you to be honest."

My senses were still open. I knew that because I felt a foreign sensation coming through the connection, but it was too brief for me to figure out what it was.

And then he kissed my temple, and I thought about the odd, ashy feeling that had coated my throat. "I was seconds from taking you to the ground and becoming a very, very bad guard."

Air caught in my throat as a pulse of warm heat went straight through me. I didn't know a lot, but I knew enough to know what he meant. "Really?"

"Really," he answered seriously.

I should've felt relief that he'd stopped, and I did. But I also didn't. What I felt was a confusing mess. But I knew one thing for sure.

"I don't think I would've stopped you," I whispered. I would've let him take me to the ground, and I would've welcomed what he did, consequences be damned.

Hawke's body shook as he moaned. "You're not helping."

"I'm a bad Maiden."

"No." He kissed my other temple. "You're a perfectly normal girl. What is expected of you is what's bad." He paused. "And, yes, you're also a very bad Maiden."

Instead of being offended—because there was no way, even if I didn't count tonight, that I could deny that—I laughed and was rewarded by his arm coming back around me. Hawke pulled me back to his body, sliding his hand to my nape. I settled my cheek against his shoulder as his grip briefly tightened, and then his fingers moved, working the muscles of my neck. I wasn't sure how long we stayed there like that, quiet and hidden away under the willow, but I did know that it was far past the point where my blood had cooled, and my heart had slowed. I didn't move then, and neither did Hawke. I thought that maybe…maybe being held like this, so close and so tight, felt just as good as the kissing and the touching.

Perhaps even better, but in a different way.

But it was getting late, and unsurprisingly, Hawke was the responsible one. He kissed the crown of my head, causing my heart to squeeze in a way that was so sweet, it was almost painful.

"I need to get you back, Princess."

"I know." But still, I held onto him.

He chuckled, and I grinned into his shoulder. "You have to let me go, though."

"I know." I sighed, yet I remained where I was, thinking that the moment we stepped outside of the willow, we would be back in the real world, no longer in our haven where I was Poppy, and who I was mattered. "I don't want to."

He was silent for so long that I feared that I'd said the wrong thing, but then his arm tightened around me again. When he spoke, his voice was strangely rough. "Neither do I."

I almost asked why we had to, but I managed to stop myself. Hawke stood then, taking me with him, and I reluctantly lowered my legs. We stood there for another all-too-short moment, his arm around me, my arms stretched above me, and our bodies still connected.

Then I took a deep breath, opened my eyes, and took a step back. I couldn't see him, but I wasn't surprised when his hand found mine, and he led me toward the willow branches.

He stopped. "Ready?"

Not at all, but I said yes, and we walked out from underneath the willow, my chest threatening to become heavy. I refused to let that happen. At least not right this moment. I had all night for everything I felt to become memories.

I had many nights ahead for that.

We found our way back to the gas-lamp-lit walkway, the garden silent except for the sound of the wind and our steps. I looked down the shadowy paths, wondering what had happened to the hushed conversations and soft moans. We rounded the corner, nearing the fountain—

And came face to face with Vikter, sans mask.

My heart lurched in my chest as I stumbled back a step. Hawke turned as if to catch me, but I gained my footing. "Oh, my gods," I whispered, looking up at Vikter. "You about gave me a heart attack."

He stared at me for a long moment and then turned to Hawke. A muscle in his jaw clenched as he looked down to where Hawke still held my hand.

Oh, shit.

Slowly, Vikter looked up while I tried to pull my hand free. Hawke held on for a moment and then let go. I clasped my hands together, my eyes wide behind my mask.

"It's time to go back to your room, *Maiden*." Vikter bit out, voice low.

I winced at his tone.

"I was in the process of escorting *Penellaphe* back to her room," Hawke replied.

Vikter's head snapped in his direction. "I know exactly what you were in the process of doing."

My mouth dropped open.

"Doubtful," Hawke murmured.

Which was the wrong thing to say. "You think I don't know?" Vikter stepped into Hawke's space, and while Hawke was an inch or two taller, they were eye to eye. "It only takes one look at both of you to know."

One look at both of us? Blinking, I lifted my fingers to my lips that were still humming and felt puffy. My gaze flew to Hawke's mouth. His lips *did* look swollen.

Hawke held his ground and Vikter's stare, and I really had no idea what he could say. "Nothing happened, Vikter."

Well...

"Nothing?" Vikter snarled. "Boy, I may have been born at night, but I wasn't born last night."

I blinked.

"Thanks for pointing out the obvious," Hawke retorted. "But you're stepping way over the line."

"*I* am?" Vikter laughed, but there was no humor to the sound. "Do you understand what she is?" he demanded, voice so low it was barely audible. "Do you even understand what you could've caused if anyone other than I had come upon you two?"

I stepped forward. "Vikter—"

"I know exactly who she is," Hawke shot back. "Not what she is. Maybe you've forgotten that she's not just a godsdamn inanimate object whose only purpose is to serve a kingdom, but I haven't."

"Hawke." I whirled on him.

"Oh, yeah, that's rich, coming from you. How do you see her, Hawke?" Vikter stepped in more. Suddenly, they were as close as Hawke and I had been under the willow. "Another notch in your bedpost?"

I gasped, spinning back around. "*Vikter.*"

"Is it because she's the ultimate challenge?" Vikter continued, and my lips parted.

Hawke's chin dipped. "I get that you're protective of her. I understand that. But I'll tell you just one more time, you're way out of line."

"And I'll promise you this…it will be over my dead body before you spend another moment alone with her."

Hawke smiled then, one side of his lips curling up. There was no dimple. His features seemed to sharpen in the moonlight, creating shadows under his eyes and on his cheekbones. "She thinks of you as a father," he said, his voice so soft it sent a chill down my spine. "It would hurt her greatly if something unfortunate were to happen to you."

"Is that a threat?" Vikter's brows lifted.

"I'm just letting you know that is the only reason I'm not making your promise come true this very second," he warned. "But you need to step back. If you don't, someone is going to get hurt, and that someone won't be me. Then Poppy will get upset"—he turned to me—"and that's the sixth time I've said it," he added, and all I could do was stare at him. "I don't want to see her upset, so step. The fuck. Back."

"Both of you need to stop," I whispered, grabbing Vikter's arm, but he didn't budge. "Seriously. This is escalating over nothing. Please."

They didn't look away from each other, and it was almost like I wasn't there. Finally, Vikter stepped back. I didn't know if he saw something in Hawke's face, or if it was me tugging on his arm, but he took another step away, his skin unusually pale in the moonlight.

"I'll be guarding her for the rest of the evening," Vikter stated. "You're dismissed."

Hawke smirked, and I shot him a glare he didn't even seem to notice. He said nothing as Vikter took my arm and turned. I went with him, having taken only a couple of steps before I looked over my shoulder.

The space where Hawke had stood was empty.

I looked around quickly, not seeing him. Where had he—?

"I don't even know what to say to you right now," Vikter stated. "Gods. After I finished talking to the Commander, I couldn't find you, but I ran into Tawny. She said you returned to your room. I went to check on you, and when you weren't there, I figured you could be here. But I did not expect to find *this*."

It seemed as if he knew exactly what he wanted to say.

"Dammit, Poppy, you know better than this. You know what's at risk, and I'm not talking about the fucking kingdom."

Hearing him curse caught my attention. I looked up as he stalked along, bringing me with him.

"If anyone had seen you with him, missing a few days of training would've been the least of my fears," he went on, and my stomach dropped. "And Hawke knows better. Dammit, he never should've laid a hand—"

"Nothing happened, Vikter."

"Bullshit, Poppy. You looked like you'd been thoroughly kissed. I hope that was all."

"Oh, my gods," I exclaimed, my face flaming.

"Don't lie to me."

"We were coming back in to go to my room—"

Vikter stopped, looking down at me with wide eyes and lifted eyebrows.

"Not what you're thinking," I insisted, and that was the truth. "Please. Just let me explain what happened," I said, desperately trying to figure out how to fix this.

"I don't think I want to know."

I ignored that. "After you left to speak to the Commander, I felt bad because Tawny wouldn't leave my side. I knew that as long as I stayed at the Rite, she would feel as if she had to stay with me. So, I told her I was going back to my room so she could have fun."

"That doesn't explain how you ended up out here with him."

"I was getting to that," I said, trying to be patient. "Hawke knew I didn't want to go back to my room, and he knew how much I used to love the gardens. So, he brought me out so I could...so I could get past what happened here with Rylan. That's why we were out here."

"I feel like you're leaving a lot out."

At this point, I knew I couldn't continue lying, at least not about everything. "We walked around, and Hawke showed me a place he enjoyed in the garden. I...I asked him to kiss me."

Vikter looked away, jaw locking.

"And we did kiss. Okay? It happened, but that was all. He stopped it before it went any further," I told him, speaking the truth. "I know I shouldn't have asked him—"

"He shouldn't have been so willing to oblige you."

"That's not the point."

"That *is* the point, Poppy."

"No, it's not." I pulled my arm free, closing my hands into fists before I picked something up and threw it. "He's not the damn point!"

Shock flickered over his face.

I made an effort to lower my voice. "This whole stupid thing is the point. The fact that I can't do anything is the point. That I can't have one night to do something normal and fun and enjoyable. That I can't experience anything without being warned to remember what I am. That every privilege you have, and Tawny has, and everyone else has, I *don't* have." My voice cracked as the back of my throat started to burn. "I have *nothing*."

His expression softened. "Poppy—"

"No." I took a step back, his features blurring. "You don't understand. I can't celebrate my birthdays because that's ungodly. I'm not allowed to go to picnics at the Grove or to supper with others because I'm the Maiden. I'm not allowed to defend myself because that would be unseemly. I don't even know how to ride a horse. Nearly every book is forbidden to me. I can't socialize or make friends because my sole purpose is to serve the kingdom by going to the gods—something no one will even explain. What does that actually mean?"

Breathing heavily, I tried to rein my emotions back in, but I couldn't. Something in me snapped, broke wide-open, and I couldn't stop. "I don't even know if I'll have a future beyond my Ascension. In less than a year or even sooner, I may lose every chance I have to do everything everyone else takes for granted. I have no life, Vikter. Nothing."

"Poppy," he whispered.

"Everything has been taken from me—my free will, my choice, my future—and I still have to suffer through the Duke's *lessons*," I spat out, shuddering. "I still have to stand there and let him hit me. Let him look at me and touch me! Do whatever he or the Lord wants—" Sucking in a fiery, painful breath, I lifted my hands, grabbing fistfuls of my hair, pulling them back as Vikter closed his eyes. "I have to stand there and take it. I can't even scream or cry. I can do nothing. So I'm sorry that choosing something that I want for myself is such a disappointment to you, the kingdom, everyone else, and the gods. Where is the honor in being the Maiden? What exactly should I be proud of? Who would want this? Point me in their direction, and I'll gladly switch places with them. It should be no shock that I want to be found unworthy."

The moment those words left my mouth, I smacked my hands over my lips. Vikter's eyes snapped open, and for a long moment, we stared at one another, the truth a double-edged sword between us.

"Poppy." Vikter looked around and then reached for me. "It's okay. It's going to be okay."

I danced out of his reach, curling my fingers against my mouth. It wasn't fine. It wasn't going to be all right. I'd said it. The truth. Out loud. Heart thumping and stomach churning, I turned and started walking toward the castle. I thought I might be sick. "I want to go back to my chambers," I whispered, lowering my hands. Vikter started to speak. "Please. I just want to go back to my room."

He didn't respond, thank the gods, but he followed directly behind me. All I could focus on was putting one foot in front of the other. If I didn't, the angry, messy, and violent ball of emotion lodged in my throat would erupt. I would erupt. That was how I felt. I would explode everywhere in a shower of sparks and flames, and I didn't care what I looked like when we entered the hall and moved into the light, or what people saw if they looked at me and realized that I was the Maiden. My entire body was trembling with the force to keep—

A loud, cracking sound reminding me of wood splintering drew us to a halt. We turned to the Great Hall just as a shout sounded, followed by screams—piercing screams, one after another. My heart dropped.

Someone—a Lady in Wait—backed out of the Great Hall, her red gown fluttering around her feet as she pressed her hands to her mouth.

Vikter started toward the entryway but stopped. He turned to me, and I knew he was going to take me back to my room, but the screams kept coming, followed by shouts of panic and horror. Another joined the Lady in Wait. Then another, a servant carrying an empty tray. He turned and vomited.

"What happened?" I demanded, but no one answered. No one could hear me over the *screams*. My wide gaze met Vikter's. "Tawny is in there."

The set to his jaw said that he couldn't care less. He moved to grab me, but I was fast because he'd taught me how to be when I needed speed. I evaded his reach as I raced for the entryway, his muttered curse ringing in my ears.

A rush of people came out of the entryway, knocking into my shoulder. A blur of masked faces came from every direction. I was thrust to the side, my slippered feet slipping on the polished floors, but I pushed forward. Tawny was still in there. That was all I could think as I broke through the panicked crowd.

I slid to a stop, my gaze landing on the dais, to what was *behind* the dais. "Oh, my gods," I whispered.

I knew what had made the cracking sound. One of the wooden rods that held the heavy banners had cracked. The Rite banner had fallen, pooling on the floor of the dais, but red still streaked the wall.

I saw what had broken the rod, what hung from the remaining one. Rope stretched arms outward, and so much red streaked pale skin. I knew who it was. I knew why the Duchess stood in the center of the Great Hall, her arms at her sides, and why everyone else was frozen in shock. It was the hair so blond that it almost looked white.

It was the Duke.

Even from where I stood, I knew what had been shoved into his chest—through his heart. I would recognize it anywhere.

It was the cane he'd lashed me with.

And above him, written in red—in *blood*—was the mark of the Dark One.

From Blood and Ash....
We Will Rise.

Chapter 26

The Duke of Masadonia was dead.

Murdered.

I couldn't pull my gaze from him, not even when I became aware of Vikter coming to stand beside me. He said something, but I couldn't hear him over the pounding of my own heart.

The Duke had been staked through the chest in the same manner the cursed or a Craven would be killed—with wood fashioned from a tree that had grown in the Blood Forest.

With the same cane he'd often stroked lovingly right before it whistled through the air, bruising my back and sometimes even splitting the skin.

Dumbly, I wondered how someone could get the cane through the Duke's chest. The ends were not sharp but smooth and rounded. The effort and strength that would've required... Not to mention, the Duke would've fought back unless he'd been incapacitated beforehand.

Only an Atlantian could've accomplished that.

Vikter touched my arm, and slowly, I tore my gaze from the Duke's remains. "He's dead," I said. "He's really dead." A very inappropriate giggle welled up, and I clamped my mouth shut as I turned back to where the Duke was impaled.

I didn't think it was funny. Not at all. I didn't like the man—frankly, I hated him with every fiber of my being—but an Atlantian had gotten into Castle Teerman yet again, and that was frightening. Because of that, this wasn't funny.

It also wasn't sad.

Gods, I truly was unworthy, and probably a terrible person, but I sighed softly, a sound of...relief passing my lips. No more *lessons*. No more lingering stares and touches. No more pain at his hands. No more heavy, sticky shame. My gaze shifted to where a tall, dark-haired Ascended joined the Duchess. No more Lord Mazeen.

Without the Duke, he had little sway over me, and I almost smiled again.

Movement to my left snagged my attention, and I turned, seeing Tawny pushing through a group of Ascended and the Lords and Ladies in Wait. She hurried across the room, her eyes wide behind her mask.

Curls bounced off her cheeks as she shook her head. "I can't believe what I'm seeing." She clasped my hands, glancing toward the dais. Shuddering, she quickly looked back at me. "This can't be real."

"It's real." I turned to the dais once more. Guards were trying to get the Duke down, but he was too far up on the wall. "They need a ladder."

"What?" Tawny whispered.

"A ladder. They're not going to be able to reach him," I pointed out. I could feel Tawny's gaze on me. "Do you think he was up there for the whole Rite? The entire time?"

"I don't even know what to think." She turned so her back was to the dais. "At all."

"At least we know why he didn't show," I said.

"Poppy," she exclaimed in a low voice.

"Sorry." I watched the Duchess turn to the Lord, her lips moving fast. "The Duchess doesn't seem all that torn up, does she?"

Vikter stepped in then. "I think it's time that I get you back to your chambers."

It probably was, so I nodded and started to turn—

Glass shattered. I spun toward the sound as pieces flew through the air. It was one of the windows facing the garden. Tawny's grip tightened on my arm. Another window broke, this time to our left, and we both whirled to see shards piercing, cutting into the group standing there—the gathering Tawny had been a part of. Screams of shock gave way to ones of pain as jagged chunks of glass sliced into skin. A girl stumbled out from the scattering group, her hands trembling as she lifted them to her bloodied face. Numerous tiny cuts marked her cheeks and brow. It was Loren. She doubled over, screaming as the blond girl in front of her slowly turned around.

Glass jutted from her eye, and red streamed down her face. She crumpled like a paper sack.

"Dafina!" cried Tawny, letting go of my arm and starting toward her.

I snapped out of the shock and lurched forward, grabbing Tawny's arm as a Lord in Wait dropped to his knees and fell forward. Had he been hit by glass, too? I wasn't sure. She cranked her head around. "What? I have to go to her. She needs help—"

"No." I pulled her back while Loren went to her friend, trying to get her to stand—to move. Another window exploded. "You can't go near the windows. I'm sorry. You *can't*."

Tawny's eyes glistened. "But—"

Something whizzed through the air, striking a Lord. The impact spun him around, and Tawny screamed. An arrow had struck him through the *eye*. He was an Ascended, but he went down, dead before he hit the floor. Blood pooled under him.

The Ascended could die.

Their head and heart were as vulnerable as a mortal's, and whoever had released that arrow knew just that.

Short sword unsheathed, Vikter shoved Tawny and I behind him as the Duchess, surrounded by Royal Guards, screamed, "Get her out of here! Now! Get—"

An arrow pierced the Royal Guard standing in front of her. Blood spurted from his neck as he reached for the arrow, his mouth open and closing soundlessly.

Gods...

I staggered into Tawny as Vikter turned us around and herded us toward the opening. We started forward as I reached for the dagger on my thigh—

The shrieks that came from outside the Great Hall stopped all of this for just a handful of seconds. The sounds...

Pain.

Terror.

Death.

Then a wave of people rushed the Great Hall, Ascended and mortal, commoner and Royal alike, all running toward us. The gowns and tunics of some were a deeper red now, faces either leached of color or splattered with crimson. Some fell before they made it to the steps, arrows and...*knives* embedded deep into their backs. Others toppled down the stairs in their panicked run.

We were about to be overrun.

I didn't even reach for my dagger. I couldn't fight them. They weren't the enemy.

"Shit," Vikter growled, spinning toward me as Tawny stood frozen. My eyes met his, and I knew what was about to happen. My heart dropped. "Protect the Maiden!" he shouted.

Grabbing hold of Tawny by both her arms, I tugged her against me and wrapped my arms around her, holding her as tightly as I could. Vikter's arms went around me. Guards pressed in, and because of how close I held Tawny to my body, they were forced to form a barricade around both of us.

"I'm scared," Tawny whispered against my cheek.

"It's okay," I lied as I forced my eyes open, even though I wanted to close them. My heart slammed against my ribs. For a brief second, I prayed to the gods. I sent up a prayer that Hawke was nowhere near here. That he'd left to blow off some steam and had gone into the city. "Brace your—"

It was like being hit by falling rocks.

Bodies slammed into the guards from seemingly every direction, pushing them into Tawny and me. Hilts of swords cracked into ribs and other bones. Elbows knocked against flesh. Vases shattered. People *broke*. The crush of the crowd, of the hundreds who had fled the Great Hall and now returned was too much—

It was as if a massive wave rolled across the floor, tearing free one guard and then another and another until I felt Vikter's grip loosen. And then he was gone, and something—*someone*—hard hit me, crashed into Tawny and me. She was ripped away, carried off with the wave of screaming, shrieking people as they ran from whatever it was that had scared them.

That was my last thought as the room seemed to turn upside down. My feet left the floor, and I experienced a boneless, airy moment. I saw the painted gods on the ceiling, then terror-stricken faces and blood and foam. I came back down, slipping and cracking my knees on the hard floor.

I tried to push up, knowing I couldn't stay down. "Tawny!" I screamed, looking for her, but all I saw was red...everywhere.

A knee connected with my ribs, knocking the air out of my lungs. A booted foot landed on my back, slamming me to the floor. Pain shot down my spine. I scrambled blindly over spilled food, crushed roses, and gods...oh, gods, over wet and warm bodies as I tried to stand. Something caught my skirt, causing me to fall forward.

I came face-to-face with Dafina, and it seemed like time stopped as I stared down at her one beautiful blue eye open and glazed over. That mask of hers, just as gaudy as Loren's, more red than any other color now that it was drenched in blood. I reached forward, wanting to wipe the blood from the crystals—

I saw Loren then, curled into herself behind Dafina, her arms over her head. I scrambled forward, grabbing her arm. Her head jerked up. Alive. She was alive.

"Get up," I said, pulling on her as I struggled to stand, but something held me down. I looked over my shoulder and wished I hadn't. It was a body. I grabbed my skirt, ripping it. I turned back to Loren as the faintest scent of something sulfuric, something acrid reached me. My stomach dropped. "Get up. Get up. Get up!"

"I can't," she cried. "I can't. I can't—"

Screaming as someone fell over me, I grabbed Loren by her dress, her arm, her hair—anything I could grab onto and pulled her over Dafina. My senses had cracked wide-open, and terror and pain came from her, came from everywhere. I gained my footing, hauling Loren to her feet. I saw a pillar and headed for that.

"See the pillar?" I asked Loren. "We can stay there. We can hold onto it."

"My arm," she gasped. "I think it's broken."

"I'm sorry." I shifted my grip so it was around her waist.

"I need to get Dafina," she said. "I need to get her. She shouldn't be left like that. I need to get her."

A knot lodged in my throat as I kept pulling Loren toward the pillar. I couldn't think of Dafina and that mask and that one beautiful remaining eye. I couldn't think about the bodies I crawled over. I couldn't. "We're almost there."

Someone fell into us, but I held on—Loren held on, and we were almost there. Just a few more steps, and we'd be out of the crush. We'd be—

Loren jerked, and something wet and warm sprayed the right side of my face and my neck. Loren's arms loosened, and I caught her, her sudden weight pulling at the tender skin around my ribs. "Hold on," I told her. "We're almost there—" I looked down, peered at her because she was falling, and I couldn't hold her.

She fell, and I couldn't believe what I was seeing. I refused to reconcile what I saw as I was jostled to the left and then to the right. There couldn't be an arrow through the back of her head, the fletching vibrating.

"We were almost there," I whispered.

A piercing whistle sounded from outside, followed by another and another. Slowly, I lifted my chin and stared out into the shadows of the garden, some deeper and darker than others. They drew closer.

I'd just been out there with Hawke. Had he gotten out in time? Or had he been felled by—

I couldn't think like that. He must have left. He had to.

Someone grabbed my arm, spinning me around.

"The side entrance." Commander Jansen's face appeared in front of me. "We must get to the side entrance now, Maiden."

I blinked slowly, numbly. "Vikter, Tawny. I must find them—"

"They don't matter right now. I need to get you out. Dammit," he cursed as I turned away, desperately scanning the mass of people for those I cared about. He grabbed for me, but my arm was too slippery. He lost his grip as I raced into the churning mass of people.

"Tawny!" I screamed, shoving past an older man. "Vikter! Tawny—"

"Poppy!" Hands grabbed my back, and I spun. Tawny clutched me, her mask gone, and her hairdo half fallen. "Oh gods, Poppy!"

Holding onto her, I looked over her shoulder and met Lord Mazeen's icy stare. "Good to see you're still alive," he said.

Before I could respond, Vikter shoved through, pulling me away from Tawny. "Are you hurt?" he shouted, wiping at the blood on my face. "Are you injured?"

My lips parted. I saw the Duchess behind us, surrounded by guards. Beyond them, I saw the Duke.

Flames crawled and licked up his legs, climbing over his torso and spreading across his arms.

"My gods," Tawny said. I thought she saw what I did, but then I realized that she was facing the entrance. I turned.

They stood in the entryway and at the broken windows, dozens dressed in the ceremonial garb of the Rite, their faces shielded by silver masks. *Wolven.* Their facial coverings had been designed with the characteristics of the wolven—ears, snouts, elongated fangs. Those at the entryway were armed with daggers and battleaxes. Those at the windows had been the ones to fire the arrows. There were Descenters, possibly even Atlantians among the masked.

It struck me then.

They had been among us the entire night. I thought of Agnes, of what she had said and how nervous she'd looked, and how Vikter had felt as if there'd been more she hadn't told us. Had she known and tried to warn me? Not the guards and the commoners who lay injured and dead on the floor. Not the Ascended who'd fallen. Not Loren and Dafina, who'd never harmed a single person.

My hands curled into fists.

"From blood and ash," one of them shouted.

Another yelled. "We will rise!"

"From blood and ash!" several yelled as they started down the steps. "We will rise!"

Vikter grabbed me as I took hold of Tawny's hand. "We need to move fast," he said, nodding at the Commander, who was now beside the Lord.

The Royal Guards surrounded the Duchess and us, pushing back through the masses. Every part of me was sickened as they guided us through the crowd toward the open door, where people were being thrown back. We were escaping, and they were being held in.

"This isn't right," I said, and then I yelled it over the screams as I was pulled through the door. "They're going to be massacred."

Ahead of me, the Duchess's head whipped around, and her black eyes met mine. "The Royals will take care of them."

Normally, I would've laughed at that. The Royals? The Ascended, who never seemed to raise a hand, would take care of them? But there was something in her eyes, almost where her pupils would be if I could see them. It was like burning coal.

We went through the doorway, and...and others went out into the Great Hall. They weren't guards. They were Ascended, male and female, their eyes carrying that same unholy light.

Racing along, I looked over my shoulder as the last of the Ascended swept through the door, her crimson gown like a cape. A Royal Guard closed the door behind her and then stood with his back pressed against it, his short swords crossed.

Guards streamed past us then as we ran through the foyer, around the statues, and I looked at every one of them, hoping and fearing that I'd see Hawke. Each face that passed me was unfamiliar.

And then the screams from the Great Hall ceased.

My steps faltered. Tawny looked back, too. The screams had simply...stopped.

"Come, Poppy," Vikter urged.

We spilled into the banquet hall. A guard came running over, his face and arm spotted with blood. "They're at the back entrance, surrounding the whole damn castle. The only way out is through them."

"No," The Duchess argued. "We wait them out. Here. This room will do." She stalked forward. "They won't make it to us."

"Your Grace—" Vikter started.

"No." The Duchess turned to him, that same odd fire I'd seen earlier in her eyes. "They will not make it to us." Her gaze snapped to me. "Bring Penellaphe."

The skin around Vikter's mouth tightened, and we exchanged looks. He shook his head. I held onto Tawny's hand as we crossed the room and moved into one of the greeting rooms. In the back of my mind, I was at least grateful that it hadn't been the room Malessa had been murdered in.

Because there was a good chance that we were all going to die in here.

The Commander remained outside, sword drawn, and I knew he was going back to the Hall. My dagger practically burned against my thigh.

As the door closed behind us, I let go of Tawny's hand and looked around. There was only one window, but it was far too small for anyone but a child to climb through.

The Duchess dropped into a settee, her lips pressed into a firm line. Lord Mazeen went to her, and I saw that several Royal Guards remained inside.

"Dear girl, you look like you're about to pass out from fright," the Duchess said to Tawny. "We will be just fine in here. I assure you. Come." She patted the seat. "Sit with me."

Tawny glanced at me, and I gave her a discreet nod. She drew in a shallow breath and then joined the Duchess, who turned to the Lord. "Bran, why don't you pour us some of the whiskey."

As the Lord rose to obey the Duchess, I looked at Vikter and whispered, "This is incredibly stupid."

His jaw flexed.

"If they make it in here, we are sitting ducks." I kept my voice low. "That is if we don't burn alive from the flaming Duke."

He turned from the Duchess as he nodded. "Are you armed?"

"Yes."

"Good." His gaze fixed on the door. "If anyone makes it in here, do not hesitate to use what you've been taught."

My gaze lifted to his in question.

"I don't care who sees you," he whispered. "Defend yourself."

Exhaling slowly, I nodded, and then there was only the sound of glass clinking against glass and then nothing more. The guards remained focused on the door, and I stayed near Vikter, checking on Tawny every so often. She was staring straight ahead, the drink virtually forgotten in her hand. Each time I looked, the Lord was staring back at me.

How unfair that he still breathed when so many others did not.

I didn't care how unworthy that thought was. I meant it. I didn't know how much time passed, but my thoughts wandered to Hawke. Fear trickled through my blood like ice.

Lightly touching Vikter's back, I waited until he faced me. "Do you think Hawke is okay?" I whispered.

"He's good at killing," he answered, refocusing on the door. "I'm sure he's fine."

A lot of the guards who'd fallen had been good at killing. All the talent in the kingdom meant nothing when an arrow came out of nowhere.

I forced myself to take a deep, slow breath. The Duke was dead. Masadonia had become the next Goldcrest Manor, but Tawny was okay. So was Vikter. And Hawke had to be. This…this wasn't going to turn out like the night the Craven had come, when my mother—

Something hit the door, causing Tawny to gasp. She clasped her hand over her mouth.

Vikter lifted his finger to his lips. I held my breath. It could've been anything. No need to panic. Yes, we were fish in a barrel, but we were—

The door rattled with the next impact, shaking the hinges. Tawny rose, as did the Duchess. The guards moved to block the entryway, drawing their swords.

Wood cracked and splintered as the deadly edge of a battleax breached the portal.

"What did you say, Your Grace?" the Lord said, sighing. "That they wouldn't make it to us?"

"Shut up," she hissed. "We're fine."

A chunk of wood fell. We were *not* fine.

Vikter looked over his shoulder at me. Our eyes met, and I let go of the breath I had been holding. I turned, planting my foot on the seat of an empty chair. I gathered up my skirt—

"Now, this is getting interesting," the Lord remarked.

My gaze met his as I unsheathed the dagger, wishing I could shove it through his heart. He must've seen that in my stare because his nostrils flared.

"Penellaphe," gasped the Duchess. "What are you doing with a dagger? And under your skirt no less? This whole time?"

A high, panicked giggle snuck out from around Tawny's hand where it covered her mouth, and her eyes widened. "I'm sorry. I'm sorry."

Duchess Teerman shook her head. "What are you doing with a dagger, Penellaphe?"

"Doing my best not to die," I told her. Her mouth dropped open.

Knowing I would hear about this later—if there *was* a later— I turned back to the door. The hall had quieted. Nothing moved beyond the gash in the wood. One of the Royal Guards crept forward and bent down to peer out.

His head tilted to the side. "Shit," he exclaimed, turning. "Get back!"

I jumped, as did Vikter, but two of the guards weren't fast enough. The door blew off its hinges and smacked into them, taking one of them down while the other was caught in the chest by the battering ram. I heard a sickening crunch.

Vikter swung his sword, cutting through bone and tissue. The battering ram hit the ground, along with an arm. A man screamed, stumbling back as blood pumped from the severed limb. He fell to the side, and then they swarmed, swallowing Vikter and the guards. There was no time to give in to panic or fear as one of the Descenters stalked forward, flipping the battleax in his hand. I had no idea if they were here for me or to just shed blood, but with the mask and how I was dressed, they had no idea that I was the Maiden.

The man behind the wolf mask chuckled. "Pretty dagger."

They had no idea I knew how to use it.

He raised the battleax, and I thought the Duchess screamed. Maybe it was Tawny. I wasn't sure, but the sounds they made faded into the background as I let instinct take over.

Waiting until the axe blade whistled through the air, I then shot forward, darting under his arm. I spun behind him just as he turned, slamming the dagger into the back of his neck, right in the area I used to end the cursed.

He was dead before he even realized that I'd killed him.

As he fell forward, I saw the Duchess staring back at me, her mouth hanging open.

"Behind you," Tawny shouted.

Whirling around, I hit the ground as another axe swept through the air. I kicked out, sweeping the man's leg out from under him. He went down just as Vikter turned, his sword arcing through the air as he brought it down. I popped to my feet as a Descenter moved to shove a dagger into Vikter's back.

I shouted a warning, and Vikter threw out his elbow, catching the man under his chin, snapping his neck back.

A Descenter rushed me, axe swinging. I darted to the left just as something—a glass—smacked into the Descenter's metal mask. I glanced over my shoulder to see Tawny sans glass, but she wasn't emptyhanded for long. She grabbed the decanter, holding it like a sword.

I shot forward, thrusting the dagger deep into the Descenter's chest. He went down, taking me with him. I landed on him with a grunt and started to rise. A booted foot kicked out, catching my hand. Fiery pain erupted as the dagger was knocked from my grasp.

It hurt and punched the air from my lungs. Gods, it stung. I reared, falling on my butt. I looked up, scrambling backward. My aching hand rubbed over the handle of an axe.

Above me, the Descenter lifted a sword with two hands, prepared to bring it down. My heart lurched in my chest.

"She's the Maiden!" the Duchess shrieked. "She's the Chosen!"

What the...?

The Descenter hesitated.

Hand tightening around the handle of the axe, I shot forward, dragging the heavy weapon through the air. He tried to move back, but I caught him in the stomach. Blood sprayed as he shouted, dropping the sword to cradle his midsection, his—

Bile hit the back of my throat as I brought the axe down on his neck, ending what would've surely been a painful death from disembowelment.

Hand aching, I gripped the axe as a Descenter took down one of the guards and then moved toward Tawny, his sword dripping blood. Lifting the axe over my head, I did just as Vikter had taught me. I made sure the blade was perfectly straight as I brought it back over my head and then heaved it forward, releasing it. It winged through the air, striking the Descenter in the back. He toppled forward, his sword falling to the floor.

"Gods," Lord Mazeen uttered, staring at me with wide eyes.

"Remember that," I warned, sweeping down to pick up the fallen short sword. "And *this*," I spat. Light and double-edged, I sliced open the throat of the next Descenter.

Breathing heavily, I turned back to the door just as Vikter thrust his sword through the last Descenter. Only one other guard remained standing. I lowered the sword, my chest rising and falling as I stepped over the body...parts. "Is that all?"

Vikter glanced out to the hall. "I think so, but we shouldn't stay here."

There was no way in the world I would stay in this room. The Duchess and the Lord could do whatever they wanted. I turned to Tawny.

"How?" the Duchess demanded, her hands and clothing free of blood and gore while I had to be swimming in it. "How is this possible?" she demanded, staring down at the mess. "How?"

"I trained her," Vikter answered, shocking me. "I've never been more glad that I did than I am right now."

"I do not believe she is in need of any Royal Guards," the Lord commented dryly, his nose wrinkling as he flicked something off his tunic. "But so very unbecoming of a Maiden."

I was two seconds away from showing him just how *unbecoming* I could be.

Vikter touched my arm, drawing my attention to him. *Later*, he mouthed. "Come." He glanced at Tawny. "This isn't safe."

"Really?" whispered Tawny, still holding the decanter as she came forward. "I would've never noticed that."

Vikter's gaze shifted back to me, and even though his cheeks were more red than golden, he smiled. "You make me proud."

I'd wanted to throw something at him while we'd been in the garden, but now I wanted to hug him. I stepped toward him just as Tawny shouted.

Time slowed to a crawl, and yet there wasn't enough time to stop any of what was happening.

Vikter twisted at the waist, facing the door, looking to where a wounded Descenter had risen to his feet, his sword lifted. It hummed through the air, the blade shiny with blood.

"No!" I shouted, but it was too late.

The sword found its target.

Vikter's body jerked, his back bowing as the sword punched through his chest, just above his heart. Shock crawled across his face as he looked down. I stared too, unable to process what I was seeing.

The Descenter tore the sword free, and my own weapon slipped from my hand as I tried to catch Vikter. He couldn't fall. He couldn't go down. He staggered as I wrapped my arms around him, his mouth opening and then closing.

His legs went out from under him, and he toppled. He fell. I didn't remember joining him as I pressed both hands against the wound. I looked up, tried to call for help.

Without warning, the Descenter's head flew in the opposite direction of his body, and I saw Hawke standing there, his eyes a fiery amber, his cheeks speckled with blood and…and soot. Behind him were more guards. As Hawke's gaze swept the room, it landed on us and then stopped. I saw the look on his face, in his golden eyes as he lowered his bloodied sword.

"No," I told him.

Hawke's eyes closed.

"No. No. No." My throat hurt as I pressed my hand to Vikter's wound, and blood gushed against my palm, streaming down my arm.

"No. Gods, no. Please. You're okay. Please—"

"I'm sorry," Vikter rasped out, placing his hand over mine.

"What?" I gasped. "You can't be sorry. You're going to be okay. Hawke." I snapped my head up. "You have to help him."

Hawke knelt at Vikter's side, placing a hand on Vikter's shoulder. "Poppy," he said quietly.

"Help him," I demanded. Hawke said nothing, did nothing. "Please! Go get someone. Do something!"

Vikter's grip tightened on my hand, and when I looked down, I saw the pain settling into his features. I felt his pain through the gift. I was so shocked, so thrown, I hadn't even thought to use it. I tried taking his pain, but I couldn't concentrate, couldn't find those happy, warm memories. I couldn't do anything.

"No. No," I said, closing my eyes. I had this gift for a reason. I could help him. I could take his pain, and that would help calm him until help came—

"Poppy," he wheezed. "Look at me."

Opening my eyes, I shuddered at what I saw. Blood darkened the corners of his too pale lips.

"I'm sorry, for…not…protecting you."

His face blurred as I stared at him. The blood wasn't pouring from the wound as freely now. "You have protected me. You still will."

"I…didn't." His gaze trekked over my shoulder to where Lord Mazeen stood. "I…failed you…as a man. Forgive me."

"There's nothing to forgive you for," I cried. "You've done nothing wrong."

His dulling eyes fixed on me. "Please."

"I forgive you." I rocked forward, dropping my forehead to his. "I forgive you. I do. I forgive you."

Vikter shuddered.

"Please don't," I whispered. "Please don't leave me. Please. I can't…I can't do this without you. Please."

His hand slipped from mine.

I drew in air, but it went nowhere as I lifted my head, looking down at him. I frantically searched his face. His eyes were open, his lips parted, but he didn't see me. He didn't see anything anymore.

"Vikter?" I pressed down on his chest, feeling for his heart, for just a beat. That's all I wanted to feel. Just a heartbeat. *Please.*

"Vikter?"

My name was whispered softly. It was Hawke. He placed his hand over mine. I looked at him and shook my head.

"No."

"I'm sorry," he said, gently lifting my hand. "I'm so sorry."

"No," I repeated, my breath now coming in short, rapid pants. "*No.*"

"I do believe our Maiden has also crossed a certain line with her Royal Guards. I don't think her lessons were at all effective."

A wave of ice swept from the top of my skull and moved down my spine as Hawke looked up at the Lord. His mouth moved, and I thought he said something, but the world simply fell away. I couldn't hear Hawke over the buzzing in my ears, over the absolute burning rage pounding through my veins.

Forgive me.

I failed you.

Forgive me.

I failed you.

I was moving, my hand finding metal. I rose from the blood, turned around. I saw Lord Mazeen standing there, barely a speck of blood on him, hardly a strand of hair out of place.

He looked at me.

Forgive me.

He smirked.

I failed you.

"I won't be forgetting *that* anytime soon," he said, nodding at Vikter.

Forgive me.

The sound that tore from me was a volcano of fury and pain that cut so deep, it irrevocably fissured something inside of me.

I was quick, just like Vikter had taught me to be. I swung the sword around. Lord Mazeen was unprepared for the attack, but he moved as fast as any Ascended could, his hand snapping out as if he planned to catch my arm, and I bet he thought he could. The smirk was still there, but rage was faster, stronger, deadlier.

Fury was pure power, and not even the gods could escape it, let alone an Ascended.

I cut through his arm, through tissue, muscle, and then bone. The appendage fell to the floor, useless like the rest of him. The surge of satisfaction was bliss as he howled like a pitiful, wounded animal. He stared at the blood geysering from the stump just above his elbow. His dark eyes went wide. There was shouting and screaming, so much yelling, but I didn't stop there. I brought the sword down over his left wrist, severing the hand that had held mine down on the Duke's desk, ripping away the last shred of modesty I had as the Duke brought the cane down on my back.

I failed you.

The Lord stumbled back against the chair, his lips peeling back as a different sound came from them, one that sounded like the wind when the mist came in. Spinning the sword, I swept it in a wide arc. This sword—Vikter's sword—found its target.

Forgive me.

I sliced Lord Brandole Mazeen's head from his shoulders.

His body slid to the floor as I raised the sword and brought it down, hacking into his shoulder, his chest. I didn't stop. I wouldn't until he was nothing but pieces. Not even when the screams and shouts became all I knew.

An arm came around me from behind, hauling me back as the sword was wrestled from my hands. I caught the scent of pine and woods, and I knew who held me, knew who pulled me back from what was left of the Lord. But I fought—clawing, swinging to be free. The hold was unbreakable.

"Stop," Hawke said, pressing his cheek to mine. "Gods, stop. Stop."

Kicking back, I caught him in the shin and then the thigh. I reared, causing him to stumble.

Forgive me.

Hawke crossed his arms around me, lifting me up and then bringing me down so that my legs were trapped under me.

"Stop. Please," he said. "Poppy—"

I failed you.

The screaming was so loud it hurt my ears, my head, my skin. In a distant, still-functioning part of my brain, I knew I was the one screaming like that, but I couldn't make myself stop.

A flash of light exploded behind my eyes, and oblivion reached for me.

I fell into nothingness.

Chapter 27

Half resting on the inner ledge, I stared out the window at the torches beyond the Rise, eyes aching and weary with the pressure of tears that wouldn't fall.

I wished I could cry, but it was like the cord that had connected me to my emotions had been severed. It wasn't that Vikter's death didn't hurt. Gods, it ached and throbbed every time I even thought his name, but that was almost all I'd felt in the week and a half since his death. A sharp slice of pain that cut through my chest. No sorrow. No dread. Just pain and anger…so much anger.

Maybe it was because I hadn't gone to his funeral. I hadn't made it to any of the funerals, and there had been so many dead that ten or more were held at a time—or so I had heard from Tawny.

It hadn't been my choice not to attend the services. I'd been asleep. I'd been sleeping a lot this week. Entire days just gone in a blur of sleep and drugged consciousness. I didn't even remember Tawny helping me bathe away the blood and gore or how I got back to bed. I knew she'd talked to me then, but I couldn't recall a single thing she'd said. I had this weird impression that I hadn't been alone while I slept. There was a sensation of callused palms against my cheek, fingers brushing hair back from my face. I had the faintest memory of Hawke talking to me, whispering when the room was filled with sunlight and when it had been taken over by night. Even now, I could feel the touch against my face, my hair. It had been the only grounding connection I'd had while I slept.

I squeezed my lids shut until the phantom sensations vanished, and then I reopened my eyes.

It wasn't until about four days after the attack on the Rite that I'd learned that Hawke had used some kind of pressure point on my neck to render me unconscious. I'd woken up sometime later in my room, unable to use my voice. The screaming…it had torn up my throat. Hawke had been there, so had Tawny, the Duchess, and a Healer.

I was offered a sleeping draught, and for the first time in my life, I took it. I might've kept taking it if it hadn't been for Hawke removing the powder from my room four days ago.

It was then I learned that the attack on the Rise hadn't been the only one that night. The Descenters had set fire to several of the opulent homes along Radiant Row, drawing guards from the Rise and the castle. That was where Hawke had been after he'd left the garden, which explained the soot on his face.

The fires had been a smart move by the Descenters. I had to give them that. With the guards distracted, the Descenters were able to move through the night, taking out guards stationed around the castle before they even knew they were there. They were able to commence wholesale slaughter before the guards who'd gone to Radiant Row could even be summoned.

No one could be positive what message the attack on the Rite had been meant to send, or even if they had been searching for me. None of the Descenters were taken alive that night, and any of those who had escaped, had slipped back into the shadows.

The Ascended had done what the Duchess said they would do. They got their hands dirty, but their assistance had come too late. Most who'd been left in that room had died. Only a few had survived, most so traumatized that they couldn't even recall what had happened.

Well over a hundred had died that night.

Gods, I'd rather be asleep than awake.

At least when I slept, I didn't think about the Duke burning from where he had been hung and impaled. I couldn't think about Dafina's one blue eye, or how Loren had tried to go back to her friend, only to be struck down. I wouldn't remember how it had felt to crawl over people who were dead or dying, unable to do anything to help him. The metal wolf masks didn't haunt my sleep. Neither did that smile Vikter had given me, or how he'd told me that he was proud. Asleep, I didn't think about how the last words he'd ever spoken were a plea for forgiveness for him not protecting me. And I couldn't remember how my gift had failed me when I needed it the most.

I wished I had never said what I did in that garden.

I wished...I wished I'd never gone to the Rite or gone out into the willow. If I'd been in my room where I was expected to be, we wouldn't have been in the thick of it. The attack still would've happened, and people still would've died, but maybe Vikter would still be here.

However, a tiny voice in the back of my mind whispered that the moment Vikter learned of what was happening, he would've gone down there anyway, and I would've followed. Death had come for him, and that voice also whispered that death would've found a way.

In the days I spent lost to the deep nothingness, I couldn't acknowledge what I'd done to Lord Mazeen and how I felt about it now.

Or how I *didn't* feel.

There wasn't an ounce of regret. My nails dug into my palms. I would do it again. Gods, I wished I could, and that disturbed me.

When I was out of it, I didn't think, and I didn't care about anything.

But now I was awake, and all I had were my thoughts, the pain, and the anger.

I wanted to find every single Descenter and do to them what I'd done to the Lord.

I'd tried the second night I was awake. I donned my cloak and mask and grabbed the short sword Vikter had given me years before since my dagger was lost to the chaos of that room the night of the Rite. I'd planned to pay Agnes a visit.

She'd known. Nothing could convince me otherwise. She'd known, and her attempts to warn me hadn't been enough. The blood that had been spilled that night was on her hands—Vikter's blood tainted her skin. My mentor and friend, who'd drunk her hot cocoa and comforted her. She could've stopped all of this.

Hawke had caught up to me halfway through Wisher's Grove and all but dragged me back to the castle. The chest of weapons had been removed from my room at that point, and the servants' access barred from the stairwell.

And so, I sat. I waited.

Each evening I'd been awake, I waited for the Duchess to summon me. For punishment to be rendered. Because I'd done something so expressly forbidden that it made everything I'd ever done before an afterthought.

I'd killed an Ascended.

Maiden or not, there had to be some kind of punishment for that. I had to be found unworthy.

A knock drew my gaze from the window. The door opened, and Hawke strode in, closing the door behind him. He was dressed in the uniform of the guards, all black except for the white Royal Guard mantle.

No one had replaced Vikter's position yet. I didn't know why. Maybe after seeing what I was capable of, the Duchess realized that I no longer needed as much protection. But protecting myself would be kind of hard to do without access to any weapons. Or maybe it was the fact that I'd already gone through three guards in one year. Or it could be because so many had died during the attack, and they were shorthanded.

My back tensed as Hawke and I stared at one another from across the room.

Things had been weird between us.

I wasn't sure if it was because of what had happened in the garden and then with Vikter, or if it had been what I'd done in that room after Vikter's death. It could've been all of that. But he was quiet when he was around me, and I had no idea what he was feeling or thinking. My gift was hidden away behind a wall so thick that it couldn't even crack.

He said nothing as he stood there. Just crossed his arms over his chest and stared at me. He'd done that a time or five hundred since I woke. Probably because when he tried to talk to me, all I did was stare at him.

Which was also probably why things were weird.

My eyes narrowed as the silence stretched between us. "What?"

"Nothing."

"Then why are you here?" I demanded.

"Do I need a reason?"

"Yes."

"I don't."

"Are you just checking to make sure I haven't figured a way out of the room?" I challenged.

"I know you can't get out of this room, Princess."

"Don't call me that," I snapped.

"I'm going to take a second to remind myself that this is

progress."

My brows furrowed. "Progress with what?"

"With you," he answered. "You're not being very nice, but at least you're talking. That's progress."

"I'm not being mean," I shot back. "I just don't like to be called that."

"Uh-huh," he murmured.

"Whatever." I tore my gaze from his, feeling...I didn't know what I was feeling. I squirmed, uncomfortable, and it had nothing to do with how hard the stone was beneath me.

I wasn't mad at Hawke. I was just angry with...everything.

"I get it," he said quietly.

When I looked at him, I saw that he'd moved closer, and I hadn't heard him. He was only a few feet from me now. "You do?" I lifted my brows. "You understand?"

Hawke stared at me, and in that moment, I felt something other than anger and pain. Shame burned through me like acid. Of course, Hawke knew, at least to some extent. But still, he probably knew better than a lot of other people.

"I'm sorry."

"For what?" The hardness had eased from my tone.

"I said this to you before, shortly after everything, but I don't think you heard me," he said. I thought about those vague sensations of him being beside me. "I should've said it again sooner. I'm sorry for everything that has happened. Vikter was a good man. Despite the last words we exchanged, I respected him, and I'm sorry that I couldn't do anything."

Every muscle in my body locked up. "Hawke—"

"I don't know if me being there—like I should've been— would've changed the outcome," he went on, "but I'm sorry that I wasn't. That there was nothing I could do by the time I *did* get there. I'm sorry—"

"You have nothing to apologize for." I rose from the ledge, my joints stiff from sitting for so long. "I don't blame you for what happened. I'm not mad at you."

"I know." He looked above me and out the window to the Rise. "But that doesn't change that I wish I would've done something that could've prevented this."

"There are a lot of things I wish I would've done differently," I admitted, staring at my hands. "If I'd gone to my room—"

"If you'd gone to your room, this still would've happened. Don't put this on yourself." A heartbeat later, I felt his fingers under my chin. He lifted my gaze to his. "You're not to blame for this, Poppy. Not at all. If anything, I—" He cut himself off with a low curse. "Don't take on the blame that belongs to others. You understand?"

I did, but that changed nothing, so I said, "Ten."

His brows knitted. "What?"

"Ten times, you've called me Poppy."

One side of his lips tipped up. The faintest trace of the dimple appeared. "I like calling you that, but I like calling you *Princess* more."

"Shocker," I replied.

He dipped his chin. "It's okay, you know?"

"What is?"

"Everything that you're feeling," he said. "And everything that you're not."

My breath caught as my chest squeezed, and it wasn't just pain doing that. It was something lighter, something warmer. How he knew was proof that, in some way, he'd been where I was right now. I didn't know if I moved or if he did, but my arms were suddenly around him, and he was holding me just as tightly as I was him. My cheek was plastered to his chest, below his heart, and when his chin dropped to the top of my head, I shuddered in relief. The tender hug didn't fix the world. The pain and anger were still there. But Hawke was so warm, and his embrace was...gods, it felt like *hope*, like a promise that I wouldn't always feel this way.

We stood there for some time before Hawke pulled back, and as he did, he smoothed the unruly strands of hair back from my face, sending a shiver of recognition through me.

"I did come here with a purpose," he said. "The Duchess needs to speak with you."

I blinked. So, it was time. "And you're just telling me now?"

"Figured what we had to say to each other was far more important."

"I don't think the Duchess would agree," I told him, and the expression on his face said that he didn't really care. "It's time for me to find out how I'll be punished for what I...for what I did to the Lord, isn't it?"

Hawke frowned at me. "If I thought I was delivering you for

punishment, I wouldn't be taking you there."

Surprise flickered through me, proving it was yet another emotion I could feel. "Where would you take me?"

"Somewhere far from here," he said, and I believed him. He'd do what no one else would, not even…not even Vikter. "You're being summoned because word has come from the capital."

It felt strange when Tawny arrived to help me with the veil, to be wearing it after everything, and even more weird to realize that the castle looked the same as it had before the attack. All except for the Great Hall. It had been barricaded from what I could gather. One brief glance at the room Vikter had died in told me that the door had been replaced.

That was all I needed to know.

The Duchess wore white, like I did, but while I wore the clothing of the Maiden, she wore the color of mourning. She sat behind what had been the Duke's desk, looking over a piece of paper. Not the desk that had been in the Duke's more private office. If we'd been meeting there, I had no idea what I would've done.

I still couldn't believe how the Duke had been killed. Surely, the weapon had been coincidental, but it still pecked away at something in the back of my mind.

The Duchess glanced up as the door closed behind us. She looked…different. It wasn't the color, or that her hair was pulled back sharply from her face in a simple twist. It was something else, but I couldn't place it as I walked past the benches. There were two other people in the room, the Commander, and a Royal Guard.

Her gaze flickered over me, and I wondered if she could tell that I had left my hair down beneath the veil. "I hope you're doing well." She paused. "Or at least better than the last time I saw you."

"I am well," I said, and that felt like neither a lie nor the truth.

"Good. Please. Take a seat." She gestured at the bench, and I did as she asked.

Tawny sat beside me, but Hawke remained standing to my left. I did everything in my power not to think about how Vikter belonged here.

"A lot has happened while you've been…resting," the Duchess started. "The Queen and King have been notified of recent events." She tapped one long finger on the parchment.

The message must have been sent through carrier pigeon to the capital, but only a Huntsman would deliver a Royal message here. He had to have ridden night and day, changing horses along the way to have made it back. It generally took several weeks to travel that distance.

"After the abduction attempt and the attack on the Rite, they no longer believe it's safe for you here," the Duchess announced. "They have summoned you back to Carsodonia."

I knew this was coming. Since the abduction attempt, I'd accepted that there was a high chance that the Queen would summon me to the capital, and I knew that could mean an earlier than expected Ascension. That was probably why I wasn't surprised, but it didn't explain the lack of dread and fear.

All I felt was…acceptance. Maybe even a little relief because this castle was now the last place I wanted to be, and I wasn't thinking about what could happen when I got to the capital. I wasn't even thinking about seeing Ian again. I knew what else I felt, though. And that was confusion.

"I'm sorry," I blurted out. "How am I not punished?"

Hawke turned to me, and without looking, I knew he probably had the same expression on his face that Vikter would have had.

The Duchess didn't respond for a long moment until she said, "I assume you're speaking about Lord Mazeen."

My stomach tightened as I nodded.

Her head tilted. "Do you think you should be punished?"

I started to respond as I would've two weeks ago before the attack, back when I was still trying so damn hard to be what I was beginning to believe I was never meant to be. "I don't think I can answer that question."

"Why not?" Curiosity marked her features.

"Because…there was a history there." I settled on that, aware of how Tawny shifted so her leg pressed against mine. I drew in a deep breath. "I know I *should* be punished."

"You should," she agreed. "He was an Ascended, one of our

oldest."

Tension radiated from Hawke as I felt him move just the slightest bit toward me.

"You cut him up like a butcher would a slab of meat," she continued. I should've felt horror or disgust—anything other than the surge of gratification that swamped me. "But I'm sure you had your reasons."

My mouth dropped open.

The Duchess leaned back as she picked up a quill. "I've known Bran for many, many years, and there is very little about his...personality that I am unaware of. I had hoped that he would've known better given what you are. Apparently, I was wrong."

I tipped forward. "Did you—?"

"I would not ask that question," she interrupted, her unflinching stare locking on mine. "You would not like my answer, nor would you understand. Neither would I expect you to. Take this as a much-needed lesson, Penellaphe. Some truths do nothing but destroy and decay what they do not obliterate. Truths do not always set one free. Only a fool who has spent their entire life being fed lies believes that."

Chest rising and falling, I snapped my mouth shut and sat back. She knew. She'd always known about the Lord and the Duke. Maybe not what they'd done exactly, but she knew. My fingers dug into the skirt of my gown.

"You're the Maiden," she continued. "That is why you will not be punished. Count your blessings, and do not speak of them ever again." A muscle twitched under her eye. "And do yourself a favor. Do not waste another moment thinking of either of them. I know I will not."

I stared at her as her white-knuckled grip on the quill eased. It struck me then. If the Duke had treated me as he did, why had I assumed he would treat his wife any differently? After all, I'd never seen them being loving towards one another, and that went beyond the almost cool nature of the Ascended. I'd never seen them touch. Being an Ascended didn't mean you were no longer in a position to be abused.

Lowering my gaze, I nodded. "When...when do I leave for the capital?"

"Tomorrow morning," she answered. "You will leave with the rise of the sun."

Chapter 28

"I am not leaving Tawny here," I stated, squaring off with Hawke. "There is no way."

"She is not coming with us." His eyes flashed a fiery amber. "I'm sorry, but no."

We were in my chambers no more than thirty minutes after we'd left the Duchess's office. We also had an audience. Tawny was there. So was the Commander, but it was like they weren't even in the same building.

Hawke and I had been arguing for the last ten minutes.

"It's a good thing you're not the one in charge," I pointed out, turning to the Commander. "I need—"

"I'm sorry, Maiden, but I am not traveling with you." Commander Jansen stepped into the room from the doorway. "Only a small group is going, but Hawke is your personal Royal Guard. He takes the lead."

"How can he possibly take the lead?" I almost shouted. "He hasn't even been my Royal Guard for that long."

"But he is your only Royal Guard."

That statement threatened to sting, so I whirled on Hawke and did the only completely immature thing I could. I took it out on him. "You seriously expect me to leave her here? Where Descenters are murdering people left and right?"

"You seriously expect me to bring her out beyond the Rise?"

Tawny stepped forward. "If I may—"

"Yes!" I exclaimed. "You're taking *me* out beyond the Rise."

"Exactly. Only a handful of guards can be spared to escort you. All of them will be focused on keeping you safe. Not her."

"I can—"

"I know you can protect yourself. Everyone in this room knows that, trust me, but we're going out there, Princess. Out beyond the Rise. Do you know the path we will have to take?" he demanded. "We'll have to travel through the Barren Plains and the Blood Forest."

Trepidation had my stomach dipping. "I know."

"And we will also be traveling through areas heavily populated by Descenters. This will not be a smooth trip, and I will not risk your safety," he said as he glared down at me. Gone was the Hawke who'd held me so tightly and so tenderly only hours before. In his place was...

In his place was a Royal Guard Vikter would've been proud of. There was no stopping that sting. Hawke wasn't my friend or...or whatever he was to me in this moment. He was a Royal Guard duty-bound to keep me alive and deliver me safely to the Queen and King.

He dipped his chin, eyes latched to mine. "If we take Tawny with us, we may as well just send her ahead and use her as Craven bait."

I gaped at him. "That was possibly the most absurd statement ever."

"No more absurd than standing here arguing with half of your face," he retorted.

I threw up my hands. "That sounds like your problem, not mine."

Jaw working as he stared down at me, he barked out a short laugh and then turned to where Tawny stood. "I know you want to accompany her. I understand that, but this is not going to be like a normal caravan. There won't be dozens of guards, and we won't be staying at the finest inns. Our pace will be fast and hard, and there is an extremely high likelihood that the Rite will not be the last time you see bloodshed."

I turned to Tawny, but before I could speak, she said, "I know. I understand." She came forward. "I appreciate that you want me to come with you, Poppy, but I can't."

A feather could've knocked me over. "You...you don't want to?"

She'd been so excited about seeing the capital.

But if I wasn't here, then her time would become hers, at least a good majority of it. I pressed my lips together.

"I want to. Badly." She stopped in front of me, clasping my hands. "And I hope you believe that, but the idea of going out there like this terrifies me."

I...I wanted to believe her.

She brought our joined hands up to her chest. "Not only that, but what Hawke said is true. So many guards are...they are gone. And the ones going with you cannot be focused on me. I can't fight. Not like you can. I can't do what you did."

What I did? Did she mean when I defended myself or...or what I'd done to the Lord?

"I can't go," she whispered.

Closing my eyes, I exhaled raggedly. She was right. So was Hawke. It would be irresponsible and illogical for Tawny to travel with us. And while I was worried about leaving her behind in a city in such a state of unrest, I was arguing because...because...

I was leaving everything familiar behind.

So much had happened. So many losses. And while I didn't have the brain space or the emotional capacity to worry about the possibility of the Ascension moving up or even being found unworthy by the gods, I wasn't borrowing tomorrow's problems. But everything kept shifting and changing, and Tawny was...she was the last of what used to be.

What if I didn't see her again?

Drawing in a shaky breath, I couldn't let myself think like that. I couldn't let Tawny think that. I opened my eyes. "You're right."

Tears gathered in her eyes. "I hate being right."

"Thank the gods, there's someone rational in this room," Hawke muttered.

My head shot in his direction. "No one asked you for your input."

Commander Jansen whistled under his breath.

"Well, you got it, Princess." He smirked when I dropped Tawny's hands and turned to him. He walked to the door and then stopped. "And I have more input for you. Pack lightly. And don't bother taking that damn veil. You won't be wearing it."

Eyes closed and chin lifted to the rising sun, I reveled in the feel of the cool morning air kissing my bare cheeks and brow as I stood beside the black walls of the Rise. It was such a small thing, but it had been *years* since the sun and wind had touched every part of my face. My skin prickled pleasantly, and even the reason I was able to do this didn't tarnish the moment.

The veil made me a very obvious moving target as we traveled to Carsodonia. The best way for us to avoid Descenters and the Dark One was to ensure that no one we came into contact with realized who I was, which was why our group was gathering near the Rise, and I wore a plain dark brown cloak with a heavy sweater underneath it, and my lone pair of breeches and boots. I had no idea what people would think when they saw me, but they definitely wouldn't think of the Maiden.

It was also why I'd said my goodbyes to Tawny in my room. The few castle staff that would be moving about may recognize Tawny as my companion, and Hawke was taking no chances by ignoring the possibility that Descenters could still be among those who worked in the castle.

And that made it even harder to say goodbye to Tawny. Anything could happen between now and when she joined me in the capital, and I'd have no idea until someone decided to tell me. That caused my stomach to twist with helplessness because there was nothing I could do about any of that. I could only *hope* that I would see her again. I could *believe* that I would.

But I wouldn't pray.

The gods had never answered my prayers before.

And it no longer felt right to ask them for anything when I…I could no longer deny what Vikter had claimed.

That I wanted to be found unworthy.

I sighed, concentrating on the sensation of the wind lifting the wisps of hair from around my forehead and temple.

The Duchess hadn't come to say goodbye.

It didn't surprise me. And it didn't hurt like it had before. There wasn't even disappointment, and I wasn't sure if that was a good thing or a bad one.

"You look like you're enjoying yourself."

Opening my eyes at the sound of Hawke's voice, I turned around and almost wished I'd kept my eyes closed.

Hawke wasn't dressed like a guard as he stood next to a massive black horse. His dark brown breeches hugged his long legs, showcasing the strength of his body. His tunic was heavy and long-sleeved, suited for cold weather, as was the fur-lined cloak. In the sunlight, his hair was the color of a raven's wings.

Somehow, he looked even more striking dressed as a commoner.

And he was staring at me, one eyebrow raised while I was…well, I was just gawking at him. My cheeks heated. "It feels nice."

"For the air to touch your face?" he asked, figuring out what I was talking about.

I nodded.

"I can only imagine that it does." His gaze flickered across my face. "I much prefer this version."

Biting down on my lip, I reached out and lightly rubbed the side of the horse's nose. "He's beautiful. Does he have a name?"

"Been told it's Setti."

I smiled at that. "Named after Theon's warhorse?" Setti nudged my hand for more pets. "He has big hooves to fill."

"That he does," Hawke replied. "I'm assuming you can't ride a horse."

I shook my head no. "I haven't been on one since…" My smile widened. "Gods, it was three years ago. Tawny and I snuck out to the stables and managed to climb on one before Vikter arrived." My smile faded as I dropped my hand and stepped back. "So, no, I can't ride."

"That will be intriguing." He paused. "And torturous since you'll be riding with me."

My heart skipped over itself as I looked over at him. "And why is that intriguing? And torturous?"

One side of his lips curved up. The dimple appeared. "Besides the fact that it will allow me to keep a very close eye on you? Use your imagination, Princess."

My imagination didn't fail me then. "That's inappropriate," I told him.

"Is it?" He dipped his chin. "You're not the Maiden out here.

You're Poppy, unveiled and unburdened."

My gaze met his, and the surge of anticipation and relief proved that under the pain and anger, other emotions simmered. "And what of when I arrive at the capital? I will become the Maiden once more."

"But that's neither today nor tomorrow," he said, turning back to one of the saddlebags on his horse. "I brought something for you."

I waited, wondering what it could be since the only thing I'd been able to pack was underclothing and two additional sweater-tunics.

Opening one of the leather bags, he reached inside and pulled out something folded in a cloth. He unwrapped it as he turned to me.

My heart stopped and then sped up when I saw what he held in his hand, recognizing the ivory-hued handle and the reddish-black blade.

"My dagger." My throat clogged. "I thought...I thought it was lost."

"I found it later that night." A sheathe lay under it. "I didn't want to give it to you when I had to worry about you running off and using it, but you'll need it for this trip."

The fact that he was making sure I was equipped to defend myself in case it was needed meant the world to me. But the fact that he'd found the dagger and kept it safe for me...

"I don't know what to say." I cleared the hoarseness from my throat as he handed it over. The moment my fingers curled around the handle, I let out a shaky breath. "Vikter gave me this on my sixteenth birthday. It's been my favorite."

"It's a beautiful weapon."

The clog dissipated, and all I could do was nod as I carefully sheathed the dagger and then secured it to my right thigh. It took a moment for me to speak. "Thank you."

Hawke didn't respond. When I looked up, I saw a small group approaching. Two unfamiliar men on horses and six other men, leading their mounts toward us.

I recognized two of the guards immediately. I'd played cards with them at the Red Pearl. Phillips, and I believed the other was called Airrick. If they recognized me, it didn't show as they greeted me with curt nods, neither meeting my eyes.

My scars tingled, but I resisted the urge to touch them or to turn so they weren't visible.

I was surprised to see them, knowing that they weren't

Huntsmen, but I supposed there hadn't been enough available to join us, and I was happy to see Phillips. He was someone who'd faced Craven time and time again and was still standing.

"The party has arrived," Hawke murmured, and then louder, he began to make introductions. He rattled off names, most a blur beyond the two I knew, but then he said another name that tugged at my memory. "This is Kieran. He came from the capital with me and is familiar with the road we must travel."

It was the guard who'd knocked on the door the night at the Red Pearl. It was like a reunion, I thought as I finally got to see him. He looked to be about the same age as Hawke, his dark hair trimmed close to the skull. His eyes were a striking shade of pale blue, reminding me of the sky during winter, a startling contrast to his warm, beige skin, reminding me of Tawny.

"A pleasure to meet you," Kieran said as he mounted his horse.

"Same," I murmured, noting that he had the same slight accent as Hawke, a lilt I still couldn't place.

He looked toward Hawke, the angles of his face sharp and more than pleasing to the eye. "We need to be on our way if we have any hope of crossing the plains by nightfall."

Hawke turned to me. "Ready?"

I glanced west, toward the center of Masadonia. Castle Teerman reached high above the Lower Ward and the Citadel, a sprawling structure of stone and glass, of beautiful memories and haunting nightmares. Somewhere in there, Tawny roamed, and the Duchess assumed control of the city. Somewhere in there, my present had become the past. I turned to the Rise. Somewhere out there, my future awaited.

Chapter 29

Within a few hours of our trek across the Barren Plains, I no longer had to rely on my imagination to know what Hawke had meant when he'd said that I'd be riding with him.

There was little space between our bodies. It hadn't started out that way as the heavy doors of the Rise had opened and we passed the torches. Aware that the men traveling with us knew who I was, I sat straight and desperately ignored the feeling of Hawke's arm around my waist, but the pace was hard. It wasn't a dead run, but unused to how a horse moved, the stiff position quickly became awkward and painful. With each passing hour, I ended up closer to Hawke until my back was pressed to his chest, and my hips were cradled by his thighs. The hood of my cloak had slipped at some point, and I left it down, partly because I wanted to feel the wind on my face.

And in part because I could feel Hawke's warm breath against my cheek every time he leaned down to speak to me.

I'd been right. For a Maiden, this was wholly inappropriate. Or, at least the way it felt to be held by him was inappropriate for a Maiden.

But after a while, I relaxed and cherished the sensation of being in his arms, knowing that when we reached our destination, this would be over, no matter how well Hawke believed his skills were.

Things would be different in the capital.

I stared out over the empty land. At one time, there'd been farms here, and inns where people could stop and rest. But now, there was nothing but endless grass, bent and twisted trees, and tall reeds climbing over the broken ruins of farmhouses and taverns.

I was convinced that everyone we passed was haunted.

The Craven had destroyed the Plains, tainting once fertile ground with blood, and slaughtering anyone who dared to set down roots outside the Rise.

And so close to the Blood Forest.

I kept my eyes peeled for the first glimpse of the forest and did everything not to think about where the sun was currently at and where we'd end when night fell.

Hawke shifted, and somehow, half of his arm ended up slipping between the folds of my cloak. My mouth dried as the horse slowed. Hawke's palm was against my hip, and although the wool sweater and my pants separated our skin, the weight of his hand was like a brand.

"You doing okay?" he asked, his breath dancing over my cheek.

"I can't really feel my legs," I admitted.

He chuckled. "You'll get used to it in a couple of days."

"Great," I said, drawing in a deep breath as I felt his thumb move over my hip. My grip on the horn of the saddle tightened.

"You sure you ate enough?"

We'd snacked on cheese and nuts as we rode, and while I'd typically have had a much larger lunch by now, I wasn't sure I could learn how to eat while being jostled by the horse. I nodded, noting that Kieran and Phillips, who were at the front, had also slowed. They'd been speaking to one another on and off, but they'd been too far away from me to hear what they said.

"Are we stopping?" I asked.

"No."

My brows knitted. "Then why are we slowing?"

"It's the path—" Airrick, who rode to our left, cut himself off, and I grinned. I knew he was about to call me *Maiden*. Something he'd done so many times over the last couple of hours that Hawke had threatened to knock him off his horse if he did it one more time. Luckily, he'd caught himself this time. "The path gets uneven here, and there's a stream, but it's hard to see through the growth."

"That's not all," Hawke added, his thumb still moving, catching the wool and dragging it in a slow, steady circle.

"It's not?"

"You see Luddie?" Hawke was talking about one of the

Huntsmen who rode to our right. The man hadn't said much since we left. "He's keeping an eye out for barrats."

My lip curled. Barrats weren't your average rodents. Rumored to be the size of a boar, they were the things of nightmares. "I thought they were all gone."

"They're the only thing the Craven won't eat."

Didn't that say something? I shuddered. "How many do you think are out here?"

"I don't know." Hawke's arm tightened around my waist, and I had a feeling he knew exactly how many.

I looked at Airrick.

He averted his gaze.

"Do you know how many, Airrick?"

"Eh, well, I know there used to be more," he said, sending a nervous glance at Hawke. He immediately faced forward. "They didn't used to be a problem, you know? Or at least that was what my grandfather told me when I was a boy. He lived out here. One of the last ones."

"Really?"

Airrick nodded as Hawke's thumb continued moving. "He grew corn and tomatoes, beans and potatoes." A faint smile appeared. "He would tell me that the barrats used to be nothing more than a nuisance."

"I can't imagine rats that weigh nearly two hundred pounds being only a nuisance."

"Well, they were just scavengers and were more scared of people than we were afraid of them," Airrick explained. I was confident that I would be scared of them, whether they left people alone or not. "But with everyone moving out, they lost their…"

"Food source?" I finished for him.

Airrick nodded as he scanned the horizon. "Now, anything they come across is food."

"Including us." I really hoped Luddie had perfect eyesight and a sixth sense when it came to barrats.

"You're intriguing," Hawke commented as Setti trotted ahead of Airrick.

"Intriguing is your favorite word," I told him.

"It is when I'm around you."

I let myself grin because no one was watching, and I wanted to.

"Why am I intriguing now?"

"When are you *not* intriguing?" he said. "You aren't afraid of Descenters or Craven, but you're shuddering like a wet kitten at the mere mention of a barrat."

"Craven and Descenters don't scurry about on all fours, and they don't have fur."

"Well, barrats don't scurry," he replied. "They run, about as fast as a hunting dog locked onto prey."

Another shudder made its way through me. "That is not helping."

He laughed. "You know what I would love right about now?"

"For there to be no talk of giant, people-eating rats?"

Hawke squeezed me, and I felt a dip in my chest. "Besides that."

I snorted.

"Do me a favor and reach into the bag by your left leg. Be careful, though. Hold onto the pommel."

"I'm not going to fall off." I held on, though, stretching forward and lifting the flap of the bag.

"Uh-huh."

I ignored that and reached inside. My fingers brushed over something smooth and leather. Frowning, I grabbed hold of it and pulled it out. The moment I saw the red cover, I gasped and shoved it back into the bag.

"Oh, my gods." I sat up straight, my eyes wide.

Hawke burst out laughing, and ahead, Kieran looked over his shoulder at us. Could he see how red my face was?

"I can't believe you." I turned at the waist, and for a moment, I got a little lost in that dimple in Hawke's right cheek. The left one was starting to appear, too. And then I remembered what was in the bag. "How did you even find that book?"

"How did I find that naughty diary of Lady Willa Colyns? I have my ways."

"How?" The last I'd seen it, it was shoved under my pillow, and with everything that had happened, it hadn't even occurred to me that someone might find it and have questions.

Lots of questions.

"I'll never tell," he replied, and I smacked his arm. "So violent."

I rolled my eyes.

"You're not going to read to me?"

"No. Absolutely not."

"Maybe I'll read to you later."

That was even worse. "That's not necessary."

"You sure?"

"Positive."

His laugh was low and soft against my neck. "How far did you get, Princess?"

I pressed my lips together and then sighed. "I almost finished it."

"You'll have to tell me all about it."

That wasn't likely to happen. I couldn't believe he'd not only found that damn book but had also packed it. Out of everything he could've brought with him, he'd grabbed the diary. The corners of my lips twitched, and before I knew it, I was smiling and then I was laughing. When his arm tightened around me again, I relaxed against him.

Hawke was...intriguing.

Our pace picked up after that, and it almost felt like we were racing the moon. I didn't have to look ahead to know that we were losing.

And then I saw it.

Ice drenched my skin at the first glimpse of red. And then it rose into sight. A sea of crimson stretched as far as the eye could see.

We'd reached the Blood Forest.

The horses carried us forward even though every instinct in my body screamed in warning. I couldn't tear my eyes from the forest, even though it felt like a sight that would haunt my dreams for many, many years to come. I'd never seen it up close, having come to Masadonia through a different route that would've added days to our trip. What I saw was a twisted mass of red and a deeper shade that reminded me of dried blood. Under the pounding hooves, the ground became rockier. Something crunched and snapped. Was it twigs? Branches? I started to look down—

"Don't," ordered Hawke. "Don't look down."

I couldn't stop myself.

My stomach churned. The ground was *littered* with sun-bleached bones. Skulls that belonged to deer and smaller animals. Perhaps rabbits? There were also longer bones, too long for an animal, and—

Sucking in a sharp breath, I tore my gaze away. "The bones..." I said, swallowing. "They're not all animal bones, are they?"

"No."

My hand went to the arm around my waist. I held on. "Are they the bones of Craven who died?" If they didn't feed, they withered away until there was nothing left but bones.

"Some of them."

A tremor coursed through me.

"I told you not to look."

"I know."

But I had.

Just like I couldn't close my eyes now. The red leaves glistened in the fading sun, looking like a million leaves had captured tiny pools of blood. It was a sight as horrifying as it was disturbingly beautiful.

The horses slowed, and Airrick's mount reared, shaking its head, but he pushed forward. We advanced, my heart thundering as the branches stretched toward us, their slick leaves rippling softly, seeming to beckon us forward.

The temperature dropped the second we passed under the first branches, and nearly all the sun that remained couldn't penetrate the leaves. Goosebumps pimpled my skin as I looked up. Some of the branches were so low that I thought I could possibly reach up and touch one of the leaves shaped like the ones found on a maple tree. I didn't, though.

No one spoke as we fell into line, two by two, side by side, following the path that had been worn into the ground. Everyone kept their eyes peeled. Since there was no crunching, I felt safe looking down.

"No leaves," I said.

"What?" Hawke leaned into me, keeping his voice low.

I scanned the rapidly darkening floor of the forest. "There are no leaves on the ground. It's just grass. How is that possible?"

"This place is not natural," Phillips answered.

"That would be an understatement," Airrick added, looking around.

Hawke leaned back. "We will need to stop soon. The horses need rest."

Pressure clamped down on my chest, and my grip on Hawke's arm increased. I knew my fingernails were beginning to dig into his arm, but I couldn't make myself let go.

I exhaled raggedly and saw my breath in the air.

We rode for another hour, and then there was nothing but silvery streaks of moonlight when Hawke signaled to the group. The horses slowed to a trot and then eventually stopped, their breathing heavy.

"This seems like a better place than many to camp," Hawke commented.

The strangest urge to giggle hit me, but there wasn't anything funny about what we were about to do.

We were going to spend the night here, inside the Blood Forest, where the Craven roamed.

Chapter 30

I didn't think I'd ever been this cold before.

The bedroll did nothing to stop the chill from seeping up from the ground, and the blanket, as heavy as the fur was, couldn't fight back the iciness in the air. My fingers felt like ice cubes inside my gloves, and no amount of shivering warmed my skin.

It had to be at least twenty degrees cooler at night inside the Blood Forest, and I imagined if it rained, it would turn to snow here.

For the last twenty or so minutes, I'd tried to will myself asleep. Because if I were unconscious, I wouldn't be so worried about turning into a chunk of ice. But every crunch of grass and stir of wind had my hand going to the dagger stowed under the bag I was using for a pillow. Between the cold, the possibility of free-roaming barrats, and the threat of a Craven attack, there was no way I was getting any sleep tonight. I didn't know how anyone would. I'd barely been able to eat any of the food during our quick, quiet supper.

Four guards slept. Four guards stood watch several yards away, one at each corner of the camp. Hawke had been speaking to one of them, but now he was striding toward me. A tiny part of me thought I should pretend to be asleep, but I had a feeling he'd know.

Stopping in front of me, Hawke knelt. "You're cold."

"I'm fine," I muttered, teeth chattering.

A moment later, I felt his ungloved fingers brush my cheek. I tensed. "Correction. You're freezing."

"I'll warm up." I hoped. "Eventually."

He let his hand dangle between his knees. "You're not used to this kind of cold, Poppy."

"And you are?"

"You have no idea what I'm used to."

That was true. I stared at the shadowy shape of his hand. For such rough, callused hands, his fingers were rather long and graceful. Digits that belonged to an artist and not a guard. A killer.

Hawke rose, and for a moment, I thought he might walk off to join the others keeping watch, but he didn't.

Holding the coarse blanket as close as I could around me, I watched him unhook the rolled blanket from his bag and then drop the bag on the ground. Without saying a word, he stepped over me like I was nothing more than a log. Before I could take my next breath, he was lying down behind me.

I cranked my head around. "What are you doing?"

"Making sure you don't freeze to death." He unrolled the heavy fur blanket, tossing it over his legs. "If you did, that would make me a very bad guard."

"I'm not going to freeze to death." My heart started thumping erratically. He was close enough that if I shifted onto my back, my shoulder would touch his.

"What you're going to do is lure every Craven within a five-mile radius with your shuddering." He rolled onto his side, facing my back.

"You can't sleep beside me," I hissed.

"I'm not." With the edge of his blanket in hand, he draped it, *along* with his arm, over me.

The heavy weight of his appendage settled at my waist, stunning me for a few precious moments. "What do you call this, then?"

"I'm sleeping *with* you."

My eyes opened wide. "How is that any different?"

"There's a huge difference." His warm breath coasted over my cheek, causing my pulse to dip and then rise.

I stared at the darkness, every part of my body focused on the feel of his arm around me. "You can't sleep with me, Hawke."

"And I can't have you freezing or getting sick. It's too dangerous to light a fire, and unless you'd rather I get someone else to sleep with you, there really aren't many other options."

"I don't want anyone else to sleep with me."

"I already knew that," he replied, his tone both teasing and smug.

Heat blasted my cheeks. "I don't want *anyone* to sleep with me."

In the darkness, his gaze found mine, and when next he spoke, his voice was even lower. "I know you have nightmares, Poppy, and I know they can be intense. Vikter warned me about them."

Sorrow pierced the embarrassment before it could even form, shattering it. "He did?" My voice was thick, hoarse.

"He did."

My eyes squeezed shut against the burn of pain. Of course, Vikter would've filled Hawke in. He'd probably done so the very first night Hawke had to watch over me. I knew in my heart of hearts that Vikter had shared this information for my benefit instead of preparing Hawke for the night one of the nightmares drove me from sleep. He'd done it so Hawke wouldn't react in a manner that would cause me embarrassment or stress.

Vikter was…gods, I missed him.

"I want to be close enough to intervene in case you have a nightmare," he continued, and I opened my eyes. "If you scream…"

He didn't need to finish. If I screamed, I could draw nearby Craven.

"So, please, relax and try to rest. We have a hard day ahead of us tomorrow if we have any hope of not being forced to spend two nights in the Blood Forest."

A hundred refusals rose to the tip of my tongue, but I was cold, and if I did have a nightmare, someone needed to be nearby to stop me before I started screaming bloody murder. And Hawke's heat…the warmth of his body was already seeping through the blanket wrapped around us, sinking into my chilled skin and bones.

Besides, all he was doing was sleeping *beside* me. Or sleeping *with* me, as he'd said. But neither of those things was forbidden.

And it wasn't like we hadn't already done things I *should've* protested or avoided. Compared to the night at the Red Pearl and during the Rite, this was extraordinarily chaste, no matter that I shivered now for an entirely different reason than the cold.

"Go to sleep, Poppy," he urged.

Exhaling as loudly and obnoxiously as I could, I plopped my

cheek back onto the bag and winced. The material had chilled significantly while I had my head up. I ended up staring straight ahead, focusing on the vague shape of one of the guards standing in the moonlight.

I closed my eyes, and immediately, my entire focus went to where Hawke's body touched mine.

Hawke's arm was all but curled around my waist, but his hand didn't touch me. It must've dangled in the space in front of me. That was surprisingly...polite of him. His chest rested beside my back, and with every breath he took, it brought his body more into contact with mine.

The only sound other than my pounding heart—which I wondered if he heard—was the rattle of the wind stirring the leaves, reminding me of dry bones rubbing together, and the soft neighing of the horses.

Was Hawke asleep already? If he was, I was going to be *so* irritated.

"This is wildly inappropriate," I muttered.

His answering chuckle stroked my nerves in all the wrong—and right—ways. "More inappropriate than you masquerading as a wholly different kind of maid at the Red Pearl?"

My jaw snapped shut so quickly and tightly, I was surprised I didn't crack a molar.

"Or more inappropriate than the night of the Rite, when you let me—"

"Shut up," I hissed.

"I'm not done yet," he said, his chest pressing against my back. "What about sneaking off to fight the Craven on the Rise? Or that diary—?"

"I get your point, Hawke. Can you stop talking now?"

"You're the one who started this."

"Actually, no, I did not."

"What?" A low laugh left him. "You said, and I quote, 'this is wildly, grossly, irrefutably...'"

"Did you just learn what an adverb is today? Because that is not what I said."

Hawke sighed. "Sorry."

He didn't sound sorry about it at all.

"I didn't realize we were back to pretending we hadn't done all those other inappropriate things," he said. "Not that I'm surprised. After all, you're a pure, untainted, and untouched Maiden. The Chosen."

Oh, my gods....

"Who's saving herself for a Royal husband. Who, by the way, will *not* be pure, untainted or untouched—"

I moved to jab him with my elbow, but forgot I was currently wrapped in one blanket and draped with another. All I managed to do was uncover the front of my body, revealing it to the cold air.

Hawke laughed.

"I hate you." I scrambled to fold myself back up into my blanket cocoon.

"See, that's the problem. You don't hate me."

I had no response to that.

"You know what I think?"

"No. And I don't want to know."

He ignored that. "You like me."

My brows knitted together as I stared out over the small clearing.

"Enough to be *wildly inappropriate* with me." A pause. "On multiple occasions."

"Good gods, I'd rather freeze to death at this point."

"Oh, right. We're pretending none of that happened. I keep forgetting."

"Just because I don't bring it up every five minutes doesn't mean I'm pretending it didn't happen."

"But bringing it up every five minutes is so much fun."

The corners of my lips tipped up as I lifted the edges of the blanket above my chin. "I'm not pretending none of that stuff happened," I admitted in a low voice. "It's just that..."

"That it shouldn't have happened?"

I didn't want to say that. I felt like once I did, I couldn't take it back. "It's just that I'm not supposed to...do any of that. You know that. I am the Maiden."

Hawke was quiet for several moments. "And how do you really feel about that, Poppy?"

After several false starts when I tried to answer him, I closed my eyes and just answered truthfully. "I don't want it. I don't want to be given to the gods and then, after that, if there is an after part, I don't want to be married off to someone I've never met, who will probably…"

"Probably what?" His voice was quiet, soothing even.

I swallowed hard. "Who will probably be…" I sighed. "You know how Royals are. Beauty is in the eye of the beholder, and flaws, well, they are unacceptable." Warmth finally crept into my cheeks. The words tasted like ash. "If I end up as an Ascended, I'm sure whoever the Queen pairs me with will be the same."

Hawke didn't say anything for a long moment, and I was so grateful, I almost rolled around and hugged him. Nothing he could've said would've made what I said any less humiliating to admit.

"Duke Teerman was a cunt," he said. "And I'm glad he's dead."

A shocked laugh burst from me, loud enough that I saw the pacing guard stop. "Oh, gods, that was loud."

"It's okay." He sounded as if he smiled.

Grinning into the blanket, I said, "He was definitely that, but it's…even if I didn't have these scars, I wouldn't be excited. I don't understand how Ian did it. He barely even knew his wife, and I…I don't think he's happy. He never speaks about her, and that's sad, because our parents loved each other. He should have that."

I should have that, Maiden or not.

"I heard that your mother refused to Ascend."

"It's true. My father was a firstborn son. He was wealthy, but he wasn't chosen," I said. "Mom was a Lady in Wait when they met. It was accidental. His father—my grandfather—was close to King Jalara. My father went to the castle with him once, and that's when he saw my mother. Supposedly, it was love at first sight." My smile faded. "I know that sounds silly, but I believe it. It happens—at least for some."

"It's not silly. It does exist."

A slight frown pulled at my lips. His voice sounded off. I couldn't explain it exactly, but it made me wonder if he'd seen someone and had fallen in love with them after just one conversation. I thought of how he'd admitted to being in love before.

The center of my chest burned.

"Is that why you were at the Red Pearl? Looking for love?"

"I don't think someone goes looking for love there."

"You never know what you'll find there." He was quiet for a moment. "What did you find, Poppy?"

His question was so soft, it was almost…seductive. "Life."

"Life?"

I closed my eyes again. "I just want to experience things before my Ascension." Before whatever happened *during* the Ascension. "There's so much I haven't experienced. You know that. I didn't go there looking for anything in particular. I just wanted to experience—"

"Life," he answered. "I get it."

"Do you? Really?" I didn't think even Tawny got it.

"I do. Everyone around you can do basically whatever they want, but you're shackled by archaic rules."

"Are you saying that the word of the gods is archaic?"

"You said it, not me."

My nose wrinkled. "I've never understood why it is the way it is." I opened my eyes. "All because of the way I was born."

"The gods chose you before you were even born." He felt closer, like if we weren't wrapped up, I'd feel his breath on the back of my neck. "All because you were *'born in the shroud of the gods, protected even inside the womb, veiled from birth.'*"

"Yes," I whispered, opening my eyes. "Sometimes, I wish...I wish I was..."

"What?"

Someone different. Someone other than the Maiden. Thinking it was one thing. Saying it out loud was another. I'd come close to admitting it to Vikter, but that was as close as I would let myself get with those words.

It was far past time to switch gears. "Never mind. And I don't sleep well. That's another reason why I was at the Pearl."

"Nightmares?"

"Sometimes. Other times, my head doesn't...go quiet. It replays things over and over," I said, the shivering easing a little.

"What is your mind so loud about?" he asked.

The question caught me off guard. No one other than maybe Tawny—not even Vikter—had ever asked me that. Ian would've if he were still near. "Lately, it's been the Ascension."

"I imagine you're excited to meet the gods."

I snorted like a piglet. "Far from it. It actually terrifies—" I sucked in a sharp breath, shocked that I had so willingly admitted that out loud.

"It's okay," he said, seeming to sense my disbelief. "I don't know much about the Ascension and the gods, but I'd be terrified to meet them."

"You?" Disbelief compounded on top of itself. "Terrified?"

"Believe it or not, some things do scare me. The secrecy around the actual ritual of the Ascension is one of them. You were right that day when you were with the Priestess. It is so similar to what the Craven do, but what is done to stop aging—stop sickness for what has to be an eternity in the eyes of a mortal?"

My stomach shifted with unease. "It's the gods—their Blessing. They make themselves seen during the Ascension. To even look upon them changes you," I explained, but my words sounded uncomfortably hollow.

"They must be a sight to behold." While I sounded empty, he sounded as dry as a whole swath of the Wastelands. "I'm surprised."

"About?"

"You." His chest touched my back again when he took a deep breath. "You're just not what I expected."

I wasn't.

Most would look forward to meeting the gods, to possibly becoming an Ascended. Ian did, just like Tawny, and all the Ladies and Lords in Wait, but not me or my mother, and that made us different. Not in a unique way. Not in a special way. But in a way that made it...difficult to be who we were, even if our reasons were vastly different.

I shook my head. "I should be asleep. So should you."

"The sun will be up sooner than we realize, but you're not going to sleep anytime soon. You're as tense as a bowstring."

"Well, sleeping on the hard, cold ground of the Blood Forest, waiting for a Craven to attempt to rip my throat out, or a barrat to eat my face isn't exactly soothing."

"A Craven will not get to you. Neither will a barrat."

"I know. I have my dagger under my bag."

"Of course, you do."

I smiled into the night.

"I bet I can get you relaxed enough that you sleep like you're on a cloud, basking in the sun."

I snorted again, rolling my eyes.

"You doubt me?"

"There is nothing anyone or anything in this world could do that would make that happen."

"There is so much you don't know."

My eyes narrowed. "That may be true, but that is one thing I do know."

"You're wrong. And I can prove it."

"Whatever." I sighed.

"I can, and when I'm done, right before you drift off to sleep with a smile on your face, you're going to tell me I'm right," he told me.

"Doubtful," I said, wishing that he could actually do—

The hand that had been dangling in the air was suddenly flat against my upper stomach, startling me.

My head jerked back around. "What are you doing?"

"Relaxing you," he said, and all I could tell was that his head was dipped.

"How is this relaxing me?"

"Wait, and I'll show you."

I started to tell him that he didn't need to show me anything, but then his hand began to move in slow, small circles. My mouth fell shut. Somehow, he'd gotten that hand between the folds of my blanket, through the cloak, and under the sweater to move against my thin undershirt. He moved those fingers in circles, first in small, tight ones, and then larger arcs until his fingers reached below my navel and his thumb almost brushed the undersides of my breasts. All he was doing was rubbing my belly, but it was new and different and it felt like…like more than that. A warm, shivery sensation radiated from his hand.

"I don't think this is making me relaxed."

"It would if you'd stop trying to strain your neck." Suddenly, his head lowered, and his lips touched my cheek. "Lay back down, Poppy."

I did what he said only because of how close his mouth had been to mine.

"When you listen to me, I think the stars will fall." He followed me down so he spoke just above my ear. "I wish I could capture this moment somehow."

"Well, now I want to lift my head again."

"Why am I not surprised?" The sweep of his touch drifted lower, now below my navel. "But if you did, then you wouldn't find out what

I have planned. And if I know anything about you, it's that you're curious."

An answering warmth bloomed under his hand and spread lower. I sent a nervous glance to the guard. "I...I don't think this should happen."

"What is *this*?" His fingers brushed the band of my breeches, causing me to jerk. "I have a better question for you. Why did you go to the Red Pearl, Poppy? Why did you let me kiss you under the willow?"

I opened my mouth, but his lips brushed the curve of my cheek, stealing my words.

"You were there to live. Isn't that what you said? You let me pull you into that empty chamber to experience life. You let me kiss you under the willow because you wanted to feel. There's nothing wrong with that. Nothing at all." His lips coasted back up my cheek, sending a fine shiver over my skin. "Why can't tonight be that?"

My eyes closed briefly and then reopened, fixed on the guard.

"Let me show you just a little of what you missed by not coming back to the Red Pearl."

"The guards," I whispered, and it wasn't lost on me that they were my concern. Not the gods. Not the rules. Not what I was.

"No one can see what I'm doing." His hand moved, slipping down and between my thighs. I gasped as he cupped me through the pants that no longer felt thick at all. "But we know they're there."

I could barely breathe around the sharp swirl of sensation that settled low in my stomach and made my chest feel heavy, achy.

"They have no idea what's going on. No clue that my hand is between the thighs of the Maiden." His voice was a hot whisper as he pulled me back and pressed against me, causing another puff of air to escape my lips. My rear nestled into the cradle of his hips. He made a deep, rumbling sound that sent a flash of heat through me. "They have no idea that I'm touching you."

And then he was no longer just palming me. He *was* touching me, rubbing two of his fingers over the seam of the pants, over the very center of me. A rush of damp heat flooded me. My gaze dropped, and I almost expected to see what he was doing under the blanket.

I saw nothing in the darkness.

But I felt everything.

How did we get here? I couldn't quite figure it out, and I wasn't sure I wanted to. I'd had a taste before of what I was feeling now, and just a tease seemed so unfair. And wasn't that what living meant? Taking more than a sip here and small bite there. It was all about gulping and swallowing as much as you could.

I wanted to feel as much as I could, especially after feeling nothing but pain and anger for so long. I felt none of that now.

I would be in the capital soon, and it was quite possible that my Ascension would happen sooner than expected. And if I came back from it, I knew beyond a doubt that whoever I ended up with wouldn't make me feel half of what Hawke always seemed to elicit from me, whether it be irritation and anger, laughter and amusement, or this—this consuming, rippling wave of acute pleasure.

His fingers toyed with the stitching, pushing in just hard enough that I felt the touch all the way to the tips of my toes. Every part of my body became hyperaware.

How did he think this was going to help me sleep?

I was wide-awake now, pulse pounding and heart crashing, and he was touching, rubbing me in a way that caused my hips to twitch.

He dragged his hand up the front of the breeches. His palm brushed along the bare flesh of my lower stomach. Those long fingers settled over a throbbing point and moved in slow, steady circles. "I bet you're soft and wet and ready." His voice was a lush growl in my ear. "Should I find out?"

I shuddered, half afraid that he would.

Partly scared that he wouldn't.

The friction of his fingers, the rough material against my flesh...and his words... Oh, gods, they were decadent, purely sinful, and I never wanted it to end.

"Would you like that?" he asked, and my hips rolled instinctively, seeking his touch. He made that sound again, that rumble of approval that was so raw and primitive. "I would do more than this."

Eyes open only a slit, I watched the not-too-distant shape of one of the guards slowly patrolling the north-facing side of the camp, my skin and body flaming with forbidden heat as my hips moved again. This time, it wasn't only a reaction I couldn't control. I moved them purposefully, rocking them against that slow, steady circling of his fingers. I reveled in the spike of aching, biting pleasure that followed.

I shouldn't allow this. Not even in the privacy of a room, and surely not where someone could just turn around. I imagined if they paid close enough attention, they'd know that something was happening. I was almost positive that the guard closest to us, the one I watched even now, was Kieran. He seemed as alert as Hawke.

This was wrong.

But how could it…how could it feel so right, then? So good? I was becoming a being of liquid, pulsing fire, all due to just two long, graceful fingers.

"You feel what I'm doing, Poppy?"

I nodded.

"Imagine what my fingers would feel like with nothing between them and your skin."

I shuddered.

"I would do this." His fingers pressed in, a little harder, a little rougher, and my legs jerked. "I would get inside of you, Poppy. I would taste you. I bet you're as sweet as honeydew."

Oh, gods….

I bit down on my lip as my grip eased off the blanket. I reached down, placing my hand over his forearm. He stopped. He waited. Wordlessly, I lifted my hips to his hand as my fingers dug into his skin. The ache was becoming unbearable.

"Yes," he breathed. "You would like that, wouldn't you?"

"Yes," I whispered, forcing the word out past my lips.

His fingers started moving again, and I almost cried out. "I would work in another finger. You'd be tight, but you're also ready for more."

My breath was coming out in quick, shallow pants as I felt the tendons in his arm flex under my hand, as my hips moved in the same circles he was making against me.

"I would thrust my fingers in and out." His lips brushed the skin just below my ear. "You'd ride them just like you're riding my hand right now."

That's what I was doing, shamelessly so. Clutching his arm, I rocked against his hand, chasing that unbelievable tension that kept building and tightening.

"But we won't do that tonight. We can't. Because if I get *any* part of me in you, *every* part of me would be in you, and I want to hear every sound you make when that happens."

Before I could even feel disappointment, before I could truly process the silky promise in his words, he shifted his hand lower, pressing his fingers against the very center of me while his thumb rolled over the part that throbbed. There was nothing slow about his movements then. He knew exactly what he was doing with all that swirling, inescapable tension. Hawke shifted beside me, somehow, working his other arm under my shoulders. He hauled me flush against his front, and I was no longer just moving against his hand, but against *him*, the rolls of my hips erratic and sharp. Soft, low moans escaped my lips. I felt trapped, wonderfully pinned between his hand and the hard, unyielding length of his body. Something…something was happening. It was what his kisses and brief touches before had hinted at and promised. My body suddenly went as tight as a bowstring taking aim, and my lips parted a second before Hawke folded his hand over my mouth, silencing the moan I wouldn't have been able to suppress. His hot mouth moved against the side of my throat, his lips, his teeth. There was a wicked sharpness—

The tension broke. I broke. Pleasure whipped out, intense and sudden. It was like standing on a ledge and then being pushed over. I fell, shuddering in pulsing, throbbing waves, and I kept falling until the hand between my legs slowed and then stopped. I wasn't sure how much time had passed, or when Hawke's fingers slipped from my thighs or his hand eased away from my mouth. My heart was only beginning to slow when I became aware of his hand pressed against my stomach, and his arm curled around my shoulders, keeping my boneless body snug against his.

I thought maybe I should say something but…what? *Thank you* seemed inappropriate. And I thought that it wasn't entirely fair that he had given me this, while I gave him nothing of the sort. Plus, I thought that I should probably look to see if Kieran or any of the other guards had noticed what Hawke had done—what *we'd* done under the blankets, but I couldn't keep my eyes open. I couldn't get any words out.

"I know you're not going to admit it," Hawke said, voice low and thick. "But you and I both will always know that I was right."

My lips curved into a faint, sleepy smile.

He *was* right.

Again.

Chapter 31

When I woke just before dawn, I couldn't believe how soundly and deeply I'd slept. It was as if I hadn't been lying on the hard ground but in the lushest of beds.

I didn't think I would've woken up on my own if it hadn't been for the sound of hushed conversation near me.

"We made it farther than I thought we would," Hawke said, his voice low. "We should reach Three Rivers before nightfall."

"We can't stay there," came the response, and I recognized Kieran's voice. "You know that."

There was a lot of Descenter activity at Three Rivers, so that made sense. I blinked open my eyes. Through the gloom, I saw them standing a few feet from me. I flushed when my gaze lifted to Hawke. There wasn't much I could see of his face, but I thought about what we'd done.

"I know." Hawke's arms were crossed. "If we break halfway to Three Rivers, we can ride through the night and make it to New Haven by morning."

"You ready for that?" Kieran asked, and my brows knitted.

"Why wouldn't I be?"

"You think I haven't noticed what's been going on?"

My heart kicked against my chest. Immediately, my mind conjured up the image of Kieran patrolling while Hawke had whispered such indecent, wicked words in my ear. Had Kieran seen us?

Oh gods. My skin prickled and turned hot, but under the embarrassment, I was surprised to find there wasn't a single ounce of regret. I wouldn't take back a second of what I felt.

Hawke didn't answer, and my mind quickly went to the worst-case scenarios. Did he regret it? What we'd done wasn't just forbidden for me. While I wasn't aware of the exact rules established for Royal Guards, I was pretty sure that what Hawke and I had done, what we'd been doing, wasn't something the Commander would overlook.

But Hawke had to know that.

Just like I knew. And yet, I still did it.

"Remember what your task is," Kieran stated when Hawke didn't respond.

Kieran stared at Hawke and repeated. "Remember what your task is."

"I haven't forgotten for one second." His voice hardened. "Not one."

"Good to know."

Hawke started to turn toward me, and I closed my eyes, not wanting them to realize that I'd heard their conversation. I felt him stop, followed a moment later by the touch of his fingers on my cheek.

I opened my eyes, and I had no idea what to say as I looked up at him. All thoughts scattered as he dragged his thumb along the curve of my cheek and then over my lower lip, sending a shivery wave of awareness through me.

"Good morning, Princess."

"Morning," I whispered.

"You slept well."

"I did."

"Told you."

I grinned even as my cheeks heated and despite the conversation I'd overheard. "You were right."

"I'm always right."

"Doubtful."

"Do I have to prove it to you again?" he asked.

My body woke up and was fully on board with that idea. However, my brain also started functioning. "I don't think that will be necessary."

"Shame," he murmured. "We have to get moving."

"Okay." I sat up, wincing at the stiffness in my joints. "I just need a couple of minutes."

Hawke's hand found mine after I peeled myself free from the blanket. He helped me stand, straightening the tunic I wore. His hands lingered on my hips in a familiar, intimate way that tugged at my chest. My gaze lifted to his, and even in the shadows of the Blood Forest, the intense way he looked down ensnared me.

"Thank you for last night," he said, his voice pitched low for only me to hear.

Surprise flickered through me. "I feel like I should be thanking you."

"While it pleases my ego to know you feel that way, you don't need to do that." His fingers threaded with mine. "You trusted me last night, but more importantly, I know that what we shared is a risk."

It was.

He stepped closer to me, and all I could smell was that pine and dark spice of his. "And it is an honor that you'd take that risk with me, Poppy. So, thank you."

That sweet, swelling motion swept through me, but there was a strange heaviness to his voice. With our hands joined, I opened my senses, something I hadn't done since the night of the Rite.

I felt the now-familiar razor-sharp sadness that cut so deep inside him, but there was something else. It wasn't regret, but it tasted lemony. I concentrated until his emotions became mine, and I could filter through them and understand what I was feeling. Confusion. That was what I felt. Confusion and conflict, which wasn't surprising. I felt a lot of that myself.

"You okay?" Hawke asked.

Severing the connection, I nodded as I let go of his hand. "I should get ready."

Feeling his gaze on me as I stepped to the side, I looked up. The faintest gray light was filtering through the leaf-heavy branches. My gaze connected with Kieran's.

He'd been watching us the entire time, and the set to his jaw said that he wasn't happy.

Kieran looked concerned.

Whatever worry I had that the conversation with Kieran would change Hawke's behavior faded before it could even take form. The relief swirling through me should've been a warning that things were…well, they were escalating.

They had already escalated.

I shouldn't be comforted. If anything, both of us being reminded of our duties was very badly needed, but I wasn't just relieved. I was thrilled and hopeful.

But what could I be hopeful for? There was no future for us. I may be Poppy now, but I was still the Maiden, and even if I was found to be unworthy upon the Ascension, that didn't mean there'd be a happily ever after for me with Hawke. I'd most likely be exiled, and I would never expect anyone else to suffer that.

It wasn't like I thought that what we were or what we meant to one another had grown to a place where Hawke would go into exile with me. That was silly. That was…

That sounded like the kind of epic love my mother had felt for my father.

Either way, last night had felt like a dream. That was the only way I could describe it. And I wasn't going to let the what-ifs or the consequences ruin the memory and what it had meant to me. I'd cross that bridge when it came time to do so.

Right now, all I could really focus on was not falling off Setti.

My cheeks stung from the icy wind as we traveled through the Blood Forest, the red maple leaves and gray-crimson bark a blur.

We had moved into the heart of the forest, where the trees were less dense, allowing more light rays to come through. The sun didn't warm the air, though. If anything, it got cooler the farther in we went, the trees even odder.

Trunks and branches twisted, spiraling upward, their boughs tangling. It couldn't be the wind. All the trees stood straight, and the bark…it seemed *wet*, almost as if the sap was leaking.

I'd been right earlier about snow falling if it rained. A few hours into the ride, flurries swirled and drifted, blanketing the lush, vibrant green grass on either side of the beaten path. I'd put my gloves back on, but I didn't think my fingers had ever thawed from the night. I secured my hood, but it could only shield my face to a certain degree, and I had no idea how much longer we had to go. The forest seemed endless.

We slowed as thick, gnarled roots broke free from the ground and climbed across our path as if they were trying to reclaim the patch of earth used by the living.

Loosening my grip on the pommel, I looked down, somewhat awed by the strength of the roots as the horses carefully navigated the obstruction. Something along the ground caught my attention. I looked to my right, beyond Airrick's horse. Next to one of the trees was a pile of rocks placed so neatly, that I couldn't imagine they'd naturally gotten that way. A couple of feet farther, there was another grouping of stones. But this time, they weren't in a pile but placed in a perfect pattern. To my left, I saw another pristine circle of stones. There were more, some with a rock placed in the center, others empty, and even some where the stones had been placed in a way that looked like an arrow slashing through the circle.

Like the Royal Crest.

Unease trickled down my spine. There was no way these stones had fallen in these patterns naturally. I turned in the saddle to point them out to Hawke—

Suddenly, one of the horses up front reared, nearly throwing Kieran from his seat. He held onto the lead, calming the horse as he rubbed its neck.

"What is it?" asked Noah, a Huntsman who was riding in front of us as we all came to a stop.

Phillips lifted his finger, silencing the group. Holding my breath, I looked around. I didn't hear or see anything, but I felt Setti's muscles twitch under my legs. He began to prance, backing up. I placed my hand on his neck, trying to calm him as Hawke pulled on the reins. The other horses started to move nervously.

Hawke quietly tapped the area where my dagger was attached, and I nodded. Reaching into my cloak, I unsheathed the blade and took hold of it. I scanned the trees, still—

It came out of nowhere. A burst of black and red, leaping into the air and slamming into Noah's side. Startled, the horse rose up, and Noah went down, hitting the ground hard. Suddenly, the thing was on top of him, snapping at his face with jagged teeth as he struggled to hold it off.

It was a barrat.

I managed to stifle the scream that had climbed into my throat. The thing was huge, bigger than a boar. Its slick, oily fur rose along its curved spine. Ears pointed and snout as long as half my arm, its claws dug into the grass, ripping it from the ground as it tried to get at the Huntsman.

Phillips turned in his seat, bow in hand and arrow nocked. He let it go, the projectile whizzing through the air, striking the creature in the back of its neck. The thing shrieked as Noah tossed it from him, its legs kicking as it rolled, attempting to dislodge the bolt.

Scrambling to his feet, Noah pulled his short sword free. The bloodstone glinted in the beam of sunlight as he brought it down, silencing the beast.

"Gods," he grunted, wiping the spray of blood from his forehead. He turned to Phillips, who still held his bow, a new arrow nocked. "Thanks, man."

"Don't mention it."

"If there's one, there's a horde," Hawke advised. "We need to get—"

From every direction, it sounded like the forest had come alive. A rustling grew louder, coming from the right.

I jerked back, all but plastering myself to Hawke as the horde did indeed arrive. Noah cursed as he leapt to a low-hanging branch, pulling his legs up as the rodents burst from the shrubs and moved in between the trees.

They didn't attack.

They ran *past* us, darting between the agitated horses. There had been dozens of them, chattering and squeaking as they crossed the roots and then disappeared into the brush and trees.

Nothing about what had just happened gave me relief. If they were running, it was because they were running *from* something.

Glancing at the ground, I saw thick tendrils of mist gathering. Tiny hairs all over my body rose. The sudden scent...

It smelled like death.

"We need to get out of here." Kieran had noticed the same thing I had. "Now."

Noah dropped to the ground in a crouch, his feet disappearing in the rapidly thickening mist. My heart leapt into my throat as I leaned forward, gripping the pommel. I felt Setti tense under me as Noah ran to his horse, grabbing the reins near the horse's neck with one hand, his sword with the other. He lifted the blade into the air.

The Craven was as fast as the arrow that had struck the barrat, rushing out from between the trees. His torn and ragged clothing flapped as he caught Noah, digging clawed fingers into the Huntsman's chest as it latched on to his neck. Crimson poured down Noah's front as he screamed and fell back, dropping his sword as his horse ran, blowing past the guards at the front of our group.

A howl turned my blood to ice, and my stomach seized as it was answered by another and another—

"Shit," growled Hawke as Luddie turned his horse around, catching the Craven who'd downed Noah in the head with a bloodstone spear.

"We won't make it if we run." Luddie flipped the blade of his weapon upward. "Not in these roots."

Heart thumping, I knew what that meant. The mist was now at our knees, and our luck had run out.

"You know what to do," Hawke told me. "Do it."

I gave a curt nod, and then he swung one leg off Setti, dropping to land on the roots. I slid from the horse, stepping down so I wasn't in the twisted mass. I glanced to see the others doing the same. Airrick spotted the dagger in my hand, his brows raised.

"I know how to use it," I told him.

He gave me a boyish grin. "For some reason, I'm not surprised."

"They're here." Kieran lifted his sword.

He was right.

They flew from the trees, a mass of gray, sunken flesh, and decayed clothing. There was no time to feel panic. Despite being almost nothing more than skin and bones, they were frighteningly fast.

"Don't let them get to the horses," one of the guards shouted as Hawke stepped forward, thrusting his sword through a Craven's chest.

I braced myself, seeing nothing but blood-stained fangs, and then one came straight for me. Snapping forward, I slammed a hand into its shoulder, ignoring how the skin and bone seemed to cave under my palm, and then shoved the dagger into its chest. Rotten blood spurted as I yanked the blade free. The Craven fell, and I spun, grabbing the torn shirt of another Craven who was making a run for Setti. Shoving the dagger into the base of its skull, I grimaced as I pulled the blade free.

I looked up, my gaze snagging with Hawke's. He gave me a tight smile that hinted at the dimple. "Never thought I'd find anything having to do with the Craven sexy." He swung, lopping off the head of the one nearest him. "But watching you fight them is incredibly arousing."

"So inappropriate," I muttered, letting go of the Craven. I turned and danced out of the grasp of another. I shot toward it as it grabbed hold of my cloak, slamming the dagger into its chest. It went down, nearly taking me with it

My blade was effective. Unfortunately, however, it required close contact. I quickly scanned the area and saw Kieran moving with the grace of a dancer, a sword in each hand as he took down one Craven after another. Luddie was making great use of his spear, as was Phillips with his bow. Airrick stayed close to me, the mist now to our thighs.

Wailing, a Craven rushed me. Grip tightening on the wolven bone handle, I waited until he was within grasp and then darted to the left as I shoved the bloodstone up under its chin. Sucking in a sharp breath, I took a step back as I willed my stomach to settle. The smell...

"Princess. Got a better weapon for you." Picking up Noah's fallen bloodstone sword, Hawke tossed it to me, and I caught it.

"Thanks." Sheathing the dagger, I turned and struck out, slicing through the neck of the closest Craven.

I loved the dagger, but the lightweight bloodstone sword was far more useful in this situation. Able to keep a bit of distance, I cut down another Craven as my heart thumped against my chest. The back of my leg bumped into something, and I jerked to my right, putting my foot down. My boot slipped into the roots as I swung out, catching the Craven in the chest. It wasn't a clean blow. I'd missed its heart. I yanked the sword free and shifted my legs to brace myself as I went for his neck.

I'd forgotten about the roots.

Foot snagged, I tripped and tried desperately to catch myself, but I went down as someone crashed into me, knocking me free of the roots. Airrick. He caught the Craven as I fell, tackling him as they both disappeared under the mist.

My head slipped under the fog, and for a moment, there was nothing to see but a white film. Panic exploded in my stomach. My free hand hit the ground. It was too slick under my palm. I was thrown back through the years, to when I was tiny and frightened, my grip on my mother desperate and slipping—

I heard Vikter's voice in my mind. A warning he'd given me in training at the very beginning. *Never cave to panic. If you do, you die.* He'd been right. Fear could heighten the senses, but panic slowed everything down.

I wasn't a child.

I wasn't tiny and helpless anymore.

I knew how to fight back, knew how to protect myself.

With a shout, I pulled myself free of the memory and pushed to my feet just as a hairless Craven reached me. I jammed the sword forward, slicing into its heart. It didn't even so much as whimper as its soulless eyes met mine. All it did was shudder and then fall backward. I turned to find Airrick, realizing that the mist had retreated, slipping down our legs and thinning. That was a good sign as I stalked toward a now visible, wounded Craven crawling across the ground toward one of the horses. I planted my boot on its back, shoving it to the ground as it howled. I jabbed down with the sword, silencing it. The mist was all but gone now.

Breathing heavily as Hawke thrust his sword through the chest of the last remaining Craven, I turned to survey the damage. Only five guards were standing, not including Hawke. I saw Kieran and Luddie above a Huntsman who was very clearly dead. I saw the guard whose sword I held, and I knew that Noah had been gone the moment the Craven had sunk its teeth into his neck. I kept turning until my gaze found Phillips. He knelt beside...

Airrick.

No.

He was on his back, both his and Phillips' hands pressed against his stomach. His pale skin made his brown hair seem so much darker, and there was...there was so much blood. Lowering the sword, I walked over to where Airrick lay, stepping around the fallen Craven.

"Is...she...is she okay?" Blood trickled out of his mouth as he stared up at Phillips. "The..."

Phillips glanced up at me, his brown skin taking on a shade of gray. His eyes were somber as he nodded. "She's more than okay."

"Good." He let out a wheezing breath. "That's…good."

Heart sinking, I lowered to my knees and placed the sword beside me. "You saved me."

His eyes flicked to me, and he coughed out a bloody, weak laugh. "I don't…think you…needed saving."

"I did," I told him, glancing at his stomach. Craven claws had caught him, digging in deep—too deep. His insides were no longer *in*. I hid my shudder as Hawke drew closer. "And you were there for me. You did save me, Airrick."

Hawke knelt beside Phillips, his gaze meeting mine. He shook his head, not that I needed to be told. This wasn't a survivable wound, and it had to be so painful. I didn't need my gift to tell me that, but I opened my senses, shuddering at the raw agony pulsing through the connection.

Keeping my attention focused on Airrick, I picked up his hand and folded both of mine around it. I couldn't save him, but I could do what I hadn't been able to do with Vikter. I could help Airrick, and make this easier. It was forbidden and not exactly wise to do it when there were witnesses, but I didn't care. I couldn't sit here and do nothing when I knew I could help.

So, I thought of the beaches and how Hawke made me laugh, how he made me feel like I was living, and I pushed that warmth and happiness through the bond and into Airrick.

I knew the moment it hit the guard. The lines of his face relaxed, and his body stopped trembling.

He looked at me, his eyes wide. He looked so terribly young. "I don't…hurt anymore."

"You don't?" I forced a smile as I kept the connection open, washing him in waves of light and warmth. I didn't want even the slightest bit of pain to sneak through.

"No." A look of awe settled in his expression. "I know I'm not, but I feel…I feel good."

"I'm relieved to hear that."

He stared at me, and I knew Phillips and Hawke were watching. I knew without even looking at them that they realized his sudden relief had nothing to do with the stages of death. No one with that kind of wound slipped away peacefully.

"I know you," Airrick said, his chest rising heavily and then slowly settling. "Didn't think...I should say anything, but we've met." More blood leaked out of his mouth. "We played cards."

Surprised, the smile became real. "Yes, we did. How did you know?"

"It's...your eyes," he told me. There were too many moments between when his chest settled and when it rose again. "You were losing."

"I was." I leaned down, keeping his pain at bay. "Normally, I'm better at cards. My brother taught me, but I kept being dealt bad hands."

He laughed again, the sound even weaker. "Yeah...they were bad hands. Thank..." His gaze shifted to my shoulder. Whatever he saw was beyond me, beyond all of us. It was welcome. Airrick's lips trembled as he smiled. "Momma?"

His chest didn't settle. It rose, but it didn't come back down. Airrick passed some seconds later, his lips still curved into a smile, his eyes now dull but glistening. I didn't know if he saw his mother, saw anything, but I hoped he did. I wished for him that his mother had come for him and not the god, Rhain. It was nice to think that loved ones were there to greet those passing over. I wanted to believe that Vikter's wife and their child had been waiting for him.

Slowly, I lowered his hand and placed it on his chest. I looked up then to find both Phillips and Hawke staring at me.

"You did something to him," Hawke stated, his gaze searching mine.

I said nothing.

I didn't need to. Phillips said it for me. "It's true. The rumors. I heard it, but I didn't believe it. Gods. You have the touch."

Chapter 32

Our group rode hard, the pace aggressive and jarring, and we were three guards short of when we left Masadonia. A few hours later, we found Noah's horse grazing, and once he was tethered to Luddie's mount, we were on our way once more.

Having stopped just outside of Three Rivers for only a few hours to rest the horses, we traveled straight through the night. My heart was heavy, my legs numb and sore, and I was worried.

Phillips didn't speak of what I'd done once the others joined us, but he kept stealing glances at me. Each time, he looked at me as if he weren't sure I was real, reminding me of the glances the servants had sent my way whenever they saw me veiled.

It made me uncomfortable, but it was nothing like Hawke's response to my gift.

He'd stared at me over Airrick's body as if I were a puzzle missing all the edge pieces. Obviously, he was surprised, not that I could blame him. I'd figured he'd have questions. When we stopped outside of Three Rivers, I tried to speak to him about what I'd done, but all he did was shake his head. Just told me "later" and said to get some rest. I, of course, resisted, which ended with him either pretending to fall asleep beside me or actually going to sleep.

I didn't know if he was mad or disturbed or…upset that I hadn't told him, but I didn't regret using my gift to ease Airrick's passing. Hawke and I would talk, and later may come sooner than he wanted.

But I managed to resist using my gift to determine how he felt. I'd rather him tell me than for me to cheat.

Because reading his emotions right now would feel like cheating.

By the time we reached New Haven, dusk was quickly upon us. We passed through the small Rise with little issue. Hawke dismounted and walked ahead to talk to one of the guards before swinging back up onto the horse behind me, leading the way through the cobblestone street.

Kieran had taken Airrick's place, riding alongside us as we traveled through the sleepy town surrounded by a heavily wooded area. We passed shuttered businesses, closed for the evening, and then entered a residential area. The homes were as small as the ones in the Lower Ward but not nearly as stacked on top of one another. They were also in much better condition. The small trading town was obviously profitable, and the Royal who ruled over this city, apparently had a better grip on maintenance than the Teermans did.

It was about a block into the neighborhood when the door to the first house opened, and an older, brown-skinned man stepped out. He said nothing, simply nodded at Kieran and Hawke as we passed. Behind the man, a young boy ran out and to the house next door. He banged on the door, and shutters swung open. Ahead of us, Phillips' hand moved to his sword as another young lad stuck his head out. "My papa is—" He broke off, eyes widening as he saw our little caravan. He whooped, and with a toothy grin, he disappeared back into the house, yelling for his father.

The boy from the first house ran two doors down, summoning another child, this one a girl with hair redder than mine. Her eyes grew as wide as saucers when she saw us.

Then, across the street, another door opened, this time revealing a middle-aged woman with a small child on her hip. She grinned, and the child waved. Lifting a hand, I gave an awkward wave back, and then I noticed that the first boy had gained quite a crew. An entire group of children followed our progress on the sidewalk now, and more and more doors opened as the people of New Haven came out to watch. None of them called out. Some waved. Others smiled. Only a few looked on wryly from their front stoops.

I leaned back and whispered, "This is a little odd."

"I don't think they get a lot of visitors," Hawke answered, squeezing my waist, and my stupid heart jumped a little in my chest in response.

"This is an exciting day for them," Kieran commented drolly.

"Is it?" murmured Hawke.

"They behave as if royalty is among them."

Hawke snorted. "Then they truly must not get many visitors."

Kieran slid him a long, sideways look, but Hawke seemed to have relaxed behind me, and I took that as a good sign.

"Have you been here before?" I asked.

"Only briefly."

I glanced over at Kieran. "You?"

"I've passed through a time or two."

I raised a brow, but then Haven Keep came into view. Situated near the woods, it didn't employ a secondary wall like Teerman Castle did, but it was also nowhere near its size. Only two stories tall, the greenish-gray stone structure looked like it had survived a different era.

Barely.

We rode forward just as something cold touched the tip of my nose. I looked up. Snowflakes fell haphazardly as we crossed the yard, heading toward the stables. Several guards in black waited, nodding as we entered the open space that smelled of horse and hay.

I exhaled raggedly, briefly closing my eyes as I loosened my grip on the saddle. The trek across the kingdom was nowhere near complete, but at least for the night, we had a bed, four walls, and a roof.

Things I would no longer take for granted.

Hawke dropped down behind me and turned, lifting his arms as he wiggled his fingers. I arched a brow and then slid off the other side of the horse.

Hawke sighed.

Grinning, I rubbed Setti's neck, hoping he would get a tummy full of the best hay and some rest. He deserved it.

With the saddlebag draped over his shoulder, Hawke came to my side. "Stay close to me."

"Of course."

He shot me a look that said my quick agreement was not to be trusted. Once the others joined us, we exited. The snow was coming down a little harder now, dusting the ground. I pulled my cloak around me as the front entrance opened, revealing another guard—a tall blond with pale, wintry-blue eyes.

Kieran greeted the guard with a handshake. "It's good to see you," the guard said, his gaze flickering to Hawke and then to me. His attention lingered for a few seconds on the left side of my face before coming back to Kieran. "It's good to see all of you."

"Same, Delano," Kieran answered as Hawke placed his hand on my lower back. "It's been too long."

"Not long enough," boomed a deep voice from inside the keep.

I turned to see a wide-open area lit by oil lamps. A tall, bearded, dark-haired and broad-shouldered man strode out from two large wooden doors. He wore dark breeches and a heavy tunic. A short sword was strapped to his waist even though he wasn't dressed as a guard.

Kieran smiled, and I blinked. This was the first time that I'd seen him smile, and he'd gone from coldly handsome to strikingly attractive as he did it. "Elijah, you missed me more than anyone else."

Elijah met Kieran halfway, capturing the younger man in a bear hug that lifted the guard clear off his feet. Eyes that were hazel, more gold than brown, landed on where Hawke and I stood.

One side of the man's lips kicked up as he let go of Kieran. Or rather, dropped him. Kieran stumbled back a step, catching himself as he shook his head. "What do we have here?" Elijah asked.

"We're in need of shelter for the night," Hawke answered.

For some reason, this Elijah found Hawke's response funny. He threw back his head and laughed. "We have plenty of shelter."

"Good to hear." Hawke's hand stayed while I glanced around the entryway, confused.

Several people had come from beyond the doors, men and women. Like the townsfolk, there were varying degrees of looks. Most smiled, but a few stared in a way that reminded me of the blond Descenter who'd thrown the Craven hand.

Where was the Lord or Lady who oversaw the city? The sun was still up, but the space was windowless and, therefore, would not be an affront to the gods if they moved about. I didn't see any Ascended among the gathered people. Perhaps this man was one of the Lord's stewards and the Lord was otherwise occupied? I noted that Kieran was looking around with a narrowed gaze, probably thinking the same thing as I was.

"We do have a lot of…catching up to do," Elijah said, clapping

Kieran on the shoulder with a heavy hand that caused my brows to rise.

A black-haired woman in a deep forest green, knee-length tunic and matching breeches strode forward, a heavy cream shawl draped over her shoulders. Immediately, my gaze was pulled to her footwear.

They were boots.

She drew closer, and I noted that her eye color was very similar to Elijah's, if not exact. Were they related? She seemed at least a decade younger, closer to Hawke's and my age. Maybe a niece? She gave all of us a close-lipped smile, her gaze, like Delano's, falling and catching on my visible scars. There was no pity in her face, just...curiosity, which was far better than the former.

"I must speak with a few people, but Magda will show you to your room." Hawke turned to the dark-haired woman before I could respond. "Make sure she has a room to bathe in, and she's sent hot food."

"Yes—" She started to dip, almost as if she were sinking into some sort of curtsy, but then stopped halfway. Her cheeks flushed prettily as she glanced at me. "Sorry. I'm a little off balance somedays." She patted her slightly rounded stomach. "I blame baby number two."

"Congratulations," I said, hoping that was the appropriate response as I turned to him. "Hawke—"

"Later," he said, and then pivoted, stalking off to join where Kieran stood with Elijah, now joined by Phillips, who was eyeing every inch of the keep.

"Come." Magda lightly touched my arm. "We have a room on the second floor that has its own bathing chamber. I'll have hot water sent up, and you can bathe while Cook prepares your dinner."

Unsure of what else to do, I followed Magda from the entryway and through the side door that fed into a stairwell. Surprised that Hawke had left me alone, I figured it was because he knew I was more than equipped to defend myself, but it still seemed odd. Unless he felt confident about there being no Descenters here.

But even if that was the case, it didn't explain how Hawke had known this woman's name when he'd only been to the town briefly, and we hadn't been introduced.

The room was surprisingly large and airy despite the only source of natural light being a small, narrow window overlooking the yard. I liked the exposed wooden beams on the ceiling, and the bed looked like the most inviting thing I'd ever seen.

I didn't dare go near it, not when my cloak and clothing were stained with Craven blood, dirt, and sweat. I'd draped my cloak over a heavy, wooden chair and then made sure my sweater covered my dagger.

A fire was lit, and the food, a rich and savory beef stew, had come before the hot water. I ate every drop of the stew and the accompanying biscuits, and would've probably licked the bowl clean if it hadn't been for the small army of servants commanded by Magda.

As the tub was filled with steaming-hot water, Magda hung a light blue robe on a hook in the bathing chamber. I stared at it, my throat suddenly clogged with emotion.

It wasn't white.

I closed my eyes.

"Poppy," the woman said, and I snapped my eyes open. She'd asked earlier what to call me, and that was the name I'd given her. "Are you all right?"

"Yes." I blinked. "It's taken…a lot to get here."

"I can imagine," she replied, though I doubted she could. "If you leave your clothing here by the door, I'll make sure it is cleaned this night."

"Thank you."

She smiled. "Fresh soap and towels have been placed by your bath. Is there anything else you need?"

I wanted to ask where Hawke was, but I didn't think she'd know. I shook my head, and she started for the door. Then I thought of the Ascended. "Magda?" I called out. "Who is the Lord and Lady in residence here?"

"Lord Halverston has gone hunting with some of the men," she answered. "He would've been here to greet you, but he was already preparing to leave with it being so close to dusk."

"Oh." The Lord went hunting with the men? The people here were…odd.

"Is there anything else?"

This time, I shook my head and didn't stop her. I quickly undressed, leaving my clothing by the door and then hurried across the chilled floor that the fire hadn't yet warmed, dagger in hand.

The large tub had to be the second-best thing I'd ever seen.

My sore muscles immediately welcomed the hot water, and I stayed longer than necessary, scrubbing myself with the lilac-scented soap and washing my hair twice before I worried that I'd wrinkle like a prune if I stayed one minute longer. Toweling off, I slipped on the warm robe and padded on bare feet to the small vanity, pleased to find a comb. I roamed out to the bedroom, idly combing out the knots and tangles in my hair, and placed the dagger on the end table. When that was done, there was nothing to do but wait.

I sat on the edge of the bed, wondering what Tawny was doing right now. Was she making friends with the other Ladies and Lords in Wait? Sadness tugged at my chest, and I welcomed it. That was far better than feeling only anger and pain, but I missed her.

I missed Vikter.

The knot of emotion was back in my throat as I smoothed my hand over the soft blue material. My eyes burned, but the tears…they wouldn't come. I almost wished they would. I sighed, glancing back at the head of the bed. There were two pillows as if the bed were meant for two people to—

A knock on the door startled me. I jumped from the bed and was in the process of moving to the end table when the door opened. Snatching up the dagger, I whipped around.

"Hawke," I breathed.

He lifted his brows. "I thought you'd be asleep."

"Is that why you barged in?"

"Since I knocked, I don't consider that barging in." He closed the door behind him and stepped into the light. He'd bathed and changed, his damp hair curling against his cheeks. "But I'm glad to see that you were prepared just in case it wasn't someone you wanted to see."

"What if you're someone I don't want to see?"

That half-grin appeared. "You and I both know that's not the case." His gaze roamed over me. "At all."

"Your ego never fails to amaze me." I placed the dagger back and then looked around. Since the only other place to sit was the very uncomfortable-looking chair, the bed was the only option. I sat on the edge.

"I never fail to amaze you," he replied.

I smiled. "Thank you for proving what I just said."

He chuckled as he strode forward. "Did you eat?"

I nodded. "You?"

"While I bathed."

"Multi-tasking at its finest."

"I am skilled." He stayed where he'd stopped, several feet from me. "Why aren't you asleep? You have to be exhausted."

"I know the morning will come sooner rather than later, and we'll be back out there, but I can't sleep. Not yet. I was waiting for you." Suddenly nervous, I toyed with the sash on the robe. "This place is...different, isn't it?"

"I imagine if one was used to only the capital and Masadonia, it would be," he answered. "Things are far simpler here, no pomp and circumstance."

"I noticed that. I haven't seen a single Royal Crest."

His head tilted. "Did you wait up for me to talk about Royal banners?"

"No." I sighed, letting go of the sash. "I waited up to talk to you about what I did to Airrick."

Hawke said nothing.

My nervousness gave way to irritation. "Is this later enough for you? A good time?"

There was that curl of his lips. "This is a good time, Princess. It's private enough, which is what I figured we would need."

I opened my mouth and then snapped it shut. Dammit. Was that why he'd kept pushing it off? If so, that made sense.

"Are you going to explain why neither you nor Vikter ever mentioned that you had this...touch?"

My jaw came unlocked. "I don't call it that. Only a few who have heard...the rumors about it do. It's why some think I'm the child of a god. You, who seems to hear and know everything, haven't heard that rumor?"

"I do know a lot, but no, I have never heard that," he replied. "And I've never seen anyone do whatever it was that you did."

My gaze searched his, and I thought I saw the truth in his stare.

"It's a gift from the gods. It's why I'm Chosen." Or at least one of the reasons. "I have been instructed by the Queen herself to never speak of it or to use it. Not until I am deemed worthy. For the most part, I have obeyed that."

"For the most part?"

"Yes, for the most part. Vikter knew about it, but Tawny doesn't. Neither did Rylan or Hannes. The Duchess knows, and the Duke knew, but that was all," I told him. "And I don't use it often...*ish*."

"What is this gift?"

I blew out a long breath. "I can...sense other people's pain, both physical and mental. Well, it started off that way. It appears that the closer I get to my Ascension, the more it evolves. I guess I should say I can sense people's emotions now," I corrected, tugging at the blanket beside me. "I don't need to touch them. I can just look at them, and it's like...like I open myself up to them. I can usually control it and keep my senses to myself, but sometimes, it's difficult."

"Like in crowds?"

Knowing he was thinking about when the Duke had addressed the city, I nodded. "Yes. Or when someone projects their pain without realizing it. Those times are rare. I don't see anything more than you or anyone else would see, but I feel what they do."

"You...just feel what they feel?"

I looked up at him.

He was staring at me with slightly wide eyes. "So, you felt the pain that Airrick, who had received a very painful injury, felt?"

I nodded.

Hawke blinked. "That had to be..."

"Agony?" I supplied. "It was, but it's not the worst I've felt. Physical pain is always warm, and it's acute, but the mental, emotional pain is like...like bathing in ice on the coldest day. That kind of pain is far worse."

Hawke walked over and sat on the bed beside me. "And you can feel other emotions? Like happiness or hatred? Relief...or guilt?"

"I can, but it's new. And I'm not often sure what I'm feeling. I have to rely on what I know, and well..." I shrugged. "But to answer your question, yes."

For the first time since I met Hawke, he looked speechless.

"That's not all I can do," I added.

"Obviously."

I ignored the dryness in his tone. "I can also ease other people's pain by touch. Usually, it's not something the person notices, not unless they're experiencing a great deal of obvious pain."

"How?"

"I think of…happy moments and feed that through the bond my gift establishes through the connection," I explained.

Hawke stared at me some more. "You think happy thoughts and that's it?"

"Well, I wouldn't say it like that. But, yes."

Something flickered over his face, and then his gaze shot to mine. "Have you sensed my emotions before?"

I wanted to lie. I didn't. "I have."

He sat back.

"I didn't do it on purpose at first—well, okay, I did, but only because you always looked like… I don't know. A caged animal whenever I saw you around the castle, and I was curious to find out why. I realize I shouldn't have. I didn't do it…a lot. I made myself stop. Sort of," I added, and his brows climbed up on his forehead. "For the most part. Sometimes, I just can't help it. It's like I'm denying nature to not…"

To not use what I had been born with.

That was why it was hard to control sometimes. Sure, curiosity often drove me to use it, but it felt like going against nature to deny it and keep it locked down. It was stifling.

Just like the veil and all the rules and the expectations and…the future I never chose for myself.

Why did my entire life seem so wrong?

"What did you feel from me?"

Pulling myself from my thoughts, I looked over at him. "Sadness."

Shock rolled across his expression.

"Deep grief and sorrow." I lowered my gaze to his chest. "It's always there, even when you're teasing or smiling. I don't know how you deal with it. I figure a lot of it has to do with your brother and friend." When Hawke said nothing, I thought I'd said too much. "I'm sorry. I shouldn't have used my gift on you, and I probably should've just lied—"

"Have you eased my pain before?"

I flattened my hands on my legs. "I have."

"Twice. Right? After you were with the Priestess, and the night of the Rite."

I nodded.

"Well, now I understand why I felt…lighter. The first time it lasted—damn, it lasted for a while. Got the best sleep in years." He coughed out a short laugh, and I peeked over at him. "Too bad that can't be bottled and sold."

I wasn't sure what to say.

"Why?" he demanded. "Why did you take my pain? Yes, I do…feel sadness. I miss my brother with every breath I take. His absence haunts me, but it's manageable."

"I know. You don't let it interfere with your life, but I…I didn't like knowing that you were hurting," I admitted. "And I could help, at least temporarily. I just wanted—"

"What?"

"I wanted to help. I wanted to use my gift to help people."

"And you have? More than just me and Airrick?"

"I have. Those who are cursed? I often ease their pain. And Vikter would get terrible headaches. I would sometimes help him with those. And Tawny, but she never knew."

"That's how the rumors got started. You're doing it to help the cursed."

"And their families sometimes. They often feel such sorrow that I have to."

"But you're not allowed."

"No, and it seems so stupid that I can't." I threw up my hands. "That I'm not supposed to. The reason doesn't even make sense. Wouldn't the gods have already found me worthy to have given me this gift?" I reasoned.

"One would think so." He paused. "Can your brother do this? Anyone else in your family?"

"No. It's only me, and the last Maiden. We were both born in a shroud," I told him. "And my mother realized what I could do around the age of three or four."

He frowned and went back to staring at me like I was a puzzle missing pieces.

"What?"

Shaking his head, his expression smoothed out. "Are you reading me now?"

"No. I seriously try not to, even when I really want to. Doing so feels like cheating when it's someone I..." I trailed off. I was going to say: "*when it's someone I care about.*"

My stomach twisted as my wide-eyed gaze swung back to him. I cared about Hawke. A lot. Not in the same way I cared about Tawny or Vikter, though. It was different.

Oh, gods.

That probably wasn't a good thing, but it didn't feel bad. It felt like anticipation and hope, excitement and a hundred other things that weren't bad.

"Now, I wish I had your gift because I would love to know what you're feeling at this moment."

I couldn't be grateful that he didn't know. "I feel nothing from the Ascended," I blurted out. "Absolutely nothing, even though I know they feel physical pain."

"That's..."

"Weird, right?"

"I was going to say disturbing, but sure, it's weird."

"You know?" I leaned in, lowering my voice. "It always bothered me that I couldn't feel anything. It should be a relief, but it never was. It just made me feel...cold."

"I can see that." He inched forward, lowering his voice, too. "I should thank you."

"For what?"

"For easing my pain."

"You don't have to."

"I know, but I want to," he said, his mouth so incredibly close to mine. "Thank you."

"It's nothing." My eyes drifted halfway shut. He smelled like pine and soap, and his breath was so warm on my lips.

"I was right."

"About what?"

"About you being brave and strong," he explained. "You risk a lot when you use your gift."

"I don't think I've risked enough," I admitted. "I couldn't help Vikter. I was too...overwhelmed. Maybe if I wasn't fighting it so much, I would've at least taken his pain."

"But you took Airrick's. You helped him." He dipped his head, and his brow kissed mine. "You are utterly nothing like I expected."

"You keep saying that. What did you expect?"

"I honestly don't know anymore."

My eyes closed, discovering that I liked this closeness. I liked being...touched when it was my choice.

"Poppy?"

I also liked the way he said my name. "Yes?"

He touched my cheek with his fingers. "I hope you realize that no matter what anyone has ever told you, you are more worthy than anyone I've ever met."

My heart squeezed in the best way. "You haven't met enough people, then."

"I have met too many." He lifted his chin, kissing my forehead. He leaned back, sliding his thumb along my jaw. "You deserve so much more than what awaits you."

I should.

My eyes opened.

I really should.

I wasn't a bad person. Under the veil and behind my title and my gift, I was like anyone else. But I was never treated as such. As Hawke had pointed out before, every privilege everyone else had was something I couldn't even earn. And I was...

I was so damn tired of it.

Hawke drew back, his voice heavy as he said, "Thank you for trusting me with this."

Unable to answer, I was too caught up in what was happening within me because something was shifting, changing. Something enormous and yet also small. My heart started pumping as if I'd just been fighting for my life, and...dear gods, that's what I was doing. Right now. Fighting not for my life but to be able to live it. That was what was clicking into place inside me.

Maiden or not, good or bad, Chosen or forsaken, I deserved to *live* and to exist without being cloistered by rules I never agreed to.

I looked at Hawke, *really* looked at him, and what I saw went beyond the physical. He'd always been different with me, and he never tried to stop me. From the night on the Rise to the Blood Forest when he'd thrown me the sword, he didn't only protect me. He believed in me and respected my need to defend myself. And like he'd said before, it was as if we'd known each other for ages. He...he understood me, and I thought I might understand him. Because he was brave and strong, and he felt and thought deeply. He'd suffered losses and survived and continued to do so even with the agony I knew he carried with him. He accepted me.

And I trusted him with my life.

With *everything.*

"You shouldn't look at me like that." His voice had thickened.

"Like what?"

"You know exactly how you're looking at me." He closed his eyes. "Actually, you might not, and that's why I should leave."

"How am I looking at you, Hawke?"

His eyes opened. "Like I don't deserve to be looked at. Not by you."

"Not true," I told him.

"I wish that was the case. Gods, I do. I need to leave." He rose and backed up, his stare lingering. I didn't think he wanted to leave at all. He took a deep breath. "Goodnight, Poppy."

I watched him start for the door, his name on the tip of my tongue. I didn't want him to leave. I didn't want to spend tonight alone. I didn't want him to believe that he wasn't deserving.

What I wanted was to live.

What I wanted was him.

"Hawke?"

He stopped but didn't turn.

My heart was racing once more. "Will you…will you stay with me tonight?"

Chapter 33

Hawke didn't respond, and I wasn't sure if he'd even taken a breath, reminding me of the night of the Rite with us under the willow. That memory didn't bring with it the sharp stab of pain.

Then he spoke. "I want nothing more than that, but I don't think you realize what will happen if I stay."

I felt a little dizzy. "What would happen?"

He turned then, his stare piercing. "There is no way I could be in that bed with you and not be all over you in ten seconds flat. We wouldn't even make it to the bed before that happened. I know my limitations. I know that I'm not a good enough man to remember my duty and yours or that I'm so incredibly unworthy of you it should be a sin. Even knowing that, there is no way I wouldn't strip that robe from you and do exactly what I told you I'd do when we were in the forest."

Heat swept through me as I stared at him. "I know."

He sucked in a sharp breath. "Do you?"

I nodded.

Hawke took a step away from the door. "I'm not just going to hold you. I won't stop at kissing you. My fingers won't be the only thing inside you. My need for you is far too great, Poppy. If I stay, you will not walk out this door the Maiden."

I shivered at the bluntness of his words. They weren't a shock, but his need was. I didn't see myself as someone who could be the object of something so fierce. I'd never been allowed to.

"I know," I repeated.

He took one more step toward me. "Do you truly, Poppy?"

I did.

And it was strange to know myself and be so certain when I'd spent so long *not* knowing myself—never really being allowed to discover who I was, what I might like or dislike, what I'd want or need. But I knew now.

I had known the moment I asked him to stay. I knew what the consequences could be. I knew what I was, and what was expected of me, and I knew I could no longer be that. It wasn't what I wanted in life. It had never been my choice.

But this...this I wanted.

Hawke was who I wanted.

This was my choice.

I was reclaiming my life, and it had started long before him. When I demanded to be taught how to fight, and when I made Vikter include me when he went out to help the cursed. Those were significant steps, but there had been smaller ones along the way. In a way, they were even more important. I'd been changing, evolving just like the gift I was forbidden to wield but remained determined to use. It was in every adventure and risk I took. It was in my desire to experience what I'd been told was not for me.

That was why I'd initially stayed in the room at the Red Pearl with Hawke.

It was the way I'd met the Duke's stare and smiled at him when I'd been unveiled.

It was when I'd spoke to Loren for the first time, and when I went out to the Rise. My evolution kept me quiet as the Duke delivered his *lessons,* and when I sliced Lord Mazeen's arm and hand and head from his body, I'd been cutting through the chains I never chose to wear. I just hadn't realized it then. There were so many little steps over the years and especially in recent weeks. I didn't know when it had finally happened, but I knew one thing for certain.

Hawke wasn't the catalyst.

He was the reward.

I lifted my surprisingly steady hands to the sash. I didn't look away as I undid the knot. The robe parted and then slipped over my shoulders. I let it puddle at my feet.

Hawke didn't look away for one second. He didn't even blink as he stared at me, his eyes locked to mine. Slowly, his gaze traveled the length of my body. I knew there was enough light for him to see everything. All the dips and swells, the shadowy, hidden areas, and all the scars. The jagged tears on my arms and across my stomach, and the ones on my legs that looked like wounds from sharp nails but were proof that I had been chosen by the gods.

Because those marks on my legs weren't from claws but from fangs that had ripped into my skin. I'd been bitten that night.

But I was not cursed.

Hawke wouldn't see the truth in those scars. Two of those who knew were now gone, and only the Queen and King, the Duchess, and my brother knew now. For the first time in my life, I wanted to tell someone the truth behind them. I wanted to tell Hawke.

But now was not the time for that.

Not when his gaze was slowly tracking back to mine. Not when he was looking at me as if he were soaking in every inch of me. I couldn't help but shiver when his eyes finally met mine.

"You're so damn beautiful," he whispered, his voice thick. "And so damn unexpected."

Then he moved in that way that always made it hard to believe he wasn't an Ascended. In a heartbeat, I was in his arms, and his mouth was on mine. There was nothing slow and sweet about the way he kissed me. It was like being devoured, and I wanted that. I kissed him back, holding onto him tightly, and just when I felt the touch of his tongue against mine, he pulled away.

Things became a blur then. His tunic came off with my help, and then his boots, and his breeches. I trembled at the first sight of him.

He was…beautiful.

All sun-kissed skin and long, lean muscles. His chest and stomach were defined by years of training, and there was no mistaking the power and strength of his body. There was also no mistaking how his life had left its imprint behind in the form of faint nicks and longer scars on his flesh. He was a fighter like I was, and now I truly saw what I'd been too nervous to notice before. His body was also a record of everything he'd survived, and the deeper, redder scar just below his hip on his upper thigh was proof that he likely had his own nightmares. It looked like a brand of some sort, as if something hot and painful had been pressed into his skin.

"The scar on your thigh," I asked. "When did you get it?"

"Many years ago, when I was dumb enough to get caught," he answered.

It was so weird how he sometimes talked as if he'd lived dozens of years longer than I was sure he had. I knew that, for some, a year could feel like a lifetime. My gaze strayed, and my eyes widened.

Oh, my.

I bit down on my lip, knowing I probably shouldn't stare. It seemed indecent to do so, but I wanted to.

"You keep looking at me like that, and this will be over before it starts."

Cheeks heating, I dragged my gaze away. "I...you're perfect."

His expression tightened. "No, I'm not. You deserve someone who is, but I'm too much of a bastard to allow that."

I shook my head, unsure how he couldn't see that he was deserving. "I disagree with everything you just said."

"Shocker," he said, and then he curled his arm around me.

In a heartbeat, I was on the bed, and he was above me, the rough hair of his legs abrasive against mine in the most surprising, pleasant way. But the feel of him against my hip caused a nervous swallow, and also brought a reminder of a very real consequence that could come from this.

"Are you—?"

"Protected?" His thoughts obviously following the same path as mine. "I take the monthly aid."

He was talking about the herb that rendered both males and females temporarily infertile. It could be drunk or chewed, and I heard that it tasted like sour milk.

"I assume you're not," he added.

I snorted.

"Wouldn't that be a scandal?" he said, skimming his hand along my arm.

"It would." I grinned. "But this..."

Those eyes met mine. "This changes everything."

It did.

It really did.

And I was ready for that.

Hawke kissed me, and I wasn't thinking of anything beyond how his lips had an almost drugging effect. We kissed until my heart was pounding, and my skin hummed with the pleasure of it. Then, only when I felt breathless, did he begin to explore.

His fingers trailed over every inch of exposed skin, and when his hand moved between my thighs, I cried out, quickly discovering that what he'd done with his fingers in the forest, over my breeches, was absolutely nothing compared to his skin against mine.

He worked his way down, using his mouth and then his tongue to follow the path his hands had blazed. He stayed in particularly sensitive areas, wringing sounds from me that made me briefly wonder just how thick the walls were, and then he lingered over the scars on my stomach, kissing them, *worshipping* them until I was sure that he didn't find them disturbing or ugly in any way.

But then he moved lower still, past my navel.

My heart stopped as I felt his breath against where I ached so fiercely. I opened my eyes to find him settled between my legs, his golden gaze locking onto mine.

"Hawke," I whispered.

One side of his lips curled up in a wicked, smoky half-grin. "Remember that first page of Miss Willa's diary?"

"Yes." I would never forget that first page.

Then, his gaze remaining on mine, he lowered his mouth.

My back bowed at the first touch of his lips, and my fingers dug into the sheets at the glide of his tongue. I thought my heart might stop, that maybe it already had. The riot of sensations he conjured up seemed unfathomable until that moment. It was almost too much, and I couldn't hold still. I lifted my hips, and his rumbling growl of approval was nearly as good as what he was doing.

Gods…

My head fell back against the mattress, and I was aware that I was writhing, squirming, and there was no sense of rhythm behind my movements. But that sharp tightening deep inside me was coiling and twisting, and then it all unraveled, stunning me with its intensity. I might've said his name. I might've actually screamed something incoherent. I didn't know, and it took what felt like a small eternity before I could even open my eyes.

Hawke lifted his head, lips swollen and glossy in the candlelight.

The intensity in his stare scorched my skin as his gaze caught and held mine. He never looked prouder of himself as his mouth parted and the tip of his tongue glided over his lips. "Honeydew," he growled. "Just like I said."

My breath caught, and I shuddered. He didn't so much move as he *prowled* up the length of my boneless form. I watched him, unable to look away as the hardness of his body caressed mine, unable to stop the shiver when the rough hairs of his legs tickled sensitive skin.

"Poppy," he breathed, his lips touching mine. He kissed me, and my skin heated at his flavor, the taste of me and those strangely sharp teeth of his. My senses whirled at the feeling of him settling between my legs, prodding, pressing in just a bit. "Open your eyes."

They had closed? Yes. They had. I opened them to see that one side of his lips was curved up, but the teasing tilt normally present was gone. He said nothing as he stared down at me, his hips and body still. "What?"

"I want your eyes open," he said.

"Why?"

He chuckled, and I sucked in a gasp at how the sound felt with him so very close to where I throbbed. "Always so many questions."

"I think you would be disappointed if I didn't have any."

"True," he murmured, dragging his hand down the length of my neck and then lower. His hand curled around my breast.

"So, why?" I persisted.

"Because I want you to touch me," he said. "I want you to see what you do to me when you touch me."

A shiver danced over my skin. "How…how do you want me to touch you?"

"Any way you want, Princess. You can't do it wrong," he whispered hoarsely.

Uncurling my fingers from the sheet, I lifted a hand, touching his cheek. His gaze remained latched to mine as I drew my fingers along the curve of his jaw, over his soft lips, and then down his throat. I was still feeling too much for my gift to be remotely functional as I glided the tips of my fingers over his chest. His breaths pushed it against my hand, and I kept exploring, soaking in the feel of the taut, coiled muscles of his lower stomach, and the dusting of hair below his navel and then lower. My fingers brushed silky hardness, and his entire body jerked. I hesitated.

"Please. Don't stop," he rasped, jaw clenched as his fingers stilled on my breast. "Dear gods, do not stop."

I focused on his face as I touched him. There were so many tiny reactions throughout his entire body. His jaw popped, and his lips parted slightly. The lines of his face became sharper, and the tendons in his neck stretched as I curled my hand around him. He kicked his head back, and his large, powerful body trembled. I noted how rapidly his breathing had become as I slid my hand down to where our bodies were almost joined. He gave a full-body shudder then, and I was awed by how much my touch affected him. I tightened my grip, becoming more confident.

"Gods," he growled.

"Is this okay?"

"Anything you do is more than okay." His voice had deepened even more. "But especially that. Totally that."

I laughed softly, and then I did it again, drawing my hand up and down his length. His hips moved then, much like mine had, rolling against my palm, against me. He made a sound, a deep, dark rumble that sent a flush of pleasure through me.

"You see what your touch does to me?" he asked, his hips following my hand.

"Yes," I whispered.

"It kills me." His head dropped, and those eyes... They seemed almost luminous as he stared down at me, and then his thick lashes lowered, shielding them from view. "It kills me in a way I don't think you'll ever understand."

My gaze searched his face. "In a...in a good way?"

Hawke's features softened as he lifted his hand to cup my cheek. "In a way I've never felt before."

"Oh."

He dipped his head, kissing me as he shifted onto his left arm. His hand left my cheek and slid down the length of my body until it was between us. "Are you ready?"

Breath catching, I nodded.

"I want to hear you say it."

The corners of my lips tugged up. "Yes."

"Good, because I might have actually died if you weren't."

I giggled, surprised by the light sound in such a tense, important moment.

"You think I'm kidding. Little do you know," he teased, kissing me again before he pushed in just a little bit. He stopped, making that sound again. "Oh, yeah, you're so ready."

My entire body flushed and trembled.

Hawke's gaze lifted to mine once more. "You amaze me."

"How?" I whispered, confused. I'd done almost nothing while he...he shattered me with the kind of kisses I'd only ever read about.

"You stand before Craven with no fear." He dragged his lips over mine. "But you blush and shiver when I speak of how slick and wonderful you feel against me."

I was definitely flushing even more now. "You're so inappropriate."

"I'm about to get really inappropriate," he promised. "But first, it may hurt."

I knew enough about sex to know that. "I know."

"Reading dirty books again?"

A flutter started in my stomach and spread. "Possibly."

He chuckled, but it ended in a groan as he began to move.

There was pressure and a moment when I wasn't sure how he could go any farther, and then a sudden, sharp sting stole my breath as I squeezed my eyes shut. Fingers digging into his shoulders, I tensed. I knew there'd be some pain, but all the languid warmth turned to chips of ice.

Hawke stilled above me, breathing heavily. "I'm sorry." His lips touched my nose, the lids of my eyes, my cheeks. "I'm sorry."

"It's okay."

He kissed me again, softly, and then rested his forehead against mine. A shallow breath lifted my chest. That was it. I'd crossed the final, forbidden line. There was no shock of guilt or burst of panic. Truthfully, I'd crossed that line when Hawke had kissed me before knowing who I was, and everything that led to this very moment had slowly erased that barrier until it no longer existed. There'd been no going back since the night at the Red Pearl, and this...this felt too right for it not to be, in some way, destined. I felt like I was supposed to be right here, in this very moment, with Hawke, where it mattered who I was and not *what* I was. It didn't matter if the gods found me unworthy because I was worthy of this—of laughter and excitement, of happiness and anticipation, of safety and acceptance, of pleasure and experience, of everything Hawke made me feel. And he was worthy of whatever consequences came from this because this wasn't just about him. I knew that from the moment I'd asked him to stay.

It was about me.

What I wanted.

My choice.

I took a deep breath, and the burning lessened. Hawke remained still above me, waiting. Tentatively, I lifted my hips against his. It stung, but not as severely as before. I tried it again. Hawke shuddered, but he didn't move. Not until my grip on his shoulders loosened, and my breath caught for an entirely different reason. There was a burning friction, but it wasn't the same. Muscles low in my stomach tightened as a ripple of pleasure skittered through me.

Only then did Hawke move, and he did so carefully, so gently that I felt tears prick my eyes. I closed them as I curled my arms around his neck, letting myself get lost in the madness once more, in the building crescendo of sensations. Some kind of primal instinct took hold, guiding my hips to follow his. We were moving together, the only sound in the room that of my softer sighs and his deeper moans. That exquisite, almost painful coiling sensation returned. My legs lifted of their own accord, curling around his hips. The pressure was building inside me once more, but it was more potent this time.

Hawke worked his arm under my head and curled his hand around my shoulder as the grip of his other hand tightened on my hip. He began to move faster, deeper, his thrusts stronger as he held me in place under him. I held onto him, my mouth blindly finding his as his hand slipped between us. His thumb found that sensitive area, and when his hips churned against mine in tight circles, the tension exploded once more. I cried out as the sensation whipped through me, more intense and biting than before. The release he'd given me earlier somehow felt like nothing compared to this. I was shattering into pieces in the best possible way, and it was only when the last wave seemed to have crested that I became aware of those intense golden eyes fixed to my face as he slipped his hand out from under me. I knew at once he'd been watching the entire time, and a breathy moan left me.

I placed a trembling hand on his cheek. "Hawke," I whispered, wishing I could put to words what I'd just felt—what I was *still* feeling.

His features turned stark, and his jaw tensed, and then he…he seemed to lose whatever control he had left. His body pounded against mine, moving us across the bed. Under my hands, his muscles flexed and rolled, and then his head kicked back, and he cried out, shuddering.

He dropped his head to mine, to the sensitive space along the side of my throat. I felt his lips against my thrumming pulse as the roll of his hips slowed. There was a scrape of his teeth that sent a shiver through me, and then the press of his lips.

I didn't know how long we stayed like that, our damp skin cooling, and our breathing slowing as I threaded my fingers through his hair. His muscles had relaxed, and his weight was on his elbows, but I slowly became aware of the tension in his body. It was the gift, slowly poking through my heady emotions.

Hawke's lips grazed my cheek and then found mine. He kissed me softly, sweetly. "Don't forget this."

I touched his jaw. "I don't think I ever could."

"Promise me," he said, seeming to not hear me as he lifted his head. His gaze snagged with mine. "Promise me you won't forget this, Poppy. That no matter what happens tomorrow, the next day, next week, you won't forget this—forget that this was real."

I couldn't look away. "I promise. I won't forget."

Chapter 34

Some hours later, a noise stirred me from sleep. I was on my side, and a long, warm body was wrapped around mine. One leg was thrust between my thighs, and I was tangled in arms. Although I was still half-asleep, every part of me immediately became aware of the unfamiliar sensations of being in someone's hold. The feeling of skin against skin, the rough, short hairs against my flesh, the biceps under my head, and the warm breath glancing off my cheek. All of it was wonderful and new. Even with the cobwebs of sleep still clouding my thoughts, I knew this feeling wouldn't be something easy to walk away from.

The last thing I remembered was lying facing Hawke, him toying with my hair while he told me how he'd gotten some of his smaller scars. Most of them had been earned through fighting, though a few were from when he was a reckless, adventurous child. I'd meant to share with him the truth about some of mine, but I must've drifted off.

Hawke shifted behind me, lifting his head as the sound came again. It was a soft knock on the door. Carefully, he slipped his leg out from between mine. He stilled for a second, and then I felt his fingertips on my arm. They coasted down and then over the flare of my hip to where the blanket lay. He tugged it up over my chest as he eased himself free, making sure the pillow had replaced his arm under my head. A sleepy, pleased smile tugged at my lips.

The bed dipped as he rose, and I heard him stop by the foot of the bed. I blinked open my eyes. One of the oil lamps still burned, casting a soft buttery glow around the room. It was still pitch-black beyond the small window, though I saw Hawke straighten as he pulled on his breeches, leaving them unbuttoned. My stomach dipped at the sight. He went to the door like that, shirtless and half-undressed. Wouldn't that make it obvious to whoever was out there what had transpired in here?

I waited for the panic to set in, the concern and fear of being discovered in a very compromising, forbidden position.

It didn't come.

Maybe it was because I was still only half-awake. Perhaps the pleasant languidness in my muscles had somehow infiltrated my brain and melted my common sense.

Maybe I just didn't care about being caught.

Hawke cracked open the door, and whoever was outside spoke too low for me to hear. I didn't pick up Hawke's response, but I saw that he accepted something he had been handed. He was only at the door for a couple of moments before he closed it again, placing whatever he carried on the chair.

Seeing that I was awake, he came to my side. Wordlessly, he reached down, catching a strand of hair and brushing it back from my face.

"Hi," I whispered, closing my eyes as I pressed my cheek to his palm. "Is it time to get up?"

"No."

"Is everything okay?"

"Everything is fine. I just need to go handle something," he answered. I opened my eyes. He stared down at me as he dragged his thumb across my cheek, just under the scar. "You don't need to get up yet."

"Are you sure?" I yawned.

A faint grin appeared. "I am, Princess. Sleep." He tucked the blanket around me once more and then rose. "I'll be back as soon as I can."

I wanted to say something, somehow acknowledge what had transpired between us, and what it meant to me, but I wasn't sure how to say it, and my eyes were getting heavy. I fell back to sleep, but I didn't stay there long. I woke for a second time, the lamp still burning, and the bed empty beside me.

Stretching my limbs, I pressed my lips together at the strange, dull ache between my legs. I didn't need the reminder of last night, but there it was. I glanced around the room, my gaze snagging on the chair. My clothing was folded there. Had it been Magda who'd come to the door? Or someone else? Either way, whoever it was, the state of undress in which Hawke had answered the door revealed everything.

I bit down on my lip as I lay there, staring at the small window. Like before, there was no panic or dread. People talked. One way or another, what had happened here would travel beyond the cobblestone streets. It would eventually make its way to the capital, and then to the Queen. Even if by some small chance it didn't, the gods had to know that I was no longer an actual maiden. Whether or not that meant I was still *the* Maiden in their eyes, I had no idea.

But I was no longer the Maiden in mine.

I couldn't go back to that life.

A brief burst of fear pierced my chest, but that was okay because a surge of determination quickly doused it like water does flames.

I *wouldn't* go back to that life of no rights, of hiding my gift and being unable to help people, of allowing others to do whatever they wanted with me and to me because I had no choice or was constantly put in a position where I had to accept whatever was done out of fear for someone else. Because even though I knew the Queen would never treat me poorly, I would still be expected to hide my gift, to be quiet and unseen, amicable, and appeasing. Every single one of those things went against the very core of my nature.

I couldn't Ascend.

And that meant there were two options ahead of me. I either attempted to disappear and hid—living behind the veil for so long would be a benefit here since so few people knew what I looked like. However, there were enough that could give a description. I was sure that every city and town would be notified to keep an eye out for me, but I knew how to remain unseen.

But where would I go? How would I survive? And what would happen to Hawke if I disappeared while he was supposed to be escorting me?

I didn't assume that my now very unknown, uncertain future included Hawke. However, my chest still fluttered. What we'd shared last night had to mean something more than simply seeking physical gratification. He could find that anywhere, but he had chosen me.

And I chose him.

That had to mean something that went beyond last night—something that I never thought I'd get the chance to experience.

Whether or not Hawke was a part of my life or not, the only other option was to go to the Queen and be honest. Now *that* scared me because I...I didn't want to disappoint her. But she had to understand. She had with my mother, and I was the Queen's favorite. She had to understand that I couldn't be this. And if she didn't, I needed to make her.

Sitting up, I kept the blanket wrapped around me.

I knew what I couldn't do, but I didn't know what that meant in the long-term for the kingdom or for me. The sky outside the window started to lighten. I would talk to Hawke about it, and I wouldn't wait. He needed to know, and I wanted to know what he thought.

What he'd say.

Knowing that dawn was fast approaching, I rose and got ready, using the remaining water to quickly wash up. The water was cold, but since I had no idea when we'd have access to clean water again, I wasn't complaining. Relieved to be wearing clean clothes, I strapped the dagger to my thigh. I was just finishing braiding my hair when the knock came.

Figuring Hawke would've just come in, I approached with caution. "Yes?"

"It's Phillips," came the familiar voice.

I opened the door, and he rushed in, forcing me back as he closed the door behind him. He turned, his cloak parting to reveal his hand on the hilt of his sword.

Warning bells went off as I took a step back.

"Are you alone?" he demanded, his gaze going to the bathing room.

"Yes." My heart kicked up. "Has something happened?"

He turned back to me, his eyes wide. "Where is Hawke?"

"I...I don't know. What's going on?"

"Something about this place isn't right."

My brows lifted.

"Things haven't been right about this whole damn thing. Should've listened to my instincts. They've kept me alive this whole time, but I didn't listen this time," he rattled on as he went to where a small saddlebag was placed. "I did some looking around here. Didn't see one single Ascended. And Lord Halverston? Seen no evidence of the Royal."

"I was told he's hunting with his men," I assured him. "I asked Magda where he was yesterday."

My bag in hand, he faced me, his dark brows arched. "What Ascended do you know that would go hunting?"

"I don't know any that would, but we don't know every Ascended."

"You know who we don't know? This Kieran fellow." He stopped in front of me. "We know nothing about him."

Confused by where he was going with all of this, I shook my head. "I don't know any of you."

Except for Hawke. Him, I knew.

"You're not understanding what I'm saying. I've never seen Kieran. Not until the morning he showed up at the Rise. Couldn't get anything from him other than that he worked in the capital. Everything else was short, vague answers."

I recalled how I'd seen them speaking often throughout the trip. Still, Kieran's unwillingness to answer questions from a stranger meant nothing. "A lot of guards are on the Rise. Do you know everyone?"

"I know enough to find it suspicious that a new transfer is part of the team tasked to escort the Maiden," he stated. "He was personally requested by Hawke, another relatively new transfer that, somehow, in a matter of months, became one of the most important people in the entire kingdom's Royal Guard."

I sucked in a sharp breath. "What are you talking about?"

"Hawke is another that no one knows hardly anything about. But he showed up, and now you're down not one but *two* personal Royal Guards."

My mouth dropped. "I was there when both Rylan and Vikter were killed—"

"And I know it's not normal that several guards were passed over to become your guard in favor of a boy who's barely a man," he cut me off. "I don't care what recommendations he came to Masadonia with, or whatever the Commander said about him. Hawke requested Kieran, and here we are, in a keep where no Ascended can be found."

"What are you trying to say, Phillips?"

"I'm trying to say this is a trap. We walked right out of the city with them and right into a godsdamn trap."

"Them?" I whispered.

"Kieran," he answered. "Hawke."

For a moment, all I could do was stare at him.

"I know you don't want to hear this. You and Hawke seem…close, but I'm telling you, Maiden, something is not right about this place or about them, and—"

"And what?"

"Evans and Warren are missing." He referenced the two guards while looking back at the door. "Neither Luddie nor I have seen them since about an hour after we got here. They went to their assigned rooms, and now they have disappeared. Their beds have not been touched, and there's been no sight of them anywhere in the keep."

That… If it was true, it was not good. But what he was suggesting was unbelievable. I didn't know Kieran, but I knew Hawke, and if Hawke trusted Kieran, then I did, too. So, what would Phillips have to gain by saying these things?

My skin chilled when the only option formed in my mind. Phillips had to be a Descenter. Shocked, I didn't want to believe it, but I remembered how the Descenters at the Rite had been dressed for the celebration. They had been mingling with everyone the entire time. It wasn't impossible.

Because nothing was.

And if Phillips was a Descenter, then this…this was bad. He was exceptionally well trained. Worse yet, he knew that I was armed and trained, as well, so I didn't have the element of surprise. I also didn't like the idea of being in this room alone with him, especially where I didn't know who was nearby.

I needed to be around people.

"Okay. You've…you've been at Masadonia for a long time. And Vikter…he always had nothing but good things to say about you," I told him. As far as I could remember, Vikter had never mentioned Phillips at all, but I needed him to believe me. I opened my senses then. "What am I supposed to do?"

"Thank the gods, you're smart. I was afraid I would have to drag you out of here." He glanced at the door once more as his emotions filtered through me. "We need to get out of here and fast."

"And then what?" It took a moment for me to make sense of what I felt. There was no remarkable pain, but I tasted the tang of…fear.

"Come." He motioned me toward the door, hand still on the hilt of his sword. He cracked the slab open and checked outside, too quick for me to take advantage of him having his back turned to me. "It's clear." His eyes met mine. "I want to believe that you know I'm telling you the truth, but I'm not stupid. I know you're probably armed, and I know you can use it. So, I want you to keep your hands where I can see them. I don't want to harm you, but I will incapacitate you if that means getting you out of this place and to somewhere safe."

Being threatened didn't exactly make me feel safe, but he was scared.

He was frightened. I knew that much as he stepped aside, and I realized that he wanted me in front of him. My hand twitched to reach for the dagger. What was he afraid of? Getting caught?

"Luddie and Bryant are waiting for us in the stables. They're readying the horses."

I nodded, stepping out into the hall just as the door at the other end of the hall opened.

Kieran walked out as cold air rippled down the corridor. Without my cloak, I wouldn't make it far. Did Phillips not realize that? Or was that not relevant? Kieran came to a stop, his brows raised. "What are you doing out here?"

Before I could answer, I heard Phillips unsheathe his sword. My heart started pounding.

"What are *you* doing out here?" Phillips demanded. "It's not time to leave."

He started forward. "I was going to my room." His gaze moved back to me. I didn't think he realized that Phillips had readied his sword. "And you didn't answer my question."

Phillips was behind me, and I knew I had to be careful. He may want to keep me alive, but I was just as effective as a message if I were dead. He'd have the sword in my back before I could get a grip on my dagger.

I stared at Kieran silently, hoping to the gods that he was able to see what I couldn't say.

He came forward, his hand casually going to the sword at his side. "What's going on here?"

Phillips grabbed hold of my arm, tugging me back. He was fast as he thrust his sword forward. So was Kieran. He deflected the blow, but the deadly point of the blade was only knocked off course. Instead of penetrating his chest, it sliced into his stomach and leg. I cried out as Kieran stared down at himself—

The sound that came from Kieran as he stumbled back raised every single hair on my body. I froze. It started out as a low rumble that was not even remotely a sound a mortal should make. I'd heard it before—the night Rylan had been killed in the Queen's Garden. The Descenter had made that same sound.

The rumble rose, turning into a deep growl that stole my breath. When he lifted his head, my heart nearly stopped.

His pale blue eyes...

They glowed iridescent in the dim light.

"You really shouldn't have done that." The voice that came out of him was garbled and all wrong as if his throat were full of gravel. "At all."

Kieran tossed his sword aside, and it clattered off the wooden floorboards. I couldn't understand why he'd throw down his weapon, but then I saw why.

He'd *changed*.

His skin seemed to thin and darken. His jaw popped up, elongating along with his nose. Bones cracked and reformed as fawn-colored fur sprouted from every inch of skin I could see. The tunic he wore split across his chest. His breeches tore as his knees bent. He pitched forward, fingers growing, claws replacing nails. Ears lengthened as he opened his mouth in a cold, violent snarl. Fangs punched out from his jaw as his hands—his *paws*—smacked down on the floor.

It took seconds—only seconds—and a man no longer stood before us. A huge creature stood on all fours, nearly as tall as Phillips in a solid mass of muscle and sleek fur. What I saw was impossible, what I saw was something that had been extinct for *centuries*, killed off during the War of Two Kings.

But I knew what Kieran was.

Oh, my gods.

Kieran was a *wolven*.

"Run!" Phillips shouted, grabbing hold of my arm.

I didn't need to be told twice.

Phillips was utterly wrong about Hawke, but he wasn't when it came to Kieran. There was obviously something incredibly *not right* about him.

Kieran's claws scraped across wood as he lurched toward us, sweeping out and narrowly missing Phillips' cloak. I ran faster than I'd ever run in my entire life. I looked over my shoulder as Phillips yanked open the door. Every instinct inside screamed for me not to, but I couldn't stop myself. I *looked*.

The wolven leapt, twisting in midair. He landed on the *wall*. Claws dug into the stone, and then he launched himself off, landing halfway in the hall.

"Go!" Phillips tugged me into the stairwell in front of him.

The space was dark with only the faintest light to lead the way. My boots slipped over the stone. I grabbed the railing as I swung onto the landing, nearly falling. But I didn't stop.

We blew through the final set of stairs and burst out the door, my brain finally spewing out something helpful, reminding me that I had a weapon. Bloodstone. It could kill a wolven if the heart or head were struck, just like a Craven.

My feet pounded off the frozen ground as I yanked the dagger free.

"The stables." Phillips ran, his cloak billowing out behind him like waves of black water.

Hawke.

Had Kieran done something to Hawke? My heart lurched—

The howl from above shattered the early morning silence, jerking up my head just as the wolven came over the railing.

He landed on the ground behind us, letting out another spine-tingling howl.

From the woods or from the keep, I heard an answer. A roar that sent a bolt of cold terror through me.

There was more than one.

"*Gods.*" I gasped, pushing harder than I'd ever pushed before. There was no way I was leaving here without Hawke, but I needed to get as far away from that thing as possible. That was all I could focus on because if I slowed down for even half a second, he would be on me.

We rounded the corner, Phillips slipping but regaining his balance as we rushed toward the stables, not a single guard in sight, and that wasn't right. There should be guards out at this time.

I saw Luddie and the other guard.

"Shut the doors!" Phillips shouted as we exploded into the stables, startling the saddled horses. "Shut the godsdamn doors!"

The two men turned as I skidded to a stop, whipping around. I knew the moment they saw the wolven.

"Holy shit," Bryant whispered, the blood draining from his face.

Kieran was gaining on us.

I shot forward to one side of the doors just as Luddie and Bryant snapped out of their shock. Grasping one side along with Luddie, we swung it closed a second before Bryant and Phillips closed their side.

"Bar it!" yelled Luddie, and the other two turned, grabbing the heavy wooden support. They brought it down, and the wood groaned into place.

Panting, I backed up—I kept backing up until I walked into one of the poles. The hilt of the dagger pressed into my palm. I looked down at it, at the wolven bone—

I jumped as the large, double doors shuddered as the wolven crashed into them.

"Is that what I think it is?" someone asked. I think it was Bryant. "A wolven?"

"Unless you know of another large wolf-like creature, then yes." Phillips turned as Kieran hit the door again, shaking the wooden slab. "That door isn't going to last. Is there another way out?"

"There's a back door." Luddie came forward. "But the horses won't fit through it."

"Fuck the horses." Bryant picked up his sword. "We get out of here, first and foremost."

"Have you all seen Hawke? He was called away in the middle of the night," I told them. Three sets of eyes settled on me, and I didn't care what they thought. "Have any of you seen him?"

A wood board splintered as a clawed, fur-covered hand punched through. Kieran grabbed the chunk of wood, tearing it free.

"We need to go." Phillips started for me.

I moved out of his way. "I'm not leaving until I find Hawke—"

"Did you just see what I saw?" Phillips demanded, his nostrils flaring. "You told me you understood what I was telling you. Hawke is one of them."

"Hawke isn't a wolven," I argued. "He isn't a part of *that*." I pointed at the door as the wolven took out another section. "You were right about Kieran but not Hawke. Have either of you seen him?"

"I have."

My head jerked toward the sound of the voice. A man stood in the shadows, and something…something inside me shrank back.

He stepped into the light. Shaggy brown hair. A trace of a beard. Pale, winter blue eyes. A flash of pure, unadulterated rage pulsed through me.

It was him.

The man who'd killed Rylan was here, and he smiled. "Told you I'd be seeing you again."

My gaze flicked over him, and my brows rose as the three guards pointed their swords at him. "You seem to be missing a *hand*. I wish I had done that."

He lifted his left arm that ended in a stump just above his wrist. "I manage." Those eerie pale eyes flicked to me as the sounds of Kieran ceased behind us. I could only hope that was something that would put the odds of us walking out of this in our favor. "Remember my promise?"

"Bathe in my blood. Feast on my entrails," I said. "I haven't forgotten."

"Good," he rumbled, taking a step forward. "Because I'm about to make good on that promise."

"Stay back!" Phillips demanded.

"He's a wolven," I warned, now knowing there were at least three at the keep.

"Smart girl," the man said.

Phillips held his ground. "I don't care what kind of ungodly creature you are, you take one more step, and it will be your last."

"Ungodly?" He threw his head back and laughed, lifting his arms at his sides. "We are created in the gods' very image. It is not us who are the ungodly ones."

"Whatever you need to tell yourself to feel better," I replied, tightening my grip on the dagger. "The head or the heart, right, Phillips?"

"Yes." Phillips dipped his chin. "Either will—"

Behind us, the slab splintered as the doors blew off their hinges, slamming into the sides of the barn. The horses reared, but tethered, they had no place to go. I twisted sideways, keeping my dagger pointed at the wolven as I looked, fully expecting to see Kieran tearing across the straw.

What I saw almost brought me to my knees.

"Hawke!" I cried out, too relieved to be embarrassed about how I sounded as I started toward him. "Thank the gods, you're okay."

"Stay back from him." Phillips caught my arm.

I went to pull free of Phillips as I saw that Hawke carried something in his hand. It looked like a curved bow, but it was mounted to a handle of some sort, and a bolt was already nocked, somehow held in place. Whatever. It would work. "Kill him!" I shouted, slipping free of Phillips. "He was the one—"

A hulking shape appeared behind him, so huge it nearly reached Hawke's chest. Kieran prowled toward him. My heartbeat stuttered. "Hawke, behind you!" I screamed.

Phillips caught me around the waist, dragging me back as Hawke lifted the strange bow. Kieran was almost on him, and I didn't see any bloodstone on the bow. It wouldn't kill him.

Hawke's gaze met mine. "It's okay."

Without any warning, Phillips was torn away from me. I fell forward, landing on my knees. My braid slipped over my shoulder as I looked behind me, half expecting to see the wolven with Phillips in his grasp.

The wolven from the Queen's Garden hadn't moved, but Phillips…

Phillips was leaning against the pole, the sword lying on the straw. Wait. He was leaning because his feet weren't even touching the ground, and something dark dripped onto the straw. I looked up.

I couldn't even scream as my stomach roiled. Hawke had fired the bow. I hadn't even seen him do it, but he had. The bolt had gone through Phillips' mouth and through the pole, pinning him there.

Shuddering, I heard Luddie shouting. I dragged my gaze from Phillips as I turned back to Hawke.

In wolven form, Kieran stalked right past him, his large head low to the straw as he sniffed the air. Luddie charged him, but he lost his footing, falling forward.

I took a breath, but pressure squeezed it right back out of me.

Luddie hadn't tripped.

The black bolt had caught him in the back. Stepping out from behind one of the horses was the guard who'd greeted us at the door the day before. Delano. He had those pale eyes, too. Eyes that I now knew belonged to the wolven. He lowered the bow.

Bryant bolted.

Spinning around, he made a run for it, but he didn't make it far. Kieran crouched and then launched into the air. As sleek and as fast as any arrow—and just as accurate. He landed on Bryant's back, taking him to the straw. The guard didn't even have a chance to scream. The wolven bared his teeth and lunged—

I cranked my head away at the wet crunch that echoed through the barn.

Then there was silence.

I saw the man who'd killed Rylan stride forward, his long-legged pace loose and relaxed. He smirked down at me. "I'm so glad I'm here to witness this moment."

"Shut up, Jericho," Hawke replied, tone flat.

Slowly, I looked at Hawke. He stood where he'd stopped, the wind lifting and tossing those dark strands of hair back from his striking face. He appeared as he had when he left the room in the middle of the night, like he had hours before that when he'd kissed me, touched me, and held me in his arms.

But he stood there with a bloodied wolven standing next to him.

"Hawke?" I whispered, my free hand grasping at the damp straw under me.

He stared at me, and my gift came alive. The invisible cord reached out, forming a connection, and I felt...I felt nothing from him. No pain. No sadness. *Nothing.*

I drew back, my chest rising and falling. Something had to be wrong with my gift. Only the Ascended lacked emotions. Not mortals. Not Hawke. But it was like the connection had hit a brick wall as thick as the Rise.

As formidable as the wall I built around myself when I tried to keep my gift locked inside. Was he...was he *blocking* me? Was that even possible?

"Please tell me I can kill her," Jericho said. "I know exactly what pieces I want to cut up and send back."

"Touch her, and you'll lose more than a hand this time." The coldness in Hawke's tone chilled me to my very soul. "We need her." His gaze never left me. "Alive."

Chapter 35

On my knees, I stared up at Hawke, hearing his words and seeing what was happening, but it was like my brain couldn't process any of it.

Or my brain was processing it and my heart…my heart was denying it.

We need her.

Alive.

We.

"You're no fun," Jericho muttered. "Have I told you that before?"

"A time or a dozen," Hawke answered, and I flinched. My entire body recoiled. His jaw tightened, and he looked away, scanning the barn. "This mess needs to be cleaned up."

Beside him, the wolven shook itself, a lot like a dog after coming in from the rain. And then it rose on its hind legs and shifted, fur curling inward to reveal skin that was thickening. Legs straightened, and fingers returned to their normal sizes. The jaw snapped back into place. Shirt lost somewhere, Kieran stood in torn breeches, the wound in his stomach from Phillips' sword nothing more than a pink mark.

I sat back.

Kieran twisted his neck from left to right, cracking it. "This isn't the only mess that needs to be cleaned up."

A muscle flexed in Hawke's jaw as he looked at me. "You and I need to talk."

"Talk?" A laugh escaped me, and it sounded all wrong.

"I'm sure you have a lot of questions," he replied, and I heard a shade of the teasing tone I was familiar with.

It caused me to flinch again. "Where...where are the other two guards?"

"Dead," he answered without an ounce of hesitation as he rested the bow on his shoulder. "It was an unfortunate necessity."

"I'm good at what I do."

"And what is that?"

"Killing."

I knew without a doubt that when he'd left the room, that was what he'd done. There was a buzzing in my ears as I became aware of others gathering behind him in the yard, their bodies still in the filtered morning sun.

He took a step toward me. "Let's—"

"No." I popped to my feet, surprisingly steady. "Tell me what's going on here."

Hawke stopped. When he spoke, his voice had softened just a fraction. "You know what's going on here."

The next breath I took scorched my throat and lungs because I realized that I did. Oh, gods, I did know what was going on here. The buzzing increased as I saw Elijah standing outside, arms folded across his barrel chest. I saw Magda, one hand protectively cradling her baby bump as she stared into the barn, her face pinched with...with sympathy and *pity*.

You deserve so much more than what awaits you.

That's what he'd said to me last night. And me, stupid, naive me, thought he'd meant my Ascension. No. He'd meant *this*.

Magda turned, brushing past Elijah as she walked back to the keep.

"Phillips was right," I said, my voice trembling as I said it, as I gave life to what I already knew.

"He was?" questioned Hawke, handing the strange bow to one of the men who'd appeared behind him.

"I do believe Phillips had begun to figure things out," Kieran answered as he stared down at his stomach. The faint pink marks were already gone. "They were coming out of the room when I went up to check on her. She didn't seem to believe whatever it was he'd told her, though."

I hadn't.

I hadn't believed Phillips at all because I believed Hawke. I trusted him—trusted him with my life, and with…

There was a sudden pain in my chest that felt as if someone had shoved a dagger through me. I looked down because it felt too real, but there was no blade, no bloody wound that equaled the agony radiating through me. When I looked up, a muscle flexed in Hawke's jaw.

"Well, he's not going to be figuring anything out again." Jericho gripped the bolt, tearing it free. Phillips slumped over. Jericho nudged the guard's body with his boot. "That's for sure."

I turned back to Hawke, feeling as if the ground were splitting and shifting beneath me.

"You're a Descenter."

"A Descenter?" Elijah laughed deeply, causing me to jerk.

Kieran smiled.

"And here I said you were smart," Jericho said.

I ignored them. "You're working against the Ascended."

Hawke nodded.

Another fissure formed in my chest. "You…you knew this…this thing that killed Rylan?"

"Thing?" chuffed Jericho. "I'm insulted."

Hawke said nothing.

"That sounds like your problem, not mine." I fully faced Hawke. "I thought the wolven were extinct."

Hawke gave a casual shrug. "There are many things that you thought to be true that are not. However, while the wolven aren't extinct, there aren't many left."

"Did you know he killed Rylan?" I shouted.

"I thought I could speed this up and grab you, but we know how that turned out," Jericho chimed in.

My head snapped in Jericho's direction. "Yes, I clearly remember how that turned out for you."

His upper lip curled as a snarl of warning sent a wave of goosebumps through me.

"I knew he was going to create an opening," Hawke answered, drawing my gaze back to him.

"For you…to become my personal Royal Guard?"

"I needed to get close to you."

I sucked in a shuddering breath as my heart seemed to split open. "Well, you succeeded at that, didn't you?"

That muscle in his jaw flexed again. "What you're thinking…you could not be further from the truth."

"You have no idea what I'm thinking," I shot back, my hand tightening painfully around the dagger. "And all of this was…what? A trick? You were sent here to get close to me?"

Kieran's brows lifted. "Sent—"

Hawke quieted him with a look, and Kieran rolled his eyes.

I knew what he was going to say. "You were sent by the Dark One."

"I came to Masadonia with one goal in mind," Hawke answered. "And that was you."

I shuddered. "How? Why?"

"You'd be surprised how many of those close to you support Atlantia, who want to see the kingdom restored. Many who paved the way for me."

"Commander Jansen?" I suspected.

"She is smart," Hawke said. "Like I told you all."

The backs of my eyes burned, along with my throat and chest. "Did you even work in the capital?" Then something hit me as my gaze darted to Kieran. "The night at the…" I couldn't bring myself to say "*the Red Pearl.*"

"You knew who I was from the beginning."

"I was watching you as long as you were watching me," he said softly. "Even longer."

That blow nearly killed me. It was like my chest had shattered. I started to turn away, but I saw Jericho, who'd created a space for Hawke to gain more personal, intimate access to me.

It clicked into place with a tremor that almost caused me to drop my dagger. "You…you were planning this for a while."

"For a *very* long time."

"Hannes." My voice was thick, hoarse. "He didn't die of a heart ailment, did he?"

"I do believe his heart did give out on him," Hawke answered. "The poison he drank in his ale that night at the Red Pearl surely had something to do with it."

The buzzing was almost too much. "Did a certain woman there

help him with his drink? The same one that sent me upstairs?"

Hawke didn't answer. Delano, on the other hand, said, "I feel like I'm missing vital pieces here."

"I'll fill you in later," Kieran commented.

I was shaking. I could feel it. Just like I could feel the walls of the barn closing in on me. I was so incredibly naive. "Vikter?"

Hawke shook his head.

"Don't lie to me!" I screamed. "Did you know there'd be an attack on the Rite? Is that why you disappeared? Why you weren't there when Vikter was killed?"

The hollows of his cheeks became sharper. "What I know is that you're upset. I don't blame you, but I've also seen what happens when you get really angry," he said, taking a step toward me, lifting his hands. "There is a lot I need to tell—"

The pain erupted out of me like it had the night of the Rite when I turned on Lord Mazeen. I had no control over myself. I moved out of instinct, cocking back my arm and throwing the dagger.

This time, I aimed for his chest.

Hawke let out a curse as he stepped to the side, snatching the dagger out of the air. Someone behind him let out a low whistle as Hawke whirled on me, the look of disbelief on his face almost comical. But in the back of my mind, I'd known he would catch it. All I'd needed was a distraction so I could dip down and pick up Phillips' fallen sword. I swung out, aiming for the bastard who'd killed Rylan. Jericho jumped back, but he wasn't entirely fast enough. I cut him again, across the stomach this time.

"Bitch," Jericho cried out, clamping his remaining hand down on the gushing wound.

I spun just as someone crashed into me from one side and then the other. My arm was twisted around. Something hot sliced across my stomach as I reared back, using my attacker's weight against them. They fell, arms still around me. I snapped my head, cracking my skull into their face. There was a yelp, and the hold loosened enough for me to tear free. I grabbed the sword from the straw and thrust it out blindly. I only saw a flicker of shock in the brown eyes of a male not too much older than me as he looked down. I yanked the sword free and spun, coming face to face with Hawke.

I hesitated.

Like a complete idiot, I hesitated, even though I knew he was working for the Dark One. He was a Descenter. Because of him, so very many innocent people were dead. Hannes. Rylan. Loren. Dafina. Malessa—gods, had he killed her?

Vikter.

"That was very naughty," Hawke chided, snatching the sword out of my hand as if I hadn't been holding onto it. "You are so incredibly violent." He dipped his chin and whispered, "It still turns me on."

A scream of fury tore out of me as I jabbed my elbow out and up, snapping Hawke's head back. "Dammit," he said, coughing—no, laughing. He was *laughing*. "Didn't change what I just said."

I spun and started for the doors but skidded to a stop as Elijah appeared in front of me, having moved in a blink of an eye. He shook his head no, tsking softly under his breath.

Turning, I saw Kieran, who looked bored, and I whirled, seeing an opening between the poles. I took off—

Arms caught me around the waist, and I'd recognize the scent anywhere. Pine. Dark spice. *Hawke.* And the hard, earthen floor raced up toward my face. This was going to hurt. Bad.

The impact never came.

As agile as a cat, Hawke twisted so he took the brunt of the fall, but the landing still stunned me. For a moment, I couldn't move.

"You're welcome," grunted Hawke.

Shrieking, I slammed the heel of my booted foot into his shin. His gasp of pain brought a savage smile to my face as I rolled, twisting until my stomach screamed in protest, but I was able to turn in his loosened hold. I straddled him—

Hawke grinned up at me, the dimple in his right cheek appearing. "I'm liking where this is headed."

I punched him in the face, right in the godsdamn dimple. Pain lanced across my knuckles, but I drew my arm back.

Hawke caught my wrist and yanked me down until my body was almost flush with his. "You hit like you're angry with me."

I shifted, jamming my knee down between his legs and aiming for a very sensitive area. He anticipated the move, and my knee hit him in the thigh.

"That would've done some damage," he told me.

"Good," I growled.

"Now, now. You'd be disappointed later if I couldn't use it."

For a moment, I couldn't believe he'd actually said that, but he had. He totally had. "I would rather cut it from your body."

"Liar," he whispered.

The sound that came from inside me would've scared me if it had come from anyone else. I jumped up, breaking his hold. I went to bring my foot down on his throat, but Hawke caught it and pulled. I went down, landing on my side. Pain flared, but I ignored it as I slammed my fist into his side.

"Damn," Kieran drew the word out.

"Should we intervene?" Delano asked, sounding concerned.

"No," Elijah answered with a chuckle. "This is the best thing I've seen in a while. Who would've thought the Maiden could throw down?"

"This is why you don't mix business with pleasure," Kieran commented.

"Is that the case?" Elijah whistled. "My money is on her then."

"Traitors," gasped Hawke, rolling me until he was on top. I went for his face, but he caught my wrists. "Stop it."

I tried to lift my hips, and when that didn't work, I pushed my upper body up. It took everything in me, and he simply pinned my wrists to the straw.

"Get off me!"

"Stop it," he repeated. "Poppy. Stop—"

"I hate you!" I screamed at the sound of my name, ripping one hand free in my rage. I slammed my fist into his face. "I hate you!"

Hawke caught my hand, jerking it back to the ground as his bloodied lips peeled back. "Stop it!"

I stopped.

I went completely still as I stared up at him, the shock robbing me of my ability to speak for several moments. I saw him—saw him for what he really was.

He wasn't just any Descenter following the Dark One.

"That's why you never really smiled," I whispered.

Because, how could he?

He had to hide the sharp, sharp teeth.

Two of them.

Fangs.

I remembered the feel of them against my lips, my neck—recalling how oddly sharp they'd felt.

Gods.

Now I understood how he could move so fast, why he seemed to have better hearing and eyesight than anyone I'd ever met, and why he sometimes sounded as if he'd lived decades longer than I had. It was why he was quick to break a kiss whenever I came close to feeling his canines.

I'd been so blind.

He wasn't mortal.

He wasn't a wolven.

Hawke was an Atlantian.

I shuddered as something deep inside me withered. "You're a monster."

Hawke's eyes flared an intense gold, and they weren't normal. They'd never been natural. "You finally see me for what I am."

I did.

He was a thing of nightmares hidden in the guise of a dream, and I had fallen for it. I fell so hard.

The fight went out of me.

Him being a Descenter was bad enough, but an Atlantian? His people created the creatures who'd taken my mother and father from me, who'd almost killed me.

Hawke seemed to sense it because he moved swiftly, hauling me to my feet. "Delano," he called. "Take her."

I was handed over like a bag of potatoes, and Delano kept my arms clamped to my sides.

"Where should I put her?" Delano asked.

Hawke's chest rose sharply. "Somewhere where she can't escape and can't hurt herself." He paused. "Or hurt anyone else, which is more likely than the former."

"Are we holding her prisoner?" someone demanded. "We're keeping her alive? Will we feed and shelter that?"

That.

As if I were the monster, the one who supported the Dark One and could create Craven. These people were beyond help.

"She's the Maiden," another yelled. "She needs to die!"

A round of agreement sounded, and someone else said, "Send her back to their counterfeit Queen and King. Just her head so they know what is coming for them."

"From blood and ash!" shouted a young boy as he pushed to the front of the group. It was the kid from the day before, the one who had run from house to house.

My legs weakened.

Several voices answered, "We will rise!"

"No one touches her." Hawke scanned the group in the yard, silencing them. "No one," he repeated as he turned back. "No one but me."

The moment I saw the dank and gloomy cells under the keep, and the twisted, white mass of bones that covered the entire length of the ceiling, the fight in me came back. There was no way I would just allow myself to be placed somewhere it appeared people never left. Not even when they died.

Delano hadn't been prepared.

I broke his hold and made it to the end of the hall only to realize the sole exit was the entrance. I squared off with him but was cornered, and with backup in the form of another who had eyes that were almost as gold as Hawke's, I was dragged into the cell that had a thin mattress on the floor and then shackled, the cold iron snapping over my wrists.

And then I was alone.

I turned around, seeing no way out. The gaps in the bars were too narrow, and when I pulled on the chains, the hook they were connected to didn't budge.

Panic bubbled up as I took a step back. How had this happened? How did I go from anticipating a future that would be all mine, where I controlled what I did and what happened to me, to this? To being chained in a cell, surrounded by people who wanted to chop me into pieces?

I knew the answer.

Hawke.

The slice of agony cutting through my chest overshadowed the pain in my stomach. My throat and eyes burned. Hawke…he wasn't even mortal. He was an Atlantian, His people had created the Cravens that had become an unstoppable plague upon this land, the very same creatures who'd murdered my parents and almost killed me. He supported the Dark One, who had killed the last Maiden and was after me. Hawke and the wolven were the embodiment of anything the gods had turned against and the humans had rose up against. They were why the Ascended had been Blessed by the gods.

How had I not seen him for what he was? Could I be that foolish? Or was he simply that clever?

Or a mixture of both?

Because Hawke had been good. He'd said and done all the right things, and I'd been so desperate to make a real connection with someone, to experience life and feel alive. So desperate that anything that may have served as a warning wasn't even acknowledged. He'd come to Masadonia with one order: gain access to me. He had done that and more. Gained my friendship, my trust, my...

A pulsing, pounding anger and sorrow swept through me. I wanted to scream, but the sound couldn't make it past the knot of emotion in my throat.

Why did he have to...do what he had? Everything he'd said and done was nothing more than clever artifice. When he told me that I was brave and strong. When he said I was beautiful. His seemingly single-minded focus hadn't been based on duty but on orders. And I'd believed it. I'd fallen for it.

Was anything true?

His pain was.

That much I knew, but the source of it? I could no longer be sure.

Lifting trembling hands to my face, I tucked back the hair that had escaped my braid. Why did he have to go so far, though? Why did he have to get under my skin and into my heart? I didn't just trust him. I'd given myself to him. All of me.

And it had been a lie.

He'd known from the beginning who I was, from the very first night in the Red Pearl, and I'd unknowingly exposed so much about myself to him.

Moving to the corner of the cell, I sat on the mattress and slowly leaned against the wall, breathing out a slow, measured breath as a fiery ache sliced over my stomach. I glanced down at my right hand. The knuckles were bruised and swollen from the punch I'd delivered. My smile was quick to fade. I doubted Hawke showed any sign of injury. He was an Atlantian.

My stomach tumbled.

A part of me couldn't believe it. He seemed so…mortal, but why should that surprise me? Atlantians could pass for mortals, just as the wolven could. I'd kissed an Atlantian.

I'd *slept* with an Atlantian.

I squeezed my eyes shut as bile climbed up my throat. I couldn't think about that. It made screams echo in my mind. I needed to focus.

What was I going to do?

This whole town was full of Descenters and Atlantians who wanted me dead, and I couldn't be more grateful that Tawny had remained behind. Obviously, I was being held until the Dark One either arrived or sent orders. The Dark One had killed the last Maiden, and here I was, captured and ready for him. I needed to get out of here, but there was no way out.

I looked up, shuddering. The ropey, twining bones reminded me of the roots in the Blood Forest. They climbed and overlapped one another, ribcages and femurs, spines and skulls. Anyone held here had this to look at, most likely a reminder of what had happened to the prisoners housed here. Who would create such a thing? Who kept their grasp on sanity staring at that?

I didn't know how much time had passed before the door opened, and footsteps approached. It had to be hours based on how empty my stomach felt. I tensed, only relaxing minutely when I saw that it was Delano.

He stepped up to the bars, holding out a small pouch. "Hungry?"

Yes. I was, but I didn't answer.

Tossing the sack in, it landed by my feet with a soft *thunk*. I stared at it.

"It's some cheese and bread," Delano explained. "I would've brought you some stew, but I feared you would've thrown it in my face, and the stew is too good to waste."

I looked over at him.

"There's nothing wrong with it. It's not poisoned or anything."

"Why would I trust anything you say?"

"He said no one touches you." He leaned against the bars. "No leap of logic to assume that would also include harming you."

My lip curled. "Why wait? The Dark One is going to kill me eventually."

Those pale eyes met mine. "If the Prince wanted you dead, you'd already be dead. You should eat."

The *Prince*. Just because the Descenters believed Casteel was the rightful heir, didn't make it true.

My gaze fell to the sack. I was hungry, and I needed my strength...and possibly a Healer because while the wound had stopped bleeding, it would probably get infected down here.

I moved gingerly, picking up the sack. "Are you going to stand there and watch me eat?"

"Wouldn't want you to choke."

I had the strangest urge to laugh, but I opened the pouch and ate the cheese and bread. The food settled in my empty stomach like clumps of stone.

Delano didn't speak after that. Neither did I, and I returned to leaning against the wall. Some time later, the door opened once more, and I looked out even though I didn't want to. I saw the tall, too-recognizable form garbed in black, looking so much like the...like the guard who'd teased me over Miss Willa Colyns' diary. My heart squeezed as if it were captured in a fist.

Hawke stopped in front of the barred door, his striking face both familiar and that of a stranger.

"Leave," Hawke commanded, and Delano hesitated for only a moment before he issued a curt nod and was gone. Then there was just us, separated by bars.

"Poppy," Hawke sighed, and I shuddered. "What am I to do with you?"

Chapter 36

As if he didn't already know.

"Don't call me that." Pushing to my feet, the chains clanked against the stone floor as I ignored the tender pull of skin around my wound. Standing hurt, but I wouldn't let him see that.

"But I thought you liked it when I did."

"You were mistaken," I replied, and he smirked. "What do you want?"

His head tilted, and a heartbeat passed. "More than you could ever guess."

I had no idea what he meant by that, and I didn't care. Not at all. "Are you here to kill me?"

"Now why would I do that?" he asked.

Lifting my hands, I rattled the chains. "You have me chained."

"I do."

Fury blasted me at his blasé response. "Everyone outside wants me dead."

"That is true."

"And you're an Atlantian," I spat. "That's what you do. You kill. You destroy. You curse."

He snorted. "Ironic coming from someone who has been surrounded by the Ascended her whole life."

"They don't murder innocents, and they don't turn people into monsters—"

"No," he cut me off. "They just force young women who make them feel inferior to bare their skin to a cane and do the gods only know what else to them. Yes, Princess, they are truly upstanding examples of everything that is good and right in this world."

I sucked in a sharp breath as my lips parted. No. I shuddered. No way.

"Did you think I wouldn't find out what the Duke's *lessons* were? I told you I would."

I took a step back, the humiliation of him learning the truth burning through me worse than any lashing the Duke had delivered.

"He used a cane cut from a tree in the Blood Forest, and he made you partially undress." He grasped the bars as my heart thundered against my ribs. "And he told you that you deserved it. That it was for your own good. But in reality, all it did was fulfill his sick need to inflict pain."

"How?" I whispered.

One side of his lips curled up. "I can be *very* compelling."

I looked away and, suddenly, I saw the Duke in my mind's eye, his arms stretched out, and the cane shoved through his heart. A tremor rocked me as my gaze swung back to Hawke. "You killed him."

Hawke smiled then, and it was a smile I'd never seen from him before. It wasn't closed-lipped this time. Even from where I stood, I could see the hint of fang. Another tremor rippled through me.

"I did," he answered. "And I never enjoyed watching the life seep out of someone's eyes more than I did while watching the Duke die."

I stared.

"He had it coming, and trust me when I say his very slow and very painful death had nothing to do with him being an Ascended. I would've gotten to the Lord eventually," he added. "But you took care of that sick bastard yourself."

I didn't... I didn't know what to think of that. He'd killed the Duke, and he would've killed the Lord because—

Cutting off those thoughts, I shook my head. I couldn't understand why he would've felt driven to do what he'd done, considering where we stood now. I didn't need to understand. At least that's what I told myself. It didn't matter. Neither did the deep, hidden part of me that was thrilled to know that there was a possibility that what he'd done to me had played a part in the Duke's ultimate demise.

"Just because the Duke and the Lord were horrible and evil, that doesn't make you any better," I told him. "That doesn't make all Ascended guilty."

"You know absolutely nothing, Poppy."

My hands curled into fists as I resisted the urge to shriek, but then he unlocked the door. Every muscle in me tensed.

I glared at him as he entered the cell. I wished there was some sort of weapon, though I knew even if I was armed to the teeth, there would be very little I could do. He was faster, stronger, and he could take me with a flick of his wrist.

But I would go down fighting.

"You and I need to talk," he said as he closed the doors behind him.

"No, we don't."

"Well, you really don't have a choice, do you?" His gaze dropped to the cuffs around my wrists. He took a step toward me and then halted. His nostrils flared as the pupils of his eyes dilated. "You're injured."

My blood. He *scented* my blood. Mouth dry, I stepped back. "I'm fine."

"No, you aren't." His gaze swept over me, stopping at my midsection. "You're bleeding."

"Barely," I told him.

Within the blink of an eye, he was directly in front of me. Gasping, I stumbled against the wall. How had he hidden such speed before? He reached for the hem of my tunic, and panic exploded.

"Don't touch me!" I side-stepped him, wincing as pain radiated up my side. He stiffened, staring down at me as my heart slammed against my ribs. "Don't."

He arched a brow. "You had no problem with me touching you last night."

Heat swamped my skin as my lips pulled back in a snarl. "That was a mistake."

"Was it?"

"Yes," I hissed. "I wish it never happened."

Gods, that was the truth. I wanted nothing more than to forget how what we'd done had felt beautiful and life-altering, how it had felt so incredibly right.

I was a fool.

His jaw hardened, and a long moment passed. "Be that as it may, you are still wounded, Princess, and you will allow me to look at it."

Breathing heavily, I lifted my chin. "And if I don't?"

His laugh reminded me of before, but now it was tinged with cold amusement. "As if you could stop me," he stated softly, and the truth of what he said was soul-shattering. "You can either allow me to help you or..."

My fingers tingled from how tightly I'd balled my hands into fists. "Or, you will force me?"

Hawke said nothing.

A burn started in my chest as I stared back at him, hating him, hating myself for feeling what I'd promised I would never feel again.

Helpless.

I could refuse and make this very difficult, but what good would that do in the end? He would overpower me, and all I would accomplish is further injuring myself. I was furious enough to do just that, but I wasn't stupid.

Looking away, I forced a long breath out of my lungs. "Why do you even care if I bleed to death?"

"Why do you think I would want you dead? If I did, why wouldn't I have agreed to what was demanded outside?" he asked, and my head jerked back to him. "You are no good to me dead."

"So, I'm your hostage until the Dark One gets here? You all plan to use me against the King and Queen."

"Clever girl," he murmured. "You are the Queen's favorite Maiden."

I didn't know why, and I didn't want it to, but the knowledge that he wanted to tend to my wound only because he planned to use me stung profoundly.

"Will you let me check you now?"

I gave him no answer because what he'd said wasn't truly a question. There was no choice. He seemed to be satisfied that I understood because he reached for me, and this time, my body went rigid, but I didn't move.

Hawke's hands curled around the hem of the dark tunic. He lifted the cloth, and I bit down on the inside of my cheek when the backs of his knuckles brushed over my lower stomach and hip. Had he done that on purpose? I stared at his glossy dark waves as he continued inching the shirt up. He stopped just below my breasts, exposing what was likely to leave yet another scar.

If I lived that long.

Because after I served whatever purpose they had in mind, I doubted I'd be released. It made no sense for that to occur.

Hawke stared at me, at the bloody, seeping cut, for too long. My pulse picked up, and I could too easily recall how his teeth—no, his *fangs*—had felt against my skin. I shivered. Was it revulsion? Fear? A leftover, unwanted sensation that the memory triggered? Maybe all of them. I had no idea.

"Gods," he said, his voice guttural as thick lashes lifted, and his gaze met mine. His cheekbones seemed sharper as shadows blossomed under them. "You could've been disemboweled."

"You've always been so observant."

He ignored that comment as he stared down at me like I was nothing more than a silly girl. "Why didn't you say anything? This could become infected."

It took everything in me to keep my arms at my sides. "Well, there really wasn't a lot of time, considering you were busy betraying me."

His eyes narrowed. "That's no excuse."

I barked out a harsh laugh and wondered if I was already developing a fever. "Of course, not. Silly me for not realizing that the person who had a hand in murdering the people I care about, who betrayed me and made plans with the one who helped to slaughter my family to use me for some nefarious means would care that I was wounded."

Those amber eyes turned luminous, filling with a golden fire. His features turned stark, and goosebumps pimpled my skin. Ice hit my veins at the slow reminder that he was not as I'd always assumed. Mortal. I refused to shrink back, even though I wanted to run.

"Always so brave," he murmured. He let go of my shirt and turned away, calling out to Delano, who apparently hadn't gone too far because he was in front of the cell within seconds.

I leaned against the wall, quiet as Hawke waited for Delano to return with the items he'd requested. The fact that he kept his back to me for so long said everything I needed to know about whether or not he viewed me as a threat.

Delano appeared with a basket, and it made me wonder exactly why such things were kept handy. My gaze flickered over the cell. Were they in the business of keeping their prisoners healthy? Better yet, was this where all the Ascended and the Lord from the keep had ended up?

When Hawke faced me, we were once again alone. "Why don't you lie—?" He glanced around the cell, his gaze centering on the threadbare mattress as if he just realized there was no bed. His shoulders tensed. "Why don't you lie down?"

"I'm fine standing, thanks."

Impatience brimmed just under the surface as he stalked toward me, basket in hand. "Would you rather I get on my knees?"

A terrible razor-sharp smile pulled at my lips as I started to agree—

"I don't mind." His gaze dropped as he bit down on his lower lip. "Doing so would put me at the perfect height for something I know you'd enjoy. After all, I'm always craving honeydew."

Air punched out of my lungs in shock, but anger quickly crashed into it. I peeled away from the wall, hurrying to the cot. I sat down slower than I stood as I shot him an icy stare. "You're repulsive."

Chuckling under his breath, he walked over to the cot and knelt. "If you say so."

"I know so."

A half-grin appeared as he placed the basket on the floor. A quick glance showed there were bandages and tiny jars. Nothing that could be fashioned into an ineffective weapon. He gestured for me to recline, and after muttering a curse, I did as he requested.

"Language," he murmured, and when he reached for my tunic once more, I lifted it myself. "Thank you."

I gritted my teeth.

A small smile appeared as he shifted onto his knees, pulling a clear bottle from the basket. He unscrewed the lid, and a bitter, sharp scent hit the musty air.

"I want to tell you a story," he said, his brows lowered as he eyed the wound.

"I am not in the mood for story time—" I gasped as he took hold of my shirt. I gripped his wrist with both hands, barely feeling the cold of the chain against my stomach. "What are you doing?"

"The blade damn near ripped out your ribcage," he said, eyes flashing an unholy gold once more. "It extends up the side of your ribs."

The wound wasn't that bad, but it did crawl up my side.

"I'm guessing this happened when the sword was wrestled from you?" he asked.

I didn't answer, and when I didn't let go of his wrists, I expected him to simply break my hold, but instead, he sighed. "Believe it or not, I'm not trying to undress you so I can take advantage of you. I'm not here to seduce you, Princess."

What should have come as a relief had the opposite effect. The burn in my chest crept into my throat, forming a knot I could barely breathe around as I stared up at him. Of course, he wasn't trying to seduce me. Not since he'd already succeeded in doing so, getting me to not only let my guard down but to also trust him. I'd opened up to him, shared with him my dreams of becoming something else, my dread of returning to the capital and—oh, gods—my gift. I'd shared so much more than just words. I'd let him into my room, into my bed, and then into me. He'd whispered that my touch had consumed him, and he'd worshipped my body, my scars. He'd told me that they made me even more beautiful, and I...

I'd liked him.

I'd done more than just like him.

Gods, I'd fallen for him even though it was forbidden. I'd fallen for him enough that I knew deep down it had played a role in my decision to tell the Queen that I would refuse the Ascension. A tremor coursed through my fingers as the burn in my throat filled the backs of my eyes.

"Was any of it true?" The question erupted from me in a hoarse voice I barely recognized, and the moment the words were set free, I wanted to take them back because I knew...I already knew the answer.

Hawke went as still as the statues that had adorned the foyer in Castle Teerman. I jerked my hands away. A muscle ticked in his jaw as his lips remained pressed firmly together.

A ragged, brittle sob climbed up my throat, and it took everything in me to keep it inside. That did very little to ease the shame that sat in the center of my chest like a hot coal. *I will not cry. I will not cry.*

Unable to look at him any longer, I closed my eyes. It didn't help.

I immediately saw how he'd gazed at me, lips swollen and glossy. Anger and shame, and a deep hurt I'd never experienced before pricked at my eyelids.

I felt his hands move then, carefully lifting the tunic, stopping short of exposing my entire chest. This time, his knuckles didn't brush my skin, and like before, even in the dim light, I knew the paler, almost shiny patches of scarred flesh were visible, especially to the eyes of an Atlantian. Last night, I'd disrobed for him and had let him look his fill, believing what he'd said. He'd been so convincing, and my stomach churned at the thought of what he must've really thought.

How he must've really felt when he touched the scars, kissed them.

He spoke into the silence then, startling me. "This may burn."

I thought his voice sounded gruffer than normal, but then I felt him lean closer, and the first splash of lukewarm liquid hit the wound. Air hissed through my teeth as scorching pain lanced the right side of my stomach and up my ribs. The bitter astringent scent rose as the liquid bubbled in the cut, and I welcomed the sting, focusing on it instead of the throbbing ache in my chest.

Tipping my head back, I kept my eyes closed as more liquid splashed along the injury, creating more foam and sending another wave of pain shuddering across my midsection.

"Sorry about that," he muttered, and I almost believed that he was. "It will need to sit for a bit to burn out any infection that may have already been making its way in there."

Great.

Maybe it would burn through my stupid heart.

Silence fell, but it didn't last long. "The Craven were our fault," he said, startling me. "Their creation, that is. All of this. The monsters in the mist. The war. What has become of this land. You. Us. It all started with an incredibly desperate, foolish act of love, many, many centuries before the War of Two Kings."

"I know," I said, clearing my throat. "I know the history."

"But do you know the true history?"

"I know the only history." My eyes opened, and I shifted my gaze away from the chains and twisted bones.

"You know only what the Ascended have led everyone to believe, and it is not the truth." He reached over, plucking up the chain that crossed a part of my stomach. I tensed as he carefully moved it aside. "My people lived alongside mortals in harmony for thousands of years, but then King O'Meer Malec—"

"Created the Craven," I cut him off. "Like I said—"

"You're wrong." He shifted so he sat back, one leg drawn up, and his arm resting on his knee. "King Malec fell hopelessly in love with a mortal woman. Her name was Isbeth. Some say it was Queen Eloana who poisoned her. Others claim it was a jilted lover of the King's who stabbed her because he apparently had quite the history of being unfaithful. But either way, she was mortally wounded. As I said, Malec was desperate to save her. He committed the forbidden act of Ascending her—what you know as the Ascension."

My heart lodged somewhere in my throat, next to the messy knot of emotion.

His gaze lifted and met mine. "Yes. Isbeth was the first to Ascend. Not your false King and Queen. She became the first vampry."

Lies. Utter, unbelievable lies.

"Malec drank from her, only stopping once he felt her heart begin to fail, and then he shared his blood with her." His head tilted, those golden eyes glittering. "Perhaps if your act of Ascension wasn't so well guarded, the finer details would not come as a surprise to you."

I started to sit up but remembered the wound and the fizzing liquid. "Ascension is a Blessing from the gods."

He smirked. "It is far from that. More like an act that can either create near immortality or make nightmares come true. We Atlantians are born nearly mortal. And remain so until the Culling."

"The Culling?" I asked before I could stop myself.

"It's when we change." His upper lip curled, and the tip of his tongue prodded a sharp canine. I knew this. It was in the history books. "The fangs appear, lengthening only when we feed, and we change in...other ways."

"How?" Curiosity had seized me, and I figured that whatever I could learn would help if I managed to get out of this.

"That's not important." He reached for a cloth. "We may be harder to kill than the Ascended, but we *can* be killed," he went on. I also knew that. Atlantians could be killed just like a Craven could. "We age slower than mortals, and if we take care, we can live for thousands of years."

I wanted to point out everything was important, especially how Atlantians changed in other ways, but curiosity got the best of me. "How...how old are you?"

"Older than I look."

"Hundreds of years older?" I asked.

"I was born after the war," he answered. "I've seen two centuries come and go."

Two centuries?

Gods...

"King Malec created the first vampry. They are...a part of all of us, but they are not like us. Daylight does not affect us. Not like it does the vampry. Tell me, which of the Ascended have you ever seen in the daylight?"

"They do not walk in the sun because the gods do not," I answered. "That is how they honor them."

"How convenient for them, then." Hawke's smirk turned smug. "Vamprys may be blessed with the closest possible thing to immortality, like us, but they cannot walk in daylight without their skin starting to decay. You want to kill an Ascended without getting your hands dirty? Lock them outside with no possible shelter. They'll be dead before noon."

That couldn't be true. The Ascended *chose* not to go in the sun.

"They also need to feed, and by *feed*, I am talking about blood. They need to do so frequently to live, to prevent whatever mortal wounds or illnesses they suffered before they Ascended from returning. They cannot procreate, not after the Ascension, and many experience bloodlust when they feed, often killing mortals in the process."

He dabbed the cloth along the wound, careful not to exert too much pressure as he soaked up the settled liquid. "Atlantians do not feed on mortals—"

"Whatever," I snapped. "You expect me to truly believe that?"

His gaze lifted to mine. "Mortal blood offers us nothing of any real value because we were never mortal, Princess. Wolven don't need to feed, but we do. We feed when we need to, on other Atlantians."

I shook my head. How could he honestly expect me to believe that? Their treatment of mortals, how they virtually used them as cattle, is what drove the gods to abandon them, and for the mortal populace to revolt.

"We can use our blood to heal a mortal without turning them, something a vampry cannot do, but the most important difference is the creation of the Craven. An Atlantian has never created one. The vamprys have. And in case you haven't been following along, the vamprys are what you know as the Ascended."

"That's a lie." My hands balled uselessly at my sides.

"It is the truth." Brows lowered in concentration as he peered down at the wound, he glanced up at me only when he laid the cloth aside. "A vampry cannot make another vampry. They cannot complete the Ascension. When they drain a mortal, they create a Craven."

"What you're saying makes no sense."

"How does it not?"

"Because if any part of what you're saying is true, then the Ascended are vamprys, and they cannot do the Ascension." Anger burned through my chest, worse than the liquid he'd used to clean out my wound. "If that's true, then how have they made other Ascended? Like my brother?"

His jaw hardened, eyes turning glacial. "Because it is not the Ascended who are giving the gift of life. They are using an Atlantian to do so."

I coughed out a harsh laugh. "The Ascended would never work with an Atlantian."

"Did I misspeak? I don't believe I did. I said they are *using* an Atlantian. Not working with one." He picked up a jar, screwing off the lid. "When King Malec's peers discovered what he'd done, he lifted the laws that forbade the act of Ascending. As more vamprys were created, many were unable to control their bloodlust. They drained many of their victims, creating the pestilence known as the Craven, who swept across the kingdom like a plague. The Queen of Atlantia, Queen Eloana, tried to stop it. She made the act of Ascension forbidden once more and ordered all vamprys destroyed in an act to protect mankind."

I watched as he dipped his hand into the jar and then set it aside. A thick, milky-white substance covered his long fingers. I recognized the smell. It was the same salve that had been used on me before. "Yarrow?"

He nodded. "Among other things that will help speed up your

healing."

"I can—" I jerked as the chilled ointment touched my skin. Hawke spread the mixture over my stomach, warming the balm and my flesh.

And then me.

My knuckles began to ache as an unwanted shiver of awareness skated over my skin. *He betrayed you*, I reminded myself. *He played you.* I hated him. I did. The knot in my throat expanded even as a heady flush swept through me.

Hawke seemed to be entirely focused on what he was doing, and that was a blessing. I didn't want him to see how his touch affected me. "The vamprys revolted," he said after scooping out more of the ointment. "That is what triggered the War of Two Kings. It was not mortals fighting back against cruel, inhuman Atlantians, but vamprys fighting back."

My gaze flew from his hand to his face. Some of what he said felt familiar, but it was a twisted, darker version of what I knew to be true.

"The death toll from the war was not exaggerated. In fact, many people believe the numbers were far higher. We weren't defeated, Princess. King Malec was overthrown, divorced, and exiled. Queen Eloana remarried, and the new King, Da'Neer, pulled their forces back, called their people home, and ended a war that was destroying this world."

"And what happened to Malec and Isbeth?" I asked, even though I didn't believe much of what he'd said.

"Your records say that Malec was defeated in battle, but the truth is, no one knows. He and his Mistress simply disappeared," Hawke claimed, returning the lid to the jar. "The vamprys gained control of the remaining lands, anointing their own King and Queen, Jalara and Ileana, and renamed it the Kingdom of Solis. They called themselves the Ascended, used *our* gods, who'd long since gone to sleep, as a reason for why they became the way they did. In the hundreds of years that have passed since, they've managed to scrub the truth from history, that the vast majority of mortals actually fought alongside the Atlantians against the common threat of vamprys."

I couldn't even speak for what felt like an entire minute. "None of that sounds believable."

"I imagine it is hard to believe that you belong to a society of murderous monsters, who take the third daughters and sons during the Rite to feed upon. And if they don't drain them dry, they become—"

"What?" I gasped, my disbelief turning to anger. "You have spent this entire time telling me nothing but falsehoods, but now you've gone too far."

Placing a clean bandage on the wound, he smoothed down the edges until it adhered to my skin. "I've told you nothing but the truth, as did the man who threw the Craven hand."

I sat up, tugging down my shirt. "Are you claiming that those given in service to the gods are now Craven?"

"Why do you think the Temples are off-limits to anyone but the Ascended and those they control like the Priests and Priestesses?"

"Because they're sacred places that even most Ascended don't breach," I argued.

"Have you seen one child that has been given over? Just one, Princess? Do you know anyone other than a Priest or Priestess or an Ascended who has claimed to have seen one? You're smart. You know no one has," he challenged. "That's because most are dead before they even learn to speak."

I opened my mouth.

"The vamprys need a food source, Princess, one that would not rouse suspicion. What better way than to convince an entire kingdom to hand over their children under the pretense of honoring the gods? They've created a religion around it, such that brothers will turn on brothers if any of them refuse to give away their child. They have fooled an entire kingdom, used the fear of what they have created against the people. And that's not all. You ever think it's strange how many young children die overnight from a mysterious blood disease? Like the Tulis family, who lost their first and second children to it? Not every Ascended can stick to a strict diet. Bloodlust for a vampry is a very real, common problem. They're thieves in the night, stealing children, wives, and husbands."

"Do you really think I believe any of this? That the Atlantians are innocent, and everything I've been taught is a lie?"

"Not particularly, but it was worth a shot. We are not innocent of all crimes—"

"Like murder and kidnapping?" I threw at him.

"That among other things. You don't want to believe what I'm saying. Not because it sounds too foolish to believe, but because there are things you're now questioning. Because it means your precious brother is feeding on innocents—"

"No."

"And turning them into Craven."

"Shut up," I growled, shooting to my feet. The sharp, sudden movement barely causing me any pain.

Rising in one fluid movement, he quickly towered over me. "You don't want to accept what I'm saying, even as logical as it sounds because it means your brother is one of them, and the Queen who cared for you has slaughtered thousands—"

I didn't stop to think about what I did next. I was just so furious and afraid because he was right, what he'd said had prompted questions. Like how none of the Ascended were seen during the day, or how no one but they entered the Temples. But, worse yet, it raised the question of why Hawke would make all of this up. What would be the point of concocting this elaborate lie when he had to know how hard it would be to convince me?

No, I didn't think about any of that.

I just acted.

The chain skidded across the floor as I swung on him, my hand curled into a fist.

Hawke's hand snapped up, catching mine before it connected with his jaw. Gods, he moved impossibly fast, twisting my arm as he spun me around. He yanked me back against the hard wall of his chest, trapping my arm between us as he grabbed my other hand. A shriek of frustration ripped from my throat as I went to lift my leg—

"Don't." His voice was a soft warning in my ear, one that sent a shiver down my spine.

I didn't listen.

He grunted when the heel of my foot connected with the front of his leg. Jerking my leg up, I kicked back.

Suddenly, I found myself pressed against the wall with Hawke at my back. I struggled, but it was no use. There wasn't an inch of space between him or the cold, damp wall.

"I said, don't." His warm breath drifted over my temple. "I mean it, Princess. I don't want to hurt you."

"You don't? You already hur—" I cut myself off.

"What?" He moved my arm so it was no longer caught between us. He didn't let go, though. Instead, he pressed my hand into the wall, just as he did with the other one.

Clamping my mouth shut, I refused to tell him that he'd already hurt me. Admitting that meant there was something to hurt, to be exploited, and he already had enough to use against me.

"You know you can't seriously hurt me," he said, resting his cheek against mine.

I tensed. "Then why am I chained?"

"Because getting kicked, punched, or clawed still doesn't feel good," he returned. "And while the others have been ordered to not touch you, it doesn't mean they'll be as tolerant as I am."

"Tolerant?" I tried to push off the wall but got nowhere. "You call this tolerant?"

"Considering that I just spent time cleaning out and covering your wound, I would say so. And a thank you would be nice."

"I didn't ask you to help me," I seethed.

"No. Because you're either too proud or too foolish to do so. You would've allowed yourself to rot instead of asking for help," he said. "So, I'm not going to get a thank you, am I?"

Thrusting my head back was my answer. He anticipated it, though, and I didn't manage to hit him. He forced my cheek to the wall. I wriggled, trying to break his hold.

"You are exceptionally skilled at being disobedient," he growled. "Only second to your talent of driving me crazy."

"You forgot one last skill."

"I did?"

"Yes," I gritted out. "I'm skilled at killing Craven. I imagine killing Atlantians is no different."

Hawke chuckled deeply, and I felt the sound all along my back. "We're not consumed by hunger, so we're not as easily distracted as a Craven."

"You can still be killed."

"Is that a threat?"

"You take it however you want."

He was quiet for a moment. "I know you've been through a lot. I know that what I've told you is a lot, but it is all the truth. Every part, Poppy."

"Stop calling me that!" I squirmed.

"And you should stop doing that," he said, his voice rougher, deeper. "Then again. Please continue. It's the perfect kind of torture."

For a moment, I didn't understand what he meant, but then I felt him against my lower back, and my breath caught as a wave of awareness stole through me. "You're sick."

"And twisted. Perverse, and dark." The rough stubble of his chin dragged over my cheek, and my spine arched in response. He seemed to get even closer as his fingers spread over mine. "I'm a lot of things—"

"Murderer?" I whispered, unsure if I was reminding him or myself. "You killed Vikter. You killed all the others."

He stilled, and the next breath he took pushed his chest against my back. "I've killed. So have Delano and Kieran. I and the one you call the Dark One had a hand in Hannes' and Rylan's deaths, but not that poor girl. It was one of the Ascended, most likely caught in bloodlust. And I am willing to bet it was either the Duke or the Lord."

The Lord.

Who'd smelled of the flower that Malessa had carried in earlier that day.

"And none of us had anything to do with the attack on the Rite and what happened to Vikter."

Gods, I wanted to believe that. I needed to believe I had not slept with the man who'd played a role in Vikter's death. "Then who did?"

"It was those you call Descenters. Our supporters," he said, his voice barely above a whisper. "There was no order given to attack the Rite, however."

"You really expect me to believe the *thing* the Descenters follow didn't order them to attack the Rite?"

"Just because they follow the Dark One, doesn't mean they are led by him," he answered. "Many of the Descenters act on their own. They know the truth. They no longer want to live in fear of their children being made into monsters or stolen to feed another. I had nothing to do with Vikter's death."

I shivered, believing what he said about his involvement and unsure why. But whether the Dark One actively led the Descenters or not, he was still the cause of Vikter's death. They'd picked up his cause and acted upon it.

"But the others you claim. You killed them. Owning it doesn't change it."

"It had to happen." His chin moved from my cheek, and then he said, "Just like you need to understand that there is no way out of this.

You belong to me."

My heart turned over slowly. "Don't you mean I belong to the Dark One?"

"I meant what I said, Princess."

"I don't belong to anyone."

"If you believe that, then you *are* a fool," he taunted, pressing his head to mine before I could lash out. "Or you're lying to yourself. You belonged to the Ascended. You know that. It's one of the things you hated. They kept you in a cage."

I never should've said anything to him. "At least that cage was more comfortable than this one."

"True," he murmured, and a heartbeat passed. "But you've never been free."

"True or not." And it was painfully true. "That doesn't mean I'll stop fighting you," I warned. "I won't submit."

"I know." There was an odd tone to his voice, one that sounded like…admiration. But that didn't make sense.

"And you're still a monster," I told him.

"I am, but I wasn't born that way. I was *made* this way. You asked about the scar on my thigh. Did you look at it closely, or were you too busy staring at my co—"

"Shut up," I screamed.

"You should've noticed that it was the Royal Crest branded on my skin," he said, and I gasped. It had looked like the Royal Crest. "Do you want to know how I have such intimate knowledge of what happens during your fucking Ascension, Poppy? How I know what you don't? Because I was held in one of those Temples for five decades, and I was sliced and cut and fed upon. My blood was poured into golden chalices that the second sons and daughters drank after being drained by the Queen or the King or another Ascended. I was the godsdamn cattle."

No.

I couldn't believe this.

"And I wasn't just used for food. I provided all sorts of entertainment. I know exactly what it's like to not have a choice," he continued, and horror followed his words. "It was your Queen who branded me, and if it hadn't been for the foolish bravery of another, I would still be there. That is how I got that scar."

Without any warning, his hands slipped off mine, and he pulled away. Trembling, I didn't move. Not for several long moments. When I turned around, he was already outside the cell.

If what he said was true…

No. It couldn't be. Gods, it could not be.

Suddenly unbearably cold, I folded my arms around myself, crossing the chains.

Hawke stared at me through the bars. "Neither the prince nor I want to see you harmed. As I've said, we need you alive."

"Why?" I whispered. "Why am I so important?"

"Because they have the true heir to the kingdom. They captured him when he freed me."

I thought that the Dark One was the only heir to the Atlantian throne. If what Hawke said was true, it could only mean…"The Dark One has a brother?"

He nodded. "You are the Queen's favorite. You're important to her and to the kingdom. I don't know why. Maybe it has something to do with your gift. Perhaps it doesn't. But we will release you back to them if they release Prince Malik."

All of what he'd just said slowly seeped into my brain. "You plan to use me as ransom."

"That's better than sending you back in pieces, isn't it?"

Disbelief thundered through me, quickly followed by that pulsing pain that came from my chest. "You just spent all this time telling me that the Queen, the Ascended, and my brother, are all evil vamprys who feed on mortals, and you're just going to send me back to them once you free the Dark One's brother?"

Hawke said nothing.

A broken, too-wet-sounding laugh left me. If what he said was true, it confirmed what was already becoming evident.

He didn't care for my safety or well-being beyond making sure I was breathing when the time came to make the exchange.

I lifted my hand to my chest to ease the throb as another laugh crept up on me.

Hawke's jaw flexed. "A more comfortable sleeping arrangement will be made."

I didn't know what to say to that, but he surely wasn't getting a thank you from me.

His chin lifted. "You can choose not to believe anything I've said, but you should so that what I'm about to say doesn't come as such a shock to you. I will be leaving shortly to meet up with King Da'Neer of Atlantia to tell him that I have you."

My head jerked upright.

"Yes. The King lives. So does Queen Eloana. The parents of the one you call the Dark One and Prince Malik."

Shocked, I couldn't move as he turned to leave, but he stopped.

And Hawke didn't look back as he said, "Not everything was a lie, Poppy. Not everything."

Chapter 37

Not everything was a lie.

Which part?

The story about Hawke's brother? The rest of his family? Farming his lands, and the caverns he used to explore as a child? That he'd been in love before and had lost? Or all the things he'd said about me?

Whatever he said that was true didn't matter. It shouldn't as I paced as far as the chains would allow, which was not very far at all.

After he'd left, I'd sat on the mattress and tried to sort truth from fiction, which had felt impossible. Somehow, even more improbable, I had drifted off to sleep. My mind hadn't shut down, but my body had simply given out on me. I'd slept until the nightmares drove me awake, my screams echoing off the stone walls.

It had been so long since the memory of the night of my parents' deaths had found me in sleep. That it would find me here was not at all surprising.

I brushed several loose strands of hair back from my face as I turned, careful to not tangle myself in the chains.

Maybe...maybe the Ascended *were* vamprys, created accidentally by the Atlantians. I could believe that. It seemed too much of an elaborate lie to not be real. And I could believe that Lord Mazeen had been the cause of Malessa's death. It wasn't as if he wasn't capable of such cruelty.

And gods, I believed what Hawke had said about how he'd gotten the brand. Maybe not the part where the Queen had been the one to deliver it, nor what he'd been held for, but the rawness in his voice couldn't be forced. He'd been held against his will, and he'd been used in ways even I couldn't comprehend.

Believing that didn't mean everything else he claimed was true. That the Ascended were feeding off mortals, sequestering them in temples and stealing into homes in the middle of the night to create Craven out of the ones they didn't completely drain dry. How in the world would they have been able to keep that a secret? People would find out.

People could've found out already.

That is if that knowledge is what drove the Descenters to support the fallen kingdom of Atlantia.

I shook my head.

But that would mean that every Ascended was aware of what was happening. That not a single one had refused the Ascension once learning what it would cost. Not even my brother.

Our mother, though, she had refused the Ascension.

My heart tripped over itself.

She'd refused because she'd loved my father. Not because she'd learned the truth and had passed on it. She'd refused because of love, and the Dark One had still killed her.

Unless…unless the Duchess had lied about that. But why? Why would she have lied? The Dark One, Prince Casteel, controlled the Craven.

Except did the Craven appear as if they were controlled by anything but hunger? Never once had I seen them stop in the middle of an attack or display any true level of cognitive thinking.

But if that wasn't true, if the Dark One couldn't control them, then did that mean the Ascended were using them to control the populace? To stop them from asking too many questions, and make them willing to hand over their children so the gods wouldn't become displeased, exposing their cities to a Craven attack?

It almost felt like I'd be struck down for even questioning that. Because Hawke was right. It was a religion.

I started pacing again.

How did the Craven make it to a town that hadn't seen an attack in decades the moment I arrived with my family unless the Dark One had sent them?

It didn't make any sense, and all of this back and forth was starting to make my head hurt. Even if some of what Hawke had claimed was true, it didn't change that they were still responsible for so much death themselves.

It couldn't all be true, because there was no way my soft, gentle brother would've Ascended if he knew what was being done. There was no way.

Hawke was...he was just messing with my head, making me weak-minded and uncertain. I wouldn't put it past him.

I stopped, staring down at my hands. He was going to return me to the very people he claimed abused him. How horrible was that?

Dampness pressed at the backs of my eyes, but I drew in a deep breath. I would not cry. I wouldn't shed a single tear for Hawke, for what may have been done to him, and for what he'd done to me. I wouldn't allow it to break me. Not when he'd already shattered my heart.

The door at the end of the hall opened, and I lifted my head. Delano came into view, along with another man with rich brown skin. His eyes were the same golden brown as some of the others.

Atlantian.

"Glad you're awake," Delano said. "Didn't want to disturb you earlier when I checked on you."

I didn't even want to think about the fact that he'd been down here while I slept.

"I'm going to open this door, and Naill and I are going to escort you to more comfortable arrangements," he explained, and my brows rose. "And you're not going to do anything foolish. Right?"

"Right," I repeated, hope sparking.

Delano smiled. "That wasn't even remotely convincing."

"It really wasn't," Naill agreed. "Not that I can blame her. If that was me, I would be thinking this is a good chance for escape."

Hope fizzled.

Delano's smile faded. "You need to understand something, Maiden. I'm a wolven."

"I figured that out already."

"Then you have to know that the only reason you outran Kieran the day before is because he didn't want to catch you. I will want to catch you."

A shiver shimmied over my skin.

"I have impeccable tracking skills. There is nowhere you can run that I would not find you," he continued.

"Truth is," Niall said, drawing my gaze to his high, sharp cheekbones, "I'm even faster than he is, and neither of us wants to harm you. That will unfortunately happen if you run because I have a feeling you will somehow turn empty air into a weapon, and we'd have to defend ourselves. I doubt *he* will make a distinction between us wanting to hurt you and us being forced to by trying to defend ourselves."

My nostrils flared on the ragged breath I exhaled. I didn't care what he wanted, did, or thought.

"He'd have us pinned to the walls in the Hall, and both of us enjoy breathing and having all our body parts. So, please, be nice," Delano said, unlocking the door. "Because even though losing my hand or certain death would be terrible, I abhor the idea of having to strike a female." He stepped into the cell. "Even someone as apparently dangerous as you."

I smiled at him, and it wasn't exactly a nice expression. It came because I was glad that they knew I was dangerous.

But I also wasn't stupid. I wouldn't be able to run from them. I knew that. There was no point in me getting myself hurt just to make things difficult. Even I could recognize that.

I lifted my wrists, rattling the chains.

Delano eyed me as he fished out a key from his tunic pocket and unhooked the shackles. They slipped, clanging off the hard-packed ground.

Naill turned away first, his head cranking toward the entrance, and then Delano followed suit. And there I was, my eyes fastened to the sword attached to Delano's waist, and my hands unbound.

"Shit," Naill said, and that drew my attention.

Delano let out a low rumble of warning that made my skin crawl. "What the fuck are you doing down here, Jericho?"

My breath caught as I saw the tall form drift out of the shadows.

"Taking a stroll," he said.

"Bullshit," Naill spat. "You're down here by yourself. You're here for her."

I tensed as Jericho looked over at me. "You're wrong," he said. "And you're right."

Footsteps came from the entrance, and I heard Delano curse again.

"I am here for her," Jericho said. "But I'm not alone."

No, he wasn't. There were six men with him, all staying close to the shadows.

"You're being incredibly stupid," Naill pointed out, blocking the door.

Jericho stared at me through the bars. "Perhaps."

"I know you think you're owed your pound of flesh. She cut you."

"Twice," I chimed in.

Delano sent me a look that said I wasn't helping.

Jericho sneered. "Don't forget the hand." He lifted his left arm. "There's that."

"That's on you," Delano answered. "Not her."

"Yeah, well, can't take it out on the Prince, now can I?" Jericho said, and I frowned, having thought it had been Hawke who'd taken his hand.

"Do you understand he will have your head if you harm her? All of your heads?" Delano said. "He said *no one* is to hurt her. You try to do what you want to do, all of you will die. Is that what you want, Rolf? Ivan?" He rattled off the names of those who were hidden. "He will see this as a betrayal, but you still have a chance to walk away from this with your lives. You won't if any of you take a step forward."

None of them moved to leave.

One advanced, an older man with brown eyes. "She's the fucking Maiden, Delano. She was raised as an Ascended, by the damn Queen herself, practically. The Ascended took my son in the middle of the godsdamn night."

"But *she* did not take your son," Naill replied.

"I get that the Prince wants to use her to free his brother, but you and I both know, Malik is most likely dead," Jericho tossed out. "And if he's not, it probably isn't a good thing. He's got to be so fucked up by now that he has no idea who he is."

"But if we send her back to the bloodsucking Royals, we send one hell of a powerful message," another argued. "It will shake them.

We need that advantage."

"And we want it," the one who was called Rolf said. "You have to. Those bastards killed your whole den, Delano. Your mother. Your father. Your sisters weren't so lucky. They waited a while before they killed them—"

"I know exactly what was done to my family," snarled Delano, and I felt my stomach twist. "But that does not change the fact that I will not allow you to hurt her."

"She was standing next to Duke and Duchess Teerman," a voice came, sending a chill down my spine. "She stood there when they told my wife and I that our son was to be given to the gods. She just stood there and did *nothing*."

I stumbled back a step when the man who spoke stepped out of the shadows. It was Mr. Tulis. So jarred by his appearance, I couldn't do anything but stare at him.

He looked at me then, with hatred in his eyes. "You cannot tell me you didn't know what they were doing. You cannot tell me that you had no idea what happened to our children!" he shouted. "What was happening to the people who went to bed and never woke up? You had to know what they were."

I opened my mouth, and the only thing I could say was, "Is your son with you now?"

"The Ascended will never get their hands on Tobias," he vowed. "We will not lose another to them."

Rattled as my gift came alive, I was barely able to pay attention to what Delano said. "And you would betray the Prince, who aided your family in escape? Who made sure that your child could grow and thrive?"

Mr. Tulis didn't take his eyes off me. "I would do anything to feel the blood of the Ascended flowing on my hands."

"I'm not an Ascended," I whispered.

"No," he sneered, brandishing a knife. "You're just their whole future."

I wanted to tell him that I planned to go to the Queen on their behalf, but I didn't get the chance. Not that it would've made a difference. Not with that kind of loathing radiating out from him.

"Don't do this," Delano warned, unsheathing his sword.

"He'll get over it," Jericho said. "And if we have to kill you two to make sure he never finds out, then so be it. It's your grave. Not mine."

Everything happened so fast.

Rolf pushed Mr. Tulis back as Naill struck like a coiled viper, grabbing the larger man by the chest. Naill sank his teeth into his neck, tearing, ripping—

A man crashed into Naill, pulling him free from Rolf, who stumbled into the bars. Blood poured, and the man laughed. "You bit me." He threw his arms out as his back bowed, cracked. "You actually bit me," he said, the last of his words turning to gravel as his knees bent. He snarled, going down on all fours.

Naill kicked the man off, baring his fangs in a hiss that sounded so cat-like that I thought of the predator I'd seen in the cage all those years ago.

The cave cat that Hawke always reminded me of.

Naill flew at the man, taking him to the ground as Delano turned to me. "Kill any of them that get close to you." He threw his sword at me, and I caught it in surprise as he turned back to those gathering at the cell door.

Delano shifted, splitting his shirt up his back as he fell forward, his lengthening hands smacking against the ground as white fur sprouted in a blinding flash over his mammoth form.

In a heartbeat, a massive wolven stood beside me just as others appeared in the hall.

"It's a party," Jericho said, and whatever hope I had that they were going to help ended right there. He winked at me. "You're popular."

"And I have two hands," I retorted.

The smirk faded from his face.

Rolf came into the enclosure, and Delano crashed into him. They rolled across the cell, a ball of brown and white fur. Delano gained the upper hand, snapping his teeth inches from Rolf's.

Naill snatched up one of the men in a run. He turned, slamming the man into the bars with such force that it cracked the iron. That man went down, and he didn't get back up.

The Atlantian turned, reaching for one of the others who'd slipped past into the cell. One quick glance at the eyes—neither ice-blue nor golden amber—told me that I was squaring off with a mortal. The one who'd spoken first.

"I don't want to hurt you," I said.

"That's okay," he said, holding a wicked sickle-shaped sword. "But I want to hurt you."

He charged forward with a cry, and it was all too easy to step aside. I spun, bringing the hilt of the sword down on the back of his head, knocking him out. Maybe doing a little more damage. I didn't want to acknowledge that his words had affected me so greatly that I hadn't delivered a purposely fatal blow.

What came through next wasn't mortal. It was a large, brindle-colored wolven. Lips peeled back, vibrating with its snarl as it bared huge teeth.

"Fuck," I whispered.

The wolven launched itself at me. I jumped back, swinging out. The edge of the sword nicked the side of the creature as he hit the wall and immediately jumped off. I spun in a panic, arcing out with the sword. It caught the massive beast in the stomach this time. Yanking on the sword, it wouldn't budge as the wolven yipped and swiped out. I let go of the sword, but I wasn't quick enough. Claws caught the front of my tunic, just below the neck. Cloth tore, and a sharp, stinging pain shot down my entire front.

Staggering back, I looked down to see half my shirt gaping open, and red dotting my exposed skin.

Naill rushed forward. "The sickle sword!" he yelled. "Get the—"

A man brought some kind of club down on the back of his head. Naill's entire body spasmed as his eyes rolled back. He went down as I dove for the sickle sword.

There was a yelp as I rose. It was Delano. Blood matted his white fur, and I prayed it was Rolf's.

Delano staggered to the side, and I knew then that it was not. It was Delano's. One of his legs collapsed under him, and he went down as Rolf prowled toward him, shaking his large head.

I didn't know why I did what I did next. I needed to focus on the others who were determined to murder me, but I shot forward, swinging the sickle sword down along the back of the wolven's neck. The blade was so sharp that it sliced through sinew and bone like a knife through butter.

Rolf didn't even yelp. There'd been no time for that.

And there had been no time to avoid the blow that landed in the middle of my back, knocking me to the ground. My back *burned*, but I held onto the sword, breathing through the fire that seemed to have ignited—

I screamed. Sharp daggers dug into my shoulder, roughly flipping me onto my back. Not daggers. Claws. I swung the sickle blade, and it sliced into the side of the wolven. Snarling, it scrambled off me, and I rolled, vision seeming to blur for a second as I pushed to my knee.

I never saw the boot coming.

Pain exploded along my ribs as the air punched out of my lungs. I fell to my side as fiery pain erupted along my left arm. I scuttled backward as I looked up.

Jericho prowled forward. "What did I promise?"

"Bathe in my blood." I wheezed, thinking my ribs were definitely broken. "Feast on my entrails."

"Yes." He knelt down. "Yes, I—"

I swiped out with the sword. Jericho jerked back quickly, falling on his ass. He shouted, his body contorting and straightening.

"You bitch," he spat, lifting his face. The sickle had split open his cheek and his forehead.

His eye.

"I'm going to rip you in two."

"Will that help you grow back that hand?" I asked, rising to my feet. It *hurt*. "Or the eye?" I shuffled around him, giving him a wide berth as I turned—

I saw Mr. Tulis, and the strangest thing happened when my eyes met his. The next breath I took seemed to be swept away in an explosion of pain that came from my stomach. My entire body spasmed, and I dropped the sword.

Confused, I looked down. Something was in my stomach. A dagger. A dagger's blade. I lifted my head. "I…I was…relieved when I didn't see you and your son at the Rite."

Mr. Tulis's eyes widened as I reached down, pulling the dagger free, tearing a scream from my throat. I stepped back, trying to catch my breath as the blood ran down my legs. I turned, hearing Jericho climbing to his feet. His right hand…it didn't look human anymore, and when it snapped out, I couldn't even move fast enough. His claws sliced through the cloth and flesh, and my foot slipped on the floor now slick with blood—my blood.

My left leg gave way, and I went down. I tried to throw my arms out to catch myself, but they wouldn't respond to the orders my brain was demanding. I fell, barely feeling the impact.

Someone laughed.

Get up.

I tried. I still held the dagger. I could feel it against my palm.

There...were cheers. I heard a *cheer* from someone.

Get up.

Nothing moved.

I shuddered at the gathering metallic taste in the back of my throat. I knew what that meant. I knew what being unable to move my arms or to stay on my feet meant.

Jericho's bleeding face appeared above me, his shaggy hair matted with blood. "You know which part I'm going to start with? Your hand." He picked up my arm. "I think I'll keep it as a souvenir." The glint of a blade appeared. "I know exactly how I'll make use of it, too. What do you all think?" he asked.

Laughter greeted him, and someone suggested other parts to keep. Parts that brought forth more laughter.

I was dying.

All I could do was hope that it was fast, that I wouldn't stay conscious through what was about to come.

"Better get started!" Jericho laughed as he swung the blade down.

The blow never landed.

At first, I thought it was simply because I'd gone numb, but then I realized Jericho was no longer standing above me. There were sounds—shouts and growls. High-pitched yelps, and then I felt a warm puff of breath against the top of my head, over my cheek. I turned my head and saw pale blue eyes and fur as white as snow. The wolven nudged my cheek with its damp nose, and then it lifted its head and howled.

I blinked, and suddenly there was a shadow falling over me. Above me, Kieran loomed. "Shit," he said. "Get the Prince. Get him *now*."

Chapter 38

Gentle arms lifted me from the dirt floor. Kieran. His face blurred, and there was buzzing in my ears. Everything around me faded out until there was nothing, and I felt no pain. I stayed there until I heard him calling for me. Hawke.

"Open your eyes, Poppy. Come on," he urged, and I felt fingers prying the dagger from my hand. It thunked off the floor next to me. His hand curved along my chin. "I need you to open your eyes. Please."

Please.

I'd never heard him say the word please like that. My sluggish heart rate picked up as awareness returned, bringing with it burning, sweeping pain. I forced my eyes open.

"There you are." A smile appeared, but it was all wrong and forced. There were no deep dimples, no warmth or laughing light to his golden eyes.

Out of lack of willpower or stupidity, I did what I hadn't since I discovered the truth about him. I reached out with my weakening senses and felt the hum of anguish from him. It ran deeper than before, no longer feeling like chips of ice against my skin but like daggers.

Like claws.

I took a breath, and it tasted of metal. "It hurts."

"I know." Misreading what I said, his gaze latched on to mine.

"I'm going to fix it. I'll make the pain go away. I'll make it all go away. You won't carry one more scar."

Confusion rippled through me. I didn't know how he could do any of that. There were too many wounds. I'd lost too much blood. I could feel it in the coldness creeping up my legs.

I was dying.

"No, you're not," he argued, and I realized I'd said the last part out loud. "You cannot die. I will not allow it."

He then lifted his arm to his mouth, and I saw those sharp teeth I'd felt before, watched in disbelief as he bit into his wrist, tearing open his skin. I cried out, trying to lift my hand to cover the wound. He'd kidnapped me. He'd killed to get to me, had betrayed me, and he was the enemy. Because of that, I'd been made helpless once more. I was dying, I shouldn't care that he was bleeding.

But I did.

Because I was an imbecile.

"I'm going to die an imbecile," I murmured.

His brows knitted. "You're not going to die," he repeated, the lines of his mouth tense. "And I'm fine. I just need you to drink."

Drink? My gaze dropped to his wrist. He couldn't mean...

"Casteel, do you—" Kieran's voice interrupted.

Casteel?

"I know exactly what I'm doing, and I don't want your opinion or your advice." Deep red blood trailed down his arm. "And I don't require either."

Kieran didn't respond to that as I stared, caught in fascinated horror. Hawke lowered his torn wrist toward me—toward my mouth.

"No." I pulled away, not making it very far with his arm around my back like a band of steel. "No."

"You have to. You'll die if you don't."

"I'd rather...die than turn into a monster," I vowed.

"A monster?" He chuckled, but it was a rough sound. "Poppy, I already told you the truth about the Craven. This will only make you better."

I didn't believe him. I couldn't. Because if I did, that meant...that meant that everything he'd said was true, and the Ascended were evil. Ian would be—

"You will do this," he repeated. "You will drink. You will live. Make that choice, Princess. Do not force me to make it for you."

I turned away, inhaling sharply. I caught a strange scent. The smell...it smelled nothing like blood, nothing like the Craven. It reminded me of citrus in the snow, fresh and tart. How...how could blood smell like that?

"Penellaphe," Hawke spoke, and there was something different about his voice. Smoother and deeper as if it carried an echo. "Look at me."

Almost as if I had no control over my body, I lifted my gaze to his. His eyes...the honey hue churned, swirling with brighter, golden flecks. My lips parted. I couldn't look away. What...what was he doing?

"Drink," he whispered or yelled, I wasn't sure, but his voice was everywhere, all around me and inside. And his eyes...I still couldn't look away from them. His pupils seemed to expand. "Drink from me."

A drop of blood fell from his arm to my lips. It seeped between them, tart and yet sweet against my tongue. My mouth tingled. He pressed his wrist more fully against my lips, and his blood ran into my mouth, coursing down my throat, thick and warm. In a distant part of my brain, I thought that I should not allow this. That it was wrong. I would become a monster, but the taste...it was like nothing I'd ever tasted before, a complete awakening. I swallowed, drawing in more.

"That's it." Hawke's voice was deeper, richer. "Drink."

And so, I did.

I drank while his gaze remained fixed on me, seeming to miss nothing. I drank, and my skin began to hum. I drank, clasping his bloodied arm and holding him to me before even realizing what I was doing. The taste of his blood...it was pure sin, decadent and lush. With each swallow, the aches and pains lessened, and the rhythm of my heart slowed, becoming even. I drank until my eyes drifted shut. Until I became surrounded by a kaleidoscope of vivid, bright blues, the color reminding me of the Stroud Sea. This blue carried startling clarity as if it were a body of water untouched by man.

But this was no ocean. There was cool, hard rock under my feet, and shadows pressing against my skin. Soft laughter drew my gaze from the pool of water to the dark-haired—

"Enough," Hawke bit out. "That's enough."

It couldn't be enough. Not yet. Latched to his wrist, I drank greedily. I fed as if I were starving, and that was how I felt. That this sustenance was what I'd been missing my entire life.

"Poppy," he groaned, breaking my hold and pulling his ravaged wrist away.

I started to follow because I wanted more, but my muscles were liquid, and my bones soft. I sank into his embrace and felt like I was floating, a little lost in the way my skin continued to buzz, and heat poured into my chest. I had no idea how much time had passed. Could've been minutes, or it could've been hours before Hawke called out to me.

My eyes fluttered open to find him staring down at me. His features were a little out of focus, fuzzy around the edges. He was leaning back against a wall, head tipped against it, and he looked utterly relaxed in that moment, as if he were the one to have tasted the magic and not I.

"How are you feeling?" he asked.

I wasn't sure how to answer that question. Was my body burning as if it were on fire? Did it sting and pulse? No. "I'm not cold. My chest...it's not cold."

"It shouldn't be."

He didn't understand. "I feel...different."

A small smile appeared. "Good."

"I feel like my body...isn't attached."

"That will go away after a few minutes. Just relax and enjoy it."

"I don't hurt anymore." I tried to steady my thoughts, but they were swirling. "I don't understand."

"It's my blood." He lifted his hand, brushing strands of hair off my cheek. His touch sent a shiver of awareness through me, and I liked the feeling. I liked the way he made me feel. I always had, but I wasn't supposed to now. "The blood of an Atlantian has healing properties. I told you that."

"That...that is unbelievable," I whispered.

"Is it?" Reaching over, he picked up my arm. "Were you not wounded here?"

My gaze followed his to my inner forearm. Dried blood and dirt smudged the surface, but where claws had ripped the tissue open, the skin was now smooth under the grime.

"And here?" he asked, moving his hand so that his thumb swirled around my upper arm, right below my shoulder. "Were you not clawed here?"

My gaze snagged on the pale scar of the old Craven attack, just inside my elbow. I forced my gaze to where his thumb continued to glide in small circles. There were no fresh marks. No gaping wounds. I stared in wonder. "There's…there's no new scars."

"There will be no new scars," he said. "That is what I promised."

He had. "Your blood…it's amazing."

And it was. My mind sluggishly delved into all that could be accomplished with it. The wounds that could be healed, and the lives that could be saved. Most people would be against drinking blood, but—

Wait.

My gaze snapped back to his. "You made me drink your blood."

"I did."

"How?"

"It's one of those things that occur during maturity. Not all of us can…compel others."

"Have you done it before? On me?"

"You probably wish you could blame your prior actions on that, but I haven't, Poppy. I never needed nor wanted to."

"But you did it now."

"I did."

"You don't even sound remotely ashamed."

"I'm not," he replied, and a hint of a teasing grin appeared. "I told you that I would not allow you to die, and you would've died, Princess. You were dying. I saved your life. Some would suggest a thank you as the appropriate response."

"I didn't ask you to do it."

"But you're grateful, aren't you?"

I snapped my mouth shut because I was.

"Only you would argue with me about this."

I hadn't wanted to die, but I also didn't want to become a Craven. "I won't turn—"

"No," he sighed, placing my arm back so it rested across my stomach. "I told you the truth, Poppy. The Atlantians did not make the Craven. The Ascended did."

My heart skipped a beat as my gaze shifted to the exposed wooden beams of the ceiling. We weren't in the cell. I turned my head, seeing a rustic bed with thick covers, and a small table beside it. "We're in a bedchamber."

"We needed privacy."

I remembered hearing Kieran's voice, but the room was now empty. "Kieran didn't want you to save me."

"Because it's forbidden."

It took me a few moments to remember what he'd told me before, and my stomach dropped. "Will I turn into a vampry?"

He laughed.

"What about that is funny?"

"Nothing." The other side of his lips now tipped up. "I know you still don't want to believe the truth, but deep down, you do. That's why you asked that question."

He had a point, but I didn't have the intellectual or emotional capacity to go there. Not right now.

"To turn, you would require far more blood than that." He returned to resting his head against the wall. "It would also require me to be more of an active participant."

Muscles low in my body clenched, proving that they were not, in fact, soft. "How...how would you be more of an active participant?"

Hawke's smile turned to smoke and became just as sinful as his blood. "Would you rather I show you instead of telling you?"

My skin flashed hot. "No."

"Liar," he whispered, eyes closing.

The warmth in my skin started to spread as if it were a spark, and I shifted, feeling less...floaty and more...weighted. I tried to ignore it. "Are...Naill and Delano okay?"

"They will be fine, and I'm sure they'll be happy to know you asked about them."

I doubted that, but something was happening, changing.

My body didn't feel like it was mine, not when the heat was seeping into my muscles, flushing my skin, and pooling in my core. I imagined it was him—Hawke's blood slowly making its way through every part of my body.

He was inside me.

I felt out of control, just like the night in the Blood Forest, and when we were in the room above the tavern.

My chest suddenly ached and became heavy, but it wasn't from pain, lack of air, or coldness. No. It was like when Hawke had touched me, when he'd stripped me bare and kissed me—kissed me everywhere. I felt loose. My insides tingled, just as my skin hummed.

Razor-sharp lust pulsed straight through me, a dark desire that burned.

Hawke's nostrils flared as he inhaled, and then his chest seemed to stop moving. His features were still hazy, but the longer I stared at him, the hotter I felt.

"Poppy," he bit out.

"What?" My voice sounded full of honey.

"Stop thinking what you're thinking."

"How do you know what I'm thinking?"

His chin lowered, and his stare was a caress. "I know."

Shivering, I shifted my hips, and Hawke's arm tightened around me. "You don't know."

He didn't respond, and I wondered if he could feel the liquid fire in my veins, and the damp heat of my core.

Biting down on my lip, I tasted his blood and moaned, closing my eyes. "Hawke?"

He made a sound, and maybe he said something, but it was indecipherable.

I stretched, taking quick, shallow breaths. The coarse shirt and breeches scraped my skin and the sensitive, hardened tips of my breasts. "Hawke," I breathed.

"Don't," he said, stiffening. "Don't call me that."

"Why not?"

"Just don't."

There were a lot of things I shouldn't do or say, but everything in me was focused on the way my entire body burned and throbbed with need. My hand moved, sliding up my stomach, over the ruined, clawed shirt, to my breast. Guided only by instinct and need, I closed my fingers over the shivery flesh, molding it to my palm. An aching shudder worked its way through me.

"Poppy," Hawke ground out. "What are you doing?"

"I don't know," I whispered, back arching as I stroked myself through the thin, worn shirt. "I'm on fire."

"It's just the blood," he said thickly, and instinct told me he was watching me, and that made me all the hotter. "It'll pass, but you should...you need to stop doing that."

I didn't stop. I couldn't. My thumb rolled over the pebbled hardness, and I sucked in air. It reminded me of what Hawke had done, but he'd used more than just his hands. I wanted him to do that again. An intense, pulsing ache between my legs twisted my insides. Hips shifting, I pressed my thighs together, but that didn't help. The pressure only made it worse. "Hawke?"

"Poppy, for the love of the gods."

Heart thrumming, I opened my eyes, and I'd been right. His gaze was fixed on me—on my other hand, the one that had a mind of its own and was slipping down my stomach.

"Kiss me?"

Taut lines formed around his mouth. "You don't want that."

"I do." My fingers reached my waist, where the breeches gaped. "I need it."

"You only think that right now." His face cleared, and there was no mistaking the way his features had sharpened. "It's the blood."

"I don't care." The tips of my fingers brushed the bare skin below my navel. "Touch me? Please?"

Hawke made a low sound in the back of his throat. "You think you hate me now? If I do what you're asking, you'll want to murder me." He paused, and his lips curved upward. "Well, you'll want to murder me more than you already do. You don't have control of yourself right now."

What he was saying made sense, but it also didn't. "No."

"No?" His brows lifted, but he didn't look away from my hand.

"I don't hate you," I told him, and there was a pained twist of the heart that told me that was the truth. I should be upset by that.

He made that sound again, and when his hand closed over my wrist, I almost wept with joy. He was going to touch me.

Except he did nothing more than hold my hand in place.

"Hawke?"

"I plotted to take you from everything you knew, and I did, but that is nowhere near the worst of my crimes. I've killed people, Poppy. There is so much blood on my hands that they will never be clean. I will overthrow the Queen who cared for you, and many more will die in the process. I am not a good man." He swallowed hard. "But I am trying to be right now."

A nervous flutter filled my stomach. His words...they should infuriate me, but I...I wanted him, and thinking was...well, it was all I ever did. I didn't want to do it anymore.

"I don't want you to be good." Without even realizing it, I had lifted my other hand, fisting the front of his shirt. "I want you."

Hawke shook his head, but when I tugged on the hand he held, he bent over me. My grip on his shirt tightened when he stopped with his mouth mere inches from mine. "In a few minutes, when this storm passes, you'll return to loathing my very existence, and for good reason. You're going to hate that you begged me to kiss you, to do more. But even without my blood in you, I know you've never stopped wanting me. But when I'm deep inside you again, and I will be, you won't be able to blame the influence of blood or anything else."

I stared at him, some of the fog of lust lifting from my mind as he lifted my hand and brought it to his mouth. He pressed a kiss to the center of my palm, surprising me. It was such a…tender act, one I imagined lovers did all the time.

I pulled on my hand, and he let go. I placed it against my chest. The tingling was fading from my skin, but the ache of unspent desire was still there. Not nearly as all-consuming as minutes before, but the part of me that felt like it was starting to wake up knew he spoke the truth. What I felt for him had nothing to do with the blood.

What I felt was…it was messy and raw. I hated him, and…I didn't. I cared for him, as idiotic as that was. And I wanted him—his kiss, his touch. But I also wanted to hurt him.

We weren't lovers.

We were enemies, and we could never be anything else. I was surrounded by people who hated me.

"I never should've left," he said. "I should've known something like this could happen, but I underestimated their desire for vengeance."

"They…they wanted me dead," I said.

"They will pay for what they did."

I shifted, feeling less…floaty and more solid. I moved my arm along my leg, still surprised that there was no pain. "What will you do? Kill them?"

"I will," he said, and my eyes widened. "And I will kill anyone who thinks to follow their path."

I stared at him, not doubting that he meant what he said. Hawke couldn't question every one of his supporters or his kind. I wasn't safe here. "And me…what are you going to do with me?"

He lifted his gaze from mine. A muscle clenched in his jaw. "I already told you. I will use you to barter with the Queen to free Prince

Malik. I swear, no more harm will come to you."

I started to speak, but then I remembered the name Kieran had called him. My entire body seemed to seize up as I stared into those beautiful eyes. "Casteel?"

He froze against me.

"Kieran...Kieran said the name Casteel." My gaze swept over his striking features as Loren's words came back to me. She claimed that she'd heard that the Dark One was handsome, and his looks had gained him entrance to Goldcrest Manor, allowing him to seduce Lady Everton....

And Hawke's own words came back to me, the ones he'd spoken to me at the Red Pearl. *They have led quite a few people to make questionable life choices.*

My heart had seemed to stop, but now it sped up, racing. Things began to click into place. Inconsequential things like little comments he made here and there, bigger things like how he'd silenced me when I called out his name the night we...the night we made love. The way everyone followed his orders, how Jericho had obeyed him in the barn, seeming to not want to cross him, even though it hadn't stopped him. How Kieran and the others said his name as if it were a joke.

Because Hawke wasn't his name.

And we hadn't made love. He'd fucked me.

"Oh, my gods." Stomach roiling, I pressed my hand to my mouth. "You're him."

He said nothing.

I thought I might be sick as I dragged my hand to my chest, to tear at the already torn shirt. "That's what happened to your brother. Why you feel such sadness about him. He's the Prince you hope to use me to get back. Your name isn't Hawke Flynn. You're him! You're the Dark One."

"I prefer the name Casteel or Cas," he replied then, his tone hard and distant. "If you don't want to call me that, you can call me Prince Casteel Da'Neer, the second son of King Valyn Da'Neer, brother of Prince Malik Da'Neer."

I shuddered.

"But do *not* call me the Dark One. That is *not* my name."

Horror rolled through me. How could I now just be figuring this out? The signs had been there. I'd been so, *so* stupid. Not just once. I hadn't gotten any wiser after I learned that he was an Atlantian. I hadn't seen what was right in front of my face.

That everything truly *had* been a lie.

I reacted without thought, slamming my fist into his chest. I hit him. My palm stung from the slap I delivered upon his cheek, and he let me. He took it as I shoved at his shoulders. I screamed at him as tears blurred my vision. I hit again and again—

"Stop it." He caught me by the shoulders, pulling me to his chest and folding his arms around me, trapping mine to my sides. "Stop it, Poppy."

"Let me go," I demanded, my throat burning.

My heart clenched with the kind of anguish I was used to feeling from others. I almost reached out to him to see if it had radiated from him, or had erupted from deep inside me, but I stopped.

I will use you.

The pain…the pain was mine. He hadn't saved me because he cared for me. He hadn't promised that no more harm would come to me because he cared for me. How did I keep forgetting this? Hawke—

Hawke.

That wasn't even his name. It was Casteel.

And he had an agenda. All of our conversations, every time he had kissed me, touched me, and told me I was brave and strong, that I intrigued him and was like no one he'd ever met. He did those things not just under a false persona but also under a false name, to gain my trust. To make me lower my guard around him, all so I would walk out of Masadonia with him willingly and right into a pit of vipers who either wanted to use me because I was the Maiden, the Chosen—the Queen's favorite—or wanted me dead for the very same reasons.

I squeezed my eyes shut.

He was worse than Jericho and the others who wanted me dead. At least there were no pretenses with any of them. Everything about Haw—everything about *Casteel*, from his name to the first night at the Red Pearl, had been a lie designed to garner my trust.

He'd succeeded, but at what cost?

Rylan was dead.

Phillips and Airrick and all the guards and Huntsmen were now dead.

Vikter was dead.

My parents were dead.

He took from me everyone I cared about, either by his hand or by his orders, through separation or death. All so he could be reunited with his brother, another Prince, something that even I could understand, could sympathize with. But he also took my heart.

And made me fall in love with the Dark One.

That was who he was, even if everything else he claimed actually appeared to be true. Even if the history I'd been taught was all a lie. Even if the Ascended were vamprys who were responsible for the Craven, for what had happened to my parents and to me. Even if my brother was now one of them.

"Poppy?"

Eyes burning, I rolled onto my side. I needed space. I needed to get away from here—from him. I wasn't safe, not from anyone here, and definitely not from him.

Because the longer he kept me here with him, the harder it would be for me to remember the truth. The more I would desperately want to believe that I was special to him because I just wanted to be special to *someone*. Anyone. To be something other than a pawn. The longer I was with him, the more likely I would be to forget about all that blood that was on his hands.

And that he had already broken my heart twice now because that was happening all over again. Even after the first betrayal, I still cared for him. Even though I wanted to hate him. I needed to hate him, but I couldn't. I knew that now because I felt like I was dying another death. How could I be so stupid?

I couldn't let him do it again. I couldn't forget that.

Panic poured into me, forcing my eyes open. My wild gaze bounced around the room. "Let me go."

"Poppy," he repeated my name, placing his fingers at my neck. I tensed before realizing that he was checking my pulse. "Your heart is racing too fast."

I didn't care. I didn't care if my heart exploded out of my chest. "Let me go!" I shouted.

His hold loosened enough for me to pull away, to sit up. His arm was still at my waist. I placed my hand on the floor to leverage my weight, but my palm glanced off the dagger—

The *dagger* Mr. Tulis had stabbed me with. It was bloodstone.

Heart dropping, I looked down at the blade. Grief swelled, closing off my throat. I couldn't breathe around it, around the knowledge that I…I loved the man who'd had a hand in the deaths of so many.

Who had left me here with these people, *his* people, who wanted me dead.

Who lied to me about everything, including who he truly was.

My heart cracked wide open, pouring icy slush into my chest. I would always be cold, from here until the end.

"Poppy—"

I twisted in his arms, moving on instinct. I didn't feel the cool hilt in my hand, but I felt the blade sink into his chest. I felt his warm blood splash against my fist as the hilt of the dagger became flush with his skin.

Slowly, I lifted my gaze to his.

His amber-colored eyes widened in surprise as he held my gaze for a moment and then looked down.

To where the dagger protruded from his chest.

From his heart.

Chapter 39

Hands trembling, I let go of the dagger and fell out of his lap. I scuttled backward, unable to look away from the glaze of shock settling over his features.

"I'm sorry," I whispered, and I wasn't sure why I even apologized. I wasn't sure why my cheeks felt damp. Was it blood? His blood?

He lifted his gaze to mine. "You're crying." A thin trickle of blood seeped from the corner of his mouth.

I *was* crying. I hadn't cried since I'd watched Vikter die, but tears now streamed down my face as I rose on numb legs. I stepped to the side. I didn't know what I was doing or where I was going, but I made it to the door. It was unlocked.

"I'm sorry," I said again, shaking.

A choked, wet laugh rattled from him as he bent forward, slamming his hand down on the floor. "No," he gasped. "No, you're not."

But I was.

I turned around, blindly staggering out the door into the empty pathway that connected to another door at the end. Cold, wet air drifted in through the open wall, but I barely felt it. I had no plan. No idea how to get out of the keep. I kept walking.

Halfway through the hall, it was like a switch was flicked inside of me. All the horror and the sorrow ceased, and instinct took over.

Breathing heavily, I threw open the door and raced down the cramped stairwell, then out through an open doorway, into—

Into the snow.

For a moment, I was struck by the beauty of the thick flakes of snow slowly drifting down. A thin layer already blanketed the ground and coated the bare trees. It was so silent, and everything was clean and untouched.

A voice from inside the keep jarred me into action. Taking off across the snow-covered grass, I ran toward the woods. In the back of my mind, I knew I wasn't prepared to make an escape. The clothing I was wearing was too thin, even if it wasn't also torn nearly to shreds. I had no idea exactly where I was or where to go from here. There could be Craven in these woods. There would definitely be Descenters. There could also be wolven, who would surely be able to track my moves, but still, I ran, the thin soles of my boots slipping on the dusted ground of the forest floor. I ran because…

I stabbed him.

I stabbed him in the heart.

He would be dead by now.

I'd killed him.

A ragged sob left me as blowing snow mingled with my tears. Oh, gods, I had to do it. Everything about him, about us was a lie. *Everything.* I had to do it. I had to—

There was no warning—no sound, nothing.

An arm circled my waist, catching me mid-run. I shrieked as my feet slipped out from under me, but I didn't go down. I was hauled back and slammed into a hard, warm chest. My feet dangled nearly a foot from the ground.

Shock stole the very breath from my lungs. I knew who it was before he even spoke. It was his scent of lush spice and pine. It was the burst of rage-laced anguish and disbelief that mirrored mine, coming through my senses that I hadn't closed down. For the first time since I'd met him, his emotions overwhelmed him and, therefore, me.

This was not the Hawke I'd fallen for so quickly that held me against him.

It was not the guard who'd sworn on his life to keep me safe, who now wrapped his fist in my hair and jerked my head back and to the side.

It was not Hawke's hot breath that caressed my exposed throat. It was *him*.

Prince Casteel Da'Neer of Atlantia.

The Dark One.

"An Atlantian, unlike a wolven or an Ascended, can't be killed by a stab to the heart," he growled, yanking my head farther back. "If you wanted to kill me, you should've aimed for the head, Princess. But worse yet, you *forgot*."

"Forgot what?"

"That it was *real*."

Then he struck.

Two twin bursts of fiery pain lanced my neck, causing my entire body to jerk. The burn traveled all the way through my body, stunning me in its intensity. I couldn't move. I couldn't even scream around the pain.

His arm around my waist was like an iron vise as he drew long and hard from the wound his fangs had created. I shook, eyes peeled wide as my hands fell to his arm. My nails dug in. The burn, the deep, staggering pull against my throat as my blood flowed freely from me into him shorted out my entire system. The building scream clawed its way around the pain—

And then, within mere seconds of when he'd sunk his fangs into me, everything changed.

The intense hurting became something else, something overwhelming in a wholly different way. A new ache erupted inside me, heating my blood until it felt like every part of me was filling with molten lava.

My wide eyes were unseeing as the heat filled my chest, my stomach, and pooled in the space between my thighs. His mouth tugged on my throat once more, and this time, that pull went straight to my very core. My body jerked with a flood of pounding arousal.

He groaned, his arm tightening around me, and I felt him, hard and thick against my rear. I gripped his arm as tension coiled inside me—

Without warning, he ripped his mouth from my neck. He let go, and I stumbled forward, nearly falling. Trembling with confusion and the desire still sparking inside of me, I turned to him.

He stood several feet from me, his chest rising and falling with rapid, short breaths. His eyes were wide. Red smeared his lips.

I lifted my hand, pressing it to my neck. Wet warmth greeted my fingertips. I took a step back.

"I can't believe it," he said, and he ran his tongue along his bottom lip. His eyes closed briefly as he shuddered, letting out a rumble that reminded me of the wolven. His lashes swept up, and his pupils were so dilated only a thin strip of amber was visible. "But I should've known."

Before I could figure out what he meant or what would happen next, he was *on* me, moving so fast I couldn't track him.

His mouth crashed into mine as one hand shoved into my hair, his other arm clamped to my waist. I wasn't just kissed.

I was *devoured.* I tasted my blood on his lips, on his tongue. I tasted him.

I wasn't sure exactly when I kissed him back. Was it after a few seconds, or had I been kissing him from the moment his mouth touched mine? I didn't know. All I did know was that I was starved for him, right or wrong, I wanted him.

That's why I didn't fight him when he brought me to the ground. The contrast of the cold snow against my back and the heat of his body pressed to my front drew a gasp from me. I didn't think he heard it as it was caught up in his hungry kisses, and I realized then that he'd been holding back when he kissed me all the times before. Now, he wasn't hiding who he was.

He rocked against me as he slid his hand over my waist to my hip. We moved, straining and gasping. His teeth caught my bottom lip. A brief sting registered, and he shuddered, groaning as the metallic taste renewed.

Breaking the kiss, he lifted up enough to look down at me. "Tell me you want this." His hips were still churning against mine. "Tell me you need more."

"More," I whispered before I could even think about what we were doing, what we'd done—who he was.

"Thank fuck," he grunted, and then he reached between us, his finger snagging the front of my breeches. He pulled on them hard enough to lift my hips. Buttons popped free, flinging into the nearby snow.

"Goodness," I murmured.

He barked out a short, harsh laugh as he shoved my pants down until one leg was completely free, and the breeches snagged on the other ankle. "You know this shirt was beyond repair, right?"

"Wha—?"

The sound of cloth tearing was my only explanation. I dipped my chin, seeing my breasts. He was staring too, his hand tearing at his own breeches as his eyes tracked the streaks of blood dried along my stomach, moving over the hardening tips of my breasts.

"I will kill them," he whispered. "I will fucking kill them all."

I didn't think he was talking about the old scars.

Then I wasn't thinking at all.

He kissed me as he settled over me, between my legs, and then things…spun. There was no slow seduction this time, no long and drawn-out caresses and kisses. There was a pinch of discomfort, but it quickly gave way to the aching, pulsing pleasure, and there was no room in my body or mind or between us for there to be anything other than what we felt. It was just him and me, the taste of my blood and his on our lips, and this *need* I didn't quite understand.

Around us, the snow fell heavier through the trees, soaking his back and my hair as we clutched and grasped at one another. There were only the sounds of our wet kisses, our bodies coming together and parting, and our moans.

One long, dragging kiss ensued, and then his mouth moved from mine to my chin and then lower, his lips and those sharp teeth gliding over my throat. His actions elicited a shiver that curled its way down my spine as he stilled above me. Was he…was he going to bite me again? Instead of fear, there was a rush of wicked heat. The pain from his fangs had been brief, and what had come afterward…

I squeezed his shoulders, too lost to even wonder if I shouldn't want him to, too far gone to think about the consequences if he did.

I felt his tongue against my skin, circling and laving over the sensitive mark he'd left behind. Then he lifted his head. I saw his eyes long enough to see that his pupils had constricted before his lashes swept down, and his mouth was on mine once more.

And then he was moving again.

His hips retreating and then pushing back in, rolling and grinding as his fingers played with my breast. He moved slowly now, so lazily that I felt as if I were being strung out. I shuddered under him, slipping my hand into his snow-damp hair.

The tension was building again, coiling until I couldn't take his slow, measured movements any longer. His teasing grinds and rolls. I lifted my hips, trying to urge him to move faster, go deeper, but he held back until I cried out and pulled at his hair.

He half-laughed, half-growled as he lifted his head. "I know what you want, but…"

Heart racing out of control, I squirmed under his weight. "But what?"

"I want you to say my name."

"What?"

His hips continued moving in maddeningly slow circles. "I want you to say my real name."

My lips parted on a sharp inhale.

He stilled once more, his eyes luminous. "That's all I ask."

All he asked? It was a lot.

"It's acknowledgement," he said, his thumb swirling and tugging. "It's you admitting you are fully aware of who is inside you, who you want so badly, even though you know you shouldn't. Even though you want nothing more than to *not* feel what you do. I want to hear you say my real name."

"You're a bastard," I whispered.

One side of his lips curled. "Some call me that, yes, but that's not the name I'm waiting to hear, Princess."

I wanted to deny him. Gods, did I ever.

"How bad do you want it, *Poppy*?" he asked.

My grip tightened on his hair as I yanked his head down. There was a flash of surprise in those glowing eyes. "Bad," I snarled. "Your *Highness*."

His mouth opened, but I lifted my legs, curling them around his hips. Taking advantage of his surprise and tapping into my own anger, I rolled him onto his back, fully intending to leave him there, but I hadn't foreseen what the move would do when I rocked back—

I sank down on his length, my body shockingly flush with his. My shout ended in his groan as I planted my hands on his chest. *Gods.* The fullness was almost too much.

"Oh," I whispered, taking ragged breaths.

His chest was moving just as unevenly under my hands. "You know what?"

"What?" My toes curled inside my boots.

"I don't need you to say my name," he said, his eyes half closed. "I just need you to do that again, but if you don't start moving, you might actually kill me.

A startled giggle burst from me. "I...I don't know what to do."

Something about his features softened even though stark need shone through the thin slits of his eyes. "Just move." His hands went to my hips. He lifted me up a few inches and brought me back down. A deep sound radiated from him. "Like that. You can't do anything wrong. How have you not learned that yet?"

I wasn't sure what he meant by that, but I mirrored his movement, moving up and down as snow fell across his shirt. My palm slipped, angling me forward. A spot deep in me was touched, sending out bolts of intense pleasure in waves. "Like that?" I breathed.

His hands tightened on my hips. "Just like that."

With each move of my hips, that spot was touched, and more streaks of bliss shot through me. Before I knew it, I was moving faster above him, and I knew he was watching me as my eyes drifted closed, and my head fell back. I knew his gaze was fastened on my breasts and where we were joined, and that knowledge was too much.

The tension whipped out, shattering me. I cried out as I shuddered, body spasming as intense shards of ecstasy sliced through me.

He moved then, rolling me back under him and thrusting his hips against mine. His mouth claimed mine as his body did the same, pounding against me, into me until the pleasure seemed to crest once more, the fierceness shocking as he seemed to lose all sense of control. His large body moved over mine, in me until he pressed hard against me, his shout swallowed in our kisses as he shuddered.

I didn't know how long we lay there in the falling snow, our hearts and breaths slow to steady, my grip still tight on his shoulders, his forehead pressed to mine. After some time, I became aware of his thumb moving along my waist in idle up and down sweeps.

The heat of passion cooled and, in its wake, was confusion. Not regret. Not shame. Just...confusion. "I don't...I don't understand," I whispered, my voice hoarse.

"Don't understand what?" He shifted above me.

"Any of this. Like how did this even happen?" I winced as he started to ease out.

He halted, brows furrowed. "Are you okay?"

"Yeah. Yes." I closed my eyes as he remained still for several moments before moving to my side.

"Are you sure?" he asked.

I nodded.

"Look at me and tell me you're not hurt."

My eyes opened, and I looked at him. He was raised on one elbow, seemingly unaware of the snow falling around us. "I'm fine."

"You winced. I saw you."

I shook my head in disbelief. My gift was utterly useless since I was feeling too much to concentrate, so I couldn't even...cheat. "That's what I don't understand. Unless I completely imagined the last couple of days."

"No, you didn't imagine anything." His gaze roamed over my face as I blinked snow off my lashes. "Do you wish that this, right here, hadn't happened?"

I could lie, but I didn't. "No. Do...do you?"

"No, Poppy. I hate that you even have to ask that." He looked away, jaw flexing. "When we first met, it was like...I don't know. I was drawn to you. I could've taken you then, Poppy. I could've prevented a lot of what has happened, but I...I lost sight of a lot of things. Each time I was near you, I couldn't help but feel as if I knew you. I think I know why it's been like that."

He said this like it was the answer to how we had gone from me stabbing him in the heart to tearing off each other's clothes. I shivered in the cold, damp air as I shook my head again.

Being drawn to one another explained none of that.

"You're cold." Rolling to his feet in one smooth movement, he fastened his pants with the one lone button that remained and then extended his hand. "We need to get out of this weather."

We did. Well, I did. He probably didn't, considering he could be stabbed in the chest and be all right minutes later.

I placed my hand in his and stated what I felt he needed to be reminded of. "I tried to kill you."

"I know." He pulled me up onto my feet. "I can't really blame you."

I stared, dumbfounded as he swooped down, tugging up my breeches as he rose. "You don't?"

"No. I lied to you. I betrayed you and played a role in the deaths of people you love," he said, listing the reasons as if it were a shopping list. "I'm surprised that was the first time you tried."

I continued to stare.

"And I doubt it will be the last time you try." The corners of his lips turned down as he tried to secure the pants but discovered that the buttons were somewhere on the snowy ground. "Dammit," he muttered, reaching for my shirt. It was torn straight down the middle. He gripped the sides and pulled them together as if that would repair the material. He cursed again, giving up. He reached up, pulling his other shirt off over his head. "Here."

I stood there, wondering if I was suffering from blood loss or post-orgasmic bliss. Maybe a combination of both because I couldn't believe this. "You're...not mad?"

He lifted a brow as his gaze met mine. "Are you not still mad at me?"

I didn't have to think about that. "Yes. I'm still angry."

"And I'm still angry that you stabbed me in the chest." He stepped toward me. "Lift your arms."

I lifted my arms.

"You didn't miss my heart, by the way. You got it pretty good," he continued, pulling his shirt on over my head, tugging it down over my stiff arms. "That's why it took a minute to catch up to you."

"It took more than a minute." My voice was muffled as my head got caught for a moment in his shirt before popping free.

One side of his lip kicked up as he tugged the other sleeve down. "It took a *couple* of minutes."

I looked down at the shirt and saw the jagged tear on the front. It didn't line up with my chest, but with my stomach. My gaze went to his bare chest. There was a wound, the skin pink and torn around it. Stomach churning, I gave a shake of my head. "Will it heal?"

"It will be fine in a few hours. Probably sooner."

"Atlantian blood," I whispered and swallowed thickly.

"My body will immediately start to repair itself from any non-fatal wounds," he explained. "And I fed. That helped."

I fed.

My hand fluttered to my throat, to the two tiny wounds that felt as if they'd already started to heal. A faint spike of pleasure pulsed through me. I jerked my hand away. "Will anything happen to me from...from you feeding?"

"No, Poppy. I didn't take enough, and you didn't take enough of mine earlier. You'll probably be a little tired later, but that's all."

I went back to staring at his wound. "Does it hurt?"

"Barely," he muttered.

I didn't believe him. Placing my palm against his chest, a few inches from the wound, I tried to tap into my gift. I felt it stretching, so I opened up my senses. He became very still. The anguish I always felt was there, heightened and stronger than before, even though he'd gotten control of it at some point. It no longer overwhelmed him, but there was a different kind of pain underneath it. It was hot. Physical pain. The wound might heal, but it hurt, and it wasn't minor.

I did what I could without thinking once more. I took his pain, both of them, and I didn't think of the beaches of the Stroud Sea this time. I thought about how I felt when he was in me, moving inside me.

And all of that did nothing but confuse me even more.

He placed his hand over mine, and when I glanced up, I saw that the lines of white tension around his mouth had vanished. There was wonder in his eyes. "I should've known then." He brought my hand stained with our blood to his mouth and pressed a kiss to my knuckles.

"Known what?" I asked, trying to ignore how the act tugged at my heart.

"Known why they wanted you so badly that they made you the Maiden."

I wasn't exactly following what he was saying, but that could've had more to do with my fog-filled brain than anything.

"Come." He tugged on my hand and started walking.

"Where are we going?"

"Now? We're going back inside so we can get cleaned up and..." He trailed off with a sigh as he noticed that I was clutching the side of my pants to keep them up. Before I even knew what he was about, he picked me up and held me in his arms, against his chest, like I weighed nothing more than a soaked kitten. "And, apparently, to find you some new pants."

"These were my only pair."

"I'll get you new ones." He strode forward. "I'm sure there is some small child around here who would be willing to part with their breeches for a few coins."

My brows puckered.

His mouth was soft, and a faint grin played across his lips as he stepped around a fallen limb.

"And after that?" I asked.

"I'm taking you home."

My heart about stopped for the hundredth time that day. "Home?" I hadn't expected him to say that. "Back to Masadonia? Or to Carsodonia?"

"Neither." He looked down, his eyes a wealth of secrets. He smiled then, a wide one that stole my breath. He did indeed have two dimples, one in each cheek, and I saw then why there'd only been half-grins before. I saw the two fine points of his canines. "I'm taking you to Atlantia."

Chapter 40

I was deposited in the same room where he'd given me his blood, and then I'd stabbed him. *Him*. I stared at the damp mark on the wood floor, where the blood had been cleaned up.

Him.

I needed to stop referring to him that way. He had a name. A real one. I may never say it when and how he wanted, but I needed to stop thinking about him as if he were Hawke or somehow nameless.

His name was Casteel. Cas.

This was where he had saved my life and the chamber where I then attempted to take his.

He succeeded.

I failed.

My gaze flicked to where Kieran stood by the door, eyeing me as if he expected me to make a rush for the window and throw myself out of it. He arched a brow at me, and I looked away.

He had left, to do the gods only knew what, leaving Kieran as a sentry. Well, I did know he'd done something. After he'd left, a dozen or so servants filled the brass tub in the bathing chamber with steaming hot water, and another placed a fresh pair of black breeches and a tunic on the bed.

A part of me was surprised that he'd brought me back here and not to the cells. I wasn't sure what that meant or if it should matter if it did mean something.

My thoughts still reeling from everything, I didn't know anything at the moment, and he hadn't answered any of the questions I'd asked on the way back. Say, for example, was Atlantia still an actual place?

Because as far as I knew, it had been all but leveled during the war.

Then again, everything I thought I knew was turning out to be false.

I rubbed my hand over my cheek as I glanced at Kieran. "Does Atlantia still exist?"

If my random question caught him off guard, he didn't show it. "Why would it not?"

"I was told that the Wastelands—"

"Were once Atlantia?" he cut in. "They were once an outpost, but that land was never the entirety of the kingdom."

"So, Atlantia still exists?"

"Have you ever been beyond the Skotos Mountains?"

The corners of my lips turned down. "Do you always answer a question with a question?"

"Do I?"

I shot him a droll look.

A faint grin appeared and then slipped away.

"No one has been beyond the Skotos Mountains," I told him. "It's just more mountains."

"Mountains that stretch so far and wide that the very tops are lost to the deepest mist? That part is true, but the mountains don't go on forever, Penellaphe, and the mist there may not contain Craven, but it's also not natural," he said, and a shiver danced over my shoulders. "The mist is a protection."

"How?"

"It's so thick, you just don't see anything. You think you see everything." A strange light filled his pale blue eyes. "The mist that blankets the Skotos Mountains is there so anyone who dares pass through will want to turn back."

"And those who don't turn back?"

"They don't make it through."

"Because...because Atlantia is beyond the Skotos?" I asked.

"What do you think?"

What I thought was that talking to Kieran was an exercise in patience and energy, two things I was running low on.

"Are you going to bathe yourself?" he asked.

I wanted to. My skin was not just dirty, it was also chilled, and I was still wearing his *bloodied shirt*.

But I also wanted to be difficult because I was so freaking confused by everything, and as *he* had warned, I was tired. "What if I don't?"

"That's your choice," he replied. "But you smell of Casteel."

I jolted at the sound of his name. His *real* name. "I am wearing his shirt."

"That's not the kind of smell I'm talking about."

It took a minute for me to get what he was referencing. When I did, my mouth dropped open. "You can smell...?"

Kieran's smile could only be described as wolfish.

"I'm going to bathe."

He chuckled.

"Shut up," I snapped, gathering up the new clothing and hurrying into the bathing room. I closed the door behind me, annoyed when I saw there was no lock.

Cursing under my breath, I looked around and found several hooks on the wall. I hung the tunic and breeches there. I quickly stripped and stepped into the bath, ignoring the twinge of pain in a very private area as I sank into the lavender-scented water. I didn't allow myself to think about anything as I got down to scrubbing off my blood and...and his. My stomach turned over as I used the bar of soap to wash my hair. When suds ran down the back of my neck, I dipped under the water and held myself there.

I stayed until my lungs and throat burned, and white spots sparked behind my closed eyes. Only then did I break the surface, gasping for air.

What was I going to do about *him*? About everything?

A strangled, hoarse-sounding laugh escaped me. I didn't know where to even begin to start figuring out this mess. I'd just learned that the kingdom of Atlantia still existed, and that seemed like the least crazy thing to have discovered. Gods, I still didn't even understand how I'd gone from learning who he truly was, stabbing him in the heart, to then willingly falling into his arms.

Squeezing my eyes shut, I dragged my hands down my face. I couldn't blame the bite, even though it had some kind of arousing effect, just like his blood had. And who, by the way, would've ever thought that would feel good?

But damn, it had...

I shivered as a tight curling motion bloomed low in my stomach.

That was the last thing I needed to think about right now if I had any hope of figuring out what I needed to do.

And I needed to come up with some kind of plan and quickly because even though he didn't seem to hold my attempt to kill him against me, I wasn't safe here. I wouldn't be safe anywhere with his people. They hated me, and if half of what he and Kieran claimed about the Ascended and what they'd done was true, I couldn't blame them, even though I'd done nothing to them. It was what I represented.

Still, it was too much to believe that the Atlantians were the innocent party, and the Ascended were the violent tyranny that had somehow managed to turn an entire kingdom away from the truth.

But...

But I'd never seen any of the third and fourth sons and daughters who were given to the gods during the Rite.

I could never understand how those like Duke Teerman and Lord Mazeen had received a Blessing from the gods.

But never once had I seen an Ascended lift a single finger to fight the Craven, the one thing the people of Solis feared more than death itself.

The one thing they'd do anything and *believe* anything to remain safe from.

He had claimed that the Royals used the Craven to keep the people in check, and if that were true, it worked. They gave up their own children to keep the beasts at bay.

It had to be true.

Worse yet, others must be involved in this. The Priests and Priestesses. Close friends of the Court, who hadn't Ascended. My parents?

Gods, I couldn't lie to myself any longer.

What had happened with him was proof enough. His blood had healed me, not turned me. His kisses had never cursed me. And so far, neither had his bite.

The Ascended were vamprys—they were the curse that had plagued this land. They used fear to control the masses, and they were the evil hidden in plain sight, feeding off those they had sworn to the gods to protect.

And my brother was now one of them.

Pulling my knees to my chest, I wrapped my arms around my legs. I closed my eyes against the burn of tears, resting my cheek against my knee. He couldn't be like the Duke. The Duchess wasn't too bad. Neither was the Queen, but—

But if they were feeding on children, almost draining innocent people and creating Craven, they were no better than the Duke.

I pressed my lips together, fighting back tears that wanted to break free. I'd cried enough today, but Ian... Gods, Ian couldn't be like them. He was kind and gentle. I just couldn't believe that he would do those things. I couldn't.

And then there was me. If it was all a lie, then I would never be given to the gods. What had they planned for me? Why did they make me the Chosen and link all these Ascensions to me? Was it my abilities? I thought about what he had said after I'd taken his pain. He knew something.

Something he needed to tell me.

I wasn't safe here, and I surely wasn't safe among the Ascended. If I did manage to escape, how could I go back to them, knowing what I knew now? How could I stay and allow him to take me to Atlantia when I would represent a kingdom who had slaughtered untold numbers of their people, who had enslaved their Prince to use him to make more vamprys?

How could I stay with him?

No matter what I felt for him, I could never trust him, and what I felt for him was also something I could no longer pretend didn't exist. I loved him.

I was *in* love with him.

And even if by some small chance I'd been able to move past the fact that he had come to Masadonia with the intention of taking and using me as a bargaining tool, I could never get over the blood that had been spilled because of him. I could never forget that Rylan and Vikter, Loren and Dafina, and so many others were dead, either by his hand, by his command, or by what he represented. I could never trust what he claimed when it came to us.

What had he claimed about us, though?

He had led me to believe that he had feelings for me. That I was anything but someone he needed to protect as Hawke, and needed to use for his own means as a Prince of Atlantia. He'd been intrigued from the start because I wasn't who he expected me to be, which apparently, was an immoral, spoiled supporter of the Ascended. He'd been kind and interested because he needed to discover all he could about me, and maybe because he was drawn to me. But what did that truly mean?

What happened in the woods may have proven that he was attracted to me, and that wasn't a farce, but lust was not love, it was not loyalty, and it was not long lasting.

Neither as Hawke nor as Casteel had he claimed anything regarding us.

The reality was jarring, and it hurt. It sliced deep because he'd made me feel *warm*, but it was reality, and it had to be dealt with.

I mulled over the options in my head. Escape. Find my brother because I had to know if he was the same and then…what? Disappear? But first, I needed to figure out how to escape.

The wolven could track me, and he…

Escaping him would be nearly impossible.

But I had to try, and there had to be a way. Maybe when my head didn't feel as if it were full of cobwebs, I would know what to do. Weary, I let my thoughts drift. I must've dozed off somehow, still curled up against the tub, because the next thing I heard was my name being called.

"Penellaphe."

Jerking my head up, I blinked rapidly as Kieran's face came into view. What the…?

"Good." He was kneeling on the other side of the tub—the tub that I was completely naked in! "I was worried you were dead."

"What?" I threw a hand over my chest and pressed my legs together as much as I possibly could. I didn't even want to think about what he could see beneath the line of water. "What are you doing in here?"

"I called out your name, and you didn't answer," he replied, tone as flat as a board. "You've been in here for a while. I thought I should make sure you were alive."

"Of course, I'm alive. Why wouldn't I be?"

One eyebrow rose. "You are surrounded by people who tried to murder you, in case you've forgotten."

"I haven't forgotten. I doubt any of them are hiding in the

bathwater!"

"One can never be too sure." He made no attempt to stand and leave.

I stared at him. "You shouldn't be in here, and I shouldn't have to explain that."

"You have nothing to fear from me."

"Why? Because of *him*?" I spat.

"Because of Cas?" he said, and I blinked, hearing the nickname for the first time from someone other than *him*. "He would be annoyed to find me in here."

I wasn't sure if I should feel good to hear that or more annoyed.

A ghost of a smile appeared. "And then he'd be…intrigued."

My mouth opened, but my mind took that and leapt with it. I had nothing to say. Absolutely nothing, but I thought about what I had read about the wolven and the Atlantians. There was a bond between some of them, and while not much was known about what that bond entailed, I was confident that a Prince was of the class that wolven would be bonded to. I wanted to ask, but considering I was in a tub and naked, now wasn't the time.

Kieran's gaze dropped, moving down my arms to the curve of my stomach and thigh. "Among my people, scars are revered. They are never hidden."

The only scar he could see was the one along the side of my waist. At least, I hoped. "Among my people, it's not polite to stare at a naked woman in a bathtub."

"Your people sound incredibly boring."

"Get out!" I shrieked.

Chuckling, Kieran rose with nearly the same grace and fluidity that he moved with. "The Prince wouldn't want you sitting in cold, dirty water. You should probably finish up your bath."

My nails were digging into the skin of my legs. "I don't care what he wants."

"You should," he replied, and I gritted my teeth. "Because he wants you even though he knows better, even though he knows it will end in yet another tragedy."

Chapter 41

After quickly drying off and changing into clean, dry clothing, I did everything in my power to forget that the brief conversation in the bathing chamber with Kieran had happened.

The breeches were a little tight, causing me to wonder if they *had* belonged to a child, but they were clean and soft, and I wasn't complaining. The long-sleeve tunic was made of heavy wool and reached my knees. The slits in the sides ended at the hips and would've made for easy access to my dagger.

But I hadn't seen my dagger since the stables, and based on what I'd done with the last one...

I winced.

I doubted I'd have access to one anytime soon, which made escaping difficult. I needed a weapon, any weapon, but what I wanted was the dagger Vikter had given me.

I added that to my plan that wasn't quite a plan. At least, not yet.

Kieran left shortly after I came out of the bathing chamber, locking the door behind him. I doubted he went very far. Was probably standing outside the door.

I started to braid my still-drying hair, but remembered the mark on my neck and let the strands hang loose. I then roamed the room aimlessly. There was no avenue of escape. I couldn't even fit through the window. Was I going to be kept here until whenever time *he* deemed fit for me to leave?

Sighing, I plopped down on the bed. It was soft, so much thicker than the straw mat in the cell. I lay down, facing the door as I curled on my side.

What would happen when he returned for me? Would his seeming acceptance of my attempted murder change? Everything he'd said about the Ascended may very well be true, but he was still the Dark One, and he was just as dangerous. He'd said so himself.

There was a lot of blood on his hands.

With how thinly my nerves were stretched, I didn't think I would doze off again, but that was exactly what happened. It had to be...it had to be the still-tender bite and its effect. Because one moment, I was alert, staring at the closed door. The next, I was out, slipping into a deep sleep where I did not dream. I wasn't sure what woke me at first. It wasn't my name being called. It wasn't words at all.

It was a faint touch on my cheek and then on the side of my neck, just above the bite. My eyes fluttered open. The room was dim except for the sconces and the single oil lamp on the nightstand, but I still saw him.

He sat on the edge of the bed, and there was a dipping motion in my chest at the first sight of him, like always happened. I imagined it always would, no matter what I knew about him.

At least, he'd found a shirt.

And had bathed somewhere, because his hair was damp, curling against his temples and ears.

Dressed in all-black, he cut an imposing, striking figure, and I no longer saw his attire that of the uniform of a guard. I saw the Dark One. I glanced down at the sleeve of the dark tunic I wore and then to my curled leg, where I expected to see the black breeches. Instead, I saw a threaded quilt draped over my legs. Unsettled, I lifted my gaze to his.

He didn't say anything. Neither did I. Not for a long time. His fingers remained on my throat, above the mark. After what felt like an eternity, he removed his hand and asked, "How are you feeling?"

I laughed. I couldn't help it. A giggle burst free.

His head cocked to the side as a half-grin appeared. "What?"

"I can't believe you're asking me if I'm okay when I stabbed you in the heart."

"Do you think you should be asking me that question?"

Yes? No? Maybe?

The grin deepened. "I'm relieved to hear that you care. I'm perfectly fine."

"I don't care," I muttered, sitting up.

"Lies," he murmured.

He was right, of course, because without realizing what I was doing, I reached out with my senses to see if he was in physical pain. He wasn't. What I'd done earlier had worn off. I knew this because I felt the anguish that always brewed just below the surface. There was something else there, though. I'd felt it before. Confusion or conflict.

"You didn't answer my question."

"I'm fine." Pulling my gift back, I looked down at the quilt. It was a faint yellow and old. I wondered who it belonged to.

"Kieran said you dozed off in the bath."

"Did he tell you that he came into the bathing chamber?"

"Yes."

Surprised, my gaze shot to his.

"I trust Kieran," he said. "You've been asleep for several hours."

"Is that not normal?"

"It's not abnormal. I guess I'm..." He frowned as if something had just occurred to him. "I guess I'm feeling guilty for biting you."

"You guess?" My brows lifted.

He appeared to mull that over and then nodded. "I believe so."

"You should feel guilt!"

"Even though you stabbed me and left me to die?"

I snapped my mouth shut as my stomach churned with nausea. "You didn't die. Obviously."

"Obviously." There was a teasing glint to his eyes. "I was barely winded."

"Congratulations," I muttered, rolling my eyes.

He chuckled.

Annoyed, I shoved the quilt off my legs and scooted to the other side of the bed. "Why are you here? To take me back to the cell?"

"I should. If anyone other than Kieran knew you had stabbed me, I would be expected to."

I stood. "Then why don't you?"

"I don't want to."

I stared at him, hands opening and closing at my sides while he remained seated on the bed. "So, what now? How is this going to work, Your *Highness*?" Satisfaction surged when I caught the way his jaw tightened. "You'll keep me locked up in a room until you're ready for us to leave?"

"Do you not like this room?"

"It's far better than a dirty cell, but it's still a prison. A cage, no matter how nice the accommodations are."

He was quiet for a moment. "You would know, wouldn't you? After all, you've been imprisoned since you were a child. Caged and veiled."

There was no denying that. I'd been kept in both comfortable cages and bare ones. The reasons were different, but the end result was the same. Folding my arms, I looked at the small window, to the night sky beyond.

"I came here to escort you to dinner."

"Escort me to dinner?" Disbelief widened my eyes as I focused on him once more.

"I feel like there's an echo in this room, but yes, I imagine you're hungry," he said, and my stomach took that exact moment to confirm that was true. "And we'll discuss what will happen next when we have some food in our stomachs."

"No."

His brows lifted. "No?"

I knew I was being difficult over something not worth it. Just like I had been with Kieran. But I was not going to be at anyone's beck and call. I wasn't the Maiden any longer. And things were not okay between us just because we had a temporary loss of rationale in the woods. He'd betrayed me. I'd tried to kill him. He still planned to use me to free his brother. We were enemies, no matter the truths.

No matter that I loved him.

"You have to be hungry," he said, pausing as he stretched out on his side, supporting his cheek with his fist. He couldn't look more comfortable if he tried.

Or more alluring.

I shook my head. "I am hungry."

He sighed. "Then what's the problem, Princess?"

"I don't want to eat with you," I told him. "That's the problem."

"Well, it's a problem you're going to have to get over because it's your only option."

"See, that's where you're wrong. I have options." I turned from him. "I'd rather starve than eat with you, *Your Highness*—" I squeaked, almost coming out of my skin when he suddenly stood in front of me, moving so fast and so quietly I nearly missed it. "Gods," I muttered, pressing my hand to my pounding heart.

"That's where you're wrong, Princess." His eyes glowed a fiery amber as he glared down at me. "You don't have options when it comes to your own well-being and your own foolish stubbornness."

"Excuse me?"

"I won't let you weaken or starve yourself because you're mad. And I do get it. I get why you're upset. Why you want to fight me on everything, every step of the way." He took that step toward me, and my spine locked up as I refused to back away. His eyes burned brighter. "I want you to, Princess. I enjoy it."

"You're twisted."

"Never said I wasn't," he retorted. "So, fight me. Argue with me. See if you can actually injure me next time. I dare you."

My eyes widened as I lowered my arms. "You're…there's something wrong with you."

"That may be true, but what is also true, is the fact that I will not let you put yourself in unnecessary danger."

"Maybe you've forgotten, but I can handle myself," I shot back.

"I haven't forgotten. I won't ever prevent you from lifting a sword to protect your life or those you care about," he said. "But I won't let you shove that sword through your own heart to prove a point."

Part of me was awed—still shocked that he wouldn't stop me from fighting. The other half was infuriated that he thought he could control any part of me. As a whole, I let out a small shriek of frustration. "Of course, you won't! What good am I to you dead? I imagine you still plan to use me to free your brother."

A muscle along his jaw flexed. "You are nothing to me if you're dead."

I sucked in a sharp, stinging breath that scorched my lungs. What in the world had I expected him to say? That he wouldn't want me dead because he cared? I knew better.

I *had* to know better.

"Come. The food will grow cold." Without waiting for my response, he grabbed my hand. He started walking, but I dug in my heels. His head cranked toward me, the grip on my hand firm but not painful. "Don't fight me on this, Poppy. You need to eat, and my people need to see that you have my protection if you have any hope of not finding yourself spending your days locked in a room."

Every part of my being demanded that I do just what he claimed he enjoyed. It wanted me to fight him every step of the way, but common sense prevailed. Barely. I was hungry, and I needed to be at my strongest if I planned to escape. Plus, I needed his people to see that I was off-limits. If eating dinner with him like we were the closest friends would provide that, then I needed to deal.

So that was what I did.

I let him lead me out of the room, and I wasn't even surprised when I found Kieran waiting for us. Based on the hint of amusement in his features, he must have heard at least half of our argument.

Kieran opened his mouth.

"Don't test me," *he* warned.

Chuckling under his breath, Kieran said nothing as he fell into step behind us. We took the same stairs we'd sped down hours earlier, and I tried not to think about my mad dash in the woods. What had happened when he caught me.

But a heatwave hit my veins nonetheless.

He glanced down at me, a questioning look in his gaze that I ignored while praying he couldn't sense where my thoughts had gone.

As soon as we entered the common area, Kieran slowed his pace so he walked directly behind me. I knew that was no unconscious act. Descenters lined the walls, their faces pale as they whispered to one another, their eyes following us. I recognized some of them who'd stood in audience outside the cell. I saw Magda. There was no pity in her eyes now. Just...speculation.

I lifted my chin and straightened my spine. The Ascended might very well be evil incarnate, and an untold number of people in Solis may be complicit, but what they did to me proved that they were no better.

We rounded the corner, and my gaze lifted—

"Oh, my gods," I whispered, I stumbled back as my free hand flew to my mouth. I bumped into Kieran.

His hand landed on my shoulder, steadying me as I stared at the walls of the hall. I couldn't move. I could barely breathe as horror choked me.

Now I understood the pale faces in the common area. Bodies lined the walls, arms outstretched, and spikes of bloodstone nailed through their hands. Some had received a reddish-brown stake through the center of their chests, others through the head. Some of them were mortal. Some were Atlantian. A half a dozen of them on either side. I saw Rolf and the man I had rendered unconscious, and I saw…

I saw Mr. Tulis.

My knees weakened as I stared up at him. He was dead, face a ghastly gray color. He was mortal, but a stake protruded from his still chest nonetheless.

All he'd wanted was to save his last child. He'd been given an opportunity to do so. He'd escaped, and now…now he was here.

Not all of them were dead.

One still breathed.

Jericho.

I locked down my senses before I could reach out and see what kind of pain he was in. His shaggy head hung as his chest rose in ragged, uneven breaths. Bloodstone pierced his palm and his forearm above his stump, but the final fatal spike was thrust through his throat. Crimson colored the front of his bare chest, his pants, and pooled on the floor below him.

"I promised you they'd pay for what they did." *He* didn't sound or look smug. He didn't sound proud. "And now the others know what will happen if they disobey me and seek to harm you."

Bile crept up my throat. "He's…he's still alive," I whispered, staring up at the wolven.

"Only until I am ready to end his life," he commented, dropping my hand. He strode forward without another look back. Two men opened the large wooden doors to the Great Room, and he entered, stalking toward the center table where several covered dishes waited.

I thought I might be sick.

Kieran's hand squeezed my shoulder. "They deserved no less."

Had they?

Even Mr. Tulis, who'd most likely delivered the fatal blow to me.

"Go." He urged with his hand. Somehow, I got my feet moving as I walked past the bodies pinned to the wall like butterflies.

In a daze, I didn't realize that I was seated to the right of him at the table, typically a place of honor. Kieran took the chair next to me. Numbly, I sat there as servants unveiled the platters of food while the rest of his entourage followed suit, seating themselves at the table. I recognized Delano and Naill, oddly relieved to see that they were okay. They had defended me, and I didn't want to think about the reasons behind it.

Laid out before us was a feast. Stewed beef. Roasted duck. Cold meats and cheese. Baked potatoes. All of it smelled wonderful.

But my stomach churned as I sat there, unable to move. Kieran offered me some of the beef, and I must've agreed because it ended up on my plate. Then came the duck and potato. *He* was the one who broke off a hunk of cheese and placed it on my plate as he reached for his glass, seeming to remember that it was one of my weaknesses.

I stared down at my plate. I didn't see the food. I saw the bodies outside the room as conversation was slow to start but soon picked up and became a steady hum. Glasses and plates clinked. Laughter sounded.

And there were bodies nailed to the walls outside the Great Room.

"Poppy."

Blinking, I looked up at him. His golden eyes had cooled, but his jaw was hard enough to cut glass.

"Eat," he ordered in a low voice.

I reached for a fork, picking it up and spearing a piece of meat. I took a bite, chewing slowly. It tasted as good as it smelled, but it settled too heavily in my stomach. I scooped up some of the potatoes.

A few moments passed, and he said, "You don't agree with what I did to them?"

I looked over at him, unsure of how to even answer the question—if it was even a question at all.

He sat back, glass in hand. "Or are you so shocked, you're actually speechless?"

Swallowing the last bit of food, I slowly placed the fork on the table. "I wasn't expecting that."

"Can't imagine you were." He smirked as he lifted the glass to his lips.

"How…how long will you leave them there?"

"Until I feel like it."

My chest twisted. "And Jericho?"

"Until I know for sure no one will dare to lift a hand against you again."

Becoming aware that several of the men around us had stopped talking and were listening, I chose my next words carefully. "I don't know your people very well, but I would think that they have learned a lesson."

He took a drink. "What I did disturbs you."

I knew that wasn't a question. My gaze shifted back to my plate. Did it disturb me? Yes. I think it would unsettle most. Or at least, I hoped so. The blatancy of the kind of violence he was capable of was shocking if not entirely surprising, further separating him from the guard I knew as Hawke.

"Eat," he said again, lowering his cup. "I know you need to eat more than that."

I bit back the urge to tell him I was capable of determining how much food I needed to consume. Instead, I opened my senses to him. The anguish there was different, tasting...tangy and almost bitter. The urge to reach out to him hit hard, causing me to curl one hand in my lap. Had what happened between us caused this? Was it what he'd done to his own supporters? It could possibly be both. I reached for my drink, closing my eyes, and when I reopened them, I found him watching me through thick lashes.

I could tell him that it did bother me. I could say nothing at all. I imagined that perhaps he expected one of those two things from me. But I told him the truth. Not because I felt like I owed it to him, but because I owed it to myself.

"When I saw them, it horrified me. That was shocking, especially Mr. Tulis. What you did was surprising, but what disturbs me the most is that I—" I drew in a deep breath. "I don't feel all that bad."

Those heavy lids lifted, and his stare was piercing.

"Those people laughed when Jericho talked about cutting my hand off. Cheered when I bled and screamed and offered other options for pieces for Jericho to carve and keep," I said, and the silence around us was almost unbearable. "I'd never even met most of them before, and they were happy to see me ripped apart. So, I don't feel sympathy."

"They don't deserve it," he stated quietly.

"Agreed," Kieran murmured.

I lifted my chin. "But they're still mortal—or Atlantian. They still deserve dignity in death."

"They didn't believe you deserved any dignity," he stated.

"They were wrong, but that doesn't make this right," I said.

His gaze drifted over my face. The muscle had stopped ticking. "Eat," he repeated.

"You're obsessed with ensuring that I eat," I told him.

One side of his lips kicked up. "Eat, and I'll tell you our plans."

That got several other people's attention. Hoping my stomach didn't revolt, I started eating instead of picking at my food. I didn't dare look at Kieran, because if I did, I would be looking outside the Great Room to the hall.

"We're leaving in the morning," he stated, and I almost choked on the chunk of cheese I'd taken a bite of. None of those around me seemed at all surprised.

"Tomorrow?" I squeaked, torn between panic and hope. I would have a better chance of escaping out on the road than I would here.

He nodded. "As I said, we'll be going home."

I took a healthy drink from my glass. "But Atlantia is not my home."

"But it is. At least, partly."

"What does that mean?" Across from me, Delano spoke for the first time.

"It means it's something I should've figured out sooner. So many things now make sense when they didn't before. Why they made you the Maiden, how you survived a Craven attack. Your gifts," he said, lowering his voice on the last part so only I and those immediately around us could hear him. "You're not mortal, Poppy. At least, not completely."

I opened my mouth and then closed it, not quite sure I heard him correctly. For a moment, I thought something was lodged in my throat. I took a drink, but the sensation was still there.

Delano's jewel blue eyes sharpened. "Are you suggesting that she's..."

"Part Atlantian?" he finished for him. "Yes."

My hand trembled, sloshing liquid onto my fingers. "That's impossible," I whispered.

"Are you sure?" Delano asked him, and when I looked at him, I could see the shock in his eyes as his gaze moved over me, stopping and lingering on my neck.

"One hundred percent," he answered.

"How?" I demanded.

A faint smile played across his full lips. His gaze too lowered and stopped…on my throat.

On the bite that I realized was barely hidden under the strands of hair. My blood. He knew after…tasting my blood?

Delano's eyes went wide as he sat back, staring at me like it was the first time he'd ever seen me. Forgetting about the Hall, I looked at Kieran. I saw none of that. He arched a brow at me. This wasn't news to him. "It's rare, but it happens. A mortal crosses paths with an Atlantian. Nature takes its course, and nine months later, a mortal child is born." Kieran paused and ran his thumb over the rim of his chalice. "But every so often, a child of both kingdoms is born. Mortal and Atlantian."

"No. You have to be mistaken." I twisted in my seat. "My mother and father were mortal—"

"How can you be sure?" Hawke cut me off—no, not Hawke. *Casteel.* The Prince. "You thought I was mortal."

My heart lurched against my chest. "But my brother, he's an Ascended now."

"That's a good question," Delano tacked on.

"Only if we're working off the assumption that he is your full, blooded brother," he said, and I gasped.

"Or that he even has Ascended," someone commented.

The glass started to slip from my fingers—

His reflexes were lightning-quick. He caught the glass before it could hit the table. Placing it down, he then covered my hand, lowering it to the table. "Your brother is alive."

My heart had stopped. "How can you be sure?"

"I've had eyes on him for months, Poppy. He hasn't been seen during the day, and I can only imagine that means he is an Ascended."

Someone cursed and then spat on the floor. I closed my eyes. Part…part Atlantian? If that was why I was the Chosen and was the source of my abilities, then had the Duke and the Duchess known? The Queen? I opened my eyes. "Why would they keep me alive if they knew?"

His lips thinned. "Why do they keep my brother?"

I jolted, my entire body freezing. "I can't do that. Right? I mean, I don't have…the, uh, parts for it."

"Parts?" Kieran coughed. "What have you been filling her head with?"

The Prince slid him a bland look. "Teeth. I do believe she means these." Curling his upper lip, he ran this tongue over one fang, and my stomach dipped and twisted in a mixture of pleasure and unease. "They don't need that. They just need your blood for them to complete the Ascension."

If I wasn't sitting, I likely would've fallen over. I wanted to refute his claim, but I couldn't come up with one good reason for why he'd lie about this. There was nothing to gain from doing so. I bent slightly in my chair, wondering if it was possible that I was having a heart attack.

"I'm curious, Cas. Why must we go home?" Kieran asked, and I swore his voice rose with purpose. "When we will be going farther away from where your brother is held."

"It is the only place we can go," he replied, those golden eyes remaining fixed on me. "Did you know that an Atlantian can only marry if both halves are standing in the soil of their land? It's the only way for them to become whole."

My lips parted as a hush descended over the entire room. Still reeling from the whole half-Atlantian thing, I couldn't believe what I was hearing. That he was saying...

That damn dimple appeared in his right cheek and then in his left. Casteel Da'Neer, the Prince of Atlantia, smiled fully as he lifted our joined hands and said, "We go home to marry, my *Princess*."

* * * *

Also from 1001 Dark Nights and Jennifer L. Armentrout, discover The Prince, The King, and The Queen.

A Kingdom of Flesh and Fire
A Blood and Ash Novel
Coming September 1, 2020

From #1 New York Times bestselling author Jennifer L. Armentrout comes a new novel in her Blood and Ash series…

Is Love Stronger Than Vengeance?

A Betrayal…

Everything Poppy has ever believed in is a lie, including the man she was falling in love with. Thrust among those who see her as a symbol of a monstrous kingdom, she barely knows who she is without the veil of the Maiden. But what she does know is that nothing is as dangerous to her as him. The Dark One. The Prince of Atlantia. He wants her to fight him, and that's one order she's more than happy to obey. He may have taken her, but he will never have her.

A Choice….

Casteel Da'Neer is known by many names and many faces. His lies are as seductive as his touch. His truths as sensual as his bite. Poppy knows better than to trust him. He needs her alive, healthy, and whole to achieve his goals. But he's the only way for her to get what she wants—to find her brother Ian and see for herself if he has become a soulless Ascended. Working with Casteel instead of against him presents its own risks. He still tempts her with every breath, offering up all she's ever wanted. Casteel has plans for her. Ones that could expose her to unimaginable pleasure and unfathomable pain. Plans that will force her to look beyond everything she thought she knew about herself—about him. Plans that could bind their lives together in unexpected ways that neither kingdom is prepared for. And she's far too reckless, too hungry, to resist the temptation.

A Secret…

But unrest has grown in Atlantia as they await the return of their Prince. Whispers of war have become stronger, and Poppy is at the very heart of it all. The King wants to use her to send a message. The Descenters want her dead. The wolven are growing more unpredictable. And as her abilities to feel pain and emotion begin to grow and strengthen, the Atlantians start to fear her. Dark secrets are at play, ones steeped in the blood-drenched sins of two kingdoms that would do anything to keep the truth hidden. But when the earth begins to shake, and the skies start to bleed, it may already be too late.

Sign up for the Blue Box Press/1001 Dark Nights Newsletter
and be entered to win a Tiffany Lock necklace.

There's a contest every quarter!

Go to www.1001DarkNights.com to subscribe.

As a bonus, all subscribers can download
FIVE FREE exclusive books!

Discover More Jennifer L. Armentrout

The Prince: A Wicked Novella

She's everything he wants....
Cold. Heartless. Deadly. Whispers of his name alone bring fear to fae and mortals alike. *The Prince*. There is nothing in the mortal world more dangerous than him. Haunted by a past he couldn't control, all Caden desires is revenge against those who'd wronged him, trapping him in never-ending nightmare. And there is one person he knows can help him.

She's everything he can't have...
Raised within the Order, Brighton Jussier knows just how dangerous the Prince is, reformed or not. She'd seen firsthand what atrocities he could be capable of. The last thing she wants to do is help him, but he leaves her little choice. Forced to work alongside him, she begins to see the man under the bitter ice. Yearning for him feels like the definition of insanity, but there's no denying the heat in his touch and the wicked promise is his stare.

She's everything he'll take....
But there's someone out there who wants to return the Prince to his former self. A walking, breathing nightmare that is hell bent on destroying the world and everyone close to him. The last thing either of them needs is a distraction, but with the attraction growing between them each now, the one thing he wants more than anything may be the one thing that will be his undoing.

She's everything he'd die for....

* * * *

The King: A Wicked Novella

From #1 *New York Times* and *USA Today* bestselling author Jennifer L. Armentrout comes the next installment in her Wicked series.

As Caden and Brighton's attraction grows despite the odds stacked against a happily ever after, they must work together to stop an Ancient fae from releasing the Queen, who wants nothing more than to see Caden become the evil Prince once feared by fae and mortals alike.

* * * *

The Queen: A Wicked Novella

The King must have his Queen....

Bestowed the forbidden Summer's Kiss by the King of the Summer fae, Brighton Jussier is no longer *just* human. What she is, what she will become, no one knows for sure, but that isn't her biggest concern at the moment. Now Caden, the King, refuses to let her go, even at the cost of his Court. When the doorway to the Otherworld is breached, both Brighton and Caden must do the unthinkable—not just to survive themselves, but also to save mankind from the evil that threatens the world.

Discover 1001 Dark Nights Collection Seven

THE BISHOP by Skye Warren
A Tanglewood Novella

TAKEN WITH YOU by Carrie Ann Ryan
A Fractured Connections Novella

DRAGON LOST by Donna Grant
A Dark Kings Novella

SEXY LOVE by Carly Phillips
A Sexy Series Novella

PROVOKE by Rachel Van Dyken
A Seaside Pictures Novella

RAFE by Sawyer Bennett
An Arizona Vengeance Novella

THE NAUGHTY PRINCESS by Claire Contreras
A Sexy Royals Novella

THE GRAVEYARD SHIFT by Darynda Jones
A Charley Davidson Novella

CHARMED by Lexi Blake
A Masters and Mercenaries Novella

SACRIFICE OF DARKNESS by Alexandra Ivy
A Guardians of Eternity Novella

THE QUEEN by Jen Armentrout
A Wicked Novella

BEGIN AGAIN by Jennifer Probst
A Stay Novella

VIXEN by Rebecca Zanetti
A Dark Protectors/Rebels Novella

SLASH by Laurelin Paige
A Slay Series Novella

THE DEAD HEAT OF SUMMER by Heather Graham
A Krewe of Hunters Novella

WILD FIRE by Kristen Ashley
A Chaos Novella

MORE THAN PROTECT YOU by Shayla Black
A More Than Words Novella

LOVE SONG by Kylie Scott
A Stage Dive Novella

CHERISH ME by J. Kenner
A Stark Ever After Novella

SHINE WITH ME by Kristen Proby
A With Me in Seattle Novella

From Blue Box Press

TEASE ME by J. Kenner
A Stark International Novel

FROM BLOOD AND ASH by Jennifer L. Armentrout
A Blood and Ash Novel

QUEEN MOVE by Kennedy Ryan

THE HOUSE OF LONG AGO by Steve Berry and MJ Rose
A Cassiopeia Vitt Adventure

THE BUTTERFLY ROOM by Lucinda Riley

About Jennifer L. Armentrout

1 New York Times and International Bestselling author Jennifer lives in Shepherdstown, West Virginia. All the rumors you've heard about her state aren't true. When she's not hard at work writing. she spends her time reading, watching really bad zombie movies, pretending to write, and hanging out with her husband, their retired K-9 police dog Diesel, a crazy Border Jack puppy named Apollo, six judgmental alpacas, four fluffy sheep, and two goats.

Her dreams of becoming an author started in algebra class, where she spent most of her time writing short stories...which explains her dismal grades in math. Jennifer writes young adult paranormal, science fiction, fantasy, and contemporary romance. She is published with Tor Teen, Entangled Teen and Brazen, Disney/Hyperion and Harlequin Teen. Her book *Wicked* has been optioned by Passionflix and slated to begin filming in late 2018. Her young adult romantic suspense novel *DON'T LOOK BACK* was a 2014 nominated Best in Young Adult Fiction by YALSA and her novel *THE PROBLEM WITH FOREVER* is a 2017 RITA Award winning novel.

She also writes Adult and New Adult contemporary and paranormal romance under the name J. Lynn. She is published by Entangled Brazen and HarperCollins.

On Behalf of Blue Box Press,

Liz Berry, M.J. Rose, and Jillian Stein would like to thank ~

Steve Berry
Doug Scofield
Benjamin Stein
Kim Guidroz
Social Butterfly PR
Dan Slater
Chelle Olson
Hang Le
Stephanie Brown
Chris Graham
Jessica Johns
Dylan Stockton
Richard Blake
and Simon Lipskar